'A warm and wonderful s[...]
that is at once nostalgic [...]
relevant' — **Adele Parks**

'Fresh, authentic and darkly funny. It's a beautifully told story
full of warmth and emotion without ever being sentimental
– I absolutely loved it' — **Ruth Hogan**

'Vivid, funny, nostalgic and utterly charming — I loved every
word of this moving story. An absolute joy and an original
new voice in fiction. I can't wait to read more from Fran Hill'
— **Veronica Henry**

'Laugh-out-loud funny' — **Frances Quinn**

'*Cuckoo in the Nest* totally evokes a Seventies childhood'
— **Joanna Nadin**

'This made my soul sing! Witty, poignant and full of heart … her
sharp mind and insightful humour had me in stitches'
— **Jessica Ryn**

'Totally absorbing and ultimately satisfying, *Cuckoo in the
Nest* is a greedy gulp of a read that leaves you hungry for
more' — **Deborah Jenkins**

'Hill's ability to take a story filled with tragedy and injustice
and inject it with wry humour, sly jokes and real emotion is
remarkable' — **Ruth Leigh**

'If you like your books to leave you part laughter, part
puddle – or you want to know why exactly a plain cheese
sandwich can be a sign of doom, read *Cuckoo in the Nest*'
— **Gráinne Murphy**

'This book is written straight from the heart, with honesty, humour and empathy for human relationships and human frailties' — **Jane Ions**

'A warm, funny, and ultimately tender exploration of family dynamics. Totally absorbing. Highly recommended' — **Emma Purshouse**

FRAN HILL

Cuckoo in the Nest

Legend Press Ltd, 51 Gower Street, London, WC1E 6HJ
info@legendpress.co.uk | www.legendpress.co.uk

Contents © Fran Hill 2023
The right of the above author to be identified as the author of this work has
been asserted in accordance with the Copyright, Designs and Patents Act
1988. British Library Cataloguing in Publication Data available.

Print ISBN 9781915643919
Ebook ISBN 9781915643926
Set in Times.

Cover by Head Design | www.headdesign.co.uk

Fran Hill is a 60-year-old self-employed English teacher and writer with two previous books: a memoir and a self-published novella. This is her first full-length work of fiction.

She has written extensively for the *Times Educational Supplement* and lives in Warwickshire with her gardener husband. She has two grandchildren.

To all the fosterers and fosterees.

FRIDAY 9 APRIL 1976

We reached the top of the stairs. 'Here you are,' she said, pointing to the half-open bedroom door. She was smiling. Perhaps she thought I should have been more pleased to need a room in a houseful of strangers.

Bobbie, my social worker, had suggested I call them Auntie Bridget and Uncle Nick.

'Suggest all you like,' I'd said.

She'd said, 'Remember that it's all strange to them, too. This is very short notice. We thought it would be weeks, not days.'

'That's not my fault.'

'Of course not. But don't give them a hard time.'

'They're not in your car on a Friday afternoon,' I'd said, 'with luggage on the back seat.'

She'd replied, 'That is true. Sorry.'

Saying goodbye to Dad and seeing him cry had made me tense. It felt like anger, but I wasn't sure. And when I wasn't sure whether I was angry, my tone turned to vinegar.

Now, not-going-to-be-Auntie Bridget pushed the door wide open and walked into a yellow bedroom. I blinked at first because sun was sweeping in through the windows, inappropriately, in my view.

'It looks different now, doesn't it?' she said. 'We moved everything back in last night. Just in time!'

I stayed in the doorway. They'd shown me the room when I'd visited with Dad earlier that week, but it had been emptied of furniture and the carpet covered in sheets. A decorator had been up a ladder, painting the ceiling.

'I love this paint we chose,' Bridget said, standing at the end of a single bed covered in a patchwork eiderdown. 'It's cheerful, isn't it?'

'I can smell it,' I told her.

'Don't you love the smell of fresh paint?' she said, stroking the wall as though it were a cat. 'It's only just dry.'

'I'm not that familiar with fresh paint lately.'

She looked uncomfortable and I felt bad, so I stepped in and ran my non-bandaged hand along the surface of a chest of drawers that was next to the bed to smooth myself down.

'Anyway,' she said. 'I hope you like the colour. I think it's called Sunflower Yellow.'

I turned my body to look first at the wall by the window, then the wall opposite the bed, near where she was standing, then the wall by the door, then the wall behind the bed. I did it slowly, as though I was at a museum or something. I needed time. 'You decorated it for me?' I said.

She smiled as though I'd given her a Christmas present.

I said, 'Even though I'm only here for a few weeks?'

'For you, and anyone else who needed somewhere… somewhere more stable to be. But you're our first foster child, yes.'

I said, 'Where's your daughter's room?'

'She's right next door,' she said reassuringly, as though she thought I'd require emergency solace in the night. She pointed to the wall behind the bed. 'She's fourteen, too, although you already know that.'

Neither of us said anything for what seemed ages. We both kept looking at the walls like idiots.

'Well,' she said, brushing down the front of her jumper as if she'd eaten a pastry. 'Time to bring your case upstairs, I suppose!'

'It's a bag, and my school satchel.'

'Your bag and satchel, then.'

'Can I have five minutes,' I said, 'on my own?'

'In here?'

I nodded.

She didn't shut the door when she left, so I closed it. But I could hear that she hadn't gone downstairs.

I waited. Sure enough, her voice, sounding as though she had one side of her face pressed to the door. 'What would you like for tea, Jackie? I've made a shepherd's pie.'

She'd done both question and answer.

'Shepherd's pie would be lovely,' I said, and this time she went downstairs.

I could imagine Bobbie's face. *That's better. Well done.*

I sat on the bed and looked at the walls again.

TWO WEEKS EARLIER

FRIDAY 26 MARCH

I could see from outside our terraced house that Dad hadn't opened the front room curtains, so even though a perfectly decent spring sun nosed at the windows, it hadn't been invited in.

I turned my key in the door then listened before I stepped into the hall, bending to pick up post Dad hadn't bothered with. His size 11 shoeprint had marked the brown envelopes.

So, he'd been out then. No need to wonder where.

Envelopes with windows. The ones he hated most. I often had to rescue them from the bin and iron them hard with my hands in case he was making things worse for himself. And for me.

'Dad?' I called, hanging my blazer on the banister. 'Happy Friday!'

Aileen, who sat next to me in English, had told me that when she walked home from school, she could hear her dad yelling while she was still four or five doors away.

'Yelling what about?' I'd said.

'How long have you got?' she'd said, but Mrs Collingworth told us to stop chatting or we'd be kept in at break, and was she boring us.

Which would be better? I'd asked myself then. A yelling dad or the silent dad, temporarily poleaxed by whisky? Silent in the way a gas attack is silent until it snaps at your lungs.

I peered around the door of the front room where, alongside the two armchairs, coffee table and telly, Dad had recently shoe-horned in the double bed he used to share with Mum. Beside the bed was one of a pair of side tables on which Mum used to put homely lamps. The lamps and the other side table now formed part of a messy pile that sat in our creaky lean-to at the back of the house.

I missed those lamps.

The front room stank – the kind of smell you get when you've left washing to ferment in a basket for three days.

He was face down on the bed, his bulky frame vanquished by the drink: on his face and off his face at the same time. He had his shirt on but no trousers, only grey Y-fronts. The usual late afternoon uniform. At first, I thought he was awake, but then he snored, suddenly, like an engine being revved.

The customary glass sat stickily on the side table beside the customary bottle with an inch of whisky left in it. That would be his first request then, once he woke up, and I'd be down at the off-licence begging for credit again, trying to pretend I was sixteen.

I left the front room and relocated to the kitchen. I had English homework and perhaps half an hour's peace.

I sat at the tiny drop-leaf table with a teacup of orange squash and two cream crackers spread with Blue Band margarine, writing a composition with the title 'A Day at the Seaside'. We were studying 'literature about places' in English. My story probably wasn't what Mrs Collingworth expected – the little boy getting buried in sand by his sisters and them forgetting about him while they paddled – but some days you're not in the mood for ice creams and donkey rides.

The parents had just discovered that the raised shape in the sand was their son when Dad woke up and announced his return to the land of the conscious by lobbing a bottle at the tiled fireplace.

I scrabbled underneath the sink for the brush and dustpan.

Dustpan but no brush.

That's the story of your life, I said to myself. Dustpan but no brush. Chips but no fish. Dad but no mum. Bed but no rest. Crackers but no cheese, and even the Blue Band was suspect.

Later, when I came back from the off-licence with two bottles of whisky, Dad poured a full glass and drank it all down.

'Doesn't that burn your throat?' I said.

'Sometimes,' he said, 'but it's a good burning.' He said it through a cough, though, so he'd never have made it in advertising.

He sat up in bed, chain-smoking. Nicotine and alcohol, when combined, loosened his tongue until it flapped like a flag in the breeze if there was nothing to watch on telly. It would last half an hour or so. He'd blather on about something he'd seen in the *Daily Mirror* or heard in the pub and I'd sit in one of our two armchairs and try to listen in the way I remembered Mum doing.

I watched some P. G. Wodehouse play once Dad had fallen asleep and was spreadeagled on the bed like a giant, pissed starfish. But it didn't grab me. I preferred stand-up comedians such as Dave Allen. I liked the way he perched on a stool, and I loved his eyes, so if I didn't catch all the jokes about the Catholics, it wasn't a big deal. Also, it intrigued me the way he obviously liked to drink but could still go on TV and tell jokes. He seemed like a normal person who wouldn't be sick in a wastepaper basket for his daughter to clear up. I hankered after that and often wondered if Dave Allen had kids of his own.

MONDAY 29 MARCH

Last lesson of the day, I was in the music room miming 'Speed Bonnie Boat' with other reluctants at the back of the group when a first-year errand boy appeared around the door. He stood obediently until Mr Court had played to the end of the chorus.

'Oh, how I *love* interruptions,' our teacher said, taking his slim hands off the piano keys.

'Sir,' said the boy. 'Miss Jones wants to see Jacqueline Chadwick.'

'Oh, does she now?' Mr Court said. 'I suppose I can lend her out, but I fear she'll be upset. She adores singing *so* much.'

I loved Mr Court's sarcasm. He used it in a way that made you like him, without scouring the dignity off you.

I was becoming familiar with the headmistress's office: its magnolia walls, the tidy desk and two reliable filing cabinets.

Miss Jones sat behind her desk. I sat opposite. She said, 'We're worried about the new bruise Mr Jackson noticed on your arm in PE. This is happening too often. How did you get it, Jackie?' She was changing the ink cartridge in her pen.

'You know who gave me the bruise,' I said.

'I need you to tell me.'

'You'll call Social Services.'

'We might have to anyway, whether you say his name or not. We need to keep you safe.'

I didn't want to say it. It made it real. I knew what the consequences could be. You hear a train approach from a long way off and for ages it seems as if it will never come and then suddenly, whoosh, it's in the station. Did I want to get on that train?

My feelings were elusive, like tiny birds that flit away under a cat's stare. I kept my hands folded firm in my lap. They wanted to pick at a new scab I knew was there, waiting at my hairline.

'What are you thinking?' Miss Jones said.

'It was Mother's Day yesterday,' I said.

'That must have been difficult.'

I shrugged. 'Having an actual mother would help with the celebrations.'

She smiled but in a sad way. 'Are there any other family members you talk to?' she said.

'Not really,' I said. 'My dad's mum lives in Devon. Dad doesn't speak to her.'

'Your mum's parents?'

'Nanna and Grandad. They're in Glasgow. Dad hasn't spoken to them either since Mum died.' I didn't know why this was. They still sent me birthday and Christmas presents, so surely this meant they wanted to stay in touch. I would have written back, but Dad said there wasn't money spare for stamps. 'Oh, there's Auntie Pat, my mum's sister. She rings Dad occasionally.'

Miss Jones' face brightened. 'Oh, that's something. Is she supportive?'

I said, 'Rings occasionally from New Zealand.'

'Oh.'

'And Dad doesn't let me talk to her.'

'Why?'

'I don't know,' I said.

Someone knocked at Miss Jones' door. She went to open it and then, rather than coming back in, slid out into the corridor, closing the door behind her.

I leaped across to put my ear against it. Another female voice said, 'Not again. Poor kid.' I recognised its squeaky tones as Mrs Caine, my head of year. She got dragged in when no one else knew what to do. The cavalry, or to continue my previous analogy, the driver of the train arriving in the station.

I listened for more, but then their heels clicked away. They'd either moved further down the corridor or into another room.

Fine. Leave me out of my own life.

I picked at my head. It left blood under my fingernails.

Ten minutes later, they returned. I sat on my hands. Miss Jones resumed her place behind her desk, but Mrs Caine stood.

'Both of you on my case,' I said. 'Things *are* bleak. Can I go back to Mr Court and sing "Speed Bonnie Boat"?'

'We have to intervene here,' said Miss Jones, 'for your protection.'

'We don't *need* your permission to contact Social Services,' Mrs Caine said. 'But we wouldn't without telling you.'

There didn't seem much to say. I didn't have a script for this.

'There's a leadership team meeting after school,' Miss Jones said, 'but we'll ring them first thing in the morning.'

Threat or promise: spot the difference.

That evening, I had to go to casualty. Dad came with me bad-temperedly. The hospital was ten minutes' walk from our house, although, on the journey there, every step had jarred my injured left wrist. I'd held it against my chest, securing it with the other hand, which helped, but had to walk quickly to keep up with Dad's never-ending legs, which didn't help at all.

A nurse sat me on a chair in a room no bigger than a cupboard, knelt and examined me. 'How did it happen?' she asked my dad, who stood by the door as though hoping for a quick exit. I'll rephrase that: hoping for a quick exit.

There was a silence, the kind that's loud.

'I fell in the kitchen,' I said, 'and landed on my hand.'

She asked what had made me fall.

'The floor was wet,' I said. That, at least, was wholly authentic and it was nice to be able to tell a truth.

'She can be careless,' my dad said.

This stung.

'Water? On the floor?' the nurse said.

'Yes,' my dad said, too eagerly.

'Did you hurt anything else?' she said to me.

'My ego,' I said.

She smiled. 'It'll need an X-ray. I don't think it's broken, but you seem to be in quite a lot of pain.'

I couldn't fault her inference skills. Mrs Collingworth would love you, I thought.

The X-ray department waiting area was rammed with patients, leaving one free seat. 'You sit there,' Dad said. 'I'll go and find a drink.'

I watched him walk down the corridor. A plump woman whose left thigh was on my seat too, like an interloper, nudged me. She said, 'Lucky you. I'm here alone. No one's going to fetch *me* a drink.'

But that wasn't what he'd meant. Fifty minutes later, he hadn't resurfaced. Gradually, the seats around me had emptied as a tall woman arrived and left, carrying a clipboard and calling out names one by one. Magazines were abandoned still open on the chairs.

The woman came back. 'Jacqueline Chadwick,' she called.

I stood up. 'That's me.'

She walked towards me. 'Is no one with you?'

'My dad's somewhere.'

'You're a minor,' she said.

'I'm sure he'll be back soon. He went to get a drink.' I nodded down the corridor.

'There's a drinks machine here,' she said, pointing the other way. 'Didn't he see it?'

He'd seen it all right.

'We'll need to wait for him,' she said. 'You need a respon-sible adult with you.'

Unintentionally funny people are the most amusing of all.

Half an hour later, Dad returned, all six-foot-three of him navigating the corridor uncertainly, like a leaning Tower of Pisa but in a grubby shirt and trousers with the flies undone. The smell of whisky was palpable. It may have carried him along on its own.

Clipboard Woman spotted his arrival and came to fetch us. I could see her looking at Dad's gaping flies, her mouth set in a thin line, like something drawn with a ruler.

A male technician who looked like a grandad positioned me at the end of the X-ray couch on a chair and asked me to lay my hand, palm upwards, on a grey board. He pointed Dad to a wooden chair by the wall and Dad sat, his head nodding forward as though it were too heavy for him.

'How did you do this, love?' the technician asked, arrang-ing my fingers.

'I slipped in the kitchen,' I said, although I don't know if Dad realised how near I was to telling the truth. There's something about being humiliated that can make you reckless.

'Don't move,' the technician called from the little room in which he operated the machine. I heard a whirr, then a click. He came back. By now, we were both trying to ignore Dad snoring like a large dog. The technician turned my hand over gently and disappeared again. Whirr. Click.

'That's her done, Mr Chadwick,' he said very loudly, and Dad jumped and said, 'Shit.'

Fifteen minutes later, the technician came to speak to us in the X-ray waiting room. Dad was restless, moaning about the wait, checking his watch as though he had somewhere to go.

'She'll need to go back round to casualty,' the technician said to him. 'It's not broken, but a nurse will bandage up her sprain and give her a sling. And some aspirin.'

'Okay,' I said.

'Bloody hell,' my dad said.

'It looks a nasty sprain, sir,' the technician said, which I think was technician for, 'I'd very much like to punch you in the face.'

'I'm off to The Roebuck for a pint,' Dad said when we were done and we'd found our way through the maze of corridors to the entrance of the hospital. It had taken long enough, especially as I'd had to wait for twenty minutes outside a men's lavatory. He'd come out yawning and bleary. I think he'd fallen asleep on the toilet.

'You've got your key, haven't you?' he said. He was leaning against a wall, trying to roll a cigarette.

'Do you want me to do that?' I was an expert, not because I smoked, but because for my father a bottle of whisky and fine motor skills didn't go together, so I often helped.

But then I remembered I had my arm in a sling.

'Fat lot of use you are,' he said, eventually taming the Rizla and tobacco into something resembling a fag. 'Use' came out as 'yoosh'.

I'm a *lot* of yoosh to you, Dad, I thought, and for a second, I was scared I'd actually said it, but I hadn't.

I left him to his evening and started trudging home, watching my step carefully in case I tripped. With one arm strapped up, something felt wrong with my balance.

I imagined him, walking in much the same unsteady way towards The Roebuck.

Like father, like daughter, I thought, but not in the way you'd hope.

TUESDAY 30 MARCH

I woke up late. All night, I'd shifted around, trying to get comfortable, but the wrist felt tender and I'd spent the dark hours afraid I would twist or bend it without realising.

And I'd forgotten to set the alarm on the tiny travel clock which had been Mum's and which sat on the floor by my bed.

I decided to leave the sling at home – wearing it to school would draw attention – and pulled on my uniform, wincing as I forced the bandaged arm into the sleeve of my school blouse. It was squeezy-tight but made the wrist feel more secure. I pulled on my blazer too.

At least it was my left arm. Small mercies. Very small, in fact.

In the kitchen, I took two of the aspirin the hospital had given me.

Dad had also slept in, but his reason was The Roebuck. I'd heard him arrive home at 11.30, needing three attempts to get his key in the door.

At school, I kept the sore wrist close against my body in the busy corridors.

English was the second lesson of the day. I arrived at Mrs Collingworth's classroom and took my usual seat next to Aileen on the front row. On each desk was a book of twentieth century poetry.

'It's very warm,' the teacher said, opening windows. 'You may take off blazers if you wish.'

A riff of relief. In Mrs Collingworth's lessons, you did nothing until given permission. She ruled her classroom like a military establishment but somehow with kindness.

Beside me, Aileen removed her blazer and draped it on the back of her chair. 'Aren't you hot?' she whispered.

I shook my head.

Mrs Collingworth stood at the front beside her desk. She wore a green corduroy skirt and matching short-sleeved green blouse. Her mid-brown hair was a neat bob. My wrist felt better for looking at her.

'Turn to page fifty-seven,' she said. 'We're studying a poem called "Adlestrop" by Edward Thomas for the next couple of lessons. It's about his impressions of a country railway station in Gloucestershire in 1914.' She explained that we'd be writing our own poems soon about a memory of a place, modelled on 'Adlestrop'.

Aileen nudged me and mouthed, 'Help!' but my heart hopped with pleasure. Mrs Collingworth also ran the Poetry Club I attended on Wednesday lunchtimes and had already praised me for my poems.

She read 'Adlestrop' to us twice. Her voice was warm and soft and she knew how to make a poem mean something. It saved us from listening to a classmate read it from the back row as though it were a shopping list.

'Who wants to tell the class what they think Edward Thomas is trying to say?' Mrs Collingworth said as we opened our exercise books to write the title 'Adlestrop' and the date.

I had my pen in my right hand so went to put my left hand up, forgetting about the wrist injury, and couldn't help crying out as it wrenched. I took it down again. But my sleeve had fallen back, revealing the bandage.

Mrs Collingworth said, 'Jackie. What did you do to your arm?'

'Nothing much,' I said, trying not to wince.

She paused.

Don't pursue it, I begged her with my eyes.

'Tell us your thoughts on the poem, Jackie,' she said at last.

When the school bell clanged at the end of the lesson, Mrs Collingworth said, 'You may pack away,' and appointed someone to collect our exercise books. She beckoned to me and said, quietly, 'Could you stay behind?'

'See you at the tuck shop,' Aileen said, clicking her satchel shut. 'What *is* wrong with your arm?'

'Nothing,' I said. 'Bandages are in fashion, like flares.'

I waited as Mrs C, as we called her when she wasn't listening, wiped the blackboard clean of chalk.

I took the chance to apologise for my seaside story homework. 'It's more like horror. I'd better warn you.'

She smiled. 'I won't mark it just before bedtime then. But – your wrist,' she said. 'What happened there?'

I was ready for her. 'I slipped in the kitchen,' I said.

'Who put the bandage on? Your father?'

'No,' I said, trying not to say the words hospital or nurse.

She picked up our pile of exercise books and tucked them under her arm. 'I see,' she said. 'I hope it's not too painful.'

'When I forget and shove it up in the air, it is.'

'Do you have PE today?' she said.

'Yes.'

'Did your father give you a note to excuse you?'

'No.'

'I'll speak to the Head of Games in the staff room,' she said.

That evening, Dad and I were in the front room together. He'd had some benefit money left over from Friday, mainly because he hadn't been to the shops to buy food for the fridge and cupboards. So he had sent me to fetch a large portion of chips and two chicken pies, which we'd eaten out of the paper on our laps in front of the telly. I'd put the sling back on when I'd arrived home, but I'd never rehearsed eating pie and chips from paper one-handed and it showed.

Dad and I ate all our meals – I'm using the term 'meals' loosely – either on trays or on plates on our laps. Increasingly over the past year or so, I'd found myself eating alone in the kitchen if I wanted my tea before it officially became a late supper. He often wasn't hungry until the middle of the evening, throwing together a clumsy pile of corned beef sandwiches or a heaped bowl of cereal when he felt like it.

Now, Dad had washed his pie and chips down with whisky. I'd persuaded him to let me buy a bottle of lemonade and him saying yes was the nearest to remorse he would offer for the wrist episode.

'I've written another poem,' I said to him. I'd spent most of my lunch break in the library on my poem homework even though Mrs Collingworth hadn't formally set it yet.

'*Another* poem?' he said, lighting a cigarette for dessert. 'That's your mother's fault.'

'It's a good one. It's based on a famous poem called "Adlestrop".'

'She caught poetry from working in libraries,' he said, blowing a smoke ring. He was proficient at them, but I'd rather he'd excelled at fatherhood.

'Poetry isn't the plague, Dad.'

'Hm.'

Mum had introduced me to poetry when I was in my Moses basket, she'd told me often, and as I was growing up, she'd read me poems at bedtime as well as stories.

I remembered a conversation we'd had when she was ill after a course of cancer treatment that obviously wasn't working. I would have been eleven. She was sitting, supported by pillows, in the bed she shared with Dad, and I was next to her. The bed was still upstairs in those days.

'You loved Dylan Thomas. Wordsworth. Ballads,' she'd told me. 'You stopped crying as soon as you heard them. You loved the rhythms, I think.'

'I had very grown-up tastes,' I'd said, 'for a baby.'

She'd laughed. 'No nursery rhymes for you. I went straight

in, training you for your future career as a poet. I couldn't be one – I had to settle for working in the library and feasting on the books there – but you can.'

'I don't think so, Mum.'

'I know otherwise,' she'd said. 'Now read me that one you wrote about winter snows again while I snuggle under this eiderdown.'

I said to Dad now, clumsily wrapping up some chips I hadn't eaten, 'Do you want to hear my poem when I've cleared up the kitchen?'

But poetry recitals work so much better when all participants are awake. His head was lolling forwards.

I took the cigarette from between his fingers and stubbed it out in the full ashtray then rescued the greasy newspaper from his lap and put it, along with mine, in the kitchen bin.

It needed emptying, but there wasn't much I could do about that with only one hand available. The lid wouldn't shut because of a whisky bottle in the top of it, so I took the bottle out and that way I could close it.

Upstairs, I sat in front of Mum's dressing table on the pink stool she used to balance on while she leaned forward to check her mascara, and I read my poem to her mirror.

'The Picnic,' I began.

'Yes. I remember the New Forest –
the place, because one afternoon
of joy, we wandered there
unhurriedly. It was summer-fine.

My mother hummed. Dad whistled.
Nothing mattered. No grief yet
to mar our picnic. What I saw
was forest, ponies. Mum called my name

to feast on bread, thick ham, tomatoes
with salt and pepper and sunshine,

23

then cake in wedges thick as love.
We ate under an approving sky.

And for that moment a future sang
close by, and hope came, whispering,
sweeter and sweeter, that we were safe
with nothing so cruel as death to fear.'

When I'd finished, I stared at my own face. What would my
mum have said?

'That's lovely, pet,' I told my reflection. 'You have such
a way with words.'

WEDNESDAY 31 MARCH

Mrs Collingworth ran Poetry Club in her classroom at lunch-time. As we trailed in, she was rearranging the desks into the usual semicircle for us: three third-year girls and five fourth-year girls. One boy had ventured along when the group had first started in September, but he'd soon scuttled back to Metalwork Club.

'Before we start,' Mrs C said now, 'I've confirmed with Mr Court in the music department that we're running our annual arts evening again in July. A mix of poetry and music. Let me know if you'd like to perform.'

'Perform in front of people?' someone said.

She replied that performing behind them might not be as effective.

The forty minutes that Poetry Club took left us barely twenty to queue for tepid beef stew and mash and shove them in our mouths, but it was my favourite forty minutes of the week.

Mrs C chose a different theme for each Poetry Club. This time it was doors. For ten minutes, we brainstormed 'doors' onto the blackboard. Entrances. Exits. Rectangles. New beginnings. Strange places. Moving house. Secrets behind doors. Doors slamming. ('Oh, these are fascinating,' Mrs C said.) Doors to bathrooms, bedrooms and gardens.

'I've got an idea,' said Molly, a fourth year sitting next to me, and she bent her head. Molly was the friendless type and smelled a little. I think Poetry Club was her way of escaping the cruelty of the playground. But she wrote good poetry, something for which, it's true, you don't need anti-perspirant.

I had written some opening lines when Miss Jones knocked and peered in. 'I'm sorry to interrupt, Mrs Collingworth,' she said. 'Could I borrow Jackie?' She smiled, I think so that I and the others knew I wasn't in trouble.

Miss Jones led me into the empty classroom next door. She sat in the chair behind the teacher's desk. 'Take a seat yourself,' she said.

'Is the news going to make me faint?' I said.

'I hope not,' she said.

I pulled out a chair and sat. 'Has something happened to Dad?'

'No. I wanted to tell you that we have been in touch with Social Services as we said.'

'Am I going to a children's home?'

'Give me a chance,' she said. 'All I know is that a social worker called Mrs Bobbie Morrison will come to visit you and your father tomorrow after school. He knows this already,' she said, 'but I wanted to tell you myself.'

'He's not keen on interference,' I said.

'I hope he'll learn to see that it's not interference.'

'What does a social worker do?' I said.

'Support you,' she said. 'She works with families who are struggling to look after themselves.'

'I'm not struggling to look after myself,' I said. 'I manage fine.'

'The problem is,' she said, 'that you shouldn't be having to look after yourself at all.'

Back in Poetry Club, there were ten minutes left before sharing time. I crossed out the lines I had started. I'd had another idea. I wrote, scribbling fast. Sometimes my ideas for poems were like pleasant dreams. If you didn't grasp them, they puffed out of reach.

'Who'd like to read?' Mrs Collingworth said. 'We've got time for three or four.'

I glanced at Molly's sheet of paper.

'It isn't finished,' she said, turning the paper over. She blushed.

Mrs C said, 'Of course it's not finished. That takes much more time. Come on, Molly. Be brave. You're a fine poet.'

Molly turned the paper back over and bit her lip. 'It's the first two verses of a ballad. I think.'

'Impressive!' said Mrs Collingworth. 'Ballads aren't easy.'

'We've been studying them in English,' Molly said.

'Ah, Mr Struthers,' Mrs Collingworth said. 'He does love a ballad. Go on, then.'

Molly read.

A maiden loved her sister so.
She loved her faithfully
except that one thing saddened her
and caused grave misery.

Her sister found a husband dear
with features strong as stone.
The maiden listened at their door
and wept alone, alone.

We all clapped, as did Mrs C. 'Well done!' she said. 'Lovely foreshadowing. I noticed 'grave' misery.'

'And strong as stone,' someone else said. 'That could mean a gravestone.'

'Anyone else?' Mrs C said.

'I'll read,' I said.

'Let's see how you fitted in the door idea,' she said.

'Okay.'

'I am the door,' I read, 'which opens to the strangers,
which grants entrance to the unknown
and allows in those about whom you know nothing.

I have no lock, only a handle which turns
while you're not looking, while you're distracted,
to admit the unfamiliar face and the alien smile.

I am the door which opens to the strangers
and, with them, their guest, the sour cold wind.'

'My, my,' said Mrs C. 'We have some true wordsmiths in the room today.'

Molly said, as we left, 'You are going to be famous one day, like Sylvia Plath,' so I forgave her for the body odour. But I also wondered whether she'd read much on Plath, someone as famous for putting her head in an oven as for her poetry.

On the walk home from school, I went to the small supermarket five minutes from our house. I hadn't visited this one for a fortnight; there were two others on my route and I tried to vary them.

I browsed the aisles, waiting for my chance, then slipped a can of baked beans and a packet of bacon into my satchel while the shop assistant dealt with an elderly customer at the front of the shop.

The bread at home was stale, but it would toast. Tea was guaranteed for another day.

I bought a Fudge bar on my way out with the few pennies in my pocket. 'It's for my dad,' I said, which was true. The shop assistant knew who Dad was. He was in the shop often, concentrating his attention on one particular aisle.

'He'll enjoy that after his tea,' she said. 'What's he cooking you? Or perhaps it's a surprise!'

'No,' I said. 'Sadly, it won't be a surprise.'

'Where did this come from?' Dad would sometimes say when he found a new block of cheese in the fridge or packet of tea in the cupboard. But I knew he didn't really want to know and I spared him the shame by pretending I hadn't heard. He played along.

THURSDAY 1 APRIL

'Your dad's been given an ultimatum, a Hobson's choice,' said Mrs Bobbie Morrison the next day. She wore red flared trousers and, on her head, an orange beret that she didn't take off, and told me to stop calling her Mrs Morrison as it made her feel middle-aged and she was only twenty-seven. She'd arrived before I got home from school and had already had a conversation with Dad. I could tell it hadn't gone well.

Call-me-Bobbie and I were in the kitchen. We'd left Dad sulking in the front room. He was staring at *Jackanory*, chain-smoking away resentment. He'd slammed the door shut. I knew he couldn't wait for Bobbie to be out of the house so that he could open another bottle, but the new one was in the kitchen, on the surface.

'Do you need me to do that?' Bobbie said, watching me fill the kettle awkwardly, putting it in the sink while it took water, then lifting it with my good arm and taking it over to the gas hob. My sling was still upstairs.

'You're all right,' I said.

'Do you know what a Hobson's choice is?' she said.

'Yes,' I said.

'We're worried about you, as were the medical staff who saw you at casualty,' she said quietly. 'As is your school. And either he accepts that you – and he – need support from Social Services, and some help with his alcohol problems, or—'

I didn't precisely know what the 'or' stood for, nor to whom it applied.

'One possibility that I've explained to your father is a short stay for you with some people who do respite fostering,' she said.

'How short?'

'Temporary. A break from looking after your dad. And we're trying to persuade him into the psychiatric hospital for a fortnight for help with the alcohol. I'm sure he'll come round to that.'

'The best of luck,' I said.

Whatever happened next, though, once a week – on Mondays – she was going to pick me up from school. 'We'll go to a café,' she said, 'and catch up. Wherever you're staying, we'll do that.'

'Okay.' I knew the word came out flat, but it was taking all my energy not to scratch at my scalp.

'You didn't slip in the kitchen, did you, Jackie?' she said, catching me off guard.

'I did,' I said.

What I didn't say was, I did slip, but only because he'd grabbed my left arm to wrench a half-finished bottle of whisky from me. I'd been replacing its cap and had intended to hide it under the sink to keep him from going over The Edge. Over The Edge, he was at his most frightening. The cap had come off and the bottle had disgorged whisky as he'd struggled to pull it from my grasp. I'd slipped on the spilled whisky and fallen. But it wasn't the fall that had sprained my wrist.

I reckoned Bobbie had more or less worked it out for herself. No need to tell then. No need to put the words out there. They didn't seem like companions for cups of tea and the digestives she'd brought with her anyway.

SATURDAY 3 APRIL

'It's Eurovision tonight,' I said to Dad. It was nine o'clock in the morning. He was sitting in one of the armchairs in his vest and pants, smoking and drinking tea. 'Can we watch it?'

'I suppose,' he said.

His mood was fairly light and his hangover didn't seem too serious. He'd picked up his benefits the day before and he liked having money in his pocket. I think it helped him to feel more like a proper person and sometimes he'd drink less because of it. Yesterday had been one of those days.

I also wondered whether he was trying to behave better so that Social Services would give a reprieve.

I was stripping his bed to wash the linen. If I didn't do it, he never would, and there's not a lot worse than spending your evenings in a room with fetid sheets. But I was having to be careful. My wrist burned and was puffed like bread dough.

I struggled as I tugged the cases off his pillows. They were stained where he'd spilled whisky. At least, I hoped it was whisky.

I said, 'Have we got enough fifty pees to put in the telly box? We don't want it switching off as the results come in.'

We rented the television. It had a box on the back that was greedy for cash.

'Only got notes,' he said. 'You can get some change at the off-licence later.'

Nice one, Dad.

I took the bandage off my wrist to wrestle Dad's laundry, my own bedsheet and some clothes, including my school uniform, through the noise and froth of Mum's old cranky twin tub then hung them on the washing line in our tiny garden. It took me twice as long as it normally would to drag the wet washing around. My wrist was multicoloured, like tie dye.

I fetched clean linen from the airing cupboard upstairs. I found Dad sitting on the edge of his mattress, slurping another mug of tea that he'd strayed into the kitchen to make while I was in the garden.

'Will you help me put this sheet on your bed, Dad? It's much easier with two.'

He hauled himself up and stubbed out his fag. 'You're a bloody pain.'

'Sorry,' I said. 'Once we've done this, I could make us some egg on toast.'

Life with Dad. Negotiation and politics of which any international ambassador would be proud.

I went to the off-licence at lunchtime to fetch whisky and twenty Benson & Hedges. These sucked up a fair proportion of Dad's money in the same way as he'd later suck up the whisky itself.

'What have you done to your wrist?' the plump woman behind the counter said as I paid her. I'd put the bandage back on, but I think she could tell I wasn't a qualified nurse.

I didn't recognise her. It was usually a man.

'Nothing serious,' I said.

'Oh, right,' she said. 'That's what they all say, love. How old are you? And who's the whisky for?'

'Sixteen. My dad.'

'If you're sixteen, I'm the pope,' she said. She handed me my bag of shopping. I took it with my right hand.

'Thank you, Your Grace,' I said.

'Cheeky bugger,' she said, but she smiled. It gave me a lump in my throat because she smiled like Mum used to, so I left before I could make a fool of myself.

Dad was never going to stay conscious for the whole of the Eurovision Song Contest. One factor that affected this was that he'd sent me out to fetch a Chinese takeaway and had ordered enough for four. 'Can we afford it?' I'd said.

'Do you want some bloody tea or not?' he'd said, so I took the money and left the house before he changed his mind because, frankly, I did want some bloody tea.

Another factor was alcohol, but perhaps I hardly need mention that. Although the day had begun well, it hadn't continued that way.

It wasn't all bad that he wasn't going to stay conscious. I wondered if he would provide a running commentary through the songs, something that used to irritate Mum. Unlike me, she'd had a decent singing voice and loved music. 'Dave, shut up, will you?' she'd say. 'Let me listen!'

I'll modify that and say that I remember her saying this when I was younger. The last couple of years before she died, she would have been more wary.

A few weeks after Mum's funeral, I'd watched Eurovision with Dad as Abba Waterlooed themselves towards the trophy. On one of our armchairs lay the blanket Mum had wrapped round herself in the evenings, having lost so much weight that she couldn't get warm. As Dad and I had watched Eurovision that evening, he'd arranged the blanket over his body and this time there'd been no running commentary. Just Dad in his whisky zone, slowly drifting from me minute by minute the way Mum had drifted from us week by week in those few months since her diagnosis, months that in some ways seemed like years and, in others, like seconds.

Now, as we watched, he made occasional remarks, but they were mainly negative – think Eeyore, not Tigger. These gradually dried up so, halfway through the show, we were watching in virtual silence, him necking whisky like a man who'd just found water in a desert and me writing down a score for each act the way Mum would have done. I asked, 'What do you think, Dad, out of ten?' a couple of times, but he didn't bite.

When Brotherhood of Man sang 'Save Your Kisses For Me' I said, 'Dad, I think they could win,' and he said, 'What, for poncing about doing a silly dance?' so I gave up.

By the time the UK song was declared the winner, Dad had shifted onto the bed. He'd woken briefly to stumble to the outside toilet which he used these days rather than risking the stairs, but now his snoring was a performance all of its own, so I missed much of their victory rendering of the song. I watched, though, as they did their funny little coordinated dance and smiled with their bright teeth. It seemed a world away from our front room and the mayhem that was life with my dad.

I took the foil trays and our cutlery into the kitchen. In one tray was the remains of some meat in a sweet and sour sauce; I couldn't remember what. The sauce had set like a dirty-brown jelly and I wondered why I had found it all so appetising earlier. It didn't look like something you'd willingly pay for and I knew that later in the week it would mean a few days on Weetabix and cheap bread or that there'd be no telly.

I pushed the trays into the bin and rinsed our spoons and forks under the tap. At least we'd squeezed in Eurovision before Dad ran out of fifty pees and, what's more, I'd predicted the winner. I wished Mum had been there so that I could tell her.

MONDAY 5 APRIL

Bobbie met me from school as she'd told me she would, collecting me in her blue Mini from the teachers' car park where I'd waited in the afternoon sunshine.

She drove me to the Happy Plate café on the edge of Leamington, which she said was one of her favourites. Its tables wore red-checked cloths and we could hear the faint tizz of a radio from the kitchen behind the counter.

A waitress brought me Horlicks, and Bobbie a pot of tea. Bobbie had taken off her cardigan but not her orange beret.

The café was crowded, most people scouring newspapers and speculating. It was the new prime minister Mr Callaghan's first day.

'It must all feel strange, Jackie,' Bobbie said, stirring the tea in the pot. 'I'm so sorry.'

'Don't apologise,' I said. 'It's not your fault about Harold Wilson.'

'You know I don't mean that.'

Bobbie wanted to tell me about some people called the Wall family. She said Bridget and Nick Wall had a daughter, Amanda.

'Any photos of them?' I said, sipping at the Horlicks. I loved its maltiness. It was like a hug.

'Sorry, no,' she said. 'We don't usually—'

'You should,' I said. 'No one wants to move in with a family of gargoyles, even for a fortnight. Have you met them?'

'Of course,' she said. 'Prospective foster parents go

through a rigorous series of interviews and form-filling before they're allocated any children.'

'You mean, I'm their first one?' I said.

'Yes,' she said. 'But they're lovely people.'

'I bet Jack the Ripper's friends said he was a lovely person.'

'I'm not their friend, remember,' she said, straining tea into her cup. 'I'm a professional. It's my duty to make sure their motivations are right and that they're suitable as foster parents.'

'You could be wrong. Everyone's got skeletons.'

'Pardon?'

'In their cupboards, I mean. Do they have jobs?'

She told me that Bridget Wall had recently left a job working at a doctor's surgery to concentrate on fostering. Her husband, Nick, used to work in a museum but had recently gone back to teaching. 'Supply teaching, for now, I think.'

'A teacher?'

'They're not all monsters.'

'That depends. I don't mind them at school – I like some of mine – but I don't think I'd like one in my house, popping out from behind doors. Where does the girl go to school?'

'I can't remember offhand,' she said. 'Not your school, I know that.' She sipped at her tea. Bright-red lipstick stained the cup. 'You and your dad can both visit the Walls before you go to stay.'

'A dream date.'

'I'll be there, too. And don't call Amanda "the girl" when we're there, will you?'

I stirred my Horlicks again.

'We try to encourage parents to meet the prospective foster family,' she said. 'It reassures them that you'll be treated well.'

I looked at my wrist. I'd taken the bandage off. The swelling had gone down and the tie-dye effect wasn't so pronounced. But, still.

'I know,' she said.

'You said "allocated",' I said. 'Is that the word they use? It's not… warm.'

'Matched with, then.' She added another spoonful of sugar to her tea.

'Matched with' wasn't much better, but I kept that thought back. She was paying for the Horlicks, after all.

WEDNESDAY 7 APRIL

I'd heard some excuses from my father before, but he excelled himself the day we were due to visit the Walls.

Bobbie had wangled me a morning off school, although I hadn't been keen because it meant I wouldn't be back in time for Poetry Club.

'Will the girl be there?' I'd said.

'Amanda has been given time off school too. It's important that you meet,' she said.

'Does she get a say once she's inspected me?'

'She's not a nit nurse.'

Bobbie said to expect her at 10. I'd slept in after a restless night, listening to Dad moving around downstairs, falling over the kitchen step on his way outside.

So, when Bobbie pitched up early, I called Dad to answer the door, but heard nothing. My bedroom was at the front of the house, so I opened my window and yelled down, 'Wait there!', dragged on my clothes and rushed downstairs.

Bobbie and I stood in the hall. 'I'm not even sure Dad's awake,' I said, trying to tame my hair with a brush.

'You have a lot of hair,' she said.

'Like Dad's,' I said. 'Depressingly black and unruly.' I tugged at it. 'I hate it.'

She took off her beret. 'Mousy and thin,' she said and put her hat back on. 'Count your blessings.'

Dad had shut the door of the front room. 'Stay here,' I said to Bobbie and nudged it open, like a sniffer dog before the bomb disposal experts go in.

The room was stuffy warm. The curtains were shut against the morning sun, as usual – shut against curious lookers-in and against any joy.

He was sprawled on his back across the bed in his underpants. The sheets and blankets were on the floor.

I turned back to Bobbie. 'He's still asleep,' I whispered. 'And he's in his pants. Don't follow me in. You could wait in the kitchen.'

'Give me a shout if you need me,' she said, and by shout I think she meant shout.

I'll give him his due; he really had overslept. He'd clearly drunk himself into oblivion the night before, and his circulatory system was doubtless still thick with whisky, but at least he hadn't had chance to start drinking that morning.

I shook him gently and he woke, edgy and wound up like some kind of clockwork toy.

'We're visiting the foster parents this morning,' I said. 'We're late.'

I think he'd rehearsed the excuses. 'I need to iron a shirt,' he said, sitting on the edge of the bed, head in hands. I was pleased to hear him getting his consonants bang on.

'Iron?' I said. 'We *have* an iron?'

It was true, though. He needed a different shirt. He surely couldn't wear the stained tee shirt and jeans that were slung on the back of an armchair.

'I feel sick,' he said.

I told him it was nerves.

'I'm knackered,' he said. 'I didn't sleep well.'

'Dad, you knew we were going. You need to get dressed.' I nodded towards his dirty clothes. 'In something decent.'

'I don't see why I have to come,' he said. 'No doubt that bloody Bobbie woman has told them some stuff. Half of it made up.'

I reminded him that that bloody Bobbie woman was in the kitchen, probably listening.

His anxiety hinted that he was ashamed about the situation he'd created, though, and I liked him a little for that.

'I want you to come,' I said. 'I want you to know who I'm being farmed out to.'

'They're probably stuck-up,' he said. 'Do-gooders. Holier-than-bloody-thous.'

'You won't know if you don't come.'

'I'll go once I've had a drink.'

'I'll make you a cup of tea,' I said.

'People who can't mind their own business,' he said. 'Messing up other people's lives.'

'I'll go and get you a clean shirt and trousers,' I said. In the kitchen, I heard Bobbie filling the kettle.

'I'll fetch my own,' he said, and I stepped back and watched him heave his body up the stairs towards what used to be his and Mum's bedroom.

I sat in the kitchen with Bobbie. We could hear him moving around above our heads, the floorboards creaking. 'I think we're going to be late,' I said to Bobbie.

She pointed towards the hissing kettle. 'I'd gathered that.'

'I'll make him a tea,' I said.

'Can I use your telephone to phone the Walls?' she said.

I nodded towards the hallway. Our telephone sat on a table at the bottom of the stairs. I hoped the bills had been paid and she'd find it connected.

'Go ahead,' I said. 'If Dad slides down the stairs, you'll be there to break his fall.'

I'd sat in the front of Bobbie's car on Monday, but after some awkward you-no-you-no-you business, Dad's frame now filled up the space between her and the front passenger door, and his knees pressed into the dashboard, even with the seat as far back as it could go. It accentuated how much room he could occupy, plus he'd substituted soft weight for his fireman's muscle over the last few years, since he'd stopped work. From my place on the back seat, behind Bobbie, I could see his hands on his thighs and I was sure his palms would be sweaty. There was dandruff on his jacket collar, but I dared not lean forward to brush it off. He could take off Bobbie's head with a sudden reaction.

A long time ago, he would have checked himself in the mirror in the hallway. But there hadn't been a mirror there for months. I couldn't remember exactly what had happened to it or maybe I could and it was best not to take myself back there.

'I think this is the turning,' Bobbie said, after a ten-minute drive during which she'd tried to make conversation with my dad about George Best and where she'd bought her Mini and about Mr Callaghan, and Dad had tried to make her stop.

We drove into a quiet road with houses like giant boxes set apart from each other, each with a tidy lawn at the front, a garage and a drive big enough for two cars.

Where Dad and I lived in Warwick was in a row of terraced houses, their rooms small and a strip of ground at the front barely enough for a tub of flowers. It was the council house we'd moved to not long before Mum died, when we realised Dad wasn't going back to work and we'd run out of money to pay the mortgage or tradesmen to mend boilers and fix loose roof tiles. Or to pay off debtors, of which there were many, including the off-licence.

Dad and I didn't, of course, have a tub of flowers. We did once have a metal dustbin that would get emptied on Wednesdays, but this had disappeared, so now Dad decorated the front of our house with a binbag full of whisky bottles and crisp packets, and sometimes he didn't bother with the binbag. I didn't understand how he wasn't embarrassed, but they say drink takes away your inhibitions and I don't know where it took his, but it hadn't brought them back.

'Here we are,' Bobbie said, tucking the car alongside the kerb in front of number 17 Hollybush Close. In the driveway, a dark-green Morris Marina was parked.

My head itched.

From the top window of the house, a girl stood, looking out. I assumed this must be Amanda, unless there were other teenagers stashed away in the house they hadn't told Social Services about. I wondered if she intended to stay upstairs.

'Shall I wait in the car for you?' Dad said.

'We're here now, Dad,' I said. 'You've made it this far.' I climbed out, went round to the passenger side and opened the door. As he stooped to clamber out, I noticed the left pocket of his jacket hung heavy.

Whisky. Dad, you sod.

There was nothing I could say without causing a scene and a Dad-scene at that.

Bobbie pressed the doorbell, but even before its bing-bong-bing-bong had binged and bonged, the green door with one of those swirly misty windows had been opened by a woman, slender and, in her tweed skirt and cardigan, looking much more official than Bobbie did. Had she dressed up? She wore a necklace and earrings. Pearls.

'Mrs Wall,' Bobbie said. 'I'm sorry we're so late. Thank you for understanding on the telephone.'

'It's no trouble,' said the woman, with her face saying something different. She looked like a woman who kept to time.

Bobbie went in first and I followed. The hall was small and square, so there was a traffic jam while the woman asked Bobbie if she'd like to hang up her jacket on a hook. Then Bobbie and I moved through a door into the living room where a stocky man in glasses stood, taking his hands in and out of his pockets as though he didn't know where to stash them.

'Can I take your jacket too?' I heard the woman say to Dad, who was still in the hallway.

He said, 'No, I'll keep it on. Actually, is there a lav?'

'It's right here,' the woman said. There must have been a downstairs toilet off the hall. I hadn't noticed the door.

Oh, Dad.

The woman came into the living room.

'Mr Wall, this is Jackie,' Bobbie said to the man.

'Jackie,' he said, putting out a hand. I liked his eyes – brown, and the kind that look as though they've heard a joke. 'It's good to meet you. I'm Nick Wall.' He had sandy-coloured hair.

I shook his hand.

'And this is Bridget Wall,' Bobbie said.

The woman shook my hand too. 'Lovely to see you,' she said.

I turned to Bobbie. 'And who are you?' and all three adults laughed far too loudly for the quality of the quip. But I'd said it because I was anxious. I was wondering where the girl was, and where my dad was. Two people missing in action and the battle only just begun.

'Settle yourselves down and I'll put the kettle on,' the woman said.

'Here, by me, Jackie,' Bobbie said, sitting on a two-seater sofa with square cushions. It was bright orange, as were its two matching armchairs. The rest of the room was in normal colours: beige and brown. It was as if the three-piece suite was shouting.

I sat by Bobbie obediently.

The man sat in one of the armchairs but had to pogo up again straight away when the woman called through from the kitchen, 'Darling, can you see where Amanda's got to?'

'Back in a tick,' he said to us and went up the stairs which led from the living room. 'Amanda?' he was calling.

Bobbie and I were left alone. I looked around the room. A bookcase. A cabinet with doors, tucked into an alcove. A dining table by French windows which led to the garden. A coffee table in the middle of the room, piled with cups and saucers, and with a small vase of flowers at its centre. A TV resting on a low cupboard in the corner.

Bobbie patted my knee. 'Okay?' she said.

'Never been better,' I said.

We heard the faint sound of a toilet flush and then Dad appeared from the hall. He stayed in the doorway and I saw him take a deep breath before venturing in, his chest rising up and down. He looked quite smart in his best clothes and I wished I could have been prouder of him.

Bridget Wall arrived with some small plates and said, 'Come in, Mr Chadwick. Sit down.'

She pointed him to the other orange armchair, and he lowered himself into it slowly as though he had backache, but I knew it was so the bottle wouldn't fall out of his pocket.

He looked incongruous in the armchair in his dark trousers and jacket, framed by orange, as though he were sitting in the middle of a sunset. Or maybe a Turner painting like the ones we'd been shown in art.

Footsteps, two sets, came down the stairs.

'I've got her,' the man said, sounding as relieved as if he'd been searching a ravine for a body and found someone alive, not checking the rooms in a suburban detached.

The girl I'd seen upstairs emerged behind him. Her smooth fair hair was in a ponytail. She wore a white cheesecloth shirt and blue cotton flares. She was taller than me and had bare feet.

I wasn't sure whether I should stand up. I didn't want to shake her hand. Who shook hands with other teenagers?

Thankfully, she seemed to think the same. 'Hello,' she said, although not warmly, and dropped to the carpet to sit cross-legged. I envied her the long legs. My dad used to call my mum short-arse and I got my genes from her. I told people 'five foot and half an inch', but the last bit was a lie.

'This is our lovely Amanda,' the man said.

'And this is Jackie,' Bobbie said, nodding in my direction.

The woman came in with a plate of cake and added it to the things already arranged on the coffee table. She poured tea, adding milk from a jug. It was good to have something to hold and I kept my hands around the cup, feeling its heat.

She fetched a dining chair and sat on that.

I said no to her offer of the fruit cake.

'She doesn't like fruit cake. She prefers sponge,' my dad said, which was the first thing he'd uttered since entering the room. I looked at him, surprised. It wasn't like him to come to my defence. In the circumstances, it was ironic, and I think the rest of the room read it that way too.

What's more, he was wrong. I loved fruit cake and didn't like sponge, but it was touching that he tried.

'Amanda's the other way,' the man said. 'You'd kill for a bit of Dundee, wouldn't you, Amanda?'

I saw her glare at him. I imagined she'd found her jovial dad embarrassing and it was the first sign that perhaps we'd have something in common.

She was supposed to pretend to be my new sister for a while, after all, if they accepted me, or I accepted them. I wasn't sure how it worked.

My first sister.

'Sister' wasn't a word I was used to. It sounded strange in my head the more I thought it, like when you take a wrong turning and don't recognise the houses.

FRIDAY 9 APRIL

Dad tried to make me stay home from school on the last Friday of term.

'Everyone skives on the last day,' he said. 'How come you're so precious about it?'

I was in the kitchen in my school uniform foraging for breakfast. I was late anyway as a button had come off my one clean school blouse, which was tight now I wore a bra. I'd hurriedly sewn it back on using a mini sewing kit Nanna had sent me in my birthday card in March. There was still an embarrassing gape that I'd safety-pinned. Dad said I had to wait until the summer for new uniform.

Sewing and safety-pinning hadn't been easy. My wrist felt sore today and my arm ached. I knew I had probably taken the bandage off too early. I wondered whether to ask Dad to help me put it back on properly but couldn't see him playing St John's Ambulance any time soon.

He had never bought me bras. I'd rescued them from Mum's drawer after she died. I wasn't even sure how I would initiate a conversation with Dad about something like that. I'd rehearsed a few starting sentences in my room, but nothing seemed feasible.

I was filling a glass with water when I heard him behind me shuffling into the kitchen. He slumped into the chair as though his body didn't do vertical any more. I had heard him moving around the house in the early hours, the clink of bottle on glass waking me from my fragile sleep. I was always worried about fire if I knew he was awake. Sometimes he fell asleep while smoking and in the morning I'd see tiny burn holes in the pillowcases like sites of mini-explosions.

He looked wrecked this morning, his eyes reddened and his face colourless.

'I need you at home today,' he said. His voice was rough, like Rod Stewart's but without the song.

I waited. I knew why this was, and it wasn't about spending quality time with his loved one. On his worst days, and when he'd exhausted his whisky supplies during the night, someone needed to fetch more in the morning. In the surprising absence of a butler, I was the only option.

And, while I was home, he'd have a list of other jobs. Changing the beds. Folding up the washing. Cleaning the kitchen. Doing the floors with Mum's battered Ewbank carpet sweeper – our vacuum cleaner had died a year before. Dusting and polishing.

I'd once pointed out that he hardly used any of the other rooms. What did it matter whether they were dusted and polished?

'Your mum would be ashamed of you, letting it all go,' he'd shouted, kicking out from where he lay on the bed but too drunk to aim a decent blow.

Now, he nodded towards my injury. 'Surely it's difficult at school with your—?'

'My arm?' I said. The words came out sarcastic without my permission and I swallowed.

'Don't bloody cheek me,' he said, which is when I knew he'd need bringing back from The Edge.

I turned away and tried to open a jar of jam with my good hand. The lid was stuck, leaked jam around its rim, no doubt because Dad had been the last one to use it. It was apricot jam: his favourite. I'd taken it from the corner shop near school.

The tension in the kitchen drifted somewhere near the ceiling.

'Dad, can you help me?' I said.

There was a pause, then, 'Give it here.'

I thought I loved him then, as I loved him for any tiny sign, like a dog looking for scraps, but tiny scraps can keep you going, if you get enough of them. Think about whales and plankton.

But when I put the jar on the table so that he could open it, he couldn't coordinate his hands to grip either. And I realised he was having trouble focusing. I watched him try and fail, try and fail, using swear words under his breath he must have learned in some sewer.

'Don't worry, Dad,' I said. 'I'll get some crisps on the way to school.'

'You're not *going* to school,' he said, and on the word 'going' he hurled the jar towards the kitchen window. It hit the tiled sill, smashed and fell into a bowl full of water in the sink.

'But I've got a history test,' I said, before I could think.

He reared up, like a bear, and seemed to fill the kitchen. He caught me by both forearms and squeezed hard with his massive fingers, as if to prove that he did have strength after all.

I yelped, despite myself. I usually tried to stay silent.

He pushed past me, crushing my body against the kitchen cupboards, and I screamed again because my wrist bent under his weight.

He went back through the hall into the front room and crashed the door shut.

I looked down at my forearms. I could see red circles where his thumbs had been and the soft underskin of my arms felt tender from his other fingers. My wrist fired up inside. I had to swallow several times not to start crying, but that would have made me weak, and I couldn't have him catch me that way.

I fetched my satchel from my bedroom and let myself out, worried that he would appear in the hall and stop me, but he didn't.

When I reached school, before I could change my mind, I went to the school receptionist and asked her if I could see Miss Jones. The receptionist's eyebrows rose so high they had a short meeting with her hairline, but she nodded straight away, so I think she knew about my situation. She pointed me to a chair.

As I waited for Miss Jones to arrive, I thought about betrayers such as Judas in the Bible and Edmund from *The Lion, the Witch and the Wardrobe*. I felt sick. But I could also feel bruises developing beneath my skin, as though Dad's fingers were still there, digging in.

When Miss Jones appeared, the tears on which I'd pressed pause came fast.

As I left the last lesson of the day, Mrs Caine appeared in the corridor to tell me that I was to wait in the school car park for Bobbie. 'In fact,' she said, 'why don't I wait with you?' which she did, like a minder but with a leather handbag and a pair of glasses on a chain.

'My dad won't turn up here,' I said.

'All the same,' she said.

When Bobbie arrived, I climbed into her car. 'I thought we were doing this on Mondays,' I said. I kept my wrist close to my chest. It had been re-bandaged by the school nurse, but it pulsed inside like a light going on and off.

'You're not going home tonight, Jackie,' she said, starting up the ignition. 'I'm sorry.'

The train in the station.

'Where am I going?' I said.

'We'll drop in at the café first and I'll fill you in,' she said. 'Then to the Walls' house. Given the situation, they're very happy to take you in at shorter notice.'

'How can I not go home?' I said. 'All my clothes are there. I haven't told Dad.'

I wasn't sure how to feel. Was I sad? Relieved? I knew

49

I felt guilty, and I'd been thinking about traitors all day, but increasingly when I considered who I'd betrayed, it had been my mum's face I saw, not my dad's. That hurt more.

'We've told your dad,' Bobbie said. 'I'll drive you home and you can pack some things. He said this morning that he'd go to the pub, so I doubt he'll be there.' We pulled out of the school car park. 'Do you have a key?'

'Yes.'

'That's something,' she said.

In the Happy Plate, Bobbie was cagey about Dad's reaction to being told that morning that I was to be whisked away. All she'd say was, 'He didn't take it well.'

'Were you on your own?' I asked her.

'No. A senior social worker came with me,' she said. 'My colleague, Peter.'

'A part-time wrestler? Judo black belt?' I said. 'Fire-eater?'

'Just senior.'

'And?'

'Suffice it to say your dad couldn't ignore the facts. And he's had a visit from the local police, too. They've given him a warning.'

That possibility hadn't occurred to me when I'd blabbed to Miss Jones.

Bobbie seemed to know how I felt. 'It's the only way he'll change, Jackie. If he knows everyone's serious about what's been happening.'

'It's because Mum died,' I said. 'Mainly. That made things worse for him, anyhow.'

She said, 'Have you been hurting other people because your mum died? Or mistreating them?'

'No.'

'But you've been grieving too.'

'I guess. I play my music in my bedroom until my

blankets tremble,' I said, 'or I would if my record player wasn't broken.'

'Oh dear.'

'And if it didn't send Dad into a rage.'

'Would you like another Horlicks before we head off?' she said.

I said no.

As Bobbie tucked her Mini into a parking space near our house, I noticed a police car also parked, two uniformed men inside it.

'What are they here for?' I said.

'They won't come in. Unless they're needed.'

Dad was sitting in an armchair staring at a blank TV screen, a whisky in his hand, so he hadn't gone to the pub. I suspected he'd seen the police car and decided to lie low.

Far from being combative, he seemed broken. 'I'm sorry,' he kept saying when I came downstairs after packing. I'd found an old sports bag in the bottom of Mum and Dad's wardrobe to put my clothes and possessions in. I'd left it upstairs for the moment with my school satchel. I didn't want to see them sitting in the hall. 'I'm sorry. I don't want you to go.' His voice was pleading.

It reminded me of when Mum was dying. He'd used the same tone.

Beside me, Bobbie stood. I could feel her apprehension – she was shuffling a sheaf of papers as though rearranging them would make things all right. She had doubtless expected him to kick off, hence the policemen, but I had the feeling his shame was keeping him calm.

'It's all my fault,' he said.

There was no disputing this. It was as true as the fact that he was wearing trousers, which was the nearest to him marking an occasion that I could hope for.

'I can maybe come and see you at the hospital, Dad,' I said, but I looked at Bobbie to check this.

'It's something we can talk about,' she said.

Dad had started to cry. I could hardly look.

'I don't want to go either, Dad. But—'

'I do love you, Jackie,' he said, gulping down whisky as though it was a cure-all for being a rubbish dad. 'I know I haven't shown it.'

His nose was running. I slid my good hand under the pillow where he kept a handkerchief the same colour as his pants. I handed it to him. He wiped his nose and sat with the handkerchief bunched up in his hand.

Did I love him, too? I didn't know. What did it feel like? If I compared it to how I felt about Mum before she died, then, no, I didn't. Still, his crying made my throat tense up as though its muscles were on standby.

'We'd better go,' Bobbie said. 'Do you have your things?'

'A bag and my satchel. They're upstairs,' I said. 'I'll fetch them.'

'No, I'll get them,' Dad said. He nodded towards my fresh bandage, wiped his nose and pulled himself up. I thought it was a bit late to play gentleman, as though it made up for my bruises. It wasn't his most successful impersonation and showed that no matter how many Mike Yarwood shows you've been drunk in front of, it isn't the best way to learn a skill.

In the car, Bobbie said, 'Do you have the addresses of your grandparents?'

'My mum's parents, yes.'

'And there's an auntie, isn't there, abroad? School mentioned her.'

'I have a little address book. I packed it.'

'Good,' she said. 'We should let them know in case your dad doesn't.'

'He won't,' I said.

I looked back to see if he was standing at the door, watching me go, but he'd shut it. If he was at the window, he was behind the closed curtains, peeping out, and I couldn't see him.

Not exactly a send-off.

After Not-to-be-Auntie-Bridget had shown me my sunflower-painted room, and I'd spent some time alone, sitting on the bed, I opened the door, wondering whether to go downstairs.

My bag and satchel had been brought up, so I spent ten minutes putting clothes on hangers in the wardrobe and folding tee shirts and jumpers into the deep drawers of the wooden chest. The drawers had flowered paper linings, and tucked in the corner of each drawer was a tiny lavender bag. I hung my satchel on the back of the door. The few books I owned were still on my window sill at home and I'd seen no point in bringing my records or the soft toys that had sat along my shelf. This was meant to be a temporary stay. Leaving them there had felt like insurance and perhaps a reminder for Dad that he had a reason to sort himself out called a daughter.

I'd intended to pack Mum's clock, though, and had forgotten. I nearly cried when I realised, but I didn't want to let tears out if I could help it. Getting them back in might prove tricky.

When I came downstairs, I perched on the sofa I'd sat on with Bobbie at the introduction visit, on the same side. It made me feel there was still a get-out clause if things went tits-up, as my dad would have put it.

Bridget turned the TV on and said, 'It's *The Magic Roundabout*. Would you like to watch it?'

'No, thanks,' I said.

She switched it off. I felt sorry for her and resistant to her all at once.

She tried again. 'Do you like *Jackie* magazine?' she said. 'There are some on that coffee table.' She pointed. 'I asked Amanda to find some back copies. She keeps them all.'

'Thanks.' At least she'd had the courtesy to pretend she

didn't realise I had the same name as the magazine. I was tired of hearing it from the girls at school. Was I named after the magazine? Was it because my mum liked the magazine? In the end, I'd looked up its first publication date in the library so I could tell them it didn't appear until 1964 when I was two, so shut your cakehole.

Bridget walked into the kitchen and I heard her fill a kettle. Then she reappeared. 'That's funny, isn't it,' she said, 'that your name is Jackie, too? Like the magazine.'

The telephone rang from the kitchen. I heard Bridget pick it up. 'Yes, she's here, safe and sound,' she said. 'Just settling in.' She dropped her voice for a minute and then, 'I'll call you in the daytime, when they're at school.'

She came in, carrying a tea towel. 'That was my friend, Gloria. She lives in Cornwall.'

'Oh?'

'She's a new foster parent, too. She and her husband.'

I waited. She was clearly going to tell me more.

'Not as new as us. They inspired us, in fact. They have two of their own children and now a foster son. They said to us, try it. It could be the making of us. And, now, here you are!'

'Here I am indeed,' I said.

'Amanda's birth was very difficult,' she said. 'We decided not to risk another child of our own.'

I hoped she'd finished.

'Amanda's often wished for a sibling,' she said. 'I suppose you have too.'

I knew Mum had miscarried twice after my birth. 'No, I haven't,' I said truthfully. I'd been happy in my family of three until things had begun to slide.

'Oh.' She waited, I think to see if I would expand on this. Eventually she said, 'Amanda should be home soon. I think she went to a friend's house after school.'

'Right.'

She folded the tea towel into a tidy square as though

planning what to say next, but she came up with nothing and went back into the kitchen.

I looked out at the garden through the French windows that led to it. It had been a warm day and the sun still covered most of the garden, so I realised it must face south. The shade was in front of a wide shed that stretched across where the square lawn ended.

The garden was neat, like Bridget's tea towel, with straight flower beds, a few shrubs, and tubs of flowers tidily placed as though someone had made a plan. My mum would have known the names of the flowers. We'd had a similar garden in the house she and Dad owned before Dad's accident.

Bridget was chopping vegetables in the kitchen. 'I'll do some carrots,' she called through – I wasn't sure how or whether to respond. But she could only have chopped one before she came back to look at me, her head on one side as though she had a cricked neck. 'Everything okay?'

I wish I'd chosen that moment to be opening a drawer or two in the cabinet in the alcove or helping myself to the sherry bottle that stood on its surface.

I picked up a magazine instead to keep her happy. In truth, I rarely got to read *Jackie* and I'd often begged Dad to let me buy it, but he'd ask me the price and then draw in his breath, presumably forgetting how much money he was sluicing away on whisky and fags.

Bridget made another visit after carrot two, but then I heard her chop at least four in succession, so she must have been feeling more relaxed.

I was reading a quiz entitled 'Are you a TRUE Donny fan?' and diagnosing myself as a liar when I heard a key in the front door. Someone came into the tiny hall – I could see their fuzzy silhouette through the frosted glass of the inner door – and I heard something drop to the floor. A satchel? The door opened and Amanda came in. A school blazer was folded over her arm. Her school skirt was short; there was the tell-tale bulge around the waist where she'd turned over the waistband. I respected her for this but once again envied her long legs.

'Hello,' she said, her voice flat. She didn't stay for conversation, leaping up the stairs instead.

I put her magazine back on the coffee table.

Her mother called from the kitchen, 'Amanda? Is that you?' and, when she had no reply, came in to ask me, 'Was that Amanda?'

'It was.' I pointed towards the stairs. 'She went that-a-way.'

'Oh, she'll come down in a minute, don't worry,' she said and went back to the chopping.

I sincerely hoped she wouldn't come down. I was very content to be left on my own. And, a couple of minutes later, I heard Slade's 'Coz I Luv You' being played upstairs and Amanda's voice joining in with the 'Ooooohs'. It sounded as though she sang as well as I did, as in, not very well.

Bridget came back in. She was beginning to remind me of one of those clocks – Dutch? – with a lady who pops out on the quarter hour, half hour, three quarter hour, and hour, but imagine half a cabbage added to the scene.

'I don't know what she's up to,' she said. She looked at the ceiling. 'That's her record player.'

I hoped Bridget wasn't going to identify all the household objects for me.

'Do you like Slade?' she said.

I felt a sense of dread.

'If you do,' she said, 'why not go up and join her? I'm sure she won't mind.'

'Have you got any orange squash?' I said.

She loved it, bustling into the kitchen, like someone given a promotion.

I followed her in.

In the corner of the spacious, gleaming kitchen, curled up but with gangly legs everywhere as though it had at least seven, was the hugest Dalmatian dog I had ever seen. When I entered, it opened its eyes, looked at me with vague interest, then closed them again.

'He's the laziest, sleepiest, most laid-back dog you'll ever meet,' Bridget said. 'Don't expect a greeting.'

'I didn't know there was a dog here.'

'Of course. I forgot,' she said. 'He was at the vets the day you visited. He'd had a minor operation. Poor Spotless. He's fine now.'

She must have seen my face when she said its name. 'I know,' she said. 'Silly, isn't it? Nick – Uncle Nick – has a strange sense of humour. Amanda and I wanted to call him Spot, but the dog was Nick's Christmas present, so—'

And that's when I knew I was going to like Uncle Nick the most.

Amanda had stayed upstairs playing Showaddywaddy after a couple of Slade hits, but she was now sitting cross-legged on the living room floor, as she had the day I visited. We were watching the evening news on TV. Spotless had wandered through from the kitchen and leaned his bulk against the sofa where I sat. I could feel his eyes scrutinising me, but with kindness.

Amanda was demolishing a bag of crisps which she must have brought down from her room as she hadn't been in the kitchen. 'I'm hungry,' she said when Bridget came in to express disapproval.

'Tea's ready as soon as Dad's home,' Bridget said.

'I'm hungry now.'

If I hadn't been there, I think this would have escalated, but Bridget drew in her lips, and, I think, most of her inner organs, and went back into the kitchen.

Amanda thrust the packet of crisps towards me as though she thought she should. 'Want one?'

'No, thanks,' I said. 'I don't like prawn cocktail.'

'Spotless does,' she said, smugly, and fed the willing dog a crisp.

'Fine,' I said. 'I hadn't viewed the dog as a source of competition.'

'What?' she said and shook her head, turning her attention back to the TV.

I heard the garage door slam and a minute later a key in the front door. Amanda's father came in and stooped to slide bicycle clips off his ankles. 'Afternoon,' he said, depositing a leather briefcase on the coffee table on top of Amanda's magazines. His forehead was damp and his cheeks were the ruddy shade that pale-skinned people's cheeks go when they're too warm. He wore a brown jacket and trousers. He had undone his tie and the top button of his shirt.

'How is everyone?' He looked at me. 'How's the new arrival? Settling in?'

I was relieved that the question had been rhetorical, as he then walked into the kitchen.

'Two minutes,' I heard Bridget say. 'And don't you dare put that tie on my kitchen surface.'

Near the French windows was the round dining table and four high-backed dining chairs. The table bore a white cloth with lace around the edge. My mum had had a similar one for special occasions. I assumed it was in Dad's lean-to in one of the boxes.

'Amanda, can you lay the table?' Bridget called.

'Do I have to?' Amanda said, tipping the bag of crisps into her mouth for the last few crumbs. But she hauled herself up, opened the top drawer of the cabinet and took out cutlery.

'Which school do you go to?' she asked me as she laid knives and forks on the cloth.

'Warwick Grammar,' I said. 'You?'

'Milverton High in town,' she said.

'Oh.'

'You passed your 11 plus, then?' she said.

'Scraped through.' This was a lie. I'd found it pig-easy.

'Congratulations,' she said, in the least congratulatory voice known to mankind. Then she went back to the cabinet. She'd forgotten she'd need four sets of cutlery.

'What have you done to your wrist?' she said.

'It's nothing,' I said.

'Nothing with a bandage on,' she said.

'If you say so.'

Uncle Nick – I was becoming more comfortable with this term of address where he was concerned – brought in glasses and a jug of water. He placed them on the table. 'There's shepherd's pie coming!' he said, as though it were making the journey independently. 'Good timing, Jackie,' he said, putting each glass to the left of each table mat, 'arriving at the beginning of the Easter holidays. Plenty of time to get settled. To get to know us. And for us to get to know you.'

'Two whole weeks off school!' Amanda said. 'At last!'

'I like school,' I said, and they both glanced at me, I think to see if I was being sarcastic.

Shepherd's pie, cabbage, and the carrots with whom I already felt I shared a history: Bridget had put it all in dishes and brought them to the table, placing them on table mats. I wondered if this was normal practice for the Walls or whether she'd usually serve it in the kitchen and this was all to mark my arrival. I supposed I would find out as the days passed.

I felt as though I were eating at a restaurant.

As she took the lids off the dishes, steam came off the vegetables and they glistened with butter. The shepherd's pie was topped with mashed potato, browned on the top so that there were crispy bits.

Mum's shepherd's pie used to look the same. Crispy bits.

I tried to think of something else while Bridget served me (first), but I couldn't. I stood up, knocking the table, which made water spill from Amanda's full glass. 'I'm sorry,' I said. 'I actually don't feel well.' I swallowed the solid lump in my throat back down.

They all looked at me.

'Oh dear,' Uncle Nick said. 'That's not good.'

Bridget went to stand, but I said, 'I'll go up to my room

and lie down. Don't come up.' I knew it sounded rude, but I had about two seconds to spare before I cried. I ran up the stairs.

Climbing into the bed, I covered myself with the sheet and blankets and pressed my face down so that no one would hear me.

I wondered what Dad was doing. Had he bought any food in? Was he even aware I wasn't there? Would he still watch Dick Emery without me?

Missing Mum was a daily occurrence. Missing Dad had come as a surprise.

Half an hour later, Bridget knocked at my door and called through, 'I've put your tea in the oven in case you feel like it.'

I'd stopped crying by then and was standing by the window, looking at an unfamiliar view of a row of houses, identical to this one, with curtains, cars parked in drives and flower tubs outside front doors. I saw one curtain twitch opposite and a face look up, which is when I remembered where Amanda had been standing the day of my visit with Bobbie. She must have been in this room, not her own, as her room was at the side of the house, not the front.

'Can I have my tea up here?' I said.

There was a pause.

'On your own?' she said.

No, you're all invited, I wanted to say. Bring some pals. A cake. But Bobbie's face came to mind. She had a way of shaking her head from side to side as though you were a disappointment to the human race.

'Yes, please,' I said.

She said she thought she could find a tray somewhere, but I read this as 'This won't be a regular occurrence' because, even after less than a day with the Walls, I'd decided that if ever a woman knew where her trays were, it would be Bridget.

I tried it in my head once more. Auntie Bridget.

No. I couldn't make it work.

SATURDAY 10 APRIL

In the morning, I woke with sore eyes after a fidgety night. I didn't know what time it was, but the room was morning-bright, with a hazy light stealing through thin curtains onto the yellow walls. I lay there, thinking again how heedless the weather is, not asking anyone's permission about what would suit your personal circumstances. It goes ahead with its own plans, roasting you to perdition, lashing down on your hatless head regardless, and sometimes chucking irony around, sending sunshine to symbolise a new beginning you'd rather not have had.

Maybe this was why Dad kept the front room curtains shut.

I looked to my right. I'd left the tray and plate from last night's meal on the chest of drawers by my bed. I'd found myself hungry after crying, in the end.

Both had disappeared. Bridget must have crept in once I'd fallen asleep. I didn't like the thought.

I could hear her and Nick talking downstairs.

I'd thought I would sleep, not having to anticipate the clink of a bottle or the thunk of a kitchen cupboard door when Dad found there was no cereal left and woke me with his rage, the kind of rage that had been the spur for my short career as a petty thief.

But instead of sleeping, I'd been alert to all the noises of someone else's house, other people's routines and familiarities. Something had hummed and clicked – a boiler? The fridge? I'd heard a front door slam in the street and a car start up while it was still dark. Twice, someone had passed my door on the way to the bathroom and the flush of the toilet broke into the night.

I tiptoed onto the landing now to check whether Amanda was in the bathroom, but it was free.

I was wiping my face with my flannel when someone knocked. I waited. It was Bridget. 'Jackie, you can leave your toiletries in there, if you like. I've cleared a space on the shelf. You know, your toothpaste etcetera.'

'Thanks for the definition of toiletries,' I called back, but I arranged my shampoo, toothbrush and toothpaste extra-neatly to make amends.

When I came downstairs, Uncle Nick was in an armchair reading *The Times* newspaper, Spotless lying across his feet, and I could hear Bridget in the kitchen. I couldn't see Amanda.

I sat on the sofa seat I'd adopted as mine.

'So,' he said, folding the newspaper untidily. 'We like school, do we?'

'Nick!' Bridget called through. 'How about, "Good morning, Jacqueline. Did you sleep well?" Don't interrogate the poor child. She went to bed upset.'

'Good morning, Jacqueline,' he said. 'I hope you slept well. And that you are feeling more settled.'

'Jackie,' I said.

'Sorry,' he said. 'Brain like a sieve.'

'I don't know why I like school,' I said. 'I like finding things out.'

'Goodness,' he said. 'Your teachers must adore you.'

There was a pause while I decided whether to say what was in my head. 'That explains the Valentines,' I said eventually, and he laughed. I mean, really laughed.

I was pleased he'd asked me about school. I preferred it to conversational rituals and being reminded I'd been upset.

Bridget came in with three boxes of cereal and some bowls and spoons. She arranged them on the table. 'I've got sausage and bacon in the oven,' she said. 'They'll be ready soon. And, as a bonus, I've popped in some of the biggest fresh tomatoes!' She smiled as though she thought she was in line for an award.

Two weeks of Easter holidays to get through, living with this family, before I could go back to school, and perhaps back to Dad. Maybe if I pretended I were on holiday, minus the sea view, it would be more bearable.

Bridget and Uncle Nick sat at the table. Did that mean we were all expected to eat breakfast together? I hesitated.

Uncle Nick patted the chair next to him and said, 'Come on. Choose some cereal. Rice Krispies? Or are you a Weetabix girl?'

I sat down. Bridget poured me half a glass of orange juice from a jug without asking if I wanted it.

'Amanda!' she said loudly, aiming her voice at the ceiling. 'Are you coming?'

I'd heard no noise from Amanda's room so thought she must still have been asleep.

'Nick,' Bridget said, 'you go.'

He rolled his eyes.

I remembered how, on the visit with Dad, it had been Uncle Nick's job to retrieve the missing Amanda, like a dog does with a stick, but with less enjoyment, and with his tongue in.

I took one Weetabix from the pack, poured milk and sprinkled a thick layer of sugar. I could sense Bridget watching. Was sugar not allowed? She was eating Bran Flakes – new to me – some kind of cornflake but with a deep tan. The portion was small.

Nick returned with Amanda behind him. She was in pyjamas, the top of which bore David Cassidy's face. She'd brushed her hair, though, into the ponytail she seemed to prefer.

'Pyjamas?' her mother said.

'It's Saturday, Mum,' Amanda said. 'Do I have to sit at the table?'

She pulled out a dining chair roughly and sat on it.

No one said anything, although the lull told me what I needed to know: they were doing things differently for my sake. While it made me uncomfortable, it would also entertain me to watch how long they could keep it up.

I declined the cooked breakfast. I'd never lived in a house where you ate a full meal within half an hour of tumbling out of bed, and I didn't intend to start now.

Amanda ate four sausages, three bacon rashers and a quivering heap of scrambled egg. She refused the tomatoes.

She wiped her plate with a piece of toast and said, 'Dad, will you drop me into town this morning?'

'Why?' That was Bridget.

'I said I'd meet Fiona.'

Uncle Nick looked at me. 'Would you like to go into town, too? Browse round the shops?'

I saw Amanda's eyes widen. 'I don't think—' She trailed off.

Bridget began stacking up our plates as though it would help with family discord. 'Dad can take Jackie round town, if she'd like to go,' she said. 'I'm staying at home to make my simnel cake. Do you like to bake, Jackie?'

I remembered Mum, in the kitchen, creaming butter and sugar and saying, 'Then I need the eggs. Can you break them for me, into this jug here?' It had made me feel heated up inside, when Mum said that.

I hadn't had a mother for a while but, even so, I wasn't finding it easy to be given a new one.

'No,' I said. 'I'm not keen on baking.'

'Into town with Uncle Nick it is, then,' she said. 'If you coordinate things, you can all come back together.' She took the plates away and I heard a tap turn on and the rush of water into a bowl.

'I've got my marking to do,' Uncle Nick said, 'but I'll try and get ahead on that this afternoon.'

'Bobbie told me you were a teacher,' I said.

'I am,' he said. 'For my sins.'

I waited to see if he would explain further.

Instead, he picked up the plate the toast had been on and took it into the kitchen.

'I don't think you'd like Fiona anyway,' Amanda said to me when we were left on our own. I think she'd meant to say she didn't think Fiona would like *me*, but got her words muddled.

Uncle Nick sat at the dining table most of the afternoon marking blue exercise books. Amanda had stayed out with her friend, so he and I had come back from town together in the car. Bridget hadn't been pleased that Amanda had not returned.

'It's a bit much,' I'd heard her say to Uncle Nick in the kitchen.

'Give them time,' he said. 'They're very different girls.'

'And I suppose it's not for ever,' she'd said.

'She's a nice kid.'

Bridget had replied, but she'd dipped her voice and all I could hear was a murmur. Uncle Nick had come back into the living room and soon afterwards Bridget had appeared with a plate of cheese and tomato sandwiches and another of Club biscuits. Again, we'd taken our places at the table to eat. Bridget had an apple instead of a Club.

'What are you marking?' I said now to Uncle Nick. 'What have they written?'

Bridget had cleared up after lunch and was sitting in one of the orange chairs, knitting something. 'He doesn't get asked about his marking very often. He'll love this.'

'Come and see.' He beckoned me over. 'It's supposed to be the diary of a soldier in World War 1, but there are too many anachronisms for my liking. There's even a nuclear bomb in this one. Do you know what anachronisms are?' I watched as he wrote '10/20. Check your facts' then slapped the book shut.

'Things out of time?'

'Bravo.'

'A guess from what you said.'

'Double bravo, then.'

I looked at the exercise book on the top of the pile. 'Where's that school?'

'Kenilworth,' he said. 'I've finished that stint now,' he

said. 'I've spent half a term there. I need to deliver these marked books after the holiday. Then I'm done.'

'You're a supply teacher all the time?'

'That's right.'

'Which school are you going to next?'

'I don't know yet.'

'What happens if no one needs you?'

'We starve.'

'Indeed,' said Bridget.

'I'm joking,' he said. 'The agency said there was something possible. Waiting to hear. Something will turn up.'

He told me he'd left a job managing a museum. I remembered Bobbie mentioning it.

'Why did you leave?' I said.

'To resume my teaching career.'

'Why did you become a teacher?'

'Quite an interrogation,' he said. 'Do you want me under a bright light?' But then, 'If I were you, I'd want to scout out the territory, too. Like checking for snipers, eh?'

'Snipers?' Bridget said. 'That's not a good analogy. She's not in danger—'

I think she was about to say 'now' and stopped herself in time.

I went over to a bookcase which was next to the television. 'Can I look at your books?' I said to Bridget.

She laughed. 'They're not mine!' she said, as though I'd accused her of something.

'Oh.'

'Bridget's not a reader,' Uncle Nick said. 'They're mine. Books in this house – my department. I don't touch Bridget's mixing bowls. She doesn't touch my books.'

I thought that strange. I was sure the marriage vows said something about 'What's yours is mine and what's mine is yours', although I may not be quoting that word for word.

'There's another stuffed bookcase upstairs in our room,' she said, sighing as though he'd moved a mistress in under her nose.

I pulled out a book. '*Jaws*,' I said. 'That's a film, isn't it?'

'It was a book first,' he said. 'Take it. Feel free.'

I put it back. It seemed too early to be borrowing their books as though we were bosom friends. I wasn't even sure yet that I wanted to live with them.

'We bought Jackie an alarm clock in town this morning,' Uncle Nick announced later. We were eating fish and chips after we'd watched the early evening news. Apparently, fish and chips were exempt from the dining table tradition. Instead, we had plates on trays on our laps. I was interested to see that Bridget had had no trouble locating four trays.

I wondered if Dad would have fish and chips tonight. What if he walked drunk to the chippie and fell? Who would know he hadn't come home?

Even so, I felt more comfortable eating fish and chips with them than I had the evening before, sitting formally at the dining table. I felt I might have more control over my emotions as a result, as long as no one pointed them out.

'An alarm clock?' Bridget said. 'Do you have trouble getting up in the morning?' She laughed but sounded very worried simultaneously. You had to admire the feat.

'No, I like to know what the time is,' I said. 'I had my mum's clock at home, but I forgot to pack it.'

'Oh,' she said.

'And we picked up a little transistor radio,' Uncle Nick said, 'so she can keep up with the charts. I did think about a record player, but I'm not sure we need two in the house, competing.'

'Goodness me, no,' Bridget said with some passion.

'Stop having a dig,' Amanda said.

'A radio suits me fine,' I said. 'I've never had my own.'

'What happened to your mum?' Amanda said. She was sloshing vinegar on her chips in a way that, if chips had breath, would have asphyxiated them.

'Darling!' Bridget said. 'Don't be tactless.'

'It's okay. It's not tactless,' I said. I turned to Amanda. 'She died. Of cancer.'

'What kind?'

'Ovarian.' She looked blank, so I added, 'In her ovaries.'

'Amanda, we told you this,' Bridget said.

Amanda speared a chip. 'Actually, that does ring a bell,' she said. 'How long ago did she die?'

'Two years ago,' I said. 'Around Christmas.'

I could see Bridget eyeing Uncle Nick as if to say, '*Say* something.'

'Make a chip butty, Jackie,' he said. 'You can't beat them.' He reached across to the coffee table where a plate sat, piled high with bread and margarine, or perhaps it was butter. He lay a pile of chips on one half of a slice then folded it over and took an enormous, inelegant bite.

'Honestly, Nick,' Bridget said.

'Come on, Bridget,' he said when he'd finished his mouthful. 'Live a little, why don't you?'

'Are you saying I'm boring?' she threw back, which I thought a giant leap from what he'd actually said.

'Of course not.'

She had taken the batter from her fish and had a scattering of chips. I counted them when she scooted back into the kitchen to fetch glasses of orange squash for me and Amanda. Ten. I wondered if she was on a diet.

I bent forwards, took a slice of bread and loaded it with chips.

'Do you need help doing that?' Uncle Nick said, looking at my wrist.

'No, thanks,' I said. 'It's feeling much better.'

'She told me there was nothing wrong with it yesterday,' Amanda said.

I took a bite of my chip butty. It was definitely butter.

Amanda was feeding chips to Spotless.

'No,' said Bridget, coming back. 'Not chips. That's how he got the gallstones.'

'It's only a few,' she said.

'The vet said cut down on fats,' Uncle Nick said. 'We've talked about this. Amanda, stop.'

She fed Spotless one more. The dog whined and turned his eyes on me.

'Forget it, pooch,' I said.

It was still light outside when we'd finished our fish and chips and Amanda and I had eaten choc ices. I stood on the patio outside the French windows and watched as Uncle Nick unwound a garden hose attached to the back wall of the house, fixed it to an outside tap, adjusted it to sprinkler mode and watered the flower beds.

'Can I do some?' I said.

'Be my guest,' he said.

I took the hose and aimed it at some dry soil. Watching it go from light brown to dark gave me the same good feeling as when I'd written a poem.

'Don't move on too quickly,' he said. 'Give each area a thorough soaking. Hopefully we'll get rain soon.'

Amanda appeared at the French windows. She said, 'What's she doing?' as though she'd never seen anyone water a garden before.

Once he'd put the hose away, I followed Uncle Nick back inside, slipping off my shoes the way he did and leaving them tucked neatly near the long curtains on a mat. 'Time for a bike ride in the evening sunshine,' he said, bending to fasten a cycle clip around his ankle. 'I deserve it. Do you have a bicycle, Jackie? I could go and fetch it from your dad's.'

'No, I don't.'

'You could use Amanda's while you're here. You never ride it now, do you, Amanda?'

Amanda was lying on her back on the sofa, her long legs hanging over its edge. 'I might,' she said.

'But you wouldn't mind Jackie borrowing it. It probably needs the tyres pumped, that's all.'

She shrugged as though she didn't care, but her face looked as though she'd been asked to donate me a kidney.

'You must have a couple of spare bikes in your shed, Nick,' Bridget said.

'I had one until I was about ten,' I said.

I thought back. My needing a bigger bike must have coincided with Dad's accident, after which we had less and less money and Mum swapped us from bakery bread to supermarket sliced bread and from canned fish to fish paste for sandwiches.

'Well,' said Uncle Nick. 'I'm sure we could sort you a bike somehow.'

When he'd gone, Bridget said, 'Uncle Nick mends bicycles.'

'But I thought he was a teacher now.'

'It's more a charitable hobby. He has a knack. Locals bring their bikes to him. He charges them peanuts. Some he doesn't charge at all.'

'Not many would do that,' I said and meant it. 'That's kind of him.'

'That's what everyone says about Nick,' she said. 'He's quite the charmer. He has hidden depths. Not like me, plain old Bridget.'

She wasn't plain. She had blue-grey eyes and wavy blonde hair that sat on her shoulders and bobbed up and down when she talked. But I did think that she dressed like someone older.

I looked out of the French windows to the end of the garden where I'd noticed the wide shed. It had double doors. It looked new, like one in a showroom.

'He's always had a shed since we married,' she said, 'but never one as big as this. It's his kingdom.'

Later, when Bridget was in the kitchen on the phone to a friend, Amanda said, 'Mum and I hardly go in Dad's shed. It's where he goes to escape us,' and she must have itched to say it, because I'd forgotten the conversation, but she had clearly held on to it, like keeping a restless spider in your palm then tossing it free.

Bridget came out of the kitchen. 'How are you girls getting on?' she said, smiling at us as though we were a couple of kittens.

'Jackie hasn't cried today anyway,' Amanda said.

SUNDAY 11 APRIL

On Sunday morning, I used the phone mounted on the wall in the kitchen to ring Dad. Bridget was in the kitchen 'supervising' the call – Bobbie's stipulation – and pretending to be absorbed by the putting-away of dishcloths into a drawer.

I shut the kitchen door. Amanda and Uncle Nick were both in the living room and I didn't want to be supervised by them too.

The first time I dialled, it rang thirteen times, but Dad didn't answer. I tried again and this time he picked it up.

'Oh, it's you,' he said. His voice sounded gruff. He had to clear his throat. 'I thought it was someone else interfering.'

'Have you caught a cold?' I said.

He laughed, but it sounded bitter. 'It's what I haven't got, not what I have got.'

'What?'

'No one to talk to, is there, in the mornings? No one to warm your voice up on.'

This was a bit rich. He hadn't exactly offered spar-kling conversation over breakfast. Mostly, he hadn't even offered breakfast.

'I took my bandage off this morning,' I said. 'My wrist feels much stronger.'

'Right.'

'How are you, Dad? Are you going into the hospital, like they said?'

'Not if I can help it.' His voice seemed distant then and I suspected he'd turned away to take a drink.

'Dad, you should. They can help you kick it. Then maybe—'

I sensed Bridget's stillness.

'Then maybe you can get the bed back upstairs. Look for a job. Look after yourself more.'

'A proper Marjorie Proops, are we now?' he said, but not in a jokey way.

'Dad,' I said. 'That's not fair.'

I felt a hand on my shoulder, patting me, but firmly, and I knew Bridget wanted me to ring off.

'I've got to go, Dad,' I said, but I said it at the same time as he said, I think, 'I miss you being here,' and then the conversation was over.

I put the receiver back.

'You can't ring if he's going to upset you, dear,' Bridget said.

'He didn't,' I said, opened the kitchen door and went up to my room, past Amanda and Uncle Nick, who both watched me as I walked through. Uncle Nick looked concerned. Amanda looked fascinated, as though I were a zoo animal.

I lay on my bed and looked at the sunshine walls.

Later that morning, I was sitting downstairs. Bridget was cooking a roast dinner. Chop, chop, sizzle, chop, stir, boil and bubble. I was stroking Spotless and Amanda was reading a magazine when Bridget called through, 'Nick, time for sherry?'

'I'll pour it,' he said. He went to the cabinet where I'd seen the bottle on Friday evening.

Bridget came through to take the tiny glass from him. 'Happy Sunday,' she said, and they clinked glasses.

'You two are alcoholics,' Amanda said.

'Don't be silly. We have this on Sundays and special occasions,' Bridget said. 'You know that.'

'And vodka. There's a bottle in the cupboard.'

Uncle Nick said, 'That's for your mother's Bloody Marys. She has about three a year, Amanda.'

Suddenly there was a lull in the room as though my dad had staggered in, a bottle in his hand and a glass in the other, singing sea shanties.

Uncle Nick looked uncomfortable. He said, 'Jackie, does the sherry bother you? Would you rather we didn't?'

I shook my head and said, 'Please don't tiptoe around me. I can't imagine anything worse.'

Bridget took another sip. 'That's reassuring. For you, Jackie, I mean.'

I scratched Spotless behind his ears. 'When you start lobbing bottles at each other or being sick in the kitchen sink,' I said, 'I'll speak up.'

Bridget looked into her sherry glass as though it didn't have quite the same pull as it had before.

FIRST WEEK OF EASTER HOLIDAYS
MONDAY 12 APRIL-FRIDAY 16 APRIL

As Uncle Nick had suggested, arriving at the Walls' house as the school holiday began gave me a chance to observe their routine and adjust myself into it as far as I could, although I assumed things would be different in term-time.

The days were punctuated by the preparation and eating of meals at regular intervals, and it reminded me that my life had been like this once, when Mum was alive and before she became too ill to go by clocks.

Uncle Nick would get up first and take Spotless out for an early walk. After breakfast, either Uncle Nick or Bridget, or both, would drive us into town to fetch groceries or visit the hardware shop, the butcher or bank. I enjoyed these shopping trips; it was refreshing not to have to eye displays of eggs or Fray Bentos pies and wonder how I could transfer them to a bag or pocket without being seen. I felt cleaner inside.

If Amanda had chosen to stay at home rather than come into town, I'd sit in the front of the Marina, checking the glovebox for the boiled sweets that Bridget kept in there. If Amanda was with us, I would climb in the back, staring at her head and her sleek hair, as shiny as though it had been buffed up like a pair of shoes, and I wished my springy black mop could be disciplined in the same way. Most mornings, in fact, Amanda had a friend to meet – Fiona was a regular – and her parents would drop her at the top of town. They'd obviously abandoned their ambition to persuade Amanda to share her friends with me.

I can't say I was distraught.

Some days, though, she'd stay with us but droop around town saying how bored she was and asking for extra pocket money.

I thought her ungrateful. Pocket money was a new concept to me and my ninety pence a week felt like treasure in the little purse Bridget had found for me. I liked to shake it to hear the coins tinkling together.

If Amanda was with friends, she would meet us in the car park at 12 noon. When we arrived home from town, we would have sandwiches and either Club biscuits or a slice of cake.

In the afternoons, Uncle Nick would do more marking and then, when he got fed up with that, which didn't take long, would disappear to the shed for time with bicycles. At least once a day, someone would knock at the back gate to deliver or collect a bike, or ask advice.

Bridget would knit or mend clothes, watch afternoon TV such as *Crown Court* or phone a friend, sometimes Gloria from Cornwall, no doubt to swap fostering anecdotes. She'd close the kitchen door for these conversations.

Bridget would start preparing the evening meal when we were still full of the lunchtime sandwiches and I couldn't imagine how we'd want to eat fish pie or egg, chips and beans, but when the time came, we did.

I'd been given Easter homework by my science and English teachers, so I worked on this some afternoons.

'Don't you have homework, Amanda?' Bridget asked her one lunchtime as we were clearing up. 'Jackie's been doing hers.'

Amanda flushed. I wished Bridget hadn't said it.

'Don't apply for a job in the diplomatic service, darling,' Uncle Nick said.

'I'll do it when I'm ready,' Amanda said.

In the evenings, the Walls would sit in the living room with the TV on, so in some ways evenings with them were not too dissimilar from life with Dad, if you took out the whisky burps and the grey underpants and the bed crowding the room. Uncle Nick often had one eye on the TV screen and another in a spy or crime novel. Spotless gravitated from his bed in the kitchen to the living room carpet. Amanda sometimes read Enid Blyton books while dipping her hand into a bag of sweets and was always saying, 'I wish I could go to boarding school. It sounds so much fun,' so I guessed she hadn't read *Tom Brown's Schooldays*.

Amanda puzzled me. She was tall and slender and yet seemed to eat constantly. 'How do you stay so slim?' I asked her one evening a few days after I'd moved in. She was snaffling her way through a box of Black Magic that Uncle Nick had won in a raffle at school and she'd eaten all the soft centres before deciding to offer them round.

I'd meant it as a compliment, but her expression said she'd misunderstood me.

'If she's not careful, she won't be,' Bridget said. 'I'm sure that skirt is tighter than it was.'

'Shut up, Mum,' Amanda said, and Uncle Nick sent her up to her room.

On the Wednesday of that week, Uncle Nick was in his shed and Bridget, Amanda and I were in the living room. I was reading a copy of *Little Women* from the school library. Amanda was flicking through a magazine. Bridget put her knitting down and told me that Wednesday evenings were her Weight Watchers nights, so she'd be leaving us with Uncle Nick that evening.

'Why do you go to that?' I said.

'I'm the group leader,' she said. 'The consultant.'

'Oh. How do you get to be one?'

'You suffer,' Amanda said, looking up from her magazine. 'You don't eat crisps or doughnuts or biscuits. You cook salad every single day.'

'It wasn't suffering, dear,' Bridget said. 'And salad isn't cooked.'

Amanda laughed, not kind laughter. 'You moaned about it the whole time!'

I could see she'd hurt Bridget, who fiddled with an earring. 'It wasn't easy,' she said.

She disappeared into the kitchen. I followed her. I wanted some squash, but I was also angry with Amanda, and it was safer to be with people I wasn't angry with. 'Did you follow the diet, then?' I said.

'Bless you,' she said, 'for being interested. Yes, that's how you can become a consultant, by successfully losing weight yourself, then encouraging others to do the same.'

I heard Amanda go upstairs in the way people who want everyone to know they're going upstairs do.

'Wait there,' Bridget said. She went into the living room and came back with a Polaroid photograph of her and Uncle Nick, dressed up as though at a wedding. I could see it was her. But in another way, it wasn't. Her face was rounder and her body plumper: Bridget but with cushions inside her clothing. Her calves were thick, looking strange in strappy, light summer shoes.

'Four stone gone,' she said, 'in a year.'

I was genuinely impressed. Weight wasn't something I thought about, but I knew I was around eight stone, so that was half of me! And if it had been as hard for her to resist a Jammie Dodger as it was for my dad not to unscrew a bottle, that deserved credit.

'Wow,' I said, looking at the photo and then back at her.

'Thank you,' she said. 'People don't usually understand how much it meant to feel good about myself at last.'

Uncle Nick came in to fetch a drink, and if he hadn't, I think she was about to cry. 'Is she showing you her "before" photo?' he said. 'I told her. She didn't need to lose weight. It made no difference.'

It seemed crass for him to say it. It had clearly made a difference to Bridget.

SATURDAY 17 APRIL

On Easter Saturday, Bridget took me to buy new school uniform for the summer term. She'd asked me to try on the uniform I had. Bobbie had mentioned that I might need an update, she said.

She'd waited on the landing outside my room while I changed. I emerged, my face burning up the way it did when we changed for PE and I had to hope none of my classmates would comment on my mother's old bra.

'That blouse is tight on you,' Bridget said. 'And the skirt is short. You're a very different shape from Amanda,' she said.

I do apologise, I said in my head.

'You'll need summer dresses, not skirts and blouses. And new sweaters. Sports kit?'

'My tie still fits, if that's of any help,' I said.

She did smile at that.

'What about underwear?' she said.

'I wear it regularly.'

'Jackie,' she said. 'I know it's embarrassing, but—'

'Okay, I need some new things.'

'I haven't seen underwear come through the wash with your other clothes,' she said, and my face, having cooled down a little, heated up again. I thought, this must be what it feels like to be a dodgy boiler.

Bridget had asked me on my first day to put any soiled clothes in a basket inside the bathroom door. But I'd been washing my bra and pants in the bathroom sink with soap, wringing them out as much as I could, and hanging them in my wardrobe.

'I'll put everything in the wash tonight,' I said. I would have to bow to the inevitable if I didn't want to have damp pants in my wardrobe for however long I'd be staying.

But these little concessions felt like giving away pieces of myself.

'What size are you?' she said, looking directly at my breasts. 'Thirty-two? Thirty-four?'

I crossed my arms over my chest. I wasn't sure about sizes. The labels on Mum's bras had faded. I knew they didn't fit me because there was still space inside each cup. I'd been willing my breasts to grow into them like cakes rising, but nothing had changed for six months now.

'I don't know.'

'We'll get you measured in the lingerie shop,' she said. 'They're very nice ladies in there, with warm hands.'

Never having been measured for a bra before, the image in my head was of a woman standing opposite me in a cubicle and stretching out her warm bare hands to cup my breasts and determine their size. In the car on the way there, I felt queasy.

We dropped Amanda into the welcome embrace of two laughing girls at the top of town. They gawped at me, so I looked the other way. Then we parked the car and went to the school uniform suppliers first to buy two dresses, two sweaters, a blazer, sports kit and some white socks.

Bridget paid with pound notes, crisp and new.

In the lingerie shop, the tape measure came as a welcome revelation and in my relief and euphoria, I let Bridget talk me into some pants with lace round the edges. 'Aren't they pretty?' she said, and she reminded me of my mother and not of my mother all at once. 'I bought some like this myself not too long ago,' she said, but then she blushed, as did I, an unwelcome recipient of such information.

As we left the shop, I took a deep breath and said, as quickly as I could, 'I need sanitary towels.' Dad would automatically throw coins towards me with alarm in his eyes if I mentioned 'personal items'. So, I'd lain awake that morning with the tell-tale ache in my belly, wondering how I could sneak to a shop with my pocket money, but it had seemed impossible. Bridget was taking her new status as child protector seriously and I was clearly going to have a lot less independence.

I'd expected Bridget to make a fuss about the sanitary towels, asking me awkward questions, but perhaps she understood more than I realised. She said, 'Ah, you remind me. Amanda will need some too next week,' and marched me to Boots, business-like. 'Do you need any painkillers?' she said while we were there.

I shook my head.

'I'll get some in case,' she said. 'Amanda can get trouble, especially in the first two days.'

I decided I wouldn't tell Amanda that her mother had shared full details of her menstrual cycle with me.

Given the inch that was this new intimacy, Bridget grabbed a furlong and suggested we go to a café together for a nice cup of tea and a biscuit. She said she needed to sit down.

I declined at first and offered to carry the shopping bags instead if she was tired, but she persuaded me inside by upgrading my biscuit to a toasted teacake.

While we waited for my teacake to turn up and she nibbled on a custard cream, I saw Amanda passing the window with her friends. She was smoking but looking the other way. I was sure she hadn't seen us.

'Hey, look at that woman, Auntie Bridget,' I said, pointing to someone sitting at the back of the café.

Bridget turned her head. 'What about her?' she said. And because there was, indeed, nothing about her, I had to make up a story about liking her tweed coat. Bridget looked justifiably baffled, but while she was busy being baffled, and no doubt pleased to have wangled an 'Auntie' out of me, at least she wasn't watching Amanda pull expertly on a fag.

SUNDAY 18 APRIL

I woke up on Easter morning to find a KitKat chocolate egg on the dining table with my name written on it. There was a Milk Tray egg labelled for Amanda.

I hadn't had an Easter egg for a couple of years. Mum always organised an egg hunt, but once she'd died Dad was usually busy hunting for oblivion instead and didn't have money or energy to celebrate the resurrection of Jesus in more traditional ways.

My instincts had been right in terms of Wall mealtime rituals. The cereal boxes and milk jug were left in the kitchen now at breakfast, although Bridget still laid the dining table with spoons and knives. In the evenings Bridget was plating up meals on the kitchen counter rather than bringing in all the dishes.

We had regular places to sit. I sat with Amanda on my left and Uncle Nick to my right, Bridget opposite. My back was to the window. The morning light concentrated itself on Bridget's breakfast face so that I could see where her foundation had been applied over a blemish or where her mascara had smudged. The sun is cruel like that. You think it's befriending you with its warmth, on your side, but simultaneously it's magnifying your flaws and weaknesses to others.

'Thank you for the Easter egg,' I said to Bridget in the kitchen. I was pouring milk onto cornflakes.

'Happy Easter, dear,' she said. 'I hope you like KitKats.'

'Who doesn't?' I said, a comment I threw out there, not insincerely, but without much commitment. However, the pleasure came off her like static.

'I'm so delighted,' she said. 'Your uncle Nick thought you'd be a Fry's Chocolate Cream girl, but I was sure he was wrong.'

Fry's Chocolate Cream. My mum's favourite.

I walked to the dining table with my cereal bowl. Amanda was on the sofa, opening her boxed egg.

'Darling,' Bridget said. 'Not before breakfast.'

'This is breakfast,' Amanda said, punching into the egg with her knuckle so that it collapsed like a lung. 'Live a little, Mum.'

Bridget said, 'Stop saying that. You're just copying your dad. I *do* live. More than you know.'

'Sorry for giving an opinion,' Amanda said.

Uncle Nick followed me into the kitchen when I went back in to fetch more sugar. I could hear Bridget and Amanda still arguing in hisses.

He filled the kettle and placed it on the hob. 'While Bridget's cooking up a storm this morning,' he said, 'we could sort you out this bicycle. I've found one in the shed that might work.'

'Amanda's?' I said. I'd worried about this. She needed no help with her antagonism.

'No, a different one,' he said. 'It's been there for a year. Someone left it with me and never picked it up. Slightly smaller than Amanda's.'

'Are you calling me a titch?' I said.

'Not explicitly,' he said, 'but any time you need help with a high shelf—'

I felt like crying. I wasn't sure why because his teasing made me happy. But then the telephone rang and Uncle Nick answered. I could hear a woman's voice on the other end, but it was faint.

'Hold on, please,' he said. He turned to me. 'It's Pat. Your auntie from New Zealand?'

'Auntie Pat? My mum's sister?' For a moment, I had trouble taking in the information. Auntie Pat in New Zealand and the kitchen of the Walls' house didn't belong together.

He said into the mouthpiece, 'Yes, she's here.'

I took the receiver. 'Hello?'

Bridget came in, clearly alarmed that Uncle Nick had allowed me to speak to a stranger, perhaps a potential abductor who would lure me outside with the promise of an ice lolly or a kitten.

I turned my back to the kitchen so that I could focus despite the crackly line.

'I had a letter from a social worker,' Auntie Pat said, 'to tell me you'd been taken away. You poor love.'

She had always been overdramatic.

'I'm fine, Auntie Pat. Honestly.'

'Are they looking after you?' she said.

'That was the plan.'

'Have you heard from your nanna and grandad? I rang my mum with your address, but they'd had a letter from Social Services too.'

'I had an Easter card from them yesterday.'

'What did they say?'

'Happy Easter,' I said.

I could hear the smile in her voice. 'Nanna's better on the phone.'

'I'll write to them,' I said.

'They'll like that. They've missed you. What about your grandma, your dad's mum?'

'I haven't heard. She and Dad weren't in touch.'

'Oh.'

She asked me how school was, and whether I was still writing poetry. That touched me, that she'd remembered.

'Your mum would have wanted me to check on you,' she said. 'Especially as your dad wasn't keen for us two to talk.'

'I don't know why,' I said.

'Don't you?' she said. She sounded upset. Or perhaps it was the line.

'No.'

I waited. I thought she was going to say something else.

'I need to go,' she said. 'Your uncle's reminding me how much this costs. I'm glad you're safe.' Her voice broke and then I heard a dial tone.

'Me too,' I said into the phone.

Later that morning, I was in the garden, scratching Spotless under the chin, when Uncle Nick came out of the house. 'Come and meet the shed and we'll see about this bike.'

Amanda had spent the morning in her room with the rest of her Easter egg, listening to music. Even though her bedroom faced the side wall of the house next door, the day was warm for April and all the doors and windows in the house were open, so Uncle Nick and I could hear the thump of a drum and the twang of guitars – the Osmonds? – as we crossed the garden.

'Here it is,' he said. 'My second home.' He'd brought a mug of coffee with him. He placed it on a workbench.

I thought back to what Amanda had said about escape.

I looked around. In the shed, shelves lined the sides and held boxes, paint pots, tools I didn't know the names of. Under the shelves leaned seven or eight bicycles of different sizes, plus some extra wheels and a couple of bicycle chassis without their wheels.

I could smell oil, but it wasn't unpleasant.

One shelf at the narrow end of the shed held a selection of books, too many, so that some were stacked horizontally on top of others. Underneath the shelf was an old wooden stool.

'My overflow library,' he said, pointing. 'But even the overflow is overflowing. I need to have a sort-out.'

'You read in here?'

'Sometimes. When I've had enough of inner tubes and tangled bicycle chains.' He pointed to a tiny portable heater. 'For my feet,' he said, 'in colder weather.'

'We did inner tubes in biology last week,' I said.

He groaned. 'Very witty.'

I peered at the titles. '*Tinker Tailor Soldier Spy*,' I said.

'John Le Carré. A genius.'

'Charles Dickens' short stories. We read one of those at school. "The Signalman", I think.'

'That's right.'

'I got eighteen for my essay.'

'Out of a hundred?'

'No, out of tw—' but then I realised he was joking.

'Got you back,' he said. 'Anyway, take a seat.'

I sat down.

'This is the bike I was thinking of,' he said. He pulled it away from the others and stood with it in the centre of the shed, testing its brakes. 'This, madam,' he said in a fake-Cockney salesman voice, 'is from our new range of bicycles for young ladies. It's a Raleigh, the best you can get. It has had a repaint and its bell is most impressive.' He rang it and it shrilled, temporarily shutting out the sound of Queen that was now bursting from the house. I wondered why Bridget wasn't telling Amanda to turn it down. No doubt she couldn't face the argument that would follow.

Uncle Nick wheeled the bike out of the shed's double doors and onto the neat lawn with its path of square stones weaving through its centre. 'Come on. Try it out.'

'I've forgotten how to do it,' I said, following him.

'You never forget how to ride a bike,' he said. 'Your legs will remind you.'

I glanced at the house. Bridget was standing on the patio outside the French windows, watching us. 'Yoo-hoo,' she called and waved, as though we were farmers in a distant field. 'How's it going? Does it fit?'

Does it *fit*?

'She hasn't tried it on yet,' Uncle Nick called back. 'We'll take it into the road and test it out properly.'

I looked up at the window of Bridget and Uncle Nick's bedroom as I thought I'd sensed movement. But I must have been mistaken.

Ten minutes later, I was wobbling along the quiet cul-de-sac on the bike with Uncle Nick jogging behind me, trying to catch his breath.

'I'm going to fall,' I called. 'I know I am.'

'Go a bit faster,' he said. 'It sounds counter-intuitive. But it'll help.'

I put more pressure on the pedals and the bike sped up. 'Arrrggh!' I yelled, but kept going.

'Now try out the brakes!' he shouted. 'Not too suddenly.'

I squeezed the brakes a little, then a little more, stopped the bike and hoisted myself off the seat so that I could look back. He was yards behind me now, smiling and holding his side as though he had a stitch. 'See?' he said. 'Your legs knew what to do.'

I turned the bike round clumsily, remounted and cycled back towards him.

'Well done,' he said. 'Next week, John O'Groats to Land's End.'

I said, dismounting, 'Enjoy your trip. I'm sure it'll be lovely.'

'You can take the bike home with you,' he said, 'when your dad's sorted out and you can go back.'

'There's nowhere to store it,' I said.

'I'm sure your dad could work something out.'

'Maybe.'

'It's great to see you smiling,' he said as we walked back down the side alley and through the back garden gate, this time with me wheeling the bicycle.

I tried to rearrange my expression to dispassionate mode but failed. You traitor, face.

The house smelled of roasting meat and I could hear pans bubbling. I was thirsty for orange squash and needed to ask Bridget a question. I went into the kitchen. She was cooking, her Sunday sherry sitting on the kitchen counter.

She pushed a long knife into a plump, steaming roast chicken that she'd taken out of the oven.

'It's got lovely crispy skin,' I said, grappling for how to ask my question.

'I put butter on it,' she said.

'It does look tasty.'

'I hope it will be.'

I made myself some squash and stood by the door.

'Is everything okay?' she said.

Bridget, you have redeemed yourself!

'Where do I put my sanitary towels?' I whispered.

'In the bathroom bin,' she said. 'Wrap them in toilet paper.'

This was a relief. Even while she'd been pointing out the sunflower yellow paint on that first day, I'd wondered.

I turned to go upstairs.

She said, 'By the way.'

'Yes?'

'Your dad called while you were out with Uncle Nick,' she said, and I realised she'd also been wondering how to start a conversation.

'Oh,' I said. I wished she hadn't made it sound as though I'd favoured Uncle Nick. 'You should have come to fetch me in.'

She looked uneasy. 'I don't think that would have been a good idea,' she said. 'He didn't sound very... very well.'

She wasn't looking at me while she wiped the knife with a cloth.

'I can ring him back,' I said.

'Not today,' she said. 'Try him tomorrow, when he's feeling better. Can you open the oven for me, dear, while I put this chicken back in? It's not quite there.'

I opened the oven door. 'I thought he would be in hospital by now. Did he say anything about that?'

'Make sure you wrap the towels up well,' she said, 'but I empty that bin every day.'

After lunch, Uncle Nick went for a long bike ride along the Warwickshire lanes. He showed me on a map where he'd go. When he'd left, Bridget said she needed a nap and went upstairs to her room. I don't know how she got on with the napping as Amanda was playing an Osmonds album so loud that even if Bridget had fallen asleep, they would have crooned their way into her dreams.

I said I'd sit downstairs and watch the sport on TV.

I turned the TV on then slipped into the kitchen, shut the door and dialled Dad's number.

He was more or less incoherent. All he kept saying was, 'I'm sorry about your mum. I'm sorry about what I did. I wish she hadn't died.'

'Don't say that, Dad. It wasn't your fault she died.'

I couldn't hear his next words because he was sobbing and then started a coughing fit.

'Happy Easter, Dad,' I said, when I couldn't bear hearing him any more, and hung up.

I rubbed my eyes, which were stinging.

As I did, the door opened and in came Amanda. She glanced at the telephone and then at my face. 'What are you doing?' she said.

'Mind your own business,' I said, slipping past her to go upstairs to my room.

'Fine,' she said to my back.

She can't have mentioned it to her mother and father as

nothing was said. So, I had a secret of hers and she had a secret of mine.

One–nil to me, though. She didn't know I'd seen her smoking.

I spent the evening in my bedroom eating some of Bridget's simnel cake and writing a letter to Nanna and Grandad, but the words didn't come easily. The last time I'd seen them was at Mum's funeral when they were punch-drunk with shock and grief, as we all were. They were preserved in my mind in that state, dressed in dark clothes and with handkerchiefs bunched in their palms. Writing about my new foster parents seemed like adding to the list of things that had gone wrong for our family. So, instead, I thanked them for their Easter card, described Mrs Collingworth, told them about Poetry Club and even stooped so low as to comment about how we'd had no rain for weeks.

MONDAY 19 APRIL

On Easter Monday, Bridget's parents came to visit from Oxford-shire. While we waited for them to arrive for lunch, Bridget told me that they'd recently returned from a trip to the Amazon rain-forest. Before that, she said, they'd been trekking in Spain.

'They're adventurous types,' she said. 'We hardly see them since Dad retired. We get postcards.'

She sounded wistful.

'Don't you ever go?' I said.

She laughed but not with her eyes. 'I've never been asked,' she said.

I suspected her parents were coming to look me over, like people inspecting a second-hand car to make sure it's roadworthy.

Bridget's mother, whom Amanda called Granny, didn't look like a granny. She reminded me of Bridget but was even leaner. I doubted that she had ever been plump, the way Bridget had. Her skin was nut-brown and had that dried-out look of those who rush out into the sun the moment it appears. She had severe grey hair, cut short. Amanda's grandpa was tall and distinguished-looking: a retired headteacher. He was dressed in a safari suit. I'd seen them worn before by people on TV and when elephants or tigers were nearby, but it looked out of place in Bridget's living room, in which the only elephant was the tension.

Bridget introduced me as Jacqueline, perhaps to elevate me to the status of normal child rather than deprived waif fit for the workhouse.

'Most people call me Jackie,' I said to her parents.

'Obviously *not* Bridget!' the woman said, as though she'd been annoyed with Bridget for a hundred years.

We sat round the table eating roast lamb, the French doors open to the garden and the dry, warm day. It was difficult to ignore Spotless, stretched inelegantly on his back on the lawn which Uncle Nick had mowed that morning. He was displaying his genitals. Bridget said, 'Honestly! That dog is so lazy!' but we all knew she meant the genitals. In the end, she pulled a curtain across so that we couldn't see out. She said it was against the sun.

'What do you want to be when you grow up?' Bridget's mother asked me, as though I were seven.

'A poet,' I said, although I'd rather have said pickpocket just for fun.

'Oh! How quaint!' she said.

'This meat is cooked perfectly,' Bridget's father said through a mouthful, and Bridget's whole face lifted as though the compliment had astonished her.

'I do mine with garlic these days,' said his wife. 'Garlic and rosemary.'

'Garlic!' Bridget said. 'What on earth for?'

'Oh, Bridget,' her mother said. 'Do keep up with the trends.'

Amanda asked her grandparents, her voice sweet, where they would travel next. I was sure she was trying to act the doting granddaughter so that I'd seem even more the cuckoo in the nest. When they'd arrived, she'd led them to the armchairs and fetched extra cushions for their comfort. 'Well!' her grandmother had said, as if she'd not expected it. 'What a welcome!'

'We're hiring a barge to explore the Norfolk Broads, so staying local,' her grandfather said now, redefining local for us all. 'With a couple of old friends.'

Uncle Nick said, 'Lovely! We could do that, Bridget.'

'Goodness, no,' Bridget's mother said. 'Bridget wouldn't cope with a Porta Potti and a two-ring hob.'

'I know you think I'm boring,' Bridget said, sounding stung. She stabbed a carrot with her fork. 'One day I might surprise you all.'

Her parents looked sceptical as though Bridget and surprises weren't concepts they'd ever put together.

'You *are* boring,' Amanda said, and no one rebuked her.

I felt sorry for Bridget. She seemed under attack. Uncle Nick appeared cowed by the older couple, perhaps by the safari suit or by their busy passports, and wasn't helping.

Still, they favoured him over Bridget in terms of starting conversations.

'You've gone back into teaching, then?' Bridget's mother asked him.

'I certainly have,' he said.

'You like to ring the changes, don't you?' she said, but admiringly.

'Too right,' her husband said. 'Don't let the grass grow under your feet. That's the best way, son.' He helped himself to more roast potatoes from Bridget's best casserole dish but perhaps to be polite. She'd overcooked them – an unusual lapse – and her best china highlighted their sadness. I concentrated hard on my food, noticing a similarity between the leathery potatoes and Bridget's mother's complexion.

'How's your dad doing?' Bridget's father said to Uncle Nick.

'He's fine. We saw him for his birthday in February. We'll visit again in the summer.' He turned to me. 'He lives in South Wales. He'd love to meet you.'

'But will Jackie still be here by the summer?' Bridget's mother said. 'I thought you were doing short-term fostering.'

Uncle Nick looked embarrassed. She was talking about me in the third person and I think he felt it. He did his best with the reply but with limited success. 'She'll be here as long as you need us, won't you, Jackie?' he said and smiled.

Bridget's mother raised her eyebrows as though she'd found what he said too sentimental for her taste, like someone who discovers four sugars in their tea.

FRIDAY 23 APRIL

On the Friday morning before Amanda and I went back to
school, I was eating breakfast, enjoying the early sun on the
back of my neck, when Bridget told me that Bobbie would
visit that morning.

'Is she coming to check I haven't burned the house down,'
I said, 'or graffitied my bedroom?'

'I don't think so, dear,' she said.

Later, I saw a Mini arrive and park outside the house.
'Bobbie's here!' I called to Bridget, who was upstairs, putting
laundry away. 'I'll get the door.'

Bridget came down the stairs as fast as though she'd slid
down on a tray. I realised she preferred to open her own front
door. But I'd won. Bobbie was stepping into the house as
Bridget came into the tiny hall behind me.

For a second, none of us moved, wondering who was going
to shift first.

'I'm in an adult sandwich,' I said, 'and I can't say I like it.'

Bridget stepped backwards and said, 'Come in, Bobbie,'
although I'd already welcomed her.

Bobbie followed me into the living room and Bridget
pointed her to one of the orange chairs, although I don't know
why, as there were four potential seats and Bobbie presumably
had enough brain function to select one for herself.

Bobbie and I sat down and Bridget fussed off into the
kitchen.

I cooperated with Bobbie in the small talk adults seemed

to think was necessary before useful human interaction. 'Actually,' she said, after that, 'I was wondering about a drive in the Mini. If you fancied it.'

She said it as Bridget brought through a plate of Nice biscuits and said, 'Do you take sugar in your coffee, Bobbie? I can't remember.'

'I thought I'd take Jackie out for a drive,' Bobbie said, 'then have coffee afterwards. If that's all right.'

'That's a lovely idea,' Bridget said, looking glumly at the plate of biscuits as though she'd never heard a worse idea and the biscuits were going soft and stale before her eyes.

Bobbie headed out into the countryside, probably along the same roads where Uncle Nick cycled. For five minutes or so, we drove in silence. She turned off a main road onto a narrow lane. I looked out of the window. 'I'm guessing we're not here to look at scenery and chat about sheep,' I said.

'Well guessed,' she said. 'I was wondering if you'd been in touch with your dad.'

'Not successfully,' I said. 'Why?'

'We really want him to get urgent help,' she said. 'He seems in a bad way.'

'Should I go and see him?' I said. 'I might be able to persuade him.'

She waited at a junction then drove over it onto an even narrower lane. 'Have you tried persuading your dad to get help before?' she said.

'A million times.'

'That's what I thought. I'm afraid it's up to him. People with alcohol problems don't usually get better unless they make the decision for themselves.'

'Have you seen him?'

'I've spoken to him on the phone,' she said. 'If we go round there, he won't let us in.'

'Oh.'

We drove round a bend and found ourselves behind a tractor which chugged away, taking all the road space. Bobbie didn't seem hassled the way some would. I liked that.

She looked at me. 'You know, don't you, that while he refuses help, you can't go back? He has to try harder if he wants that.'

'I'd guessed.'

'And if you'd like to visit him, or he visits you, we'd need to supervise.'

'He'll love that. That's his best thing, being watched.'

'So, I want to check that you're happy at the Walls' house. How are you settling in?'

The tractor driver stuck out his left arm then turned onto a farm track. Bobbie waited, then accelerated, and the Mini whizzed along once more.

'I'm not sure we're a perfect fit,' I said.

'That's probably too much to ask,' she said. 'It's all new for both parties. Tell me what the problems are.'

'I like the dog best?' I said, although this wasn't strictly true. I liked Uncle Nick and the dog equally.

She laughed. 'What's the dog called? Something silly, wasn't it? I met him when I did their interviews.'

I reminded her, and then she laughed again and began telling me about her own dog.

We turned onto a main road and began heading back.

'I'm ready for that coffee,' she said.

So, I didn't tell Bobbie I'd heard Amanda saying to Bridget in the kitchen the day before, 'Why did you let her in? I don't like her being here.' She'd made no effort to keep her voice down. They must have thought me still upstairs. But I was sitting on the bottom stair. They couldn't see me from the kitchen.

Bridget said, more quietly, 'Darling, she's not a stray cat.'

I had to stifle my laughter when I heard that. One-liners from Bridget were rare and precious.

'You're being mean, Amanda,' I heard her say.

'What did I say that was mean?' Amanda said. A kitchen drawer slammed shut and the utensils in it rattled. 'I'm trying to tell you what I think. And you don't want to hear it. As usual. No one asked *me* if I wanted her to come.'

'That's not true. We talked to you about it.'

'That's not the same as asking.'

'You've always said you wanted a sibling.'

'Not a *fake* one,' she said. 'A proper one.'

I tiptoed back to my room. I didn't want to hear it either. I wasn't aiming to antagonise Amanda and, as far as I knew, hadn't done anything to rile her.

Except for, I suppose, moving into her family home so that her parents expected her to welcome an imported sister with open arms. Like getting a scarf at Christmas in a vile lime green and having to wear it for Granny and smile even though all your friends would laugh until they peed.

MONDAY 26 APRIL

Bridget was tugging a thin cardigan from the back of a dining chair as I picked up my school satchel, ready to leave on the first morning of the summer term. Amanda had already left, a local friend calling for her to walk to their school together. I could hear Uncle Nick on the phone in the kitchen.

Bridget said, 'I'll come with you to the school bus stop.'

I thought, over my lifeless, rigor-mortis-stiffened body, you will.

'You don't need to,' I said. 'I know where to go.'

'I'm worried that the bus driver won't be expecting you,' she said. 'What if he doesn't let you on?'

'I've got the pass,' I said. I took it from my blazer pocket and pretended to read from it. 'Dear Driver. Let Jackie Chadwick on or die horribly.'

'What if there aren't any spare seats?' she said.

This was weak. What was she going to do? Drag someone off to make space?

I headed for the door.

She followed me. 'I've got to post a letter anyway,' she said, patting her handbag, which may or may not have contained a letter.

If I protested any more, I knew I'd miss the bus, so I gave in. She was going to stay with me whether I wanted her to or not, like those coughs you get after you've had a cold.

The bus stop was five minutes from Hollybush Close and picked up other Leamington students who went to Warwick

Grammar on the edge of the town. A group of them stared at me as I approached with Bridget. But they were first and second years, apart from one fifth-year boy with trousers too short and an awkward, future civil service look about him.

'You can leave me here now,' I said to Bridget.

'I'll wait,' she said, 'in case.'

In case of axe-murderers? An unexpected outbreak of cholera? A rogue typhoon?

When the bus arrived, I climbed on quickly before Bridget could consider hugging me.

I felt my face heat up as I walked down the aisle of the crowded bus but then saw a girl from my form next to a spare seat. She beckoned to me, looking surprised.

As the bus pulled away, I waved to Bridget and pointed melodramatically to my neighbour as if to say, 'See? A real non-dangerous person!' Bridget's shoulders fell, presumably with relief that I had survived climbing on a bus, and she over-waved until I couldn't see her any more. In fact, she'd waved so hard I wondered whether she'd find it hard to stop, having built up all that momentum.

'You're not usually on this bus,' my neighbour said. 'Have you moved house?'

'Yes,' I said. 'Hey, did you do the English essay?'

At lunchtime, my best friend Kim and I were picking scepti-cally at bowls of tapioca pudding in the school dining room when I thought I saw Uncle Nick sitting with a geography teacher. I looked again. Yes, it was definitely him.

'What's up?' Kim said. 'Your face went weird.' She twisted around to follow my gaze, her blonde ponytail swinging with her.

'Oh, nothing,' I said. I hadn't told anyone about the move to the foster home. Bridget had said that my teachers would have been informed, but it was up to me to tell friends.

I wasn't sure how to open such a conversation with Kim, just as I'd had difficulty starting conversations with Bridget.

Dad, this is your fault, I thought. What have you done to my communication skills?

'I don't know who that new teacher is,' Kim said. 'Do you?' But then she seemed to lose interest and pushed her chair back. 'Do you want me to take your bowl? That tapioca is vile, isn't it?'

'I think my body might reject it,' I said, 'like an organ transplant.'

By the door to the dining room, the school secretary shook the clanging metal bell that signalled the end of lunch and, for those who ate the tapioca, the beginning of indigestion.

'I'll see you in maths in Period 6,' Kim said.

After school, Kim and I left the maths classroom together and wandered to the school gates. Sometimes her mother or father collected her but, if not, she often walked half the way home with me to Dad's house.

Then I remembered and it gave me the opening line. 'Actually, I'm getting a bus today.'

'Are you?'

'I live in Leamington now.'

'Oh.'

'But not with my dad. With a foster dad, and mum. And their daughter.'

She frowned, shifting her satchel from one shoulder to the other. 'Why?'

I put on a scary voice. 'Because my dad was snatched away in the night by a *werewolf* and now I'm a poor orphan.'

'Jackie!' she said. 'Why really?'

But I saw the bus driver nudge past the queue of pupils to climb onto his bus. 'I'll tell you more tomorrow,' I said and ran.

I turned the corner into Hollybush Close and saw Bobbie's car parked up. It was Monday, the day she usually took me to the café. I should have waited in the school car park.

She was in the living room with a glass of squash. 'The wanderer returns,' she said.

'I forgot,' I said. 'I'm sorry.'

'Don't worry,' she said. 'It's understandable. And I was five minutes late anyway, or you'd have spotted me and remembered.'

I could hear Bridget in the kitchen and Amanda upstairs, playing music. I sensed that we were left alone strategically. She must have news.

I was right. Dad had been arrested the night before for being drunk and disorderly and had spent the night in Warwick Police Station.

'What kind of disorderly?' I said.

'The manager of a pub rang the police,' she said. 'Your dad wasn't keen to leave.'

'Is he going to court?' I said.

She said they'd cautioned him. 'He'll have to be careful not to reoffend,' she said. 'Remember he was already on their radar.'

'And what about hospital?'

She shrugged.

Shoulders can tell you a lot.

TUESDAY 27 APRIL

Kim and I sat on a low wall in the corner of the playground at break time, watching a group of boys kick a ball around half-heartedly. I'd confessed to her that the new geography teacher was also my foster parent. 'Don't you dare tell anyone,' I said.

'Of course I won't,' she said, and I knew I could trust her.

Kim and I had become close friends during the first year. Mum had died a few months after I'd started secondary school and Kim had found me crying in the cloakroom. She'd sat on the floor, next to me, and said nothing, asked nothing, until my sobs had dried up.

'Are you being bullied?' she'd said kindly. 'Because you're so short?' Her eyes filled with tears of their own, which is when I knew she would be a decent friend. But what she said made me laugh.

'No, it's not that.'

She tried again. 'Lost something?'

I nodded and said, 'Sort of.'

She said, 'The bell's going soon. Do you want to walk to geography with me?'

On the way, I'd told her that my mum had died. I didn't add details. I found them hard to say.

'You're going to need a friend,' she told me, 'which is good, because most of my friends went to a different school, so I need one too. And I love your crazy hair.'

I found out that she lived in a council house on the edge

of Warwick with her mother, father and two older brothers – they both attended our school – and she seemed happy. She was sporty, unlike me, and loved dancing and singing. I'd told her that my dad was often 'ill' and let her surmise, which I think she had.

I said to her now, 'The foster home situation is because Dad's too poorly to look after me. He's going into hospital to get some help. So, the fostering is temporary.'

'What's the girl like?' she said, and again, I knew she understood.

That afternoon, Uncle Nick still wasn't home by 6. 'We'll have to start without him,' Bridget said. 'He must have been called into a school.' She, Amanda and I sat down to eat Bridget's meat loaf with boiled potatoes and cabbage. The cabbage was like school cabbage, all memory of its greenness boiled away without mercy, leaving it white and floppy as though something had terrified it. It wasn't Bridget's usual standard of cookery and reminded me of the wrinkled roast potatoes when her parents had visited.

I didn't comment on the cabbage, but Amanda had less reserve. 'It's disgusting,' she said.

'The phone rang while it was cooking,' Bridget explained to her, although I didn't think Amanda's rudeness merited an explanation. 'My Weight Watchers supervisor.'

'The meat loaf is really tasty, though,' I said. 'All mushroomy.'

Amanda said, 'Creep.'

I pretended I hadn't heard, so she said it again, louder.

I said, 'Isn't it interesting that the word creep can be a noun and a verb?'

Amanda had her mouth full of potato and pointed to her bulging cheek as though to say, 'I can't answer you because I'm eating, dumbo.' But her eyes told me she didn't know what I was talking about.

'I'm not a creep,' I said while she was disadvantaged.

She swallowed. 'Who talks about nouns and verbs at teatime?'

'Girls, stop,' Bridget said, in the way teachers do when they know they've no control but feel they should comment. 'Did you hear that Sid James died last night? On stage. Isn't that shocking?'

Sid James and his family had my heartfelt sympathies, but I did think Bridget could have chosen something more light-hearted with which to distract us.

We heard the garage door shut, heralding the arrival of Uncle Nick.

Spotless loped through to greet him, his claws ssshhhing on the kitchen's lino floor.

'Something smells good,' Uncle Nick said, coming in through the hall door.

'It's not the cabbage,' Amanda said, her voice sullen.

He bent to kiss the top of Bridget's head, his customary greeting. 'Sorry I'm so late. Guess where I went today?'

'My school,' I said. 'I saw you in the dining room.'

'Oh,' Bridget said, looking at me, as did Amanda. 'Jackie didn't mention it.'

It hadn't felt like news that belonged to me.

Uncle Nick put his briefcase down and pulled his shirt out of his trousers, flapping it to cool his body down. 'It's warm out there. Is my tea in the oven?'

'I'll get it,' Bridget said. 'You go and change.'

But he was in the kitchen, getting it himself. 'I'll change afterwards,' he said. 'I could eat a field of horses.'

'Are you teaching at her school?' Amanda asked him when he'd sat down and was adding salt to his food. Spotless had returned with him and sat underneath the table in between all our feet.

'Who's her?' he said.

She pointed at me.

'I've got a name,' I said. 'I've had it a while.'

Bridget looked as though she would say something, but Uncle Nick let it go and carried on. 'They rang me this morning from the agency,' he said, 'as Jackie was leaving with Bridget this morning.'

'She came with you to the bus stop?' Amanda said and snickered.

'Only today,' I said.

Uncle Nick said, 'Apparently one of your geography teachers fell ill over Easter. I can't remember with what. They need a teacher to cover her, perhaps for the term.'

'Miss Rolfe?'

'That's the one.'

I was relieved. My geography teacher was Mr Donaldson. I liked Uncle Nick, but I didn't want to be taught by him and be teased about it once my classmates found out I was living in his house, eating limp cabbage at the same table.

'You're a history teacher,' Amanda said.

'I've done some geography, too,' he said. 'I like maps.'

'Liking maps isn't enough,' she said.

'It's a joke, darling,' he said.

'Are you sure it's for the whole term?' Bridget said.

'Why do you think I snapped it up?' he said. 'We don't have to busk outside Woolworths to pay the bills after all.'

'That's a relief,' Bridget said, as though she'd seriously considered it.

'Can either of you play guitar or sing?' I said. I put my knife and fork down, giving myself a trophy in my own head for having conquered the cabbage.

'Needs must when the devil drives,' said Uncle Nick. 'If Bob Dylan's allowed to sing in public without being able to hold a tune, I don't see why I can't.'

I found that very funny and laughed, but Bridget and Amanda were straight-faced, like Victorians in old photos.

Spotless came out from under the table and looked up at Uncle Nick, his tongue lolling.

'See?' Uncle Nick said. 'Even the dog is laughing.'

'He wants some of your food, that's all,' Bridget said.

'He can have my cabbage,' Amanda said glumly.

FRIDAY 30 APRIL

After school, I found a letter on the dining table addressed to me. It was from Nanna and Grandad. Nanna's tiny, barely legible writing covered one side of the notepaper, telling me about trouble with their milkman and about a visit to the sea last weekend. She mentioned nothing about Dad, Mum or my move to a foster home. But I wasn't sorry about that. I'd been sketchy with detail in my own letter to them. I didn't want outpourings of emotion, particularly in black and white, although I felt guilty about it. Perhaps it would have made me feel closer to Mum again. Equally, perhaps that was what I was avoiding.

I felt I knew Bridget and Uncle Nick more than I knew my grandparents now, which was a strange realisation and had something wrong about it that I couldn't identify.

Uncle Nick was already home and in the shed. His sixth formers were on a school trip, he'd told us that morning.

I made a cup of tea and took it down the garden. He was fitting a mudguard to a bike. I put the tea on a shelf near him.

'You star,' he said. He told me that Bridget had walked to the local shopping arcade for flour and Amanda was with a friend.

'Can I help you?' I said.

'How much do you know about mudguards?'

'Nothing.'

'Sit on the stool and talk to me,' he said.

'What about?'

He straightened up and stretched, picking up his mug. 'You've been here three weeks today.'

I'd been thinking the same. 'I've never stayed in anyone else's house for that long. Not even for a week.'

'Not on holiday? In bed and breakfast?'

'Usually caravans,' I said. 'We did have one long weekend in a seaside hotel. Before Mum knew she had cancer. Dad had won money on the pools, so we went to Bournemouth on the train.'

'That sounds fun,' he said.

'Some of it was.'

I remembered how each of us had tried to be authentically happy as we rustled our bags of egg sandwiches and drank flask tea, Mum giggling when it spilled as the train went over a junction. We were pretending that Mum and Dad hadn't spent days fighting about how to spend the cash.

'The hotel felt strange,' I said to Uncle Nick. 'I felt like an alien, as though we were on a film set.'

He'd bent to his task again. 'Well, if you weren't used to it.'

'There was a lady with a snooty nose and a stiff apron. My room was next door to Mum and Dad's. It had a pink bedspread and green curtains with matching pink flowers.'

'Auntie Bridget would have approved.'

I didn't respond because he was so accurate it would have seemed rude to agree.

'The dressing table had one of those brush, comb and mirror sets.'

'I know the type.'

'I remember the mirror and brush were lying face down, as though they were worried we'd be ugly.'

He stood again, laughing, and slurped down more tea. 'Who needs telly with you around?'

I loved the affirmation. It made the hairs on the back of my neck tingle.

'The lady said they were for decoration only,' I said.

He fell to fixing the mudguard on and I picked a book from his shelf and idly thumbed through the pages.

I remembered how I hadn't been sure how to behave in the hotel, where to put my shoes, or whether it was fine to leave my flannel draped over the bath as I did at home.

This must be how they felt when they landed on the Moon, I thought. They had to find a new way to be. See themselves in a different light. Find new methods of walking, talking, breathing and thinking.

'It's strange, isn't it,' I said, 'being in someone else's house?'

He stood and finished his tea. 'I suppose,' he said, 'you learn the rhythms of your own house and your own family. You fall into step with them until you don't notice you're doing it.'

That was exactly how it was. I knew he understood. It made me braver.

'Your stair carpets are softer than ours at home,' I said. 'My feet slide in the slippers Bridget bought me.'

'The ones she bought without asking.'

'Yes.'

'I haven't seen you wearing them much.'

I'd tucked them under my bed and hoped she wouldn't notice.

'And there's the key business,' I said.

'Yes, the key,' he said. 'Not your best skill: door keys. I think you've conquered it now.' He'd had to show me how to slide it in more gently, almost tricking it into working.

'My key for home is my mum's old key,' I said to Uncle Nick now.

He put his cup down. 'Is it?'

'I like having it.'

'You wanted to keep something of hers. That's understandable.' He started cleaning up the bike with an old rag. 'We all like to keep things associated with people who were special to us.'

He seemed embarrassed, almost flustered.

I said, 'Is your mum still alive?'

He looked surprised. 'My mum? She's not, actually. She died five years ago. She had a stroke. Very unexpected.'

Then I remembered that Amanda's grandpa had asked Uncle Nick about his father.

I closed the book and put it on the shelf. 'Did you see her before she died? I mean, right before? The day before?'

'Sadly, no,' he said. 'The stroke was massive. I didn't get there in time. My dad was with her, thank God.' He looked at me. 'What about you? Did you see your mum?'

I shook my head. 'Dad said I would be too upset. He wouldn't take me with him to the hospital for the last week of her life.'

'Perhaps he thought he was doing the best thing for you.'

'It wasn't, though, was it?'

'It's not for me to say, love,' he said.

'That's the problem with adults,' I said, standing up, ready to go back to the house. 'You all stick together. You're too scared of betraying other adults.'

As things turned out, I couldn't have been more wrong.

TUESDAY 4 MAY

I wavered at the edge of the school car park after my last lesson on Tuesday. The previous day had been Bank Holiday Monday, so Bobbie had postponed our usual café visit. I squinted my eyes against the afternoon sun and heard the toot of a horn. Bobbie was waving. She wore her usual orange beret. I'd begun to wonder if she kept it by her bed for use first thing, like other people did with spectacles or a blood pressure tablet.

I climbed into her car with my satchel.

She started the ignition and the Mini coughed into life. 'The usual café?' she said.

'And the usual Horlicks,' I said.

'It's a bit hot for Horlicks.'

'I would drink Horlicks in the Sahara,' I said.

As we drove, I stole a glance at her. She was humming something, tuneless but happy.

'Do you like your job?' I said.

We were at a traffic light. She turned to face me. 'I like *this* part,' she said, and I felt as I had sometimes when Mum had read me a story and hadn't been in a hurry to get away.

I swallowed hard and fixed my gaze out of the passenger window at the local shops we passed.

'We have a complication,' Bobbie said as I dunked a Bourbon into my drink. The café was empty apart from Bobbie and me and an old couple sitting in the corner eating tiny sandwiches. The café door was wedged open for air.

'A complication? My dad?' I said.

'Yes.'

'Does it mean I'm with the Walls for even longer?'

'Would that be so terrible?'

'Not terrible, no.'

She sighed and unwrapped an individual slice of fruit cake from the polythene. It looked weary, as though it had made a strenuous effort to get released into the world. She took a bite. 'We were hoping by now he would have agreed to go into hospital.'

'You don't know my dad,' I said.

'You're right,' she said. 'Not for lack of trying. He's not exactly—'

'He doesn't like talking about himself to strangers.'

'No.'

'Are you happy to tell me how he got his injury? It was at work, wasn't it?'

'He was a fireman,' I said.

I could remember how it had made me feel to see him in his fireman's uniform. Mum used to love it too and would hug him tight and say, 'I fancy you rotten.'

'Did you put out any fires, Daddy?' I'd ask when he came home at teatime or as he made breakfast for me if he'd come back from a night shift.

'Mostly little fires, but if I hadn't been there—'

'They would have been great big fires?'

It was an old routine.

'What are you thinking?' Bobbie said, and I realised she was waiting.

I chewed my lip. 'When I think about him in his uniform, I wonder whether that was someone else and I'm remembering the wrong person.'

'You were proud of him.'

'He loved being a fireman. He'd talk to me for hours about

his job. How to climb a ladder safely. How to put a pan fire out. How to roll someone in a rug if they were on fire or what to do if someone got electrocuted.'

She was quiet for a while, then poured herself more tea. 'And he had an accident at work?'

'No,' I said. Was that what he'd been telling them? 'Otherwise we would have had some money. Some compensation. He was always angry with himself about it.'

'So…?

I examined myself for betrayal. If Dad wanted them to believe it was a work accident, did I have the right to say otherwise?

At school, our form tutor had been telling us about utilitarianism and how you had to decide whether an action that seemed harsh would eventually benefit more people than it disadvantaged. He'd been using it to justify a whole class detention if we didn't shut up.

'Dad was driving home after a night shift,' I said now. 'I think he was speeding. A lorry hit him. Or he hit a lorry. I'm not sure.'

She put her hand to her mouth.

I drained the rest of my Horlicks. 'Surely you've asked him these questions.'

'We've tried. You were nine? Ten?'

'Eight.'

I told her how Mum had taken me to the hospital to see Dad, his leg hoisted up into the air, double its usual width because of bandages, and he'd had an operation on his shoulder, which had shattered with the impact of the crash in which he'd been thrown against the driver's door. The side of his head had been shaved and his face was purple with bruises.

I'd cried until my throat was sore.

'Then he got a blood clot in his lungs when he came home from hospital,' I said, 'from lying down so long and doing nothing. So that meant more time in hospital and more time off work.'

'That was hard for you and your mum too,' she said. 'How long did it take for him to get back to work?'

I shook my head. 'He did a couple of jobs in a warehouse or something. But in the end he took up whisky as his main job. I think he forgot how to be the type of person who rescues people and puts out fires.'

'That's sad.'

'We didn't live in Conway Road then.'

'Where were you?'

'In our own house nearer the town. Where we are now – where Dad is now – is a council house.'

'I see. And then your mum got—'

The old couple in the corner were paying the waitress and putting their coats on. Old people wear coats whatever the weather. The woman's was pale pink, the pink of candy floss.

'And then my mum got,' I said. 'Yes.'

When Bobbie dropped me home after our café visit and I went into the kitchen for some water, Bridget said, 'Are you hungry? I've made fairy cakes.'

I was learning that Bridget offered food as a greeting. It was odd, because she rarely ate any form of cake or biscuits herself and she certainly didn't seem keen on Amanda's new-found practice of comfort eating, if that's what it was. Maybe Bridget was just struggling to break the habit of creaming butter into sugar and adding flour as her way of showing affection, like when you wind up a child's toy but can't stop it whirring and spinning.

'I had Bourbons at the Happy Plate,' I said to her. 'But thanks.'

'The Happy Plate?' she said. 'Oh, that's good.'

'Why?'

'No reason. I mean, it's a good café.' She was ruffled and I wasn't sure what I'd said.

'It's okay,' I said. 'I can't say I'm an expert in these things. Dad's budget didn't stretch to regular outings.'

'No, I suppose not,' she said.

She asked if I'd help her make tea. 'Home-made meatballs,'

she said in a this-will-be-such-fun voice. 'You can do the mincing, if you like.' She pointed knowingly to the metal mincer as though introducing me to a potential life partner with whom I would find eternal happiness.

I hedged. I'd never seen Amanda in the kitchen playing domesticity with her mother, so why was she asking me? 'I have some homework,' I said. 'I've got a grammar test tomorrow.'

'Of course, of course. Merely a thought,' she said.

'I'll come down when I've finished revising,' I said, 'and see if you still need help.'

'Maybe you could put together the salad,' she said, but managed to make it sound like a tragic anticlimax after the rich promise of mincing.

'Jackie chopped up the salad ingredients,' Bridget announced to Uncle Nick and Amanda as we were eating later.

'How lovely for Jackie,' Amanda said.

'You can help me any time you want,' Bridget said.

'Did I say I wanted to?' Amanda said.

Clearly not, I thought, but Bridget often misunderstood sarcasm, or pretended to. I hadn't worked her out yet.

'These meatballs are tasty,' Uncle Nick said. 'Are there more?'

Bridget said there were.

'I'll get them, Bridget,' I said. She had just sat down after fetching more salad.

I saw her glance at Uncle Nick. She didn't like the fact that I wouldn't call her Auntie, but it never felt right on my tongue the way it did to say 'Uncle' Nick. I wasn't trying to be deliberately difficult and I couldn't see that it mattered, especially as my stay there was short term. Supposedly.

I'd had to stop Uncle Nick from calling me 'Jack', a habit he'd adopted. Not because I didn't like it. I did. But Bridget and Amanda didn't, I could tell, and if you jab a tiger with a stick, you're to blame when it bites off your head.

I took Uncle Nick's plate into the kitchen and put three

more meatballs on it. Spotless was in his basket in the corner, apparently sleeping, but he raised his head and sniffed as I lifted the pan lid. 'You're on a health drive,' I reminded him.

I replaced the lid. I could hear that the conversation at the dining table had gone quieter as if someone had turned the volume down.

When I walked back in, Amanda was saying, 'But how *much* longer?'

'Thank you, Jackie.' Uncle Nick took his plate and boomed out his thanks as though to drown Amanda's words.

I sat down and put my knife and fork together. I'd lost my appetite. Amanda reached over and forked my two remaining meatballs and Bridget said, 'Darling, really!'

'Take it as a compliment, Mum,' she said.

I said, 'Are you all talking about what Bobbie told me today?'

Everything went very still as though we were in a photo and not real people.

'What did Bobbie tell you, dear?' Bridget said, although I was sure she knew.

'She said I would probably need to stay longer.' I wasn't going to go into details about my dad.

'That's what I was asking. How long?' Amanda said with her mouth full, and I could sense her mother bristling.

Uncle Nick took a sip of water and said, 'I don't think that matters, does it? We said we'd give Jackie a home and that's what we'll do, as long as she needs one.'

Amanda said, 'But you told Social Services you only wanted short-term fostering.'

Bridget stood and started clearing away our plates. 'Circumstances change,' she said, as though wanting that to be the final word.

'And,' said Amanda, 'you asked them for kids younger than me. You told me they would be younger.'

This was new information to me.

Uncle Nick put a hand on Amanda's shoulder. 'Stop,' he said. 'You've gone far enough.'

At that point, Spotless trotted in, no doubt hoping there would be a reprieve on the meatball situation. He came to my chair and laid his head on my lap.

'You see,' Bridget said, 'Spotless wants her to stay,' which she no doubt meant as a comfort.

WEDNESDAY 5 MAY

After school, I climbed off the bus a few streets away from my usual stop and where I knew there was a phone box. Inside, I dialled Dad's number and pushed numerous coins into the slot when he answered. I hoped I'd have enough. I'd been saving them from my pocket money.

'Dad?'

'Oh,' he said. It wasn't a good start.

I heard a woman's voice in the background say, 'Who's that, Dave?'

'Who are you with?' I said.

'Never you mind.' His words were unclear, with no corners to them.

I didn't know what to do. This was my chance to persuade him to go to hospital. I didn't have long or Bridget would call out a search party.

'Dad, why won't you go into hospital?' I said. 'Don't you want me to come back?'

'Of course I want you back, my darling,' he said, and I knew this was a performance.

'If that's true,' I said, 'you have to get sorted out. Please.'

I heard the woman again. 'Who are you calling "darling"?'

There was a pause. 'It's my daughter,' he said eventually.

I heard a high-pitched 'Oh!'

'Dad, I want to come home,' I said, 'but you need to be well. I want us to go back to how we were.'

'That's never going to happen,' he said. 'I ruined all that years ago. You don't know the half of it.'

'What?'

But then I heard the buzz that told me he'd put the receiver down.

The telephone laughed out the change, coin after coin after coin, like someone amused that Dad hadn't told whoever the woman was that he had a daughter.

THURSDAY 6 MAY

After breakfast, I was knotting my school tie when I heard someone come upstairs. I wasn't sure who. I hadn't figured out their individual steps yet.

Knock knock. 'Jackie?' It was Bridget.

I opened the door.

'You do look smart in your uniform,' she said.

'Thank you.' I waited. Bridget didn't leave the kitchen unguarded for trivial reasons, so I couldn't believe she'd made the trip upstairs to pass judgement on my clothing.

'I need to wash your sheets and pillowcases today,' she said.

Ah. This was fallout from the first time she'd stripped my bed while I'd been at school. She had lost my mum's engagement ring, although Bridget didn't know that. Dad had reluctantly let me have the ring after Mum had died as I liked its pretty stone: an opal. I'd persuaded him one evening when he was too drunk to protest and I'd hoped too drunk to remember. I'd been right.

I'd kept the ring tucked under my pillow ever since and it was the first thing I'd rescued when I packed to move to the Walls'. I loved knowing it was there at night, under my dreaming head.

When I'd come home from school to find my bed stripped by Bridget and the ring gone, it had taken me an hour to find, lying on the floor and sweeping the carpet with my hands, and I'd cried for much of that hour before finding the ring under the wardrobe.

I'd washed my face and taken some big breaths (a tip from Bobbie, who did the same before taking part in court cases, she said). Then, in the kitchen, I'd asked Bridget if I could strip my own bed next time she needed to wash the linen.

'Oh!' she said, her eyebrows taking the lift to the fourth floor.

'I like to look after my own room,' I said. 'I'm used to it.'

'Goodness me,' she said. 'You'll be wanting to vacuum and dust it yourself next.'

I considered this. 'I would, actually. I can do it on Saturday mornings.'

She wore the kind of expression I'd expect had I announced I was really a mermaid.

'I've been in charge of the housework for two years,' I said, wondering whether she'd ever had to re-wash a clean basket of clothes because someone had been whisky-sick in it.

She opened a cupboard and started reorganising cans of soup and spaghetti that had all been in the right places. 'But that's why you came to us. So that we could look after you and save you from that.' She said this from behind a cupboard door.

'I'm fourteen,' I said.

'So am I,' said Amanda, walking in and opening the fridge. 'What's the big deal?'

'It was a private conversation,' I said, at the same time as Bridget said, 'Jackie has offered to change her own bed and clean her room.'

Spotless, in his basket in the corner, stretched and then yawned, luxurious and loud, as if to tell us that family politics really wasn't his thing and he'd much prefer a bowl of Winalot.

'What?' Amanda said, turning my way but still referring to me in the third person. 'She's insane, then.' She'd taken out a piece of leftover gateau that Bridget had put on a plate.

I said, 'Fourteen-year-olds all over the world do the family laundry and they don't have twin tubs and utility rooms. They take it to the river and scrub it. With a baby on their backs sometimes.'

Amanda picked a spoon from the cutlery drawer and started eating the gateau.

'Not standing up in the kitchen, darling,' her mother said.

'Don't give me all that stuff about Africa,' Amanda said, ignoring her.

'All over the world, I said.'

'Don't give me that stuff about all over the world.'

'You could start stripping *your* bed if you like, Amanda,' her mother tinkled.

I wished I could rewind her, like a tape cassette.

'Teacher's pet,' Amanda said, walking past me with her plate and out of the kitchen. I heard her go upstairs.

'She's going to slam her door,' Bridget said, moving seamlessly from crass to prophetic.

Spotless lifted his head again at the slam and whimpered.

I said to Bridget now, 'I'll strip the bed before I come downstairs. Where do you want me to put the linen?'

'In the bath, if you like,' she said. 'As they do in all the best hotels.'

I'd never been to a best hotel. It seemed an odd practice, almost common, like leaving your dirty socks for someone else to pick up. 'I'll take your word for it.'

She looked suddenly sad. 'I hope you are beginning to feel part of the family,' she said.

I didn't know what to say. I wondered if she was going to cry. I began to shut my door, but Uncle Nick came out of his and Bridget's bedroom, tucking in his shirt. 'Are you nearly ready to go, Jack?'

Bridget frowned, I think at the abbreviation, but what she said was, 'Go where?'

'I'm running her into school,' he said. 'We need to get going. I want to vote in the council elections on the way.'

'The bus is always late on Thursdays,' I said to her. 'The driver does another job before us.'

'She's worried about getting a black mark from her form tutor,' Uncle Nick said. 'I assume you'll go and vote later, darling.'

'Jackie's stripping her own bed,' Bridget said, as though she hadn't heard him.

'I know,' he said. 'You told me. But you'll live through it.' He patted her on the shoulder, as if to make sure she knew he was teasing, then went back into the bedroom.

Amanda had been downstairs. She took the stairs two at a time and arrived on the landing, saying to her mother, 'Did I hear right? Is Dad taking her to school?'

'Hi,' I said and waved.

'It seems so,' Bridget said. 'Amanda,' she added, 'do you need me to let out your school skirt?'

I pretended I hadn't heard Bridget's comment. 'It's only on Thursdays,' I said to Amanda, but she disappeared into her bedroom as I said it. I don't think she heard me over the hum left on the landing that was her mother's blunder.

I said to Bridget, 'Where will I find new sheets?'

Her voice was as taut as a drum. 'They're in the bathroom, in the airing cupboard. I'll fetch them.'

'I can go,' I said.

But she was already there. Click, went the cupboard door.

SATURDAY 8 MAY

At breakfast, Uncle Nick asked if I fancied a longer bike ride. So far, all we'd done was cycle around the local streets to get me used to the road. He'd taught me hand signals and how to handle the bike if I had to brake suddenly.

'I need to clean my room first,' I said.

Amanda said, slathering butter on toast, 'I thought that was a joke.'

Bridget leaped on the opportunity as people leap on ten pound notes they find on the street. 'You go with Uncle Nick,' she said to me. 'I'll clean your room.' She stood up, surprising her cornflakes as she'd just poured on the milk.

'Can you wait for me?' I said to Uncle Nick.

'Whenever you're ready,' he said. 'I'll check over the bikes first. Pump up the tyres.'

Bridget sat down and resumed normal service. She seemed resigned. 'The vacuum cleaner is under the stairs,' she said.

'Where are the dusters?' I said.

'What?' Amanda said.

'They're yellow,' I said. 'You use them to wipe surfaces.'

'Ha ha,' she said. But it didn't have the usual bite. She was in a good mood. Bridget and Uncle Nick had said she could stay overnight at Fiona's house that evening after a birthday party. I assumed she wasn't taking risks in case they reconsidered.

I switched on Radio 1 as company while I dusted every surface, standing on my chair to clean the top of the wardrobe and feeling a whoop of victory as dust puffed up because Bridget clearly hadn't done that for weeks. It was a treat to use Bridget's vacuum cleaner after trying to keep Dad's house clean with Mum's old carpet sweeper. I made sure to take it right to the edges and vacuumed under the bedside rug so that Bridget couldn't say I hadn't done it properly.

For good measure, I tidied the clothes and shoes inside the wardrobe and chest of drawers. It's funny how even though you can't see the evidence of your tidying, knowing it's there can make you feel orderly in your heart.

I made the bed as neatly as I could, which is when I found that the pillow was stained with blood.

It was around my thirteenth birthday that I'd developed a spot on the back of my head. In the evenings, while watching telly with Dad or doing homework in the kitchen, I'd started picking at it. It took two weeks to heal because I kept pulling off the scab. Eventually, it cleared up, but I started exploring my head underneath my hair for other lumps and bumps. Maybe everyone has them. I found a couple and worried at those and somehow it helped. When I was picking and scratching, I wasn't thinking about other things.

At the Walls' house, I'd managed so far not to do it in front of them. But I kept catching myself picking while reading my book at night before switching my lamp off. This was often late despite Bridget's unsubtle knocks at the door and updates on the time as though she were the Speaking Clock.

Pick, pick, scratch, pick. I knew I was making tiny wounds lately – these weren't spots that had been there before – but I couldn't stop. The wounds formed scabs and then I made more.

So, there was blood on the pillow, and it would be another fortnight before Bridget asked me to change the bedclothes again.

I took the pillowcase into the bathroom and rinsed it with water and soap, scrubbing hard. The stain was still there, but barely, like a whisper.

Should I dry it with my hairdryer? But what if Bridget heard and investigated?

I had to hope it would be dry by the time I went to bed.

I vowed not to pick again, as I had many times. Surely it couldn't be that hard, if I really put my mind to it.

When Uncle Nick and I arrived back after our bike ride around the roads, Amanda had left for Fiona's house.

'I thought the party was tonight,' Uncle Nick said to Bridget.

'Apparently, tonight started at lunchtime,' she said.

I sat on the stool in the shed, watching Uncle Nick measuring then sawing a plank of wood which he'd clamped to his workbench.

'What's it for?' I said.

'A new shelf for some of my tools,' he said, nodding towards a space on the shed's back wall. 'It'll fit nicely there.'

While he worked, I browsed his mini-library again. '*Death on the Nile*,' I read from one spine. I pulled the book from the shelf. A piece of pink paper floated out from between the pages, drifting to the shed floor.

I bent to pick it up, but he reached it first, saw still in hand, and our heads almost collided. He slid the scrap into his pocket. 'I must start using proper bookmarks,' he said.

'Agatha Christie,' I said, looking at the front of the book.

'One of my favourites. I love a good death.'

I began to read the blurb. Then I glanced at him. He'd laid down his saw. 'I'm so sorry,' he said. 'I shouldn't have said that about death. I didn't think.'

'What? It's okay.'

I waved the book in his direction to staunch his pity. 'Can I borrow this?'

'Of course. Take it.'

I sat down and read the first few pages while he rattled in tins for screws and nails, then I shut the book.

'Uncle Nick,' I said.

'That's me.'

I'd got used to this as his standard response. It was irritating, but you have to give adults some leeway.

'About death.'

'Right.'

'At my mum's funeral, I read a poem,' I said.

He was planing the wood now, smoothing its edges. He didn't stop.

I liked his lack of reaction. It encouraged me to go on. Bridget would have said, 'You poor love,' purring like a cat, and put me right off kilter.

'The vicar had a ginger beard that made him not look like a vicar. And a Scottish accent. It reminded me of a poet we'd heard on Mrs Collingworth's tape recorder.'

'Robert Burns?' Uncle Nick said.

'That was it. Something about a mouse.'

'A moosie,' he said.

I watched him stroking the wood the way he stroked Spotless, as if he didn't know he was doing it.

'I nearly couldn't read the poem,' I said. 'I walked to the front of the church with my notebook, but when I turned round, Dad was like this.' I demonstrated, bowing my head between my knees, my hands clasped around the back of my neck. I straightened up again. 'Like trying to hold himself still or stop himself from flailing about.'

'He must have been very distressed.'

'I didn't look at him or any of our family,' I said. 'I looked at one of Mum's friends, from the library. She had grey hair and spectacles, the ones with wings.'

'Reassuring,' he said, 'library ladies. What was the poem called?'

'It's called "Winter".'

He turned the piece of wood over and began planing again. The noise and rhythm of it were like friends.

'I'd love to hear your poem,' he said. 'Do you have it?'

I wanted him to hear it.

'Everything okay?' Bridget called from the kitchen as I came into the house.

'Tickety-boo,' I said.

Upstairs, I reached inside the top of the wardrobe where I kept my poems notebook tucked in between two spare blankets.

Uncle Nick nodded towards my notebook when I stepped back into the shed. 'A collection?'

I sat down and turned the pages.

'Let's hear it, Miss Poet,' he said. He stood by his workbench, hands in trouser pockets.

'Shall I start?' I said.

'I'm all ears.'

Mrs Collingworth was always saying, 'You have to slow down. Give your reader a chance to let meanings sink in.' I took a breath.

'"Winter", by Jackie Chadwick.' Straight away, I wished I hadn't announced my name like that. 'By me,' I added.

'A kind of winter came to fetch you
with his cold hands and hoar breath.
He didn't bother with a knock or bell—'

I checked he was still listening. He was staring straight at me.

'—and before you knew it or we knew it
so we could stand at the door to defend you,
he was in, his giant, icy feet
on our hallway carpet, then by your bed,
speaking frost that grasped at your skin.'

I glanced up. 'There's another verse.'

He nodded.

'The vicar had to read the second verse,' I said. 'I thought

I would be all right. But I knew that if I opened my mouth again to say the next words, it wouldn't be words that came.'

Uncle Nick had picked up a spanner and was turning it over in his palm.

'It sounded more like poetry, the second verse,' I said.

'Because of Robert Burns?'

'I can read it to you, if you like.'

'I would like,' he said. 'It's very lovely so far.'

I read.

'A kind of winter took you over
with his curious spiteful fingers
mapping you, laying down snow on snow
in your bones so you grew heavy with it.
He lay down with you, whispering numbness
until he made you fly as quiet as birds
into his winter heart that folds you now,
tight and gone where sun cannot find you.'

Uncle Nick was revolving the spanner over and over and over. 'Well,' he said. 'And your dad? How did he react?'

I closed the notebook. 'When I went back to the pew, he was trembling. You know how land does before an earthquake hits?'

He cleared his throat. I'd noticed his voice becoming scratchy.

'Did it move you?' I said.

He looked surprised.

'Poetry's meant to move you,' I said. 'I know the library lady was moved. Her lips went crazy.'

He smiled. 'Lips can be traitors in these situations, that's true.'

At 9.30 that evening, I'd been reading the Agatha Christie and trying not to pick at my head when I heard the telephone ring downstairs. Bridget's high-pitched tones told me there was an

Amanda situation. Five minutes later, the front door slammed and the Morris Marina was started up.

I'd switched off my bedside lamp at around 10 when I heard the car pull into the driveway.

'I don't need your *help* to get up the stairs, Dad,' I heard Amanda say a minute later. 'Get off me.' Her words were slurred.

'I'm worried you'll fall,' he said.

'Ssshh.' That was Bridget. 'You'll wake Jackie.'

'Jackie!' Amanda said. 'Wake up!' She giggled.

'Don't!' Uncle Nick said.

'Why did you have to come and fetch me?' Amanda said. 'It's so embarrassing.'

'Fiona's parents *rang* us, darling,' Bridget said. 'They were worried.'

'And she smells of smoke as well as cider,' Uncle Nick said, the other side of my bedroom door.

'Amanda!' said Bridget. 'Really!'

Amanda's door slammed and I heard no more. I don't think she even bothered undressing. I didn't hear the usual creak of her bedroom floor.

'Should I get her some water?' Bridget said.

'I'd leave her be,' Uncle Nick said, and I heard him go into the bathroom. 'Let her sleep it off.'

MONDAY 10 MAY

I was pleased to leave the house on Monday morning for school in the hope of seeing some people smiling. Uncle Nick and Bridget's faces had been strained and sad all day Sunday. Amanda had stayed in her room, refusing meals, although I suspected she kept plenty of snacks in there.

I was in the school dining room eating soggy cheese flan with Kim when one of the office staff found me. 'Jackie Chadwick?' she said. 'I have a personal message for you.'

She looked at Kim.

'It's fine,' I said. 'She knows the worst. In fact, she's blackmailing me and I have to hand over my pocket money.'

Kim giggled, but, if the woman was amused, she was hiding it deep, perhaps in her gall bladder. 'It's a message from your social worker,' she said. 'She apologises but can't pick you up from school today. Can you get home on your usual bus?'

I said to Kim after the woman had gone that working in a school office must siphon the smiles out of you. Kim said that working in any office would do that, which was why she was going to be a famous singer on cruise ships.

It's usually the non-famous who sing on cruise ships, but if anyone deserved a dream, Kim did.

In the heat, it seemed to take forever to walk from school to Dad's house. Bridget and Nick would think I was with

Bobbie and I had enough money on me for a bus back as long as I didn't stay with Dad too long. I'd been looking for an opportunity to go and check on him. I knew I was meant to be supervised, but I needed to know that he wasn't living in squalor, surrounded by empty bottles and full ashtrays.

By the time I arrived, I'd shed my blazer and much of my resolve. My satchel had felt heavier with every step. I had a maths test the next day so had brought home my textbook for revision. I began to hate the textbook with an unreasonable passion.

I didn't have my key. I rang the doorbell, but it was broken. I knew it didn't work, so why had I tried? How easily that detail had slipped from my mind in the same way I couldn't always recall the exact shape of my mother's eyebrows or the tone of her voice. Time is such a pillager.

The front room curtains were closed, as I'd expected, but the front windows had been nudged open. I was pleased. He was letting in air for a change. It was a good sign.

I knocked and shouted through the letter box. 'Dad. It's me.' I peered in. The door to the front room was open. I could see through to the kitchen. A box of cakes lay on the kitchen surface.

I heard him say, 'Bugger!'

'Let me in,' I called.

There was a pause.

'Can you come back later?' he called back.

I sensed the curtains in the neighbour's window move as they lapped up the free entertainment.

'I can't do that,' I said. I rapped at the door again and waited.

He answered it. He was in his usual summer wardrobe of pants and vest. As he stood there, an elderly couple walked behind me and I heard the woman say, 'No shame.'

Some of Dad's shame came off and landed on me, like a virus when you cough.

'What are you doing here?' he said.

'I've walked from school. I'm thirsty. Can I come in?'

He checked over his shoulder.

'I'm your child,' I said.

'Suit yourself,' he said, clearly the only welcome I was getting. He stepped back from the door to let me past. The house smelled of old frying oil.

'Shall I put the kettle on?' I said, but as I did, a woman came out of the front room, said, 'I'll do it,' and walked into the kitchen. She was short with dark hair, although not as short as me. She wore a thin dressing gown around a plump, soft body. It was too small for her.

I remembered the woman I'd heard on the phone when I rang Dad from the phone box. Was this the same one?

'That's Caroline,' Dad said, which didn't help me.

I hesitated, then followed him into the front room, putting my satchel on the floor. The bed was in disarray, its cover a crumpled sheet. On the bed were a couple of women's magazines. Dad's whisky bottle was on the coffee table as usual, but there were two glasses, each with an inch of amber liquid. An ashtray next to them overflowed with stubs.

'Is she living here?' I said.

'Don't be daft,' he said.

Her voice came from the kitchen. 'It'd need a bloody good clean before I ever agreed to that. And so would he.'

'I need the toilet,' I said.

'You know where it is,' he said and picked up the bottle, topping up the glasses.

'How many sugars?' said the woman from the kitchen as I emerged.

'None, thank you.'

I went upstairs. The toilet was fairly clean – no doubt he still used the one outside. But the bath was grimy. A grey rim halfway up its side told the story.

There was a pink toothbrush in a glass on the sink and a smell of perfume or talcum powder in the room, at odds with the state of the bath.

Downstairs, the woman had put my mug of tea on the

coffee table and was sitting in an armchair. Dad was propped up against the pillows in his normal position.

The scene was similar to the one I'd come home to for the last two years except for the addition of a woman in a dressing gown which showed half her breasts and which had slid off her legs so that I could see she was wearing stockings.

'I expect this is the Spanish Inquisition,' Dad said. His tone wasn't pleasant.

I had planned questions on my way there. But the heat and Caroline's presence had evaporated them.

A knock at the front door had Caroline and Dad exchanging glances.

'Who the bloody hell is that?' Dad said.

Somehow I knew who it was. I'd started from school with a scenario in my head of Dad welcoming me in, making me tea, asking how school was, telling me he was going into hospital that very afternoon and, look, here's my bag packed. All this Enid Blyton tosh had blinded me to the fact that Social Services would have let Nick and Bridget know about the changed arrangements.

I should never have come.

I went to the door. Uncle Nick stood there, pallid and sweaty with his sandy hair sticking to the sides of his face. His bike was leaning against a lamp post. 'I've found you,' he said, breathing heavily.

'I'll get my satchel,' I said.

'Who is it?' Dad said as I went back into the front room.

Caroline had lit a cigarette and was blowing smoke into the air.

'Kids messing about,' I said. I picked up my satchel. 'I'm going now.'

'You haven't drunk your tea,' Caroline said.

'Telephone before you come next time,' Dad said.

It hurt that both would have realised I had lied about kids messing about. Neither cared enough to question it or check I wasn't being collected by a child-snatcher.

As I left, I heard her voice. 'You didn't say you had a kid,' which is when I knew she couldn't have been the woman I'd heard on the phone.

'I'll walk you to the stop,' Uncle Nick said, as though he'd just met me from a shopping trip or from the park, 'and see you onto the bus. Then I'll meet you back at home.'

'Okay,' I said.

On the bus, I sat on the back seat, behind two elderly ladies gossiping about the resignation of Jeremy Thorpe from the leadership of the Liberals. ('Secrets will out,' one said.) I plucked at two spots on the back of my head until my fingernail was filled with blood. It wasn't accidental. I was fully aware and glad of something to do.

Back at the Walls', Bridget was in the kitchen on the phone. 'It's Bobbie,' she said and handed me the receiver.

'Promise me you'll never do that again,' Bobbie said to me.

'I won't,' I said.

'It's not safe,' she said.

'Honestly, I won't.'

But it wasn't about safety for me. It was about finding Carolines or perhaps Janes or Marions with my dad and wearing my mother's silk dressing gown. I didn't know Dad had kept it.

WEDNESDAY 12 MAY

Bridget was in the garden weeding when I arrived home from school. I sensed she had news by the way she sprang upright when she heard me put my satchel down in the living room as though the satchel had a magical connection to her vertebrae. 'Is that you, Jackie?' she called, even though she could see me.

'It was, last time I looked,' I called back.

She came in, discarding her sandals at the French windows.

'How was school?' she said. She was still wearing her gardening gloves.

'Has something happened to Dad?' I said.

'Nothing bad,' she said. 'Bobbie telephoned. He's agreed to go into the hospital at last for some help. Into Hatton. You know – the hospital for—'

'Oh,' I said.

'So, that's positive, isn't it?' she said but in a way that told me she wasn't sure.

'When's he going?'

'He's there already,' she said.

'Before he changed his mind,' I said.

'Perhaps.'

'Can I phone him?'

'They advise against it. I did ask. But I'm sure it won't be long until you see him. And maybe by then…'

And maybe by then. Dot dot dot. Images flitted through my mind: Dad as a strong man again in his fireman's uniform; Dad cooking a bacon and egg breakfast, whistling; Dad helping me with maths homework.

I wondered whether Caroline had influenced him. I also wanted to believe that my visit on Monday had made a difference. But we want to believe all sorts of things, don't we, the human race?

At teatime, Bridget cooked gammon slices with a pineapple sauce, but the atmosphere as we ate was not comfortable. Amanda had not been allowed out since the party on Saturday and mealtimes so far that week had been flavoured with her hangdog face. This wouldn't have been so bad, but every time I contributed to Uncle Nick and Bridget's conversation, they leaped on it as though I'd brought a present with a silver bow on it, and they said things like, 'What an interesting observation!' so that Amanda's face fell further. After doing my best on Monday and Tuesday, I'd given up and kept my contributions inside my head where they were safe. While we ate the gammon that evening, I realised that Amanda had been told about my dad's admission to hospital when I said that I liked the pineapple sauce and she said, 'Well, I'm sure Mum will be happy to give you the recipe for when you go back home.'

Later, Bridget had gone to Weight Watchers and Uncle Nick was in the shed, talking to an elderly neighbour who'd come to fetch his fixed bike.

Amanda and I were watching a John Wayne film and I'd made us a glass of orange squash each. She'd said thank you as though I'd chiselled it out of her.

I was in an armchair. She was on the floor, cross-legged, leaning against the sofa.

She said to me, 'Have you ever been drunk?'

I was surprised. She rarely initiated conversation. I wondered whether news of my potential departure had given her some kind of confidence. 'No,' I said. 'Unless I was so drunk I've forgotten.'

'I sometimes drink some of Mum and Dad's sherry and vodka,' she said. 'They haven't noticed.'

'You can't be having that much, then,' I said.

She didn't respond to that but turned to face me more squarely. 'Do you smoke?'

'No.'

'I've been smoking for a year,' she said.

'I know,' I said. 'I saw you in town with your friends. I was with your mum in a café.'

Her cheeks went instantly, fierily red. 'Did she see?'

'I think you'd know if she had.'

'Don't say anything to them, will you?'

'I'm not a snitch,' I said.

'Neither am I,' she said, 'if you want to tell me anything.'

'Nothing to tell,' I said. 'Anyway, how do you pay for cigarettes? That must use up all your pocket money.'

She smiled and tapped the side of her nose as though this were the question she'd been waiting for. 'Wouldn't you like to know?'

I drank the rest of my squash. 'It's not top of my list of things I'm curious about,' I said. 'Are you going to tell me?'

'No,' she said and hugged a cushion to herself as though it were her secret.

'I'll go upstairs and finish my homework, then,' I said. 'This film is boring.'

SATURDAY 15 MAY

Late morning, after I'd cleaned my room and Amanda and I were watching *Tiswas*, Uncle Nick asked if I'd like a country bike ride. 'You too, Amanda,' he said. 'Come along. I'm sure your bike's keen for an outing.'

I had to hand it to him; he did keep trying.

Bridget was in the garden, picking and choosing from a flower bed.

'I'm busy reading this,' Amanda said from her supine position on the sofa, waving the new *Jackie* magazine at us. It came in the post each week.

'You've shifted the concept of busy for me, poppet,' he said, 'but if you're sure.'

'I'm sure.'

He hesitated. 'You've been indoors all week, though.'

She said, 'And whose fault is that?'

I could see how desperately he wanted to answer. But he held back.

The woods were cool, the full foliage of the trees a barrier to the noon sun which had made the back of my neck hot on the roads.

After the initial cycle uphill, the shelter and the consequent drop in temperature were welcome. We biked along a path, taking our time, weaving around walkers in their serious boots and broad-brimmed hats.

'Let's stop here?' Uncle Nick said after a while, slowing his bike and pointing to a clearing. 'We could sit on those stumps for a breather.'

I stopped behind him. 'Don't we need to get back for lunch?' Saturday lunch was at 1. If it got pushed to half past, Bridget came out in hives.

He dismounted and slipped his rucksack off. 'We do not,' he said. 'I've brought a picnic.'

I could tell Uncle Nick had made and packed the lunch, not Bridget. He'd wrapped plain cheese sandwiches inexpertly in greaseproof paper and thrown in a whole box of French Fancies. Bridget would have added lettuce and tomatoes to the sandwiches and then imprisoned them in the right size of Tupperware.

He'd filled a bottle with water and made a flask of tea but had forgotten to put milk in it.

'I should really leave these things to Bridget,' he said. 'She was having a bath this morning, so I risked it myself.'

In the distance, we could hear the faint cracks of cap guns and the occasional shouts of boys.

'Nuisance, those guns,' Uncle Nick said. 'Should be banned. They bring them into school.'

I nibbled on a sandwich. 'Bridget knows we're not back for lunch?'

'Oh yes,' he said. 'I filled in all the appropriate forms.'

I smiled, but I never felt entirely comfortable saying things about Bridget behind her back. She had taken me in, after all, and made some compromises I knew she wasn't happy with, such as the room cleaning, and letting me eat the whites of fried eggs only as I hated the yolks.

'I was chatting to Mr Donaldson, your geography teacher,' Uncle Nick said, unpeeling the paper from the sides of a cake.

'Uh oh.'

'It's nothing bad,' he said. 'He says you came third in a class test last week.'

I waited.

'Why didn't you tell us?' he said.

I wasn't sure what to say. I'd got used to leaving those sorts of achievements at school, or letting them drift away on the breeze as I'd walked home, not bringing them in through a front door. People with drool on their mouths and one fag left don't take too kindly to the good news of others. Perhaps when Dad comes out of Hatton, I thought, and I go back home, he'll be more receptive. I imagined ten pence for some sweets or a celebratory pat on the head: 'Well done, Short-arse.'

I decided to ask Uncle Nick a question which had been bothering me. 'I was wondering why you stopped being a teacher. Why you left and worked in the museum instead.'

'Oh, you don't want to know about all that,' he said.

'I do.'

He took another cake from the box. 'Yellow, this time,' he said and put it in his mouth, whole.

I watched as he dealt with it. Was he using a French Fancy as a delaying strategy?

'You seem to like teaching,' I said. 'You must have done to go back to it.'

He swallowed, finally, and took a deep breath that lasted for ages. 'It's a long time ago now.'

'When?'

I was convinced he knew the date exactly, but he took his time. 'About 1965.'

'I was three.'

'Thanks for pointing that out,' he said. 'I told you it was ancient history.'

He offered me the box of cakes. I took one and held it in my hands. 'Tell me what happened.'

'It was a misunderstanding,' he said.

'Who by?'

'What is this?' he said. 'Have you thought of hosting *Mastermind*?'

Adults are so slippery, like eels. Greased eels. I didn't feel like letting him slide away. 'Who by? What misunderstanding?'

He poured the black tea into the plastic cup from the top of the flask while I unscrewed the water bottle. 'I had an argument with a boy I taught,' he said. 'It got out of hand. He made a complaint.' He said all this fast.

I didn't ask anything else at first.

He sipped from the cup. 'It was ridiculous. Absolutely ridiculous. The headmaster took his side, of course,' he said.

There was something sour in his voice. And he'd said the last sentence to the woods.

'Did you leave the school?'

'I left teaching,' he said.

'Because of that one boy?'

He shook his head slowly from side to side. I had no idea what this meant. No, not because of one boy? No, I'm not telling you. Or, despair? Such an ambiguous gesture.

He began to put the lid back on the flask.

A sudden 'crack' from a cap gun a few yards off made him start. The lid fell and hot tea spilled out onto his thighs.

'Shit!' he said, dabbing at the wet stains with his hands, then diving into his pocket for a handkerchief. 'Shit. Stupid *bloody* kids.'

It wasn't the first time I'd heard Uncle Nick swear, but it was the first time I'd seen him so angry I thought he might hit out. I'd flinched. I hoped he hadn't noticed.

'Sorry,' he said, trying to soak up the liquid with the hanky. 'My language.'

'Thanks for the picnic anyway,' I said brightly. I looked at the French Fancy I still held in my palm. It was slightly moist as though it too felt anxious. I popped it in my mouth whole, as Uncle Nick had, in an attempt to be supportive, even though I wasn't hungry.

But he was hitching his rucksack onto his back and hadn't seen.

MONDAY 17 MAY

After school, I climbed into Bobbie's car and she said we'd go to a café called Simpsons, situated in a small street leading off Leamington's main shopping parade. 'The Happy Plate is closed for refurbishment,' she told me, 'for this week. Is that okay?'

'Of course,' I said, throwing my satchel on the back seat.

'That's a relief,' she said, starting up the car. 'Some people aren't good with change they weren't expecting.'

'Because my life so far has been so orderly and routine?'

She laughed. 'Fair point.'

Simpsons was larger than our usual café and with more atmosphere. Photographs on the walls depicted glamorous film stars and a speaker in the corner played jazz. A newspaper sat on one table, its headlines obsessed with the Jeremy Thorpe story. I didn't quite understand its complexities. Bridget and Uncle Nick had talked about it but in hushed voices.

Bobbie and I sat at a table for four by the window, opposite each other. The sun grilled the sides of our faces. 'Our cheeks won't match,' I said. 'We'll have to swap halfway. Have you heard any news about my dad?'

'No,' she said. 'We won't hear anything.'

'When is he coming out?'

'They said he'd need a fortnight. At least. These things aren't straightforward.'

I calculated in my head. 'Wednesday the 26th, then?'

'Perhaps,' she said.

'That's a fortnight.'

'It is.'

'You're being evasive,' I said. 'So, I shouldn't start packing my bag?'

'Let's wait for news.'

The waitress arrived.

'A glass of cold milk for me,' Bobbie said, 'and two packets of biscuits.'

I ordered hot chocolate as they didn't serve Horlicks. I tutted. 'More change I wasn't expecting.'

'Are you coping?'

'Barely.'

I looked out of the window. 'I like this café,' I said. 'There are more people to watch.'

'Have you been reading spy novels?' she said.

'I've been reading Agatha Christie,' I said, 'and people are surprising. I didn't guess the murderer at all.'

When the waitress had moved back to the counter, I asked Bobbie why she'd ordered milk.

She looked embarrassed. 'I don't fancy anything else.'

'But you always have tea.'

I looked more closely at her face. She looked the kind of pale green people turn before they faint.

'Don't even make me talk about tea,' she said.

I wasn't sure what to say.

We sat in an uneasy silence. Usually she asked me how school was at this point.

When the waitress brought our drinks and biscuits, Bobbie grabbed at a packet of digestives, tearing it open and eating one almost whole.

She sighed. Her face changed back to her normal skin colour in front of my eyes. 'That's better.' She sipped at her milk and smiled. 'I'm sorry to worry you,' she said.

'You went like a chameleon,' I said.

She paused. 'I might as well tell you. It's morning sickness.'

'But it's a quarter to 4,' I said, looking at the clock on the café wall.

'Morning sickness can last all day at this stage,' she said.

I couldn't help staring at her abdomen. 'You're having a baby?'

She picked up another biscuit. 'I wasn't going to say,' she said, 'but you wanted me to talk about tea.'

'Why wouldn't you say?'

'I wouldn't want you to be anxious,' she said. 'When I do have the baby, it will mean—'

She left a pause as if to give me chance to catch up. Or perhaps she didn't want to voice the words herself.

'I'll have a new social worker,' I said.

'Yes, but you might not even need one by then.'

'Now you're making things up,' I said, 'to keep me happy. Earlier, you weren't so sure.'

She smiled as if in surrender.

'When will you have the baby?' I said.

'The beginning of November,' she said, 'if all goes to plan.'

'But you won't be working right up to when it's born.'

'No, probably not. But I would introduce you to my replacement in plenty of time.'

'What if I hate their guts?' I said. 'What if they don't get my jokes?'

'Neither is likely,' she said. 'Drink your hot chocolate up. I need to ask if there's a lavatory.'

She walked over to the counter. I heard the waitress say, grumpily, 'It's a staff one, but if it's desperate.'

'It's desperate,' Bobbie said. 'I have approximately thirty seconds.'

While she'd gone, I watched out of the window. A man with a dog. Two women who looked like mother and daughter, burdened with shopping bags, including an enormous white bag bearing the words 'Your Wedding'. An old lady in a headscarf, shuffling along one tiny step after another. Each person with their story – stories that you couldn't tell from the outside. Perhaps the man had stolen the dog. Perhaps it was the mother getting married, not the daughter. What if it were the old lady's last day on Earth and she didn't know it?

Two minutes away from the Walls' house, as we approached the local arcade of shops, Bobbie said, 'Do you mind if I pull in while there's parking space? I need some bread. I'm eating enough for four when I'm actually hungry.'

'Sure.'

I waited in the car.

While she was in the shop, another car parked a few spaces ahead of Bobbie's car. As it passed me, I noticed it was driven by a man with a woman in the passenger seat. When the car stopped, the man, tall and wearing a grey suit, got out of his side and walked round to open the passenger door. The woman climbed out and he held out a hand to help her, but she batted it away.

The woman was Bridget.

The two stood by the car. I couldn't hear what they said. They weren't shouting, but they were clearly arguing. After about a minute, Bridget turned and walked off in the direction of Hollybush Close. The man looked as though he would follow but didn't. He watched her for a while and then climbed back into his car. He pulled out of the space, reversed and drove off in the opposite direction.

Bobbie and I pulled up outside the house as Bridget was letting herself in. When she saw us, she launched herself into the hallway as if to pretend she'd been there all the time.

'Unusual,' Bobbie said, putting on the handbrake. 'My impression of Bridget is that she'd be waiting in the kitchen for you with a batch of warm scones or some butterfly cakes, checking the clock.'

'She usually is,' I said.

WEDNESDAY 19 MAY

At Poetry Club on Wednesday, Mrs C confirmed the date of the arts evening. 'Definitely Thursday 22 July,' she said. 'The day before term ends. Let me know soon if you'd like to perform. I'll be offering this to my English classes too, so grab your chance.'

There were murmurs of 'Not likely' and 'Not me', but I raised my hand before I could convince myself otherwise. 'Can I let you know now? I'd like to read the poem I wrote about the picnic. The one based on "Adlestrop".'

'It's beautiful,' the teacher said. 'Super choice.'

'Can I say yes, too?' said Molly beside me.

'You're both on the list,' said Mrs C, smiling. 'Bear in mind you'll need to stay after school for a couple of rehearsals.'

Molly turned to me and whispered, 'I wouldn't have volunteered if you hadn't.'

'I nearly didn't. But what's the worst that could happen?'

We looked at each other and I think we were both visualising a collapse on stage or a hostile crowd shouting, 'Off! Off!'

'Will your mum and dad come?' she said. I didn't know her well and she didn't know my circumstances.

'That might be difficult,' I said.

'I hope my mum can,' she said, but she didn't sound sure.

I was surprised to see Bobbie's car parked outside the house when I arrived back from school. I heard it warning me, 'Turn around. Walk the other way. You won't want to hear this.'

Bobbie was on the sofa and Bridget opposite her. A tray

was laid with tea and biscuits, but Bobbie was drinking squash. Bridget sipped from what I was learning were Bridget's teacups-for-special-occasions, kept for both celebratory and sad events and, probably, because this was the Walls, events which began as celebratory and turned accidentally sad.

Bridget had on her pity face, the face she wore whenever I mentioned my mother's death, for instance. She would bend her head slightly to one side and purse her mouth as if for a kiss, a threat she'd fortunately not carried through so far.

I sat next to Bobbie. Bridget poured me some tea without asking and put sugar in it even though she knew I didn't take sugar. She stirred it seventy-three times and handed it to me. I felt I should acknowledge the effort she'd put in, so I accepted it.

Bobbie gave me the facts without fuss, the way she knew I liked them. Bridget probably judged her callous.

Dad had discharged himself from Hatton Hospital on Tuesday and had now been arrested after assaulting a policeman. He'd been involved in a fight with another man in a pub, the police had been called, and Dad had grappled with the policeman in the pub car park. The policeman had then fallen and cracked his head on the pavement, fracturing his skull.

'Assaulting an officer is a serious offence,' Bobbie said soberly.

'But he didn't make him fall on purpose,' I said.

She paused. 'That's debatable if he pushed him. A fractured skull—'

'Where's Dad now?'

'On remand. Do you know what that means?'

'Not really.'

She said, 'Waiting for his court appearance.'

'At home?'

'No. He's at Winson Green. It's a prison in Birmingham. He hasn't been granted bail,' she said. 'Do you understand?'

'Yes,' I said. 'I know about bail.'

I gulped some of my tea. It was so cloying it hit a place under my earlobes.

Bridget said, 'We watch *Porridge*, don't we, Jackie? Such a funny programme.'

I said to Bobbie, 'Do you think the no bail is because he had a visit from the police after he – before I came here?'

'I'm not sure,' she said. 'It may have influenced it. And his recent caution. It's not a good picture, I'm afraid.'

I examined myself to see if I wanted to cry. If I did, I would need to excuse myself and go upstairs. Bridget had a rogue gene that meant if anyone cried near her, even on TV, she was likely to cry too, but messier.

Had the news come to me as a shock? Or had I expected it all along?

Mrs Collingworth had told us about features of Shakespeare's tragedies. 'No one went to see *Macbeth* or *Othello* expecting anything but bodies on the stage at the end of a tragedy,' she'd told us. 'It's not *whether* it ends badly. It's how and why.'

At that point, Amanda arrived home. 'What's going on?' she said, looking at the three of us as she walked past into the kitchen.

A frisson of anxiety appeared on Bridget's face as we heard the fridge being opened. I knew she was wondering what Amanda would reappear with, so the glass of cold milk came as a relief. Amanda headed upstairs.

'Don't play your music too loudly, darling,' Bridget said. 'Or at least choose something gentle.'

Bridget offered Bobbie the plate of biscuits and she took three.

'Jackie told us your exciting news,' Bridget said indulgently, nodding towards Bobbie's fistful of digestives. 'I see you've started eating for two.'

'Otherwise I'd be sick on your carpet,' Bobbie said. 'I'm sorry to be greedy.'

'Take as many as you want,' Bridget said, her eyes showing alarm.

Bobbie said to me, 'Your dad's court case won't be for a month or so.'

'Am I allowed to go and see him?' I said.

'On your own?' Bridget said. 'Is that safe?' and then she took a sip of her tea as though she'd realised, as had I, that I would be a lot safer from my dad in a prison supervised by guards and protected by a million locked doors than I had been in our terraced house.

Bobbie said, 'I will try to organise a visit. I'd come with you. It might not be for a while.'

'You could write,' Bridget said. 'Ronnie Barker's always reading letters.'

'I've got his prisoner number and the address here,' Bobbie said. She gave me a piece of paper.

I bit my lip. Prisoner number?

'Remember that someone will probably check any letters before your dad sees them,' she said.

'So, don't mention the international gun-running?'

She smiled. 'No, best not.'

'Why did he discharge himself from the hospital?'

'It happens a lot,' she said. 'I'm sorry.'

The words were out before I could put the brakes on. 'Are you sorry you didn't warn me that it happens a lot?'

'Jackie,' Bridget said.

'It's okay,' said Bobbie.

Later, at teatime, Bridget brought in our plates heaped with cold ham and potato salad. I looked at mine, wondering how I would tackle it.

What would Dad be eating? And how would he cope without whisky but this time with no doctors or nurses to help him through it? I'd seen him try to do without it before and it wasn't pretty.

I'd been in my room before tea, writing a poem to distract myself from scratching at my head, when I'd heard Bridget and

Uncle Nick go into Amanda's. The low hum of conversation was, I assume, them sharing Bobbie's news.

Amanda said to me now, picking up her fork, 'Mum says your dad's gone to prison.'

'Oh, honestly!' Bridget said, filling our glasses with water. 'How insensitive.' She paused, unfortunately not for long enough to think. 'You'll never hear Jackie being that crass.'

Amanda said, 'I don't even know what crass *is*.' On the word 'is' she banged the table with her knife. 'At least use words I know!'

'I don't mind,' I said to Bridget. 'I'd be curious if it were me in Amanda's place.'

'You might be curious,' Uncle Nick said, 'but you wouldn't charge in like a bull in a china shop.'

I was surprised at him. He often tried to keep the peace. Amanda seemed to feel it too.

'All I did was tell the truth,' she said, talking with her mouth full. She knew her mum and dad hated this. 'But seeing as nothing I do is right, I might as well ask. Does this mean she's here for ever?'

Amanda's father sent her to her room. She took her meal with her.

'Don't you want your tea, dear?' Bridget asked me. 'The potato salad has home-made mayonnaise in it.'

I pleaded a tummy ache and went upstairs to lie on my bed and, although it hadn't been in my plan for the evening, to listen to Amanda singing along to Abba songs minus Abba's actual melodies.

At nine o'clock, Bridget knocked at my door. 'Are you asleep? I don't want to disturb you.'

I opened the door, wondering if I would be confronted with my ham salad a second time like a resurrection but with dried-up pork. But she had brought me a glass of lemonade and a plate of crackers and cheese.

I sat on my bed, finishing my poem, eating the crackers and fast going off Abba.

SATURDAY 22 MAY

After breakfast, Bridget was at the other end of the garden hanging up washing. It would be dry in an hour. May was heating up like a saucepan on a slow boil. There'd been no rain for weeks now apart from an occasional thunderstorm and the lawn was giving up its green as though it had lost faith.

Amanda and I were at the table with Uncle Nick, finishing toast and jam. My appetite was making its way back after a few days in which mealtimes had been difficult. It hadn't escaped Amanda that Bridget was simultaneously trying to persuade me to eat and her own daughter not to. This morning, I'd eaten cereal and two pieces of toast. If Bridget had held sway, I would have eaten a third, fourth and fifth, and perhaps a side of bacon.

Uncle Nick had found a book for me in the school library about modern prison life which I'd found reassuring, having lain awake imagining gruel and hunks of stale bread, balls and chains and cells with mould as big as mushrooms on the walls.

Uncle Nick said now, quietly, so that Bridget didn't hear, 'Remember it's your mother's birthday tomorrow, Amanda.'

He paused, as if wondering about the next step, then turned to me. 'It's your auntie Bridget's birthday tomorrow.'

I tried to look suitably surprised a second time.

'I'll take you two into town mid-morning,' he said, 'after I've walked Spotless.' From under the table, Spotless whined and Uncle Nick bent to pat his head. 'You girls can help me choose presents.'

'That'll give me time to clean my room,' I said.

Amanda shook her head from side to side. 'I can't believe you're still doing that. Leave it to Mum!'

I ignored her. 'I'd like to buy something for Bobbie, too,' I said to Uncle Nick, 'as congratulations about the baby. I was wondering when I'd do that.'

He looked pleased. He liked solving people's problems. I think it made him feel pure inside.

Amanda said to him, 'You bought Mum a new cheese grater last year and a set of wooden spoons.'

He said, protesting, 'Mum was pleased!'

'I'd bet a million pounds she was pretending,' Amanda said.

'I'd bet a million she was not,' he said.

I know who my money would have been on. I could see Bridget being pleased with a silk scarf or perfume the same as any woman, but kitchen equipment sent her pulse throbbing.

In town, Amanda steered Uncle Nick into Woolworths and up and down the aisles, leaving me to trail behind them like unkempt ivy.

She'd suggested he get a silver photo frame and a purse for her mother and we found these first. She'd taken charge of the basket.

We passed some pretty flowered mugs. 'One of these from you, Amanda?' Uncle Nick said. 'Or is it banned because it's a kitchen item?'

Amanda added it to the basket.

'I could get some notelets,' I said. 'Bridget was saying the other day she needed more.'

'Was she?' they both said.

'And I could buy Bobbie some, too.'

We found notelets and matching envelopes, both with bright pink and purple flower patterns. They were too garish for my taste but were a similar pattern to Bridget's flowered mug. 'That's serendipitous,' I said.

'How come you know the names of flowers?' Amanda said.

Both Uncle Nick and I laughed – I don't think either of us

could have not laughed – and she glowered. I waited to see if she'd ask what serendipitous really meant but in the same way people wait to find out the true meaning of life.

We added wrapping paper and birthday cards to the basket and walked to the front of the shop.

At the cash desk, I opened my purse.

'What are you doing?' Amanda said. 'Dad will pay.'

'But the notelets are from me,' I said. 'I'll use my pocket money.'

Uncle Nick said, 'I can get them. I'm buying Amanda's mug.'

'I want to pay for them,' I said. 'I'm paying for Bobbie's anyway.'

Amanda rolled her eyes so high I was surprised they came back again so quickly.

We'd reached the exit when Uncle Nick said, 'Oh, damn and blast. I meant to buy an extension lead for the shed. Can you two wait for me?'

'Can we get some Pick 'n' Mix?' Amanda said.

I could see he was distracted. 'Yes, yes. A few pence worth.' He headed back towards the recesses of the shop. I followed Amanda to the sweets.

'You choose yours,' she said. 'I want to look at the make-up. You don't want to come, do you?'

'I hardly use make-up. It's not my thing.'

'I'd noticed,' she said, as though she'd been keeping records.

She'd been wearing more make-up lately. Sparkly green eyeshadow and lip gloss. A few times, Bridget had ordered her to remove it before school. There'd been rows.

Amanda walked down the middle aisle purposefully.

I plucked a few Fruit Salads – my favourites – dropped them in a small candy-striped paper bag and wandered along to find her.

She had her back to me. I almost said, 'There you are,' but stopped because she was slipping small items from the make-up display into her skirt pocket. One, two, three.

I turned on my heel and walked back to the sweets.

'Did you choose anything?' I said when she reappeared.

'No,' she said. 'There was nothing I liked.' She selected a large-sized bag and scooped Fruit Salads, Black Jacks, Liquorice Allsorts and Jelly Snakes indiscriminately until the bag sagged.

'That'll keep you going until lunch!' I said.

I'd tried to make it a joke, but I knew I shouldn't have said it. Her face reddened.

'I wish you'd never come to us,' she said, tossing the scoop back into the sweets. 'You think you're so smart.'

'I'm sorry,' I said. 'I didn't mean anything by it.'

Uncle Nick arrived with a full basket of electrical equipment. 'I got tempted,' he said.

He looked at Amanda and then at me. He seemed to notice something was wrong, but wasn't sure what to do about it. 'Let's pay for this jolly lot, then,' he said, looking at Amanda's bulging bag.

We followed him to the cash desk for a second time and watched him pay for his purchases and for our sweets.

All the way back to the car, Amanda dawdled behind me and Uncle Nick, hugging the striped bag to herself and dipping her hands into it. She halted several times to unwrap a sweet so that we had to keep stopping to wait for her.

'Darling, Mum will be making lunch,' Uncle Nick said on the drive home when she continued unwrapping and eating. He tried again. 'You're sweet enough.' He sounded casual, but from my seat in the back, I could see how his hands gripped the steering wheel.

She must have eaten twenty or thirty sweets by the time we arrived home. Dentists all over England, I thought, could sleep at night, certain of long careers.

SUNDAY 23 MAY

Bridget unwrapped her presents while we sat in the garden in the morning sunshine after breakfast. Uncle Nick had made coffee and Amanda and I had lemonade. The day was already heating up and the lemonade was welcome.

Bridget lapped up this family occasion as cats lap cream, professing herself delighted with each gift even before she'd revealed it, taking the paper off slowly as though to prolong the moment of family solidarity. 'Notelets!' she said when she opened mine. 'They are so bright and pretty! You must have heard me mention them. How clever of you.'

'They match the mug,' I said. 'Nearly, anyway.'

'How clever of you,' she said again.

I wanted to say serendipitous so badly but settled for 'coincidental'. Amanda already looked as though she were attending a cremation, not a birthday, except for the fact that she was wearing electric blue mascara we hadn't seen on her before.

Later that morning, Bridget said she had a headache and would lie down for a while before preparing lunch.

'Oh dear,' Uncle Nick said. 'A birthday headache.'

'It's all the excitement,' she said. 'I need to close my eyes.'

'I'll be down at the shed if you need me,' he said.

Amanda said, 'I'm going to my room.'

'Don't play music, if you wouldn't mind,' Uncle Nick said. 'Give your mum's head a chance.'

Amanda did mind and we could tell as she went up to her room, taking it out on the stairs. But the house stayed quiet.

Twenty minutes passed. I was lying on the sofa, reading another Agatha Christie I'd borrowed from Uncle Nick's living room bookcase and idly watching him mend a recalcitrant bike on the lawn, wiping sweat from his forehead.

Bridget came back downstairs. She looked hassled. She'd put on a cardigan which made her look dressed for the wrong season. 'I need to go to the post box,' she said. 'I won't be a minute.' She had her hand in one of the cardigan pockets as though she had a letter there.

'But there's no post on Sundays,' I said.

'I know, but I could do with a stroll.'

'I could go for you if you like. I've got letters to post to my dad and to Nanna.'

'No,' she said, abrupt. 'But thank you.'

She was always reluctant to let me out on my own, but on this occasion it didn't seem to be the reason.

I waited for her to offer to take my letters too, but she was already at the front door. Had she even heard me?

She'd been gone five minutes when Uncle Nick came to the French windows and peered in. 'Where's Auntie Bridget?' he said.

'She popped out somewhere,' I said.

'Well, the back of my neck is getting scorched, but my hands are dirty with oil,' he said. 'Run upstairs for me and fetch the sun cream from Bridget's dressing table.'

I'd never been in Bridget and Uncle Nick's room before. I looked around. It was spacious with a double bed and floral eiderdown, lilac walls and green curtains bearing purple flowers. Bridget, but in home decor.

As well as the dressing table where I found the cream, there was a wardrobe and, in the square bay window, a writing desk. On it, I saw the packet of notelets. They'd been opened. Beside them, a fountain pen, its lid not replaced.

FRIDAY 28 MAY

It was six o'clock in the evening and, unusually, we were sitting at the garden table on the patio to eat. The week ahead was half-term. 'At last,' Uncle Nick said, flapping at his face. 'A week off from trying to interest melting students in geography.'

'Being taught by melting teachers isn't much fun either,' I said.

'No doubt,' he said.

The sun guffawed at the tiny flowered parasol over our heads and hammered us with its rays anyway. I could see Bridget was vindicated by this, but she didn't say it. There'd been an argument in the kitchen, Uncle Nick protesting that it was far too hot to keep eating indoors. 'It's ridiculous,' he'd said. 'Yes, we can close the curtain against the sun, but the house is like a furnace.'

'The garden will be no different,' she'd said.

'At least we'll have air,' he'd said.

However, what air there was felt like a warm, damp cloth lying on our skins. May's heat seemed to be gathering strength, like an athlete in training, pushing towards the peak.

I wasn't sure why Bridget didn't like eating outside. It was as though she thought it would mean sacrificing control, the walls of the house being her allies.

She had made coronation chicken and salad. The lettuce leaves surrendered all their crispness as soon as they arrived on our plates and the sauce on the chicken had a sweat of its own. It contained tiny snips of apricot and Amanda was picking out every single one, collecting a small pile at the side of her plate, meanwhile making neat work of a huge pile of buttered new potatoes.

'I hate apricots,' she said, 'and I don't really like curry.'

'It's not curry,' Uncle Nick said. 'It's curry-flavoured.'

'It's stupid to eat curry when it's so hot,' Amanda said, presumably forgetting all she'd ever learned about India.

Two, no, three, no, four hopeful wasps arrived, not exactly lightening the general mood. Bridget went indoors and came back with some jam on a plate which she put on the grass at the other end of the garden, near the shed.

I think they were Indian wasps. They chose the curried sauce over the jam, butting at it, and Spotless loped over to lick up the jam before Bridget could stop him.

We moved indoors, lock, stock and coronation chicken, and shut the French windows.

Bridget looked much happier when we were all seated inside, although her hair was damp and lifeless and her face blotchy with the heat or perhaps triumph.

'That's better,' she said, letting out a deep breath. 'Now we can talk about arrangements for tomorrow.'

'What's happening tomorrow?' Uncle Nick said.

She looked so pleased with herself I knew it would be bad news. 'We're having our photograph taken,' she said.

'What?' he said.

'We're what?' said Amanda.

'I thought it would be lovely,' she said, putting her knife and fork down, 'if, while Jackie is with us, we had a family photograph taken. I went into Cromwell Photography in Warwick during the week and booked us in – 10.30 tomorrow morning.'

The lettuce in the salad dish gave one final wilt and died, as did my hope that Bridget would ever judge a situation correctly.

Amanda said, 'You arranged it without telling us?'

'I'm telling you now,' Bridget said. 'I thought you'd all be pleased. It will be a memento. A nice thing to do at half-term.'

Amanda helped herself to the final two potatoes. 'Count me out,' she said. 'I'm not doing it.'

I glanced at Uncle Nick. He didn't look too happy either, but if he'd protested, he would have delivered Bridget into Amanda's hands like Judas kissing Jesus to let the Romans know which one he was.

'Amanda,' he said at last. 'It won't kill you.'

She stood up. 'I'm not doing it,' she said. 'It's a stupid idea.' And she ran upstairs.

Watching her go, I realised how much weight she'd put on in the eight weeks since I'd arrived. Her thin summer clothes accentuated it. A roll of fat sat on her waist and she had hips now. I hadn't known it was possible to eat yourself out of your clothes like that in one season.

Slam! went her bedroom door.

We finished our meal in silence. The heat seemed to intensify as the evening drew on, even the air itself sagging.

Bridget brought out a dish of fruit salad which had garish red cherries in it. I didn't like cherries, but it wasn't the time to announce this, so they sat in my dish like red eyeballs, daring me to leave them behind.

Bridget put her spoon down after two bites. 'I'm going up,' she said. 'I'm sure she'll calm down if I explain.'

'Leave her,' Uncle Nick said. 'You'll—'

I think he was going to say, 'make things worse'. But she was already walking away from the table.

Within thirty seconds, there was shouting. 'I've told you not to come in without knocking,' Amanda yelled. 'Get out of my room.'

There was a pause. Uncle Nick looked at me, helplessly, as though I'd have an answer. Spotless rearranged his position under the table but made no noise.

Bridget came down again, taking the stairs quickly and

standing at the bottom of them while we stared at her. She was crying in the way people cry who have no choice about it.

I thought Uncle Nick would go to comfort her, but he didn't. 'Whatever's the matter?' he said impotently.

I was about to say, 'Can I leave the table?' hoping I could escape the scene. But Bridget said, sobbing it out, 'She says she hates me.'

Spotless slunk to the kitchen for his bed and sweet dog dreams.

'She's never said that before,' Bridget said, pulling a handkerchief from her pocket and wiping her face. 'And she said it quietly. That's how I knew she meant it.'

'Of course she doesn't mean it,' Uncle Nick replied.

'She does.'

I said nothing. My sympathies were mostly with Amanda despite her dislike of me. Unexpected cheesy family photograph plus heatwave plus recent unwanted guest – it didn't add up to the ideal half-term treat.

'What's she doing?' Uncle Nick said.

'Trying make-up on in front of her mirror,' Bridget said. She blew her nose and sank into the sofa as though motherhood was too heavy a burden to carry standing up.

SATURDAY 29 MAY

Bridget was toying with one Weetabix as cats toy with half-dead field mice while I finished my toast on Saturday morning. Whatever restraining effect Weight Watchers had had on her was clearly permanent even though she was now slim. That, or not knowing what to do with her own child, had blurred her appetite.

Uncle Nick had gone out for a bike ride. 'Before it gets too hot,' he'd said, and we laughed because you could have scrambled an egg on the pavements.

'Be back by 10, remember,' Bridget had said, and that's when I realised she didn't intend to cancel the photography session. In my certainty that she would, I'd thrown on an old shirt and some shorts, ready for my usual Saturday room-cleaning session.

I didn't want to be part of the photograph, but I wasn't sure how to protest without seeming ungrateful.

It was at moments like these when I wished Dad had stayed in Hatton, kicked his drinking habit and welcomed me back home, the kettle on and plans for a Chinese takeaway in hand.

But wishing never got anyone off the bottle, I imagine.

Amanda came downstairs in her nightie. She hadn't cleaned off the mascara and eyeliner from her make-up experimentation the day before and it showed.

'What must your pillowcase look like?' Bridget said, light on tact as usual.

Amanda poured cereal in a bowl, sloshed in milk and took the bowl upstairs.

Bridget said, as though she hadn't seen the bowl of cereal, 'We'll be leaving at 10.30, darling.'

'I'm not coming, I told you,' Amanda said and shut her bedroom door on her mother's reply.

But at 10.20, Uncle Nick having spent ten minutes upstairs persuading (threatening?) her, she sulked down the stairs. She'd cleaned the old make-up off and applied new. The eyeshadow was sparkly blue and her cheeks were over-rouged. Neither were a decent match for a face like a storm.

She'd chosen a blue sleeveless summer dress, so tight that I thought she'd need to stay vertical all day to protect its seams. I sensed Bridget was keen to say something about the dress, like a horse restrained at the starting gates, but she held onto her opinions for once.

We travelled in the car. As Amanda climbed into the back next to me, I held my breath. Would the dress cope?

'Keep all the windows open,' Uncle Nick said. 'Perspiring isn't the best look for a family photograph.'

Neither are frayed family relationships, I thought. Or just not being part of the family at all.

I'd changed into a dress, too, in a similar blue to Amanda's. Bridget had presented me with it the previous weekend. 'I happened to see this in Dorothy Perkins,' she'd said. 'I knew it would suit you.'

'What's the occasion?' I'd said.

'Why does it need an occasion?' she'd said.

But now I realised that the photographic session had been booked for a while.

The photographer, younger than I'd expected, welcomed us into the shop and announced himself as Mr Cromwell Junior. He had blue eyes and curly dark hair, reminding me of David Essex, whose picture I would linger on in *Jackie* magazine when no one was looking. Mr Cromwell Junior wore a dove-grey suit which made his eyes bluer.

He called Amanda and me 'the young ladies' and led us all into a studio with cream walls and large square windows through which the yellow light of the morning poured.

'I see that the young ladies have wisely dressed in complementary colours,' he said. 'Two peas in a pod.'

'We're not sisters,' Amanda said in the same tone in which people claim they don't have VD.

'They know that, darling,' Bridget said. 'I've already explained the... the situation.'

The photographer's camera was set up ready on a tripod. He arranged us first in various standing poses. He took off his jacket after a while. His shoulders were broad.

He had to work quite hard with us. Bridget was posing melodramatically as though she were Zsa Zsa Gabor and had to be de-Gaborred. On the other hand, Amanda was as stiff as a rod and had to be asked to bend an arm slightly. Every time the photographer spoke to her, she giggled or fawned. Uncle Nick was asked to put one hand in a pocket to make him look more comfortable and less press-ganged. At one point, Mr Cromwell Junior had us in a row, but I stepped away from the others and had to be hauled back in. 'You look as though you're making a bid for escape,' he said.

Perceptive!

'One last shot,' he said. 'We'll have the young ladies sitting for this one.'

He reached behind him for a couple of low occasional chairs covered in a soft material and dragged them in front of the cream wall. 'Mum and Dad, if you could stand behind the chairs,' he said. 'You two pretty ladies, take a seat.'

Amanda giggled again, like a child.

He pointed to the chairs. I sat on the one in front of Uncle Nick. Amanda took the other chair, coquettishly and too quickly, and there was a sound like someone ripping card.

The room winced and we all froze in our poses, which

would have been a great opportunity for Mr Cromwell Junior had it not been a catastrophe.

I looked at Amanda. Her dress had split from its armpit to her waist, showing the strap of her bra and the soft-rolled flesh of her torso, down to the waistband of a pair of Minnie Mouse knickers.

'Amanda!' her mother cried, as though she'd done it deliberately.

Amanda put her hands to her face, although they'd have been of more use holding the two edges of the material together. She leaped out of the chair and fled through the door.

'Oh dear,' said Mr Cromwell Junior. 'Forgive the pun, but she was in a *tearing* hurry.'

Suddenly, the spawn of Mr Cromwell Senior didn't look like David Essex at all. His shoulders had shrunk and I despised him. 'Your pun,' I said, 'in the circumstances, is unforgivable and you will rot in hell.'

'Jackie!' That was Uncle Nick.

'Sorry,' I said, 'although I'm not.'

'I'd better go after Amanda,' Uncle Nick said.

'I do apologise,' said the photographer. 'It was just a joke.'

'Do you think you have enough shots?' Bridget said to him. 'Or do we need to come back?'

I followed Bridget to the car where we found Uncle Nick climbing into the driving seat and Amanda in the back. Her face was streaky with tears and mascara. Despite the heat, she had wrapped herself in a tartan blanket that was kept in the boot of the car. She looked so heated up that the rouge had blended in with the skin of her face.

'Don't speak to me,' she said fiercely. 'Any of you.'

'I'm sorry that happened to you,' I said, sliding in next to her.

'*Especially* you,' she said.

As we drove home, Amanda's plight filled the car and seemed to leave no room for conversation. But Bridget risked it anyway.

'One of those photographs will look lovely on the wall by the dining table,' she said.

'I don't want to be on the wall,' Amanda said.

'But you and Jackie looked so pretty,' said Uncle Nick.

'*She* did, you mean.'

'Oh, darling,' Bridget said.

'You prefer her anyway,' Amanda said. 'You make it obvious.'

There was a pause. I waited for Bridget to demur. But she left it to Uncle Nick. 'What a silly thing to say, darling,' he said at last.

When we reached the house and Uncle Nick had pulled into the driveway, Amanda was out of the car before he had put on the handbrake, still wrapped in the blanket. When Bridget unlocked the front door, Amanda pushed in ahead of her and disappeared upstairs. She didn't appear for lunch.

By late afternoon, there was still no sign of her. She had stayed in her room, playing Queen's 'Bohemian Rhapsody' on her record player over and over until both Bridget and Uncle Nick had shouted up the stairs several times. When they started threatening reduced pocket money, she turned it down.

She didn't appear for tuna salad followed by trifle at teatime and refused to come down to watch *Dad's Army*, which she usually enjoyed.

At about eight o'clock she started moving around upstairs, back and forth along the landing. 'What's she doing?' Bridget said. We all glanced at the ceiling as though it would tell us.

Then Amanda called down, 'Mum and Dad. I need to talk to you.'

Bridget, who had been fretting and had earlier rationed herself to two teaspoons of trifle, needed no encouragement for a potential emotional reconciliation. She catapulted herself out of her chair.

'Thank goodness for that,' Uncle Nick said, also standing. 'Let's clear the air.'

Spotless shifted from his position and sighed as though he too were relieved.

Bridget and Uncle Nick went upstairs, and I heard a hissed conversation, although it didn't seem to come from Amanda's room, which was directly above the living room. There would have been the creak of footfall.

Amanda's voice was raised at one point. 'See?' I heard her say. 'She's not what you think,' and that's when I realised that this was about me.

A minute later, Uncle Nick called down. 'Jackie, will you come up, please?'

They were all in my bedroom. On my bed lay a carrier bag and a jumbled pile of eyeshadow sets, eyeliner pencils, mascaras, sweets, chocolates, tiny mirrors and pretty make-up cases. Both Bridget and Uncle Nick were looking down at the pile the way you would at ancient artefacts you'd never imagined existed.

Amanda stood with her hands on her hips. 'Now see what's she got to say for herself.'

She didn't want to meet my eyes.

'Jackie,' Uncle Nick said. He put a hand on my arm and I wasn't sure whether it was to steady me or himself. 'Amanda says she found this collection of stolen things in one of your drawers.'

'What?' I stared at Amanda, but she still wouldn't meet my gaze. 'Why would she be in my room anyway?'

'I had a suspicion,' she said. 'Anyway, that was my chest of drawers before you came.'

'That's irrelevant,' Uncle Nick said. 'Jackie, did you steal these things? You can't possibly have afforded them all.'

'I didn't think you even liked make-up,' Bridget said. 'And when would you have been in Woolworths on your own?'

'Quite,' I said. I hoped the three pieces of evidence they had come up with – let's call them Exhibit A, B and C – would lead to the truth. Also, surely they would make the link between the stolen items and Amanda's increasing use of make-up lately. I waited for their brains to catch up.

But Uncle Nick said to Bridget, 'Woolworths is where we went to buy your birthday presents,' and I could see his mind thinking back to the fact that he'd left Amanda and me unsupervised when he'd bought his electrical equipment.

'I read about people like her in *Jackie* magazine,' Amanda said. 'They're called kluptomaniacs. They steal things they don't even need. Maybe she brought it all with her when she came.'

I could have said then that I'd watched her putting make-up into her skirt pockets. I was wondering whether it would make any difference at this point, since they seemed already to have added two and two to make seven, when Uncle Nick said, 'You're not the type to go shoplifting, Jackie, are you?'

I felt my face blush so hot that my hands automatically went up to cover my cheeks.

'Have you done it before?' Bridget said. 'Before you came to us?'

There appeared no way back. 'Sometimes,' I said.

'See!' Amanda said. Her eyes were excited, like sparks. I had delivered her a gift, wrapped in gold with a bow.

'This is very serious,' Bridget said.

Uncle Nick sighed. 'We might need Bobbie's advice about it all on Monday,' he said. 'I'm not sure what to do.' He bent to gather up all the items and dropped them dully back into the carrier bag.

'It's the Bank Holiday,' Bridget said. 'She won't be in the office.'

'Damn,' he said.

'Can I be alone now?' I said. I was trying not to cry. Uncle Nick's disappointment was like something pushing on my throat.

They left me, each of them in their own brand of silence, and I closed the door.

'She can't stay now, can she?' I heard Amanda say on the landing. 'Not if she's a thief.'

But neither Bridget nor Uncle Nick answered her, unless they'd whispered. I listened as they walked downstairs and, after a pause, Amanda's bedroom door crashed shut.

I slid into bed in my clothes and cried underneath the blankets, my mum's ring in my fist, wondering where I would be sent if I couldn't go back to Dad. Would it be a children's home? Would I be in a long dormitory with others or were those workhouse images I was remembering?

I was sure Amanda would be triumphant at her exposure of me as a petty criminal, but at one point, when my crying had dried up for a moment and I was scratching at a crusty lump on my hairline, I realised that she was sobbing too, on the other side of the wall.

SUNDAY 30 MAY

My eyelids were puffy and sore in the morning and my eyes felt as though they had grit in them. I'd cried until I'd slept, falling asleep in the middle of tears so that I couldn't remember doing so. In the bathroom on waking, I held a cold, wet flannel to them to see if I could reduce the puffiness; I'd seen my mother doing this to her eyes one morning after hearing her arguing with Dad the evening before, although at the time she'd told me the soreness was because of lack of sleep.

I'd also been lying on my mum's ring all night, finding it under my body when I woke, stuck into the flesh of my upper arm like a branding.

'What's that red mark?' Bridget said when I went into the kitchen for a drink, although I suspect she chose this to comment on rather than say anything about my ravaged face.

'It's nothing,' I said, and she didn't challenge it. This hurt. I never thought I'd miss her molly-coddling, but I did then.

A few minutes later, I was at the dining table, nibbling non-committedly around the edges of a piece of toast during a conversation-free breakfast with Uncle Nick and Bridget when Amanda appeared. Her eyelids were swollen too and, despite my despair, I enjoyed the fact that we were united in this way even as she was looking for drastic methods to be separate from me.

'Darling, have you been crying?' her mother asked.

'No,' Amanda said. 'Can I take my breakfast upstairs?' She still didn't want to look at me.

'I'd rather you didn't,' Bridget said.

Amanda went into the kitchen, and we all listened as she filled a bowl with Rice Krispies. We knew they were Rice Krispies because as she passed us again to go to her room, they snapped-crackled-and-popped, so at least they were having a nice time while the rest of the household sank into deep gloom.

When she'd gone, Uncle Nick opened the weekend newspaper. From behind it, he said, 'I find it hard to believe that you stole those things, Jackie.'

'I do, too,' I said and left my toast on the plate, leaving the table without permission and going up to my room, carrying my drink.

If even Uncle Nick couldn't bear to face me and ask a direct question, I couldn't bear to be there to watch him struggle.

'What are we going to do?' I heard Bridget say as I reached the top of the stairs. 'What if she steals things from us?'

'Something isn't right,' he said.

I sat in my room, writing in my poetry book, although words were teasing me, dodging out of reach. My clock said 10.15 when Amanda's door opened and I heard her walk downstairs. 'I'm going in the garden to read my magazine,' she called to her mother who, from the noises I could hear, had embarked on comfort baking, pulling out cake tins from cupboards and using her electric whisk.

Ten minutes later, Uncle Nick's heavier footsteps climbed the stairs. He paused on the landing then I heard him go into Amanda's room. Drawers were opened and, after a pause, shut. One drawer. Two. Three. Four. A long silence made me wonder if he'd come out again, but then Amanda's wardrobe door creaked open; I knew its sound from when she dressed in the mornings. The rustle of plastic suggested carrier bags. Other noises I couldn't identify followed and there was a further long hiatus.

There was a knock at my door and Uncle Nick said, 'Can I come in?'

I opened it. I didn't feel like letting him into my room. It felt like inviting more connection between us and, if I was going to be leaving, I didn't want to do that.

He was carrying a lidded Dolcis shoebox under his arm and his face was screwed up like someone crying only without the tears. 'I am incredibly sorry,' he said.

'Why?'

'I didn't want to believe you had stolen those things and I should have gone with my first instincts.'

I felt like being brutal. I wasn't sure why or to whom: him or me. 'I have done shoplifting, though. I told you. Plenty of times. Maybe hundreds.'

'For what reason?' he said.

'I wanted to.'

He glanced at my arm and the mark Mum's ring had made. I covered it up with my hand. I didn't want to seem any weaker than I was.

'No, really, why?' he said.

'I wanted to. I love stealing.'

'I don't believe you. You know you can tell me the real reason.'

And, because he was Uncle Nick, and because I realised he had guessed the truth, my resolve crumbled like rotten wood, and I said, 'We needed food.'

'That's what I thought,' he said and pulled me towards him with the arm that wasn't holding the shoebox so that my head was on his shoulder. He stroked my hair and I had to take in huge lungsful of breath so as not to fall over with the longing or let out all the tears in the world.

'I need to talk to Amanda,' he said, eventually, and pulled away. 'I'd stay up here if I were you.'

I stood on the landing as he went downstairs and into the kitchen where Bridget was. Someone pulled its door firmly shut.

When it opened again a minute later and Uncle Nick called, 'Amanda, can you come in here, please?' I pushed my bedroom door closed and lay on my bed with a pillow over my head even though the morning was so hot that it felt as though I might suffocate. I hoped I would fall asleep, unable to hear what was said downstairs, and anaesthetise myself against Amanda's hatred which would surely now double in size like bread dough when the yeast is added.

But it was impossible to sleep. The Walls were in their kitchen, confronting the truth about Amanda and, although I couldn't hear everything they said, phrases escaped, perhaps frightened themselves to stay in the room, so they slid through the cracks. 'How could you?' came from Bridget. 'Poor Jackie,' from Uncle Nick. 'I don't want her here,' from Amanda and a loud and desperate cry, 'We don't want a thief for a daughter!' from Bridget. With those snatches of the script, I could piece together the rest.

Eventually, the kitchen door was opened. I heard footsteps on the stairs then a knock at my door. Uncle Nick nudged Amanda ahead of him as they came in.

'Say it,' he said to her.

'I don't need her to,' I said.

'I do,' he said.

She was looking at the floor, her face pink and blotched. 'I'm sorry I tried to get you into trouble,' she said with no expression. Her voice was low and nasal as though she had a cold.

'Okay,' I said.

'It's not okay,' Uncle Nick said. 'She deliberately tried to cover up her own stealing and blame it on you.'

'I've said I'm sorry,' Amanda said. 'Can I go now?'

Uncle Nick looked nonplussed as though he hadn't thought about the next steps. 'I suppose so,' he said.

She turned and went into her room. We heard her bed creak as though she'd thrown herself onto it.

'Are you all right?' he said.

'Couldn't be better,' I said.

'Bridget is in pieces.'

'Oh.' I had nothing to say about that and wasn't going to be drawn. It was their business.

'Are you coming downstairs?' he said.

'Not for the moment. I think I'll write a poem.'

'You do that, pet,' he said and turned to leave, but cautiously, as though outside my room a bear was waiting for him.

TUESDAY 1 JUNE

On Tuesday of the half-term, Uncle Nick drove me to Kim's house. Her mother had arranged it with Bridget. Kim wanted to hear the poems I planned to recite at the arts evening. I wanted to hear what she'd sing.

'This never happened with Dad when I went to Kim's,' I'd said to Bridget in the kitchen a week before, embarrassed to find there'd been a telephone conversation. 'I'm fourteen. And I doubt Kim's mother is going to abduct me. They already have a full house.'

'Bobbie's rules, not mine,' she'd said, filling the kettle. But then she'd turned to me and said, 'I'm sorry. It must feel very limiting,' and this flash of sensitivity cheered me no end.

Going to Kim's was awkward because Amanda had of course been grounded again. She'd resigned herself to this as far as I could gather. I'd expected more rows and arguments between the three of them after Sunday morning's revelations, but instead the house had been strangely muted for the rest of that day and all day Monday, the punishments and condemnations meted out in calm voices and accepted silently. Amanda had come down and joined me and her parents as usual for meals because she was ordered to and ate heaps of mashed potato or numerous slices of bread and butter, her appetite as robust as ever, while her parents picked at their food, stricken and helpless like wounded animals.

Amanda didn't speak to me, though, even while passing the salt. I'd have preferred some healthy antagonism. You'd rather hear a truck approaching before it mows you down so that you have a chance to dodge.

'We haven't mentioned outright to Amanda that you're seeing a friend today,' Uncle Nick said as we drove to Kim's house near the racecourse. I was in the front seat next to him and sucking a lemon sherbet. 'It's probably best not to say anything when you get back,' he added.

I found myself picking at the back of my head and forced my hand back to my lap. It made me angry that Amanda's emotions were being tiptoed around and I had to collude. 'I won't say anything,' I said, 'although if she asks me, I don't want to lie.'

'No,' he said, which was a poor response.

I was head-picking again as we drew up outside Kim's.

'You haven't got head lice, have you?' he said. 'That's all we need.'

Kim opened her front door before I could knock. She told me her dad was at his mechanics job in Coventry and her two older brothers were out playing tennis. She was grateful because we'd be left in peace for some of the day. I was grateful because both her brothers were gorgeous and when they were in the room, I felt as though they used up all the air. When I saw them in the corridors at school, they always said hello and I'd feel my chest go hot. They looked like twins although they were a year apart, Kevin in the fifth year and David in sixth form. They had Kim's straw-coloured hair, although theirs was curly, and they played in a school band called The Stagers. 'You must have a very noisy home,' I'd said to Kim at school, 'with you singing and them strumming.'

'I suppose so.'

'But at least it's happy noise,' I said.

'Mostly it is,' she said and I realised I'd wanted her to say that they did have rows and throw things.

'Hello, love,' Kim's mum said when I followed Kim into their tiny living room.

The house was a terrace with this family room downstairs and a tiny square kitchen. There was no space for a dining table. Upstairs were three bedrooms. Kim had told me that her parents had squeezed their double bed into the smallest bedroom to give the siblings more space.

Tucked into the corner of the living room, too, were two guitars and an electronic keyboard.

'Hello, Mrs Price,' I said.

'Every single time!' she said. 'Call me Christine. How are things going at your foster home?'

'It's fun,' I said.

We went upstairs to Kim's bedroom, which contained a single bed, a wardrobe, a chest of drawers and a desk and stool. Her walls were covered in posters, mostly of female singers from previous decades; Ella Fitzgerald was one, but I didn't know the others.

'Did you read that article in *Jackie* about being an honest friend?' she said. She was spraying cheap Avon perfume on the inside of her wrists.

'Yes.'

'Do you promise to tell me everything if I tell you everything?'

I thought about this. There were some things I wouldn't want to tell her, things that belonged to others, such as about the Walls' problems with Amanda. 'Within reason,' I said.

'Okay. You put some of this perfume on too and we'll rub our wrists together. We'll do that as a pact instead of swapping blood. I faint if I see blood.'

I did as she asked.

'Right,' she said. 'Now admit it. Tell the truth. You fancy both my brothers.'

'You tricked me!' I was hurt. I thought the perfume

covenant had meant something bigger, but I didn't say so. I'd had to learn how to handle relationship disappointments when living with my dad and could probably run my own training courses. The Walls were also providing me with further experience.

'You promised,' she said. 'Can't back out now.'

We wrestled on her bed like a couple of toddlers, screeching and slapping each other.

Kim made cheese and tomato sandwiches for lunch. I stood in the kitchen, watching. 'We'll never eat all those!' I said, seeing her slap butter expertly on slice after slice as though she worked in catering.

'Kevin and Dave will be back soon,' she said. 'They eat for England.'

We ate from trays in the living room with Christine. Even though we opened the front door and the back door to get some breeze through, the room felt claustrophobic. I wondered about Dad and assumed his cell was cool but then realised that, despite the book that Uncle Nick had borrowed for me, I still hadn't dispelled the picture in my head of medieval dungeons with thick walls, deep in the bowels of a castle.

'We've got Swiss roll,' Kim said. 'Mum made it when she heard you were coming.'

'Special occasion,' her mum said. 'We haven't seen you for so long.'

It felt like a blessing you'd get in church, but with cake instead of a priest's hand.

At 1.30, the brothers arrived, their faces blushed by the sun and their hair damp and springy. They fell on the sandwiches like starvelings and drank gallons of cold milk, then they picked up their guitars.

'Oh, it's *Top of the Pops* time, is it?' their mother said. 'No offence, but I'll be in the garden.' She took a magazine with her.

I wouldn't have defined myself as shy, but in the presence of the two boys, especially Kevin, whose eyes were as blue as seas, I felt clumsy, as though I'd have to be careful when I stood up.

'Shall we run through your possibles for the arts evening then, sis?' David said.

'Again?!' I heard Christine call from the garden, but affectionately.

Kim's first song was 'How Can I Be Sure?' which David Cassidy had made a hit, and the other, John Lennon's 'Imagine'. Kevin accompanied her on guitar and sounded the more rehearsed. David played along in parts or drummed his thighs with his hands.

Her brothers were both tall with long legs and we were sitting in close proximity in their small room. It seemed a big leap from acknowledging them across the other side of a school corridor.

Kim's voice was low for a girl's, a bit like Karen Carpenter's. I loved listening to her and it did distract me from Kevin's fingers on the guitar strings. Although my mum had loved music and sung along to the radio, the idea of a houseful of instruments was so far from my experience growing up that it seemed like a fantasy world.

When she'd sung both songs, Kevin said, 'Definitely do "How Can I Be Sure?".'

'Yep,' David said. 'It suits your voice.'

This was brother understatement. She sounded like a pop star to me.

She turned to me. 'Will you read us your poems?'

To anyone else, yes, I would have done, gladly. In front of Kevin and David, in their living room?

I widened my eyes at her in appeal. But it was too late. 'Go on,' Kevin said. 'She's already told us you're the next Wordsmith.'

'Wordsworth, you twit,' David said. He was studying English.

'She's exaggerating,' I said. 'Anyway, I think I've forgotten to bring them.'

'I can see paper sticking out of your back pocket,' Kim said.

So much for Avon perfume solidarity.

'Don't be shy,' Kevin said. 'It's only us.'

Exactly!

I knew I wasn't going to get away with it. 'I'll turn round and read to the fireplace,' I said, 'so I can't see you.'

'Do it,' Kevin said. 'The fireplace loves poetry.'

I manoeuvred my chair round and tried to pretend that the fireplace was Mrs Collingworth.

First, I read the 'Adlestrop'-inspired poem about the picnic. I messed up a couple of the words to begin with, but gradually the fireplace turned more into my teacher and the poem flowed better.

'Wow,' Kevin said when I'd finished. The three of them clapped.

'That's sad and sweet at the same time,' David said. 'What's the other one?'

'It's a ballad,' I said, turning my head to look at him.

'With a tune?' David said.

'No. Just the poem.'

I'd been working on the ballad since Molly had read hers in Poetry Club.

'What is a ballad anyway?' Kim said.

'They're usually tragic,' David said. 'Expect death.'

'It's quite long,' I said. 'You have to wait a while until someone dies.'

'We're not going anywhere,' he said.

I turned back to the fireplace and read to it:

A lady loved her soldier man
in uniform so proud.
New-married, he was sent to war
to guns so fierce and loud.

She waved him gone and hid her tears,
he marched so fine and tall.
She worshipped him, believing
that he had no flaws at all.

But young he was, his head too strong.
He thought it hard indeed,
submitting to his officers
and following their lead.

One morning, as the battle raged
the officers said 'Hold'
but he let rule his foolish head,
believing he was bold.

He lured a friend along with him
and promised glory bright
then watched the friend's blood pour away
along with all his fight.

In cold disgrace, when war was done,
he travelled home in shame,
a shadow of the man he was
and no one else to blame.

Now, cruelty was in his bones
and rage replaced his pride.
He looked for tender scapegoats
and found one in his bride.

With child, she feared for its dear life
and trembled with alarm
for he, consumed by anger,
was blind to what he'd harm.

But she was not the only one
whose soul was gripped by fear
for in the mirror he saw doom.
The time to choose was here.

He dressed up in his uniform,
so fine, but so alone.
He went down to the riverside,
filled pockets up with stone.

He slid into the water
at last relaxed, at peace,
for she and child were safe from he
who'd turned from man to beast.

'Yep, it's a ballad,' David said. They clapped again.

I turned round. 'Do you really think it's okay?'

'It's so sad, and so brilliant,' Kim said.

'It needs a tune,' Kevin said. 'Something in the minor key. Then you could sing it for the arts evening.'

'Me?' I said. 'My singing would empty the school hall.' I looked to Kim for confirmation, but she'd got there before me.

'She's telling the truth,' she said. 'Her singing is seriously bad.'

'Kim could sing it, then,' he said. 'Leave me your poem and I'll play around with it. I've got an idea in my head.'

I told them that what I'd read from was the one copy I had.

Kim stood up. 'I'll get paper,' she said. 'We can write it out.'

'Leave space for me to add chords,' David said.

Christine came back into the room. 'Is the show over?'

'Kevin's writing a tune for Jackie's ballot,' Kim said and as we all laughed together, I felt my stomach clench with sibling envy.

WEDNESDAY 2 JUNE

The next day, in the late afternoon, Amanda, Bridget and I had moved our deckchairs to the other end of the garden, in front of Uncle Nick's shed, taking refuge in the strip of shade available there. Uncle Nick had suggested this several times before, but it offended Bridget's sense of order not to use the patio even though, because we got grilled like bacon there, we often ended up indoors instead. Today, she had surrendered.

Uncle Nick was mending a bike on the lawn in front of us. Spotless was with us too, his head on his paws. Amanda and I both held books as though reading them, but I think we were dissembling. The cruelty of the heat had usurped my ability to focus on *Anne of Green Gables*. I'd reach the end of a paragraph and have to backtrack.

Amanda's usurper could have been the heat, too, but could also have been her resentment. It travelled around the house with her like a companion. For one thing, she'd thought she might persuade her parents to end her grounding early by behaving herself, but their outrage had given strength to their resolve for once and she'd been told that if she raised the issue again, they would extend the grounding, not cut it short. For another, she clearly found my continuing presence in the house hard to take and wasn't trying to hide it. She still hadn't spoken to me.

There'd been another hissed argument between Amanda and her mother that morning on the landing which I'd heard from the bathroom. I'd finished cleaning my teeth but dared not walk out, straight into the ring.

Bridget: How long have you been doing it?

Amanda: What's 'it'?

Bridget: The... stealing.

Amanda: I don't remember.

Bridget: *That* long?

Amanda: Six months? A year? Does it matter? Why does it matter? I don't see you interrogating Jackie.

Bridget: Why would I?

A long silence.

Amanda: See?

Bridget: I don't know why you've taken against her. Anyway, the stealing.

Amanda: Look, I've told you I won't do it again. Can't we stop talking about it?

Bridget: But I want to know why.

Amanda: But I don't *know* why.

Silence.

Bridget: I hope you're not still smoking.

Silence.

Amanda: Anything else you'd like to point out while you're here?

(I thought, no, Bridget, don't say it.)

Bridget: Well, have you taken my new packet of trifle sponges into your room?

Amanda shut her bedroom door so that people a mile away would know she'd done it, and I heard Bridget go downstairs, so I went back to my room.

I could hear the ripping open and rustling of a packet through the wall while I was sitting on my bed, writing a poem for the next week's Poetry Club.

'There's no *breeze*,' said Bridget now, in true revelatory style. There hadn't been breezes for weeks. Even the word sounded odd, as if out of common usage.

Uncle Nick heaved himself up from his kneeling position. 'Look,' he said, 'why don't we all go to the seaside tomorrow?'

'The seaside?' Bridget said, as though he'd suggested a two-week Himalayan climbing tour, leaving in half an hour.

'In this heat?' Amanda said.

'Precisely because of this heat!' Uncle Nick said. 'There'll be sea breezes. It's only a couple of hours to Weston-super-Mare.'

'We'd have to leave very early,' Bridget said.

'Come on,' Uncle Nick said. 'We're all tossing and turning anyway and awake with the larks.'

'Can we have fish and chips on the beach? And ice creams?' Amanda said.

I noted the plural.

'Of course,' he said. 'That's all part of the fun.'

'But I'm grounded,' Amanda said.

'You can come out if we're supervising you,' Uncle Nick said, as though she were a convict on day release.

'What about Spotless?' I said.

'Spotless loves the seaside!' he said.

There was something desperate in his tone, even while sounding so positive, the same tone you hear from people saying, 'You'll be fine' while trying to throw a lifebelt to someone fast going under.

THURSDAY 3 JUNE

I set my alarm for 6, as instructed, but I hadn't slept well, so when it rang, I was ready for it. I checked my pillow for blood. There were a few streaks, so I flipped it over.

I could hear Bridget knocking on Amanda's door and Amanda's groans of protest but, as Odysseus was lured to the islands by the Sirens, the thought of fish and chips and plural ice cream enticed Amanda to shift herself.

She arrived downstairs dressed in tee shirt and shorts, as was I.

Bridget had already been up for an hour making sausage sandwiches and filling tall Tupperware beakers with iced orange squash. She'd also packed cakes, biscuits and Salt 'n' Shake crisps into a bag 'for the journey back'; Uncle Nick pointed out that the journey back was from Weston-super-Mare to Leamington, not along the Wall of China.

Despite her initial scepticism about the trip the day before, Bridget seemed galvanised by it now, perhaps by its potential for congenial family times in the form of donkey rides and the sound of lapping waves that might block out her unhappiness.

We ate the sandwiches, still warm in kitchen foil, half an hour into the journey. Spotless was on his haunches on the back seat between me and Amanda. She fed him scraps of sausage and put her finger to her lips so that I didn't dob her in. Spotless didn't dob her in either, his eyes wide with illegal pig.

We wound all the windows down and urged Uncle Nick to drive faster so that the air would be cool, but his driving style was sensible, so all we got was warm humidity puffing at our faces. Spotless leaned across me to get his head out of the window and eventually ended up on my lap to do so, his tongue lolling. Children in passing cars pointed and laughed. A lapful of warm dog didn't help with staying cool, but that cause was lost anyway, so I put up with him.

It would have been a half-decent journey had Amanda not asked Bridget, thirty minutes from Weston, if she could open the cakes. They were in a bag at my feet.

'They're for the journey back,' Bridget said. She said 'back' as though that were the end of it.

'There are enough here for ten journeys,' Amanda said, exploring the bag.

'We're nearly there,' Bridget said. 'It won't be long before fish and chips.' On the word 'chips' her voice rose with false cheeriness, but it could equally have been anguish.

Amanda pulled out a malt loaf. 'Did you bring a knife?' she said.

'Don't open that,' Bridget said. She kept having to twist around to see what Amanda was doing. 'Open a box of small cakes, if you must.'

But Amanda had already ripped open the malt loaf and was breaking lumps off with her fingers and putting them in her mouth, like someone deprived of, or at least lacking in, something that only malt loaf would provide.

I looked away. I felt embarrassed for her but also sorry that she felt such need. I'd never thought to stanch any need of my own with cake, but I wondered whether perhaps I might have been using poetry in the same way.

Bridget flipped her sun visor down, presumably remembering the mirror by which she could observe Amanda.

I expected Amanda to demand she flip it back up, but she didn't. She ate faster.

It was the first time I'd seen anyone overeat as a revenge tactic.

Spotless climbed off my lap and sat between us again, looking at the malt loaf with longing. This time, he was unlucky.

Amanda ate half the loaf then clumsily wrapped it up again and dropped it back into the bag.

'I'd packed some butter to go with that,' Bridget said to Uncle Nick, 'with ice blocks and everything.'

No one said much else until we reached the car park. When we'd first spotted the sea, Uncle Nick had said, 'Look, there it is!' but the reaction was muted.

It was only nine o'clock. While Uncle Nick pushed coins into a parking meter, Amanda headed towards a toilet block. We put Spotless on a lead and gave him a bowl of water which he lapped up messily, splashing our feet. We laughed.

Without Amanda there, I felt more free to laugh along with Bridget and Uncle Nick.

We waited by the car for her to emerge. The heat drummed onto the backs of our necks until Bridget revealed that there were straw hats in the boot for her and Uncle Nick and floppy pink cotton hats for me and Amanda. I donned mine with reluctance, but she'd been kind to think of us, so I said nothing.

'Here she is,' Bridget said. She called as Amanda approached, 'Tummy trouble, darling?'

Amanda ignored her, understandably loath to discuss her bowel movements.

Bridget held out the cotton hat.

'No, thanks,' Amanda said, and Bridget didn't force the issue.

It occurred to me that dealing with Amanda was like dealing with the heat. You saved your energy for the essentials.

Bridget had brought buckets and spades. 'Mum!' Amanda said. 'We're not kids.'

Despite her protest, ten minutes later we were on the beach, Bridget and Uncle Nick in hired deckchairs, and Amanda and I filling buckets with damp sand ready to make castles. Tap tap tap. Dig dig dig. The sea air seemed to be tempering her animosity and at one point she said to me, 'Shall we make moats?' as though she'd forgotten that she hated me.

Bridget wandered towards the sea's edge to paddle, holding onto her straw hat with one hand. Uncle Nick sighed, patted Spotless's head and flapped open his newspaper with a flourish as though his idea for a trip to the seaside had turned out to be the agreeable family occasion he'd predicted.

And, when Amanda upended her sandcastle and yelped with success at its clean lines, it was almost as though he'd been right.

The queue at the fish and chip shop stretched down the street. The rest of the world had decided on Weston-super-Mare too and, like us, had judged piping hot greasy food suitable for consumption in heatwave conditions.

'We could try another shop,' Bridget said, peering down the road as though that would help one miraculously appear. She put the bag with our towels and buckets and spades down and wiped her forehead with her handkerchief.

'We may as well stick it out now,' Uncle Nick said. 'You three girls find somewhere to sit. I'll get the lunch.'

I knew he was happy when I heard him call Bridget a girl.

'No,' she said. 'I'll wait with you, Nick. You might forget what we want to order. Here, take the dog, you two. I'll keep the bag.'

Amanda looked at me as though wondering whether to protest at being paired up with me like this, but then she shrugged.

I took hold of Spotless's lead. His eyes said, 'Don't take me too far from the chips.'

Bridget waved me and Amanda away, saying, 'Settle somewhere near where we were sitting.' She pointed to my pink hat. 'We'll find you.'

The beach was tight with tourists and sun-worshippers, but we carved ourselves out some territory and sat down. Spotless sat with his head stretched towards the sea as though he fancied a cruise.

'Isn't your head burning?' I said to Amanda. 'Without a hat?'

'Yes,' she said.

She'd also refused Bridget's instruction to smear on sun cream.

She reached into the pocket of her shorts and took out a packet of cigarettes and a box of matches.

'You're not serious,' I said. 'They'll be back any minute.'

'They won't,' she said. 'That queue will take hours.'

She puffed on her cigarette, trying to blow smoke rings and failing. I kept checking over my shoulder for sight of her parents, wondering how I'd fallen into this informal role of minder and lookout combined.

Two boys approached who looked seventeen or eighteen. One was blond, one dark-haired and taller. They both wore shorts and punk tee shirts, their legs tanned and sandy. One carried a beach ball under his arm. 'Do you girls want to play?'

'No,' I said.

'I do,' said Amanda, stubbing out her cigarette in the sand and jumping up. She left the stub.

'I don't think you should,' I said.

'Wimp,' she called over her shoulder, following the boys.

I watched as the three of them wove their way through all the sunbathing bodies, children's inflatables and deckchairs. Soon, I realised they weren't stopping. I'd thought they would find a space to play nearby.

'Amanda!' I called. But she couldn't hear me above the sounds of the beach – the screaming of seagulls, the shouts of children. Either that, or she didn't want to.

I looked behind me, hoping, for the first time ever, to see Bridget and Uncle Nick speeding towards me.

Nothing.

Spotless and I went in hot – and I mean hot – pursuit.

I caught up with Amanda and the two boys only by running and yelling her name like a banshee. They all stopped together under the pier and I joined them.

'Leave me alone!' she said.

'Are you the big sister?' the dark-haired boy asked me. This must have stung Amanda. Her birthday had been in September, so she was the oldest in the school year.

He put out a hand to touch my shoulder and I shook him off.

'She's fourteen,' Amanda said.

'So are you, you bloody idiot!' I said. 'Where are you *going*?'

'It's none of your business,' she said.

The blond boy took a packet of cigarettes out of his pocket and a lighter. 'If we're going to be here a while—'

Amanda took one and he lit it for her, their faces too close together.

'Hello, dog,' the other said and went to stroke Spotless. I tugged the dog away.

'Touchy!' he said.

I wanted to say to Amanda, 'Your mum and dad will be worried,' but that would have been like tossing paraffin on a well-established blaze.

We stood for a while, Amanda and the boys sucking on their cigarettes. Then the dark-haired boy nodded towards me and said to his friend, 'Actually, shall we dump the blonde one and take this one? She's prettier.'

I looked at Amanda. Her cheeks were angry-red. I said to her, 'Are you really hanging around with these low-lifes?' but, rather than accept the support, she raised her hand and slapped me full across the face.

'I don't need you to protect me,' she said. 'Get lost!'

'Whoa!' the blond boy said.

I put my hand to my face. 'I can't believe you did that.'

'Well, I did!' she said, but her eyes told me that she couldn't believe it either. I saw fear.

I heard someone call and looked behind me. There, haring along the beach in her sandals, was Bridget. She was clutching a packet of fish and chips to her chest, with Uncle Nick bringing up the rear carrying the bag, its buckets and spades clanking against his leg. I wasn't sure whether they'd seen the slap.

'Amanda,' Bridget shrilled. 'Amanda, stop!'

Stop what? There was a list of options or maybe she meant just being Amanda.

'Is that your mum?' the taller boy asked. 'I think she's lost something. You!'

His friend laughed.

'You two are scum,' I said.

Amanda dropped her cigarette, far too late for conceal-ment, as Bridget was nearly upon us. But it was then that Bridget tripped.

The boys laughed more and began to wander away. Cowards, I thought. Amanda turned and faced the other direction as though she couldn't bear to watch her mother.

I ran to help.

At three o'clock, we were back at the car. No one had said, 'Let's go home now,' but we hadn't needed to. As we climbed in, I wondered how we would survive the two hours together. Perhaps prisoners feel the same. They walk into a cell on their first day to find three others already there in a space ten feet by six, sharing a toilet and quick tempers.

I thought of Dad.

Bridget spoke to Uncle Nick in half-sentences occasionally as though articulacy were a skill she *used* to have before she'd chased her errant daughter along a crowded beach, tripped over in the sand, and endured the laughter of day trippers as chips scattered and seagulls dived in for the feast.

'I don't – I honestly can't – I mean, how could – I can't believe—'

'Shut up, Mum,' Amanda said at one point, her voice like bile.

Spotless sat on my lap again and put his head out of the window. He made me insufferably hot, but it was a comfort. I hugged him.

Halfway home, we were stuck behind a lorry on an A road. Amanda asked where the bag was with the cakes and biscuits.

'In the boot,' Uncle Nick said.

'What?' she said. 'Why?'

'We can't get them now,' he said.

'Yes, we can,' she said. 'I'm hungry.'

'And whose fault is that?' he said.

'Not mine,' she said. 'It wasn't me who dropped the lunch.'

I saw Bridget's shoulders go up and down as she breathed in deeply and then exhaled.

'I'm not stopping the car, and that's final,' said Uncle Nick, and Amanda folded her arms and sulked, but kept quiet.

In fact, she had eaten a fair portion of the fish and chips that hadn't cascaded to the sand. It was the rest of us who should have been hungry. We'd picked at what was left. But the heat and the spoiled day had blunted my appetite. And it was probably the same for Bridget and Uncle Nick. They'd tried to rescue the outing, taking us to a café for ice creams and giving us coins for the slot machines in the amusement arcade. Amanda deserved punishment, but we were at the seaside. What were they to do?

So they'd pretended really hard for a couple of hours that Amanda hadn't humiliated them, defied them, mocked them. So many betrayals that I could understand their need to pretend.

At one point Bridget had said to me, 'It looks as though you've burned the side of your face.'

I saw Amanda's eyes widen in alarm.

'I think I took my hat off for a while when you were at the fish and chip shop,' I said.

'I've got some after-sun cream in my bag,' Bridget said.

'It'll calm down,' I said. 'It's nothing.'

When Uncle Nick had won a huge cuddly gorilla in the arcade, its absurdity seemed one extra reminder of the failure of the outing. It wouldn't fit in the bag and Amanda refused to carry it, so I'd ended up with it swinging from my hand.

The last hour of the journey was slow, not because of busy traffic but because the minutes ticked by inexorably towards the scene we all anticipated once we were home.

Amanda fell asleep, her head nodding forwards. She looked younger.

As we approached Warwick, Bridget said, 'The photographs! I was meant to pick them up today.'

'They'll be closed,' Uncle Nick said. 'Fetch them tomorrow.'

'We might catch them,' she said. 'While we're nearby, Nick.'

He sighed, but found a place to park opposite Cromwell's Photography. Bridget scurried out of the car and into the door. A minute later, she returned with a flat white box, hugging it to her chest as though it alone could save the day, which was giving a lot of responsibility to a set of photographs.

But, instead of a scene, Amanda, who had woken as we'd pulled away from Cromwell's, demanded to be let into the house straight away while I helped Uncle Nick and Bridget unpack the car, including the new family member, the gorilla.

'You're such a good girl,' Bridget said as we walked towards the house, in a tone I can only describe as nostalgic.

Amanda had gone upstairs.

Uncle Nick went round hurling open the French doors and the windows, welcoming all the humidity in the world into the house. I thought of Dad and all the days he'd spent in our front room with the curtains shut. The Spanish would think him the more sensible. It was a rare moment thinking 'Dad did that better' and it caught in my throat.

Bridget put the box of photographs on the dining table and went into the kitchen to sort out the bag.

Spotless followed her in and flopped into his bed.

Upstairs, Amanda began playing an Osmonds album at top volume, starting with 'Crazy Horses'. The waaaah waaaah of the guitar somehow made the house seem even hotter.

I sat on the sofa, lethargy descending, with the gorilla taking up the seat next to me.

Bridget called through, 'We did *try* with our day out.' She made a little sound as though she'd tried to laugh but the laugh hadn't cooperated.

I said nothing. I looked out at the garden as Uncle Nick walked down the path and opened his shed.

Bridget came back into the living room. 'I'm popping upstairs to freshen up,' she said.

'Okay,' I said.

I heard her running a bath.

Amanda came down the stairs, said, 'I want to see these first,' and picked up the flat box of photographs. She tucked it under her arm. Then she eyed the gorilla.

'Who's keeping that?' she said.

'Technically, your dad,' I said. 'He won it.'

'He won't want it.' She reached over and grabbed the cuddly toy. 'I'll have it.'

'Fine. It's always nice to have a reminder of a happy day out,' I said.

She paused, then in a low voice, said, 'I suppose you've told them I hit you.'

'I haven't, actually.'

'You're going to.'

'Probably not.'

'Why not?'

'What will it achieve?' I said.

She looked at the gorilla. 'You take it,' she said, dropping it on the sofa. 'It's just a stupid toy.'

She returned to her room. But at least we were speaking.

I was in the kitchen half an hour later fetching a drink when Bridget reappeared wearing a different dress, her hair wet. 'That's *much* better,' she said, as though she'd sluiced away all the family unrest. She glanced at the table. 'Did you pick up the box of photographs, Jackie?'

'Not me,' I said.

'Did Uncle Nick come in and take them? I bet he's got them in the shed.'

'I don't think so.'

She looked at the now-sleeping Spotless as though she really didn't want to acknowledge the remaining possibility and then she turned to go upstairs.

Ten seconds. Then I heard her scream, 'AMANDA!'

Uncle Nick came out of his shed and jogged towards the house, kicking off his sandals at the door. 'What's happening?' he said as he passed me.

The elderly neighbour from next door, whose name was Ken, peered over the fence and shouted, 'Is everything all right?'

I went to the French windows and leaned out to say, 'Everything's fine.'

He waved and retreated but looked unconvinced, as well he might.

There was a long silence from upstairs, as there is when people first find the body in the bath.

Then I heard the second slap of the day. I flinched.

A few seconds passed, then Amanda's bedroom door banged shut.

Above my head, I heard Bridget and Uncle Nick's bedroom

floor creak, the sound of Bridget wailing and Uncle Nick's low-toned attempts at consolation.

I went into the kitchen. 'Come on, Spotless,' I said, shaking him awake. 'Come in the garden with me. We'll sit in the shade.'

He followed me, reluctant but faithful, and lay next to my chair while I tried to ignore the whispering in next door's garden and the sound of Bridget's despair from the bedroom. Their window was open. 'Anyone would have lost their temper,' I heard Uncle Nick say at one point. 'Don't blame yourself.'

The sun stayed high in the sky, relentless and unmoved.

That evening, I didn't see Bridget or Amanda again. I spent an hour in my room writing poems. I came down at seven o'clock, hungry and wondering what was happening about tea. Uncle Nick and I sat in the living room watching *The Osmonds Show* on TV and fanning ourselves with Amanda's magazines. We ate cheese and biscuits on trays on our laps. The gorilla sat next to me.

'Did you enjoy the seaside, Jackie?' Uncle Nick said to me at one point, but I had no coherent answer for him.

I took our plates into the kitchen and opened the waste bin to scrape off crumbs. Inside it were shards of the photographs. I lifted some out to look more closely. Amanda's face. Bridget's left side. Uncle Nick's head and shoulders. Me and Uncle Nick. Me and Amanda, but without our foreheads. Bridget's smile.

Later, I realised I had a paper cut.

At bedtime, I took the gorilla up to my room and sat him on the floor in the corner. I felt guilty that I'd manipulated Amanda into rejecting him. But not for long. First, she owed me. Secondly, I knew she had plenty of cuddly toys because Bridget had washed them all in a batch not long ago and they'd hung on the line by their ears. Teddies. Rabbits. A huge fluffy lion.

I named my gorilla Weston.

TUESDAY 8 JUNE

When I returned from school the following Tuesday, there was no one downstairs. I didn't expect Amanda to be home anyway. She often stayed out after school with friends in the park, at the shops or in someone's home and, as she'd been grounded so much recently, I wasn't surprised to find she was making up for lost time. Rarely, I'd find she'd brought a friend back with her, but they'd be cloistered in her room and no one ever stayed for tea. Had this been the case before I arrived, or only since, I wondered.

Also, if Amanda was home before me, I'd usually hear her music before I put my key in the lock. There'd been an eerie silence, though, since Weston-super-Mare; her parents had confiscated her record player for a week as punishment for the dual crimes of ruining the day out and slicing up the family photographs. She'd raged, but her anger couldn't compete with theirs.

Now, Bridget wasn't in the kitchen where she should have been and I could see Uncle Nick in the shed where he shouldn't have been as he usually left school after 5, at least.

I felt as people do who walk into a room and know something's different. Has someone moved a piece of furniture? Is there a new painting on the wall?

I walked upstairs and changed out of my uniform. I sat on my bed to peel off my socks, said hello to Weston, and that's when I heard someone crying.

I peered out of my bedroom door. It wasn't coming from Amanda's room. It was from Bridget's.

Amanda's door opened before I could scuttle back off the landing and she emerged. She was wearing a nightie. Her face looked blotchy, as though she'd also been crying. She said, 'Who are *you* spying on?'

'Spying?' I said. 'Don't be melodramatic.'

The sobbing from Bridget's bedroom stopped.

'You're skulking about,' Amanda said.

'It's not skulking. I live here.'

'You don't need to tell *me* that,' she said.

'Are you poorly?' I said.

'Why should I tell you?'

'Don't, then,' I said and went into my room, shutting the door.

I waited to see if she'd go back into her room or downstairs. She did neither. She knocked on my door.

I opened it.

'Can I come in?' she said.

I nodded.

She stood at my window, looking out at the street, which reminded me of the way she'd observed my arrival on my first day.

When she spoke, I realised why she didn't want to face me.

'I was sent home from school this morning,' she said. 'Dad had to leave work and fetch me. Mum refused to.'

I didn't ask why she'd been sent home. She wouldn't have come in if she hadn't intended to tell me.

She said, 'I was… I've been selling the make-up to the girls at school. Someone dobbed me in.'

'So—'

'I've been expelled.'

'For ever?'

'I don't know.'

In the kitchen, the telephone rang. 'That might be my friend,' she said and ran to answer it.

She returned almost straight away. I pointed her to my

bedroom chair. She sat down, pulling her nightie over her plump knees.

'Not your friend, then,' I said.

'Some man whose voice I didn't recognise,' she said. 'He asked for Mum, but I said she wasn't available.'

The sobbing had begun again from Bridget's room, so Amanda had a point.

We sat in silence for a few seconds.

'You know when we went to Woolworths to get your mum's presents?' I said.

'What about it?'

'I saw you putting things into your skirt pocket.'

Her eyebrows rose and a rich red blush took over her complexion. 'You knew?'

'Yes.'

'You didn't tell Mum and Dad?'

'It wasn't my place,' I said.

'You could have.'

'I could.'

'So…' I saw her mind fitting this information into recent events and re-evaluating them. I let her do it for herself.

Her parents had forced her to throw everything she'd stolen in the dustbin. At first, Uncle Nick had threatened to make her return it all to Woolworths and confess but, as Bridget pointed out, that could have led to complications. To quote her directly, 'She could end up in borstal and how would we hold our heads up in Hollybush Close?' It had given them a moral dilemma, though, which Uncle Nick resolved by a trip to Woolworths to spend the approximate equivalent cost of the stolen goods on some tools for him and kitchen gadgets for Bridget which neither of them needed. Bridget had waited for him to return from this trip of atonement, standing at the window looking out for his car and sighing as he drew up as though she'd let go of something too.

'I hoped maybe they'd send you away,' Amanda said now, 'if they thought you were a thief.'

'So I gathered. That worked well, then.'

She fiddled with the edges of her nightie. 'I'm sorry I slapped you.'

'So am I. It hurt.'

'They do prefer you, though. Everyone prefers you.'

'I don't think so.'

Neither of us said anything for a while. Then she sighed. 'I'm hungry. Are you hungry?'

'I could eat.'

She went downstairs and came back with a packet of pink wafers. We ate them together while listening to Amanda's mother, who ran a bath then sat in it, crying.

'Someone phoned,' Amanda said at teatime, puncturing a long silence only interrupted otherwise by the clinking of our cutlery as we ate chicken with coleslaw.

Bridget's eyes were puffy, as were Amanda's still, and Uncle Nick's face was glum. I was sure some deathbed gatherings were cheerier.

Uncle Nick and Bridget said, 'Who was it?' together.

'He didn't say his name. He asked for Mum. He sounded posh.'

Bridget seemed to feel she had to cut up a piece of chicken into tiny segments.

Uncle Nick said, 'I really wish people would leave proper messages. We're not psychic.'

'I did suggest it,' Amanda said. 'It's not my fault!'

I said, 'He'll ring back if it's important.'

'I'll check on the trifle,' Bridget said, disappearing to the kitchen quickly as though she thought the trifle might be inciting a riot in the fridge.

FRIDAY 11 JUNE

Bobbie collected me from school; I'd been given permission to leave after lunch.

'How's life with the Walls?' she said as I climbed into the car.

'Nothing much to report,' I said.

'You'd tell me, wouldn't you, if anything had upset you or things were going wrong?'

'All right,' I said. 'It turns out Uncle Nick is spying for the Russians.'

'Very funny,' she said. 'But I mean it. I can't help you if you don't tell me things.'

'What if I don't need help?'

'Everyone needs help,' she said.

She found a parking space in a side street. 'I should warn you,' she said, putting on the handbrake. 'Winson Green is forbidding. You'll think you've travelled back to Victorian times.'

She was right and I wondered whether the library book about modern prison life had lied. The huge walls and prison doors brooded above us as we stood at the edge of a restless group of about twenty others, also waiting for the 2.30 visiting slot. As we'd crossed the road, we'd seen them step off a bus. They were all women, some with small children. One had a baby in a cheap pushchair. The baby was crying, but resignedly, as though she had cried for days with little result but didn't know what else to do with herself.

'I really want to pick that baby up,' I whispered to Bobbie.

Keys jangled from behind one of the giant doors. It creaked open.

'In you come, ladies,' said a tall prison officer, beckoning as if we needed to hurry, though he wasn't unkind.

We shuffled through obediently as a group. The door closed behind us and was locked. Clank. Rattle. After having our bags checked, and being led through two more clank-rattle gates ('Noisy, isn't it?' Bobbie said), we were ushered into a large, harsh-lit room with a low ceiling. Men in metal-grey tee shirts and dark trousers sat on plastic chairs, their elbows on tables that looked like those in our school dining room. I was relieved to see no green moss on the walls or shackles on anyone's ankles.

I saw Dad, at least a head taller than the men around him. He half-stood when I approached with Bobbie and then sat down again, out of nervousness or politeness, I wasn't sure.

He'd lost weight. His face was pale, but the flesh on it less puffy than it had been when irrigated by whisky.

There were two chairs opposite him. Bobbie and I sat down.

'Hello,' I said.

'Hello, Mr Chadwick,' Bobbie said.

He nodded at her, but that was all. He had both arms on the table and was holding his hands together as if in prayer. I wondered if he was trying to stop them from shaking.

'How are you, Dad?' I said.

'Been better,' he said. His voice was flat.

'It's cooler in here than it is outside,' I said, to make conversation, but then I felt stupid for suggesting he was better off in prison.

'Are they treating you well?' Bobbie said.

He looked at her. 'It's not the Ritz,' he said.

I searched my brain for another question. 'Is the food okay?' I said.

Dad stayed quiet and that's when I realised he was trying not to cry. His large Adam's apple was going up and down like a busy lift and the sight of it had me swallowing too.

'I'd like to talk to my daughter alone,' he said to Bobbie. His voice sounded grating, as though his throat was sore.

'Is that okay, Jackie?' Bobbie said.

'Of course it's okay,' Dad said.

I nodded.

'I'll wait,' she said.

I turned to watch as she walked to where a prison officer stood, his hands behind his back. I saw the suspicion on his face soften as she spoke and then she waited near him. Her orange beret looked cheeky and promising against the depression of this visiting room with its strange smell of socks and the inadequate play corner where small children bickered over toy cars.

I turned back to Dad.

'What's the matter?' I said. 'Is it horrible in prison?'

He shook his head. 'It's bearable.'

'What about not having whisky?'

'That's hell,' he said, 'but I'll survive.'

'What did you want to say that Bobbie couldn't hear?'

He said, 'You looked like your mum when you walked in. It's because I haven't seen you for so long.' He pressed his fingers into his eyes, then rubbed them with his knuckles.

I wanted to make him laugh so that I could laugh. 'Don't do that. You'll pop them out of their sockets.'

On the table next to us, the woman with the little girl was wiggling the child's pushchair to make her sleep. She'd plugged her with a dummy, but she kept spitting it out. Every time the dummy landed on the floor, the mother picked it up and shoved it back in. She was arguing in hisses with the man opposite her.

Dad said, and I saw his chest expand with a deep breath in, 'I'm going to tell you something you need to know. I didn't want Nosey Parker to hear.'

'She's all right,' I said. 'She's a good person.'

I don't think he heard me. 'Your mum. It was partly my fault. Maybe all my fault.'

A vein rose and fluttered at the side of his forehead. He'd unclasped his hands and I could see a definite shake.

'Don't say that,' I said. I reached out across the table, but he refused the contact.

'Let me talk,' he said fiercely. 'Your mum kept looking at the clock and saying, "I need to go to my hospital appointment."'

'When?' I said.

'When she was first sent to the specialist by the GP.'

'Oh.'

'But we were having a row. We were still having the row when it was time for her to leave. She kept mentioning the clock.'

'Was I at school?'

Again, he didn't listen. 'The row got worse,' he said.

'Weren't you going to the hospital with her? Surely you were going with her. What do you mean, I need to know?'

I waited this time. He didn't seem to be talking to me anyway. He was looking at the table. I noticed how his thick mat of hair was thinning. I'd never thought that would happen.

'I was drunk. She'd said something that annoyed me. I hit her face,' he said, 'harder than I thought.'

I turned my head to see if Bobbie was still where she'd been. She put a thumb up to ask if everything was okay and I nodded.

There was no point asking Dad why-did-you or how-could-you. That seemed futile. And, anyway, there wasn't time. Even now, some visitors were scraping chairs, including the woman with the baby who'd now fallen asleep but without her face being at rest.

'What are you telling me?' I said to Dad. My heart was letting me know it was doing its job in a way it didn't usually have to.

He put his face in his hands and talked through them. 'She didn't go to the appointment. She was embarrassed. Her lip was split.'

I stared at him. He took his hands away from his face and looked straight into my eyes. I felt as though he hadn't done that for years.

'She didn't go again for three months,' he said, 'and by then—'

'What?' It took a few seconds to take in what he was saying. 'Did anyone else know?'

'Only Pat,' he said. 'That's why I couldn't let you talk to her,' he added, very fast, and then his body heaved out of the chair, so that I flinched. His face was wild, screwed up as though he were holding back all the sorrow in the world. I looked up at him, startled, and ducked. But he didn't move towards me. He roared at the room as if he were charging at a bull or an enemy. Everyone fell silent, even the children.

Two prison officers appeared from nowhere. 'Come on, Dave, mate,' said one, and they took his arms. Dad was sobbing now, his nose running. He didn't struggle as they turned him towards a door that said 'Exit' and walked with him. They were holding him tightly as though afraid he'd slump to the floor without support, and for a moment I imagined he was drunk, then remembered where we were.

I felt Bobbie behind me, her hands on my shoulders, pushing down a little as though to hold me in position.

In the car, she said, 'What upset your dad? Can you tell me?'

Even if I'd wanted to, and in some ways I did, I didn't have the words. Also, I was focusing hard on keeping my hands off my scalp and in my lap.

'He said I looked like my mum,' I told her.

That afternoon, I wrote a letter to Auntie Pat in New Zealand, using one of the thin blue aerogrammes Bridget had bought for me to add to the tin of stamps and writing paper she'd already given me. 'I think I know why Dad didn't want me to speak to you,' I wrote. 'I wish you'd told me.' But I wasn't sure I meant it.

MONDAY 14 JUNE

On Monday morning, I found Amanda downstairs having her breakfast in her school uniform. Bridget was saying, 'Think of it as a fresh start, darling,' and Uncle Nick, 'You're lucky they're taking you back.' Amanda was applying a thick layer of sugar onto Weetabix with full concentration as though blocking her parents out and I couldn't blame her. They could at least have decided on a united front.

'Hope it goes well,' I said as she got up to go. I didn't get a reply either apart from a flash of something in her eyes that could have been thanks.

After school, I waited for Bobbie in the usual place. I knew she would ask me again about what happened with Dad at the prison, but I'd rehearsed what to say in response. I had decided that this was a secret I could tell no one.

I was planning to surprise Bobbie by ordering a cold drink instead of Horlicks. It was not a Horlicks day. This summer had beaten me into submission. There was no escape from the sun which had bullied its way into classrooms all day via the windows and flat roofs and punished my bare head now. The hairline at the back of my neck was wet. I'd struggled to stay awake in the last lesson, but the scorching day and trigonometry worked together to close my eyes. I would tell Bobbie about that, too.

It was unusual for her to be this late. I'd become used to spotting her Mini in the car park, the way you spot little coloured boats out on the ocean.

Someone behind me said, 'Jackie.'

It was Uncle Nick. He'd taken off his tie and had sweat patches under his arms, darkening his light shirt. He didn't have his briefcase, so I knew he hadn't finished his after-school marking and preparation yet. Why was he there?

My hand went automatically to my head to pick at a spot. I forced it back down. 'Bobbie's late,' I said.

'I know,' he said. 'Come and sit with me on the wall.'

I sat beside him, squinting against the sun which made him into a blur. But I was sure he had news, and it wasn't a win on the Premium Bonds. 'Is she poorly?' I said.

'Not as such.'

'What does that mean?'

'Social Services rang Bridget. Bobbie has had to stop work suddenly. She has something called gestational diabetes which might harm the baby if she doesn't rest.'

'Oh.'

'She's distraught not to tell you herself. Her GP ordered her home this morning after an appointment.'

I batted away a wasp which pestered my face.

'I'll take you home, don't worry,' he said. 'The buses have gone.' He took out a handkerchief from his pocket and wiped his face.

'I wasn't worried about that,' I said. 'I was worried about Bobbie.'

It was a half-lie. I was sure Bobbie would be fine. Anyone who wore an orange beret with such doggedness would be okay.

I was more worried about the substitute. I knew it was selfish but, right then, I couldn't shake selfishness off, in the same way you can't shake off a leech once it's decided you're the one it wants.

FRIDAY 18 JUNE

On Friday afternoon, I arrived home to see an unfamiliar car parked outside the house: a mustard-yellow Ford Escort.

Bridget had told me that the new social worker might visit.

I hated the car immediately but knew that was unreasonable. It wasn't the car's fault someone had sprayed it that colour.

I let myself in and peered around the edge of the living room door, not wanting to commit. But Bridget said, 'And this is Jackie!', announcing me like a prize-winner on a game show.

A woman stood up from one of the armchairs. She was short, like me, and smiley with an elfin cut in her brown hair. She wore a sleeveless shift dress – a mini, more like a 1960s dress – with large purple flowers on it and slingback shoes. She looked dressed for a party. 'Hello,' she said. 'I'm Cynthia. Your Bobbie replacement. Sorry about that.'

Unfortunately, I liked her straight away.

'You prefer Jackie to Jacqueline, I hear,' she said, putting out her hand to shake mine.

I came further in and shook it. 'Is that your car?' I said.

She sat down again. 'I know,' she said. 'Monstrous, isn't it? My husband's choice. I will never forgive him.'

She'd brought with her the smell of roses. She'd been generous with her perfume.

I sat in my place on the sofa. Bridget busied herself to the kitchen to fetch more tea and to bring me an orange squash.

I could hear Amanda's music upstairs, not disruptive but loud enough for me to know she'd been asked to turn it down.

'What's happening at school?' Cynthia said. 'Anything exciting?'

'We're rehearsing for an arts evening,' I said, although I hadn't intended to say it. The way she talked was as though we'd already been mid-conversation and I felt pulled in.

'Are you performing?'

'Reading a poem, and my friend Kim's brother has put music to a ballad I wrote. He played it to me at school. It's really haunting.'

'Are you singing it?'

'No, Kim is.'

'Impressive!' she said. 'Bobbie told me you were a poet.'

Bridget came back in bearing a tray. 'She's multi-talented,' she said, 'aren't you, darling?'

She'd never called me darling before and as far as I knew, poetry was my one talent unless you counted sarcasm. So, I knew she was nervous and it reminded me that the social worker wasn't only for the fosteree.

Also, I'd heard Uncle Nick and Bridget in discussion about whether to ask advice from Social Services about Amanda's resistance to me. 'I don't think we need to,' I'd heard Bridget say. 'Gloria says it's like when a new baby comes into a family. Eventually, things will settle down.' Neither of them sounded sure, but when Bobbie disappeared off the scene, I think that was the decision made.

In a way, it let them off the hook. 'We're having more trouble with our own daughter than with the one you sent us,' would be an awkward conversation to have.

'How's Bobbie doing?' I said to Cynthia.

'Resting in bed, where she should be,' she said.

'With her beret on?'

She laughed and I could smell roses again.

'We'll carry on Bobbie's Monday café tradition, if that still suits you,' she said. 'I have someone booked in next Monday, but we'll start the following.'

'Okay.'

Five minutes later, we heard the squeak of Uncle Nick's brakes outside then the clunk of the garage door.

'That's my husband,' Bridget said. 'Nick.'

'Nick *Wall*,' Cynthia said, which I thought strange.

He appeared through the door, tugging off his bicycle clips. His face was pink with effort and the heat. He nodded to Cynthia. 'Hello,' he said, but he sounded unsure. It wasn't his usual warmth.

She held out her hand. 'Cynthia Jones.'

He shook it. 'Nick Wall.'

'I thought so!' she said brightly. 'The name rang an instant bell.'

The room paused and held its breath for a second.

Bridget said, 'Do you two know each other?'

'I don't think—' Uncle Nick said.

But Cynthia interrupted. 'We do. We worked together at Redwood School. Early 1960s. I was an assistant in the remedial department. Don't you remember?' She turned to me and said, 'I haven't always been a social worker.'

'I'm not sure I do remember,' Nick said. 'I'm sorry.'

I was convinced he was hedging. I didn't know why. Yet.

'My sister worked there too,' she said. 'You taught in the same department. Trudie. Trudie Roberts, she'd have been then.'

He moved towards the kitchen, uncharacteristically rude. 'Ah, you may be right,' he said. 'Perhaps I do remember a Trudie.'

I waited for him to ask her how Trudie was.

After a while, Cynthia said, 'She's married now. Three kids. Lives in Scotland.' She had to say 'lives in Scotland' loudly because he was already in the kitchen. We heard him turn on a tap.

'Oh, good!' he called back.

'Small world,' Bridget said, never short of an original phrase.

'We were more acquaintances, I suppose,' Cynthia said, nibbling on a biscuit. 'He knew Trudie better. At least, I'd thought so. I must phone and ask if she remembers him.'

He came back in with a glass of water. 'I wouldn't bother her,' he said. 'It was a long time ago.' He laughed, but not happily. 'I'm not that memorable.'

'Oh, darling, you are,' Bridget said.

Everyone was darling today. I wished Amanda would come down so I could see if she got darlinged too.

'I honestly wouldn't trouble her,' Uncle Nick said again. 'Judy, did you say her name was?'

Spotless could have acted it better.

At teatime, Bridget said, pouring gravy on her sausages, 'I don't remember you ever talking about Cynthia's sister when you worked at Redwood.'

Uncle Nick speared a piece of carrot. 'I didn't. And if I did, you were probably busy with childcare.'

'With me?' Amanda said, presumably forgetting she was an only child.

'You were there for a few years, Nick,' Bridget persisted. 'And if she was in the same department—'

'It's a bit bloody hot for sausage and mash, isn't it?' he said.

Bridget's eyes widened. I felt sorry for her but also embarrassed for Uncle Nick, who was not being Uncle Nick.

He stood up. 'I'm going down to the shed. Someone's coming to fetch their bike.'

'Dad!' Amanda said. 'Finish your tea.' But he was already stepping into the garden.

I was used to seeing Amanda sullen or dissatisfied with her mother, not defending her. It showed how shocked she'd been by her father's behaviour, in the same way people are unnerved by feeling an earthquake rumble underfoot when they thought they didn't live in an earthquake zone.

Later, I took Uncle Nick a cup of tea. He was doing the promised sort-out of his bookshelf, slotting books into a cardboard box. He looked up quickly when I arrived, as though he hadn't heard me approach.

'I've brought you some tea,' I said.

He took it and pointed to the bookshelf, now less crowded. 'That makes me feel much happier,' he said, which I thought was a strange way of putting it. It was only a bookshelf.

WEDNESDAY 23 JUNE

Bridget was in the kitchen putting the finishing touches to a cheese flan when I arrived home from school.

She kept a calendar on the kitchen wall on which she recorded family events: birthdays, anniversaries, her Weight Watchers classes.

'Shall I put the arts evening on the calendar?' I said.

'Sorry?' She seemed vague.

'The arts evening. On the 22nd of July. We've been asked today to invite guests. Will you come?'

On the bus home, I'd rehearsed how to express the idea. People's families? Parents? Households? I'd settled on guests and been pleased with it.

'That'll be nice,' she said.

'I'd ask my dad,' I said, 'but I think he'll have other engagements.'

'Probably,' she said.

I glanced at the calendar. 'Nothing else is written in for that date.'

She opened a drawer and handed me a pen. 'You write it,' she said. 'I must make this salad.'

I wrote, 'Start of Jackie's worldwide tour, 7 p.m.'

Later, after we'd eaten the cheese flan and salad, Bridget brought in fast-melting dishes of jelly and ice cream for dessert but said she didn't have time to eat any. She was setting up early for her Weight Watchers meeting; they had an awards evening.

'This early?' Uncle Nick said, looking at the clock on the wall. 'You never said anything.'

'It slipped my mind,' she said tersely, but her face pinked up.

'Awards for what?' I said.

'Eating rabbit food,' Amanda said, and Uncle Nick laughed, which disappointed me.

'To celebrate people's weight loss achievements,' Bridget said. 'Slimmer of the Month. That kind of thing.' But she looked harassed and distracted, bringing only two dessert spoons at first and dropping the one she went back to fetch. I stood up, offering to help, but she batted me down again.

She didn't seem in a celebration mood to me.

We'd started the meal later than usual, having had to wait for Amanda, who'd gone to a friend's house after school and returned late, meanwhile impersonating an ashtray. There'd already been a row about that.

'We'll wash up so you can get going,' Uncle Nick called through to the kitchen when Bridget went to take her apron off. 'Won't we, girls?' he said, addressing me and Amanda with a smile on his lips but strain in his eyes.

'I've got French revision for a test,' Amanda said, nodding towards me, 'but I'm sure Florence Nightingale here will help you.'

'Florence Nightingale was a nurse,' I said, spooning up melted jelly. 'She didn't work in kitchens.'

She said, 'Know-all.'

I felt as though I'd been used. The day she'd been expelled from school, I'd let her into my room so she had someone to talk to about it. And she'd learned that I had kept her secrets quiet. Now, she'd resumed her sniping. It reminded me of living with Dad, or perhaps with chameleons or lava lamps.

Uncle Nick didn't pursue the matter of the washing-up with Amanda. He and Bridget gave in so easily some days, collapsing under the heat of her rebellion in the same way as our jelly and ice cream had yielded to the early summer's ferocity.

Ten minutes later, Bridget had left and Uncle Nick was washing the dishes while I dried.

'Have you noticed the calendar?' I said. 'Look at the 22nd of July.'

He read it and smiled. 'What's that about?'

'The school arts evening,' I said. 'The one I've been practising for.'

'Ah, yes,' he said.

'I'm reading a poem and Kim is singing my ballad. Her brother made up the tune.'

'And we're invited?'

'If you like.'

'I do like,' he said.

I preferred this Uncle Nick, not the edgy one with secrets and evasions.

'My friend Molly from Poetry Club is performing as well.'

'A song?'

'No, a poem, although she does sing.'

'You have some talented friends,' he said, and it was the first time I realised that I had a group of friends now.

I had introduced Kim to Molly one lunchtime when we met in the queue for beef casserole. 'Didn't you sing at last year's Christmas show?' Kim said to her. 'I remember. You did a solo.'

Molly nodded, shy. 'I nearly died of fright,' she said.

'But your voice is incredible,' Kim said, and Molly bent her head as though the praise was too much for her.

Once Kim and I found seats at a table, Kim had beckoned Molly over to sit with us.

Uncle Nick said now, 'You can leave this with me, pet, go and do your homework.'

'I don't have any.' I opened a cupboard to put some plates away. 'I finished it at lunchtime in the library.'

'You're a dream pupil,' he said. 'I wish—'

But he didn't get a chance to finish his sentence. A crashing sound and a yell from upstairs had him running, the dishcloth flung onto the draining board.

I followed him up the stairs, which he took three at a time.

'Don't come in, Dad!' Amanda yelled.

'Of course I'm coming in,' he said and pushed open her door. I waited on the landing. If she hadn't wanted her father, she certainly wouldn't be pleased to see me. It was a shame because this could have been the Florence Nightingale moment she'd mentioned.

I heard her say, 'Leave me. I can get up myself.' She grunted, presumably pushing herself up off the floor. 'I fell off the chair, that's all.'

'Doing what?'

'Putting the suitcase back on the wardrobe. I said don't come in.'

'What for? Why did you get it down?'

'Doesn't matter,' she said.

He softened his voice. 'Tell me.'

There was a pause, then I realised she was crying.

'Come here,' he said tenderly. I felt my gut turn over with longing.

I didn't want to overhear but was trapped now. She'd hear me if I walked downstairs or went into my room and closed the door. Anyway, I thought, she has him as her real dad. She has enough luck. I'll stay and listen.

'Don't tell Mum,' she said, her voice more muffled, as though she had her face in his shoulder. She blew her nose, loudly. I think he'd given her a starched, pure-white handkerchief from his pocket or maybe I made that up. 'My clothes—'

'What about your clothes?' he said.

Another outburst of sobbing. Then, 'Some of my things don't fit. I was putting them away. I don't want them in my wardrobe, looking at me.'

I felt uncomfortable again, being there. If she'd known, she'd never have confessed this.

'Darling,' he said.

'Are you and Mum ashamed of me putting on weight?' she said.

'Of course not,' he said. 'Of course not, love. How could you think that?' I wondered if he was stroking her hair or patting her arm.

At this point, I wished I had stayed downstairs and heard none of it. I knew he was lying. I'd heard him say to Bridget in the kitchen the day before, 'She's eating as though there's no tomorrow' and Bridget had replied, 'I find it hard to look at her.'

THURSDAY 24 JUNE

The next morning, Amanda refused to go to school. As I slid books into my satchel in my bedroom, I could hear Bridget's voice, higher and more panicked every sentence she spoke, begging Amanda to get out of bed.

Ten minutes later, I was eating cereal when Bridget came down to make a pile of buttered toast, which she took to Amanda's room. 'Honestly!' she joked as she passed me. 'That girl thinks she's the Queen!' but there was a desperation about it, and I found myself pitying her.

When I came home after school, Amanda was lying on the sofa in her nightie, staring at a tennis match on the TV.

'Who's winning?' I said.

'Who cares?' she said, so I left it.

Bridget was in the kitchen, cutting up new potatoes and crying. I stood at the door, hesitating. 'Can I get some squash, please?' I said.

She whipped round quickly and mopped at her face with a tea towel. 'I've been chopping an onion,' she said, a claim that wouldn't have stood up in court as there wasn't an onion in sight.

As I ventured in, the telephone rang, next to my right ear, and I moved to pick up the receiver, but Bridget's arm intercepted me. 'I'll get it,' she said. She recited the number.

There was a pause. I heard a man's voice, a low rumble on the other end of the line. I was sure he'd said her name.

Bridget's eyes widened and she turned away from my gaze.

'I'm sorry,' she said, 'but you must have dialled incorrectly.' She replaced the receiver and pulled on the hem of her blouse as if to straighten it. She said to me, 'Go back in the living room. I'll bring you some squash.'

I sat in an armchair. 'Haven't you been to school?' I said to Amanda.

'What does it look like?' she said.

'You might have been to school but in your nightie,' I said, bending to stroke Spotless, who had spread himself across the carpet as though auditioning to be a carpet himself. 'There are all kinds of possibilities.'

On the TV, there was a smatter of Wimbledon applause. 'You see,' I said, 'they like my jokes.'

Amanda couldn't have looked less amused.

Bridget came in with a jug of squash and two glasses, which she put on the coffee table. 'There you are,' she said, smiling.

'I didn't want squash,' Amanda said. 'I want something fizzy.'

There was an awkward break in proceedings. I carried on stroking Spotless to fill it.

'You are testing my patience, Amanda,' Bridget said eventually, and her bottom lip looked unsteady as though she'd lost control of it. 'You will be going to school tomorrow.'

But, still, she trudged back to the kitchen and brought Amanda back some lemonade.

MONDAY 28 JUNE

Some locations in England had suffered ninety-five-degree temperatures over the weekend. During breakfast on Monday, Amanda told her mother that she'd slept on her bedroom floor for several nights because of the heat. But it felt to me as though she'd made up this new revolt in exchange for having dragged herself into school last Friday.

'Darling!' Bridget said, apparently horrified, although Amanda hadn't *mentioned* a bed of nails.

Uncle Nick was reading the newspaper and eating toast. He didn't comment. More and more, he ducked out of conversations that threatened to become arguments. Amanda could form a row out of a light-hearted chat in the same way puffer fish blow up at one nudge.

'I can't sleep. It's cooler on the floor.' Amanda helped herself to orange juice from the jug and poured twice as much as Bridget normally permitted.

Amanda was right, though. The nights were oppressive, no cooler than the days. I knew she hadn't been sleeping well. I'd been awake too and had heard her moving around in her room.

Bridget said, 'But you can't possibly be comfortable on the floor.'

'That's what I'm telling you,' Amanda said. 'It's more comfortable than getting braised in a sweaty bed.'

A metaphor!

Uncle Nick turned over a page of his newspaper. 'I wouldn't want to be Jim Callaghan right now,' he said.

'Don't you wake up in the morning all achy?' Bridget said.

'No, I wake up *cooler*,' Amanda said.

'Throw your sheets off.'

'Do you think I haven't tried that?'

'But you can't sleep on the floor all summer.'

'Actually,' Amanda said, ignoring this, 'I think I'll come and sleep on the floor downstairs, in here. It doesn't get so hot. Upstairs is impossible.'

'You can't.'

'Give me one reason why not.'

Bridget nibbled at a piece of toast as though marmalade contained ideas.

'See? You can't think of anything,' Amanda said.

Bridget sighed and glanced at the coffee table which was in the centre of the room. 'You'd have to shift the furniture to make enough room,' she said weakly. She laid her unfinished toast down. I wondered whether being Amanda's mother took all the stamina she had, leaving none for eating.

Amanda collected her used plate, bowl and glass and took them to the kitchen. I thought it was a deliberate ploy to have the last word because she usually left them on the table for someone else to clear up.

Every cloud.

I sensed Bridget listening as a cupboard door in the kitchen was opened then shut with a clatter.

Uncle Nick said, 'Doesn't look as though the weather's going to break.'

Amanda came out wielding an unopened Battenberg cake. 'I need to take this to school. It's my friend's birthday,' she said.

Bridget turned to look. 'No, you can't, darling,' answering a question Amanda hadn't asked.

'You can take it out of my pocket money,' Amanda said.

'You owe *us*,' Uncle Nick said.

She was already going upstairs.

Uncle Nick folded up the paper. 'Better get my skates on,'

he said. 'Not that it's skating weather.' But he didn't leave the table.

We all moved slower these days, dragging ourselves about, fighting against lethargy as the heat sucked us dry.

I smiled at his skating comment to please him, but Bridget was staring out at the garden as though she hadn't heard.

Then she stood and began to clear the table.

'You haven't finished your toast,' Uncle Nick said.

'I've had enough,' she said.

The letter box rattled and Bridget went to fetch the post. She came back saying, 'One from the bank and one from Social Services.'

She sat down again, gave Uncle Nick the bank letter and slit open the other with a clean knife.

'What's it about?' I said as she took papers from the envelope.

Uncle Nick and I watched as she unfolded and skimmed first a leaflet then a piece of writing paper.

'That's interesting,' she said.

'What?' Uncle Nick said. He hadn't opened his bank letter.

'From Cynthia,' she said. 'She's sent me a leaflet she promised, but she's written an extra note herself. What lovely handwriting.'

Uncle Nick stood as if to go and there was a faint whiff of body odour. 'Saying what?'

'I'll read it to you.'

'There's no—'

'*Dear Bridget,*' she began, talking over him. '*My sister remembers Nick very well from when they taught at Redwood. We only had the chance for a quick phone call, but she sends her good wishes and hopes he hasn't forgotten her entirely.* Exclamation mark. *We're talking again at the weekend and she says she'll fill me in. Cynthia.*'

'What's the leaflet about?' I said.

'That's kind of her to follow it up,' Bridget said to Uncle Nick. 'I didn't think she'd remember.'

'I told her not to bother,' Uncle Nick said. His voice had a sour edge. 'It's not her business anyway.'

'Her sister remembers you better than you remember her, that's clear.'

Uncle Nick left the bank letter and newspaper on the table and headed upstairs. I turned to watch him. There was a dark line of sweat down the middle of his back where his grey shirt had stuck to him.

It was 7.45, but already the heat was having its fun.

Cynthia's mustard car was even easier to spot in the school car park than Bobbie's blue Mini had been.

Kim was waiting with me out of curiosity. I'd told her about my new social worker and she said she'd never seen a real one.

'You probably have,' I said. 'You've walked past them in the street, hundreds of times, or met them in the park. They look like normal people. Like teachers.'

We looked at each other and giggled. Teachers were never normal, even nice ones like Mr Court or Mrs Collingworth.

'You might as well come and say hello now she's here,' I said.

She shook her head furiously. 'No, I couldn't.'

But Cynthia was walking towards us.

'Jackie,' she said, waving. She was wearing another shift mini dress. Her wardrobe was clearly full of them. This time it was bright pink with a black stripe around the waist. She wore enormous square sunglasses with thick, pink rims and her hair had a red tint as though she'd had it coloured. It seemed as though she'd stepped straight from the magazine pages.

'This is my friend, Kim,' I said. I was suddenly embarrassed. This was the first time Kim would have direct contact with this part of me. You might tell a friend you had a scar, but that's different from rolling up your sleeve and letting them look.

'Good to meet you, Kim,' Cynthia said, nodding towards her. 'Have you two had a successful day? Impressed your teachers?'

'I wouldn't go that far,' I said. 'It's too hot to impress.'

Kim was staring at Cynthia and for one moment I thought she might ask for her autograph.

But then she said, as we watched a battered Ford Anglia turn into the school gates, 'Here's my dad. I'll see you tomorrow.'

Cynthia's car was untidy, unlike Bobbie's. Something went 'crunch' when I climbed into the car. It was a crisp packet in the footwell. Several carrier bags lay on the back seat.

'Oops,' Cynthia said. 'I think that was a full one.'

'Sorry.'

'My fault,' she said. 'So, Bobbie said you normally go to the Happy Plate café.'

'I liked the other café we went to recently,' I said, 'when the Happy Plate was closed. Simpsons, I think.'

'I know where that is,' she said. 'I hope they do ice creams.'

Later, I was digging into a chocolate sundae when I remembered Cynthia's handwritten note to Bridget. 'It's funny, isn't it, that Uncle Nick knew your sister?'

'Trudie's being enigmatic about it,' she said, but then she seemed to check herself. 'It's probably best for us not to speculate. How are you feeling about your dad's court case on Wednesday?'

A strange word: speculate.

We'd finished our ice creams and Cynthia was telling me how Bobbie was and how bored she was at home when the bell on the café's door went 'ting'. A man walked in and I recognised him as the man I'd seen with Bridget outside the shopping arcade when Bobbie was buying bread. Today, he wore a light-blue summer suit. He looked weary.

'Afternoon, Doctor Kite,' the waitress called over from the counter. 'Finished for the day?'

'Locum doctoring has its advantages,' he said.

'The usual?' she said.

'Yes, tea,' he said. 'I'll have a scone today, though.'

He sounded cultured, like a newsreader.

He sat at the table in the far corner, taking off his jacket and tie, folding them neatly on a chair, but not before reaching into one of the jacket pockets to retrieve an envelope. He put it on the table. It was decorated with garish pink and purple flowers. When the waitress brought him tea and a scone, he slit the envelope open with the knife. He took out a notelet.

Cynthia was trying to ask me how things were going at home and whether I was happy at school, but I couldn't concentrate.

'You seem distracted,' she said, loud enough for the man to look up from the notelet and catch my gaze. I looked away. I knew my face had reddened.

I sensed it, rather than watched, as he put the notelet back in its envelope.

Five minutes later, he'd eaten his scone and called the waitress back. 'I'll have another,' he said. 'I need cheering up.'

'Bad news?' the waitress said. I couldn't see her directly, but I wondered if she was pointing to the envelope.

'Complicated situation,' he said, and he sighed.

'I'll get you that scone, then,' she said.

WEDNESDAY 30 JUNE

Bridget said, on Wednesday morning, that if I wanted to stay home from school, I could. We were all at the breakfast table.

Amanda said, 'I bet you wouldn't say that to *me* if it was my dad in court.'

Uncle Nick said, wearily, from behind his newspaper, 'Amanda, it's not always about you.'

I was drinking tea. I didn't have an appetite for my cereal. This had clearly alarmed Bridget, who kept eyeing me as though any moment she'd attempt to spoon-feed me Weetabix or perhaps a Farley's Rusk.

Amanda said, with her mouth full, 'Will he get a life sentence?'

'Don't be silly,' Uncle Nick said.

'I can't say *any*thing these days,' she said.

'He might not get a prison sentence,' I said to her. 'You might be rid of me yet, if that's what you're thinking.' But I wasn't being sincere. Cynthia had already prepared me.

'You could spend a day on the sofa, Jackie, and I could pamper you,' Bridget said. 'Help take your mind off things. You won't be able to concentrate at school.'

Suddenly, compared to being pampered by Bridget, double maths had new appeal. 'I'm good at concentrating,' I said. 'And it's Poetry Club.'

Amanda rolled her eyes.

'One man's meat,' I said. 'Don't you go to any clubs at school?'

'They're for swots,' she said.

'Suit yourself.'

'Do your friends at school know your dad's in court?' she said.

'My best friend.'

'Kim?'

'Yes.'

She reached for more toast. 'At least you've got one,' she said. The honesty was rare.

'You still have friends, darling,' Bridget said, 'don't you?'

'I thought I did,' she said. Her bottom lip wavered.

'What about Fiona?' Uncle Nick said.

'What about her?' Amanda said.

This all made sense. I'd noticed Amanda staying out after school much less since she'd been expelled for those few days – the previous Wednesday had been the last time – and she hadn't gone shopping with friends on Saturdays for a while. Also, the girl who called for her in the mornings came less and less often.

It seemed mean of her friends to abandon her, especially after she'd supplied them all with bargain-priced glitter eyeshadow. But she seemed unhappy and, although people try to be patient, not many want to be friends with a demeanour like a wet Monday morning. I wondered, too, how many of their parents had discouraged them from spending time with her once they'd heard about the shoplifting and the expulsion.

I don't think Bridget had noticed the look on Amanda's face. She was gazing at me instead, as though it were me going to prison and as if she wanted to stroke me. 'Are you sure you wouldn't be better at home?' she said. 'I have cream slices in the fridge.' On 'slices' her voice rose a whole octave as though it were likely to tempt me to spend an extra eight hours with her.

'Do you?' Amanda said. 'I didn't know that.'

She abandoned her toast and walked into the kitchen. We

heard the fridge door open. 'You've hidden them at the back,' she said, 'behind this chicken.'

'Leave them, please, Amanda,' Bridget said.

The fridge door shut. Amanda came back in, holding one of the cakes on her palm and already using a finger to scoop up cream.

She'd had cereal and toast and couldn't possibly have been hungry. Not for food anyway.

'Nick!' Bridget said. 'Do something!'

Uncle Nick folded up his paper and drained his tea. 'What do you suggest?' he said, in a voice that weighed more than it should have.

I went upstairs to clean my teeth and pack my satchel. When I came downstairs, Uncle Nick had left and Amanda was still at the table complaining about tummy ache even though it was time to go to school.

Bridget was saying, 'Perhaps the cream slice hasn't agreed with you.' I thought it more likely that it hadn't agreed with the cornflakes and three pieces of toast and jam, but it was time for me to catch the bus.

I called 'Bye' then shut the front door so that I couldn't hear the reply.

After school, I saw Cynthia's car in the car park as I headed for the bus. She beeped her horn.

'Hello,' I said, opening the passenger door. The metal door handle was almost too hot to grasp. 'What's happening? It's not Monday.'

But I knew.

'Climb in,' she said.

Dad had been sentenced to four years, she explained as we sat in the car. There was no air, despite having the windows open. My chest felt tight. 'He pleaded guilty,' she said, 'or it could have been much more.'

I stared at the pupils streaming out of school, laughing and jostling each other.

'We've let Bridget and Nick know,' she said. 'You don't have to break the news to them.'

'I'll be eighteen when he's out,' I said.

'He might not have to do the full four. There's parole.'

'Kim said that,' I said.

Kim had asked me at break time if I was all right. 'As all right as you can be when your parent is a felon,' I'd said.

'Oh,' she'd said.

As we'd packed up our bags in the last lesson, she'd admitted to me that she hadn't known the meaning of felon. 'I had to check in my dictionary before I said anything wrong.'

'It's okay, Kim,' I said. 'I didn't have a lot to say about it.'

'He might get parole.'

'That's a long way off,' I'd said.

I said to Cynthia now, 'This makes me nearly an orphan.'

'That usually means both parents have died.'

'I know what an orphan is.'

'I'm sorry.'

No, I was sorry. I was being angry-rude. 'It feels like being an orphan,' I said. 'He might be alive, but he can't be a dad. Even a shitty one.'

'I can see that. Would you like me to drop you home?' She twisted round. 'Your bus is still there.'

'Could we go for a drive?' I said. 'If you don't think it's too hot.'

'I'd factored it in,' she said and started the car. 'You can hang your head out of the window like a dog, if you like. I told Bridget you might be late. And I've brought you a carton of orange juice and a Penguin biscuit which has probably melted.' She leaned behind her and pulled a carrier bag through. 'Here.'

'Thank you,' I said.

'I wish I could do more,' she said.

The kindness made me rash. I nearly started to tell her

what Dad had confessed about Mum's cancer. But though the words queued up in my mouth, they didn't make it past my lips, and as we drove out of the school gates, I'd changed my mind.

When Cynthia pulled up against the kerb in Hollybush Close after half an hour of country lanes, with us pointing at sheep and talking about all the fires that the arsonist sun was starting in dried-out fields and woodlands, I said, 'Are you coming in?'

'Is there someone at home for you?' she said. 'You've had upsetting news.'

'I can see Bridget in the living room.'

'I won't, then,' she said. She clearly saw Bridget's presence positively, whereas I could have done with help defending myself against the way Bridget would experience the emotions she thought I should be having.

It's your own fault, I told myself. You've let Social Services think you're having a lovely time with the Walls. You've made your bed.

Cynthia said, 'I'm coming round in a few days for a regular visit anyway. But telephone if you need me.'

Inside the house, I found Bridget hovering so near the door that we nearly collided.

'Four years,' I said, uncomfortably close to her face. I wanted her to know that I knew.

'You poor lamb,' she said, her eyes wet. 'Let me get you some nice cold Coca Cola.'

Amanda came down the stairs in shorts. She had bare feet. The shorts were too tight around her thighs and the flesh bulged.

'Are you going to ask if I want cola too?' she said, as though she was three and would have a tantrum if ignored.

Bridget didn't answer as she went to the kitchen. 'I want some too,' Amanda said, trailing behind her.

I waited.

Bridget came back out of the kitchen quickly, forcing Amanda to back up, and said, 'You are *so* selfish. I have had *enough* of your whining.' She breathed in heavily, as if she'd alarmed herself as well as us.

Amanda stared at her mother.

Bridget said, 'It's not as though you deserve Coca Cola like Jackie does. Go on, tell me. What have you done to deserve it? Nothing! You do nothing that deserves Coca Cola!' She pointed a finger towards Amanda's face. 'And all you think about is yourself! And on a day when Jackie has bad news.'

There was a long silence. Eventually, Amanda said, 'Have you finished?'

For a moment, I thought Bridget would say more. But she turned and went back into the kitchen. Her shoulders looked ashamed.

Amanda looked at me. I shrugged to apologise. I wasn't sure what I was sorry about, but I didn't like Bridget comparing us and it wasn't true that Amanda never did anything that deserved Coca Cola. Some days she was kind to the dog.

'Don't say anything,' Amanda said, and I watched in surprise as she walked to the front door and left the house in bare feet.

I told Bridget I would take the Coke up to my room and start my homework.

'Oh,' she said. 'I suppose Amanda has gone up there to sulk.'

I let her suppose.

Upstairs, I said hello to Weston. I'd promoted him to the top of the chest of drawers recently. Then I started my maths.

'How are you with equivalent fractions?' I said to Weston at one point. He had no reply, but it was a comfort to have someone in my room to share with.

Half an hour later, I heard Uncle Nick arrive home. There was a conversation in the kitchen. I couldn't hear all the words, but both voices were raised. As he came into the living room, he said, 'And I was hoping to watch the tennis. I suppose that plan's scuppered.'

He climbed the stairs. 'Amanda!' he said.

A pause. I heard him go into her room and come out again. He called down, 'She's not here, Bridget.'

He knocked on my door. 'Is Amanda in there with you?'

'No,' I said.

I listened as he checked the bathroom and his and Bridget's room, then went back downstairs.

'I thought she'd stormed up there in a temper,' I heard Bridget say.

I slipped on my flip-flops and went into Amanda's room. I'd never been in there before. It was a mess. Her bed was unmade and her school uniform had been abandoned on the floor.

Her sandals were by the bed. I picked them up and went downstairs. Bridget and Nick didn't notice me. They were both in the kitchen, speculating and trying to find things to blame. I heard my name and stopped to listen.

'What if it's all because of Jackie?' Bridget was saying.

'She was getting like it before Jackie came,' Uncle Nick said.

'Not as bad as this.'

'We can't let her hound Jackie out,' he said. 'That's not fair.'

'But Amanda's ours,' Bridget said. 'Isn't she our priority? Do you think we should talk to Cynthia after all?'

'I know I shouldn't say it,' Uncle Nick said. 'But sometimes I wish…'

'No, don't say it,' she said.

I let myself out, shutting the door with care so that it didn't click.

It was stupidly hot outside. The pavements heated up the rubber of my thin flip-flops.

In the next street, I found Amanda sitting on a small patch of grass by the kerbside, her knees drawn up to her chest, crying. A couple of older girls stood nearby. They pointed and giggled.

'Get lost,' I said to them. 'She has rabies. She could turn violent.'

'Yeah, right,' one said, but they wandered away.

'The pavements are on fire,' I said to Amanda. 'Let me see the soles of your feet.'

She shook her head.

'Here,' I said, handing her the sandals.

She stood up unsteadily and slipped them on, refusing my offer of a hand. I saw her wince.

'Can you walk?' I said.

'You think you're such a hero,' she said.

'That's not actually true,' I said blandly.

'Okay. *Mum* and *Dad* think you're such a hero.' She wiped her nose with her arm.

'I have no control over that,' I said. 'Do you need to hold my arm?'

'Drop dead,' she said. She limped along, beside me, and even though she still seemed to hate me, there was something companionable about it as we walked home, both expecting to have questions fired at us that we didn't want to answer.

'Mum told me your dad got four years,' she said as we approached the house. We could see Bridget on the front lawn, staring down the street towards us as though we were an alien invasion.

'Yep.'

'Are you upset?' she said.

'Not at all,' I said. 'Ecstatic, in fact.'

'It's sort of exciting. I wish my parents were exciting.'

'Be careful what you wish for.'

'I don't even know what that means,' she said.

Later that evening, we were all in the living room watching TV, Amanda with her feet covered in cream and resting on a thick towel. Her parents had been too horrified at her scorched soles to punish her any more and, in the fuss, neither had they acknowledged my part in her rescue. I was grateful. It helped to redress the balance and a Superwoman comparison from Bridget at that point could have tipped it back.

When the telephone rang, Uncle Nick went to answer it. 'It's Gloria,' he said, and Bridget went into the kitchen to take the call.

She was on the phone for ten minutes or more. We couldn't hear what she was saying as she'd shut the kitchen door as usual.

But when she came back, her eyelids pink, Uncle Nick said, 'Helpful?'

'Onwards and upwards!' she said determinedly, as though preparing to walk the Alps.

They got ready for bed not long after Amanda and I went up. As I turned the pages of my book, I could hear their voices murmuring into the night, and I went to sleep, still listening.

TUESDAY 6 JULY

I turned the corner into Hollybush Close after school and was reminded that Cynthia was due to visit by the brash presence of the car. It sat at the kerb, standing out from all the other modest, more muted suburban cars like someone who'd turned up to a party in fancy dress when everyone else was in work suits.

The day before, we'd had an arts evening practice after school, so Cynthia and I hadn't been to the café and Uncle Nick had brought me home instead.

Now, as I entered the living room and put my satchel on the floor, I sensed that a conversation had stopped. Bridget and Cynthia were both perched on their seats as though not comfortable with each other, but everyone was sitting like this these days, not wanting their backs to be in contact with anything. Cynthia's sunglasses were pushed back onto her head, keeping her fringe off her forehead.

A tall jug of lemon squash and fast-melting ice sat on the coffee table.

Amanda's music persisted through the ceiling. Slade.

'Hello. Were you talking about me?' I said.

Cynthia said yes and Bridget said no.

'Not in a bad way,' Bridget said.

'I was asking how you were coping since you heard the news about your dad,' Cynthia said.

'I'm coping,' I said, miming a self-strangle.

She smiled. 'I'm sure Bridget and Nick are supporting you well.'

'Let me get you a glass, Jackie,' Bridget said, going into the kitchen.

I sat on the sofa. 'I've written to him,' I said.

'Good. He'll be pleased. Letters must make a real difference in prison.'

'I sent him two of my poems.'

'Even better,' she said.

'Not that he's a poetry fan.'

'He might see that differently now,' she said.

'They'll probably be read by the officers, won't they?'

'Most likely.'

'Hurrah,' I said. 'Anything for a wider readership.' But despite my light comments, it was taking me all my concentration not to reach up to the back of my head where there was a particularly large spot which had scabbed over and which I was desperate to pick. At school, I could usually resist; I couldn't risk anyone in class seeing me do it. Sometimes, if the urge was strong, I sat in a toilet cubicle to pick, but even then older girls would bang on the door and ask if you were on your period.

Cynthia said, 'Did you all watch Borg beat Nastase at the weekend?'

We had, although Amanda had needled at her parents throughout the match about a range of complaints, as though we'd needed any more conflict what with Borg and Nastase firing tennis balls at each other, trying to knock off each other's heads. Bridget had served us all strawberries and cream so that we could pretend we were enjoying an idyllic summer day along with the crowd at Wimbledon. Amanda had quietened as the match drew on, but just as I'd thought it was all calming down and we could watch without the Amanda sideshow, she'd knocked the bowl of sugar over while helping herself to more and Bridget had had to fetch the vacuum cleaner.

Bridget came back in now and poured me a glass of squash. 'I don't think I've heard any of your poems,' she said.

Neither Cynthia nor I spoke as I think we were both certain Bridget was going to say, 'You must show me some.'

Eventually, I said, 'Am I staying here for ever now?'

Bridget said, 'Well, not for *ever*,' as though she really thought I'd meant that after my death I would still find myself at her table eating coronation chicken.

Cynthia said, 'You seem very settled.' She looked around her at the room. 'In this safe and peaceful home.' This is when I knew that Bridget had definitely not talked to her about Amanda and recent events. I'd half-expected to be told that a new foster home had been found so that the Walls could get on with sorting out the problems in their nest, minus the cuckoo.

The evening before, as I'd helped Bridget prepare the vegetables, Uncle Nick had said he'd never met such a kind and generous teenager. Amanda had said she wished they would swap me for a younger foster child as originally intended and then she'd fed a large sausage to the dog to enrage her parents further.

Also, in her assessment of said safe and peaceful home, Cynthia had overlooked Spotless, who was stretched out on the carpet in a passable imitation of a fatal trip hazard.

Cynthia stood to go and Bridget said, 'You haven't told us what your sister said. You were speaking to her over the weekend.'

Cynthia reached down to pick up her handbag. 'Yes,' she said.

'She was going to fill you in; I think was how you put it,' Bridget said. She giggled, like someone who isn't sure how what they say will be received. 'Nick's still convinced he can't remember much about her. I'm sorry. It's a bit insulting, seeing as it's your sister.'

'Oh, it was nothing in the end,' Cynthia said, but I noticed how she didn't want to meet Bridget's gaze. Who takes that long to pick up a handbag? She added, 'As Nick said, hardly anything worth worrying about.'

Bridget giggled again. 'I wasn't worrying.'

Cynthia's cheeks turned pink. She brought her sunglasses down from her head.

'Of course,' she said. 'It's all such a long time ago anyway.'

WEDNESDAY 7 JULY

I lay on my bed after school, looking at the ceiling and hoping that its whiteness would help me to stay cool. I was also trying to keep still. But being still was the worst thing for picking at my head. Being busy was the only remedy.

I'd realised the habit had become an obsession lately and I was either doing it or thinking about it. I kept my arms stiff at my sides, my hands tucked underneath my thighs, trying to resist the lure of it. If someone came in now, I thought, I'd look like one of those effigies in churches, laid on top of their tombstones as though someone had got distracted by other tasks and forgotten to bury the body.

But one row of spots at my hairline at the back of my neck was throbbing; I knew it was an infection. I'd asked Bridget if she had Germolene. 'I got bitten on my leg,' I said.

'I hope it's not bedbugs,' she said, presumably imagining shameful headlines in the local paper and an hour in the stocks.

'At school during PE,' I said.

It was difficult to apply cream to the lumps under my thick hair. On the other hand, I was grateful for its thickness because it hid them. This pleased me because opportunities to feel grateful to Dad for what he'd passed on to me weren't plentiful.

Bridget and Uncle Nick were due to attend parents' evening at Amanda's school. 'Our appointments start at 4,' Bridget had said. 'We should be back by 6, but there's pork pie and salad in the fridge, plated up.'

'Okay,' I said. Amanda was upstairs, probably avoiding

them in case they wanted a conversation about the parents' evening. I couldn't imagine they would get much happy news. Despite her reprieve after being expelled, Amanda's new resolve hadn't lasted long and her path to the status of model pupil was still rocky.

'And there are yogurts,' Bridget added.

'Come on, Bridget,' Uncle Nick said. 'We'll be late.'

After they'd gone, Amanda played through a selection of singles in her room, but she kept listening to half-songs before replacing them with another disc. I was about to shout, 'I'm fairly sure they wrote more verses,' but then I heard her go downstairs.

A few minutes later I was tossing some lines of poetry around in my mind, wondering whether to open my notebook, when Amanda knocked on my door.

I sat up, something effigies don't have the luxury of doing. 'What?'

She came in. 'You know the bookshelf in Dad's shed?'

'Yes.'

She looked awkward. I think we both knew she was only speaking to me because she needed help.

'You borrow books from him,' she said.

'It's legal. What about it?'

'Does he have any Sherlock Holmes books? I've looked on the bookcase in Mum and Dad's room and the one downstairs.'

'I'm not sure. Why?'

'I need one for my stupid homework,' she said. 'I have to write a summary of a Sherlock Holmes story, but I forgot to go to the library.'

'If there isn't one on the shelf,' I said, 'I know there are more in a cardboard box, if that's still in the shed. He was trying to make space.'

She disappeared and I stood by the window for a while,

pretending I could sense a breeze. On days as weakeningly hot as this, all we had left was imagination.

Five minutes later, she knocked and came in again. I was sitting on my bed, writing in my notebook. The book in one hand, the pen in the other, safely busy with other matters so that I couldn't scalp myself.

I'd been composing a poem based on a famous proverb: a way of writing Mrs Collingworth had introduced to us in Poetry Club. The proverb I'd chosen was 'Absence makes the heart grow fonder.' I'd written the first few lines:

It's a lie. Absence blurs
the edges of your heart
so that its memories,
once sharp as flint,
turn soft and treacherous.
A mother's perfume
migrates on the wind.
Her stories dim—

'Long time, no see,' I said to Amanda now, closing the notebook and sliding it under my pillow.

'It wasn't on the shelf. I found it in that box,' she said. 'The box was tucked in the corner, behind some gardening tools.'

'Result,' I said.

'I didn't know he had so many books in his shed,' she said, waving the Sherlock Holmes collection at me.

'He likes reading down there.'

'How come you know everything about him?' she said.

'I don't.'

'Your cosy lift to school on Thursdays, maybe.'

'There's nothing cosy about it.'

'Hm.'

I thought she'd leave to start her homework, but she flung

the book on my bed and slumped onto my bedroom chair, folding her arms across her stomach. She always sat like this now, hiding her belly.

'I can't believe you like that stupid gorilla,' she said.

'Do take a seat,' I said, 'and he's called Weston.'

'You are joking.'

'I am not. Careful what you say. He gets offended.'

'You're an idiot.'

'If you say so.'

She looked at me for longer than was comfortable. 'There's blood on your neck,' she said.

I leaped up and went into the bathroom to look in the mirror. Three streaks of blood. I wiped them away.

When I returned, she'd been to fetch food and was now standing by my window, eating cheese and onion crisps.

'What was it on your neck?' she said.

'Exactly as you said. Blood.'

I thought she'd press me for an explanation, but she didn't.

'I'll tell Dracula I don't do Wednesdays in future,' I said.

'Do you remember the day you first came to visit?' she said. 'I was standing here behind the curtains, watching you arrive in your social worker's car, with your dad.'

'I saw you watching,' I said.

'You see everything,' she said.

She screwed up the crisp packet and threw it in my wastepaper basket.

'Anyway, you're an English swot,' she said, picking up the Sherlock Holmes. 'How do I write a summary?'

Uncle Nick and Bridget came back from the parents' evening at 6.30. Amanda and I were eating from trays in front of the TV. We'd been watching news reports about someone called David Steel being elected as leader of the Liberal Party to replace Jeremy Thorpe.

'The news is boring,' Amanda had said. 'I don't even

understand the difference between Liberal and Labour and Conservatories.'

'I don't fully understand either,' I said, which was true. This had pleased her.

I didn't have much appetite and the thick jelly in the pork pie made me nauseous just looking at it.

Bridget looked strained and her pale-blue summer skirt and blouse were creased as though sharing in the tension. She went straight upstairs without speaking to either of us.

'Don't tell me what the teachers said in front of Jackie,' Amanda said to Uncle Nick.

'I'll scarper upstairs, don't worry,' I said.

'I'm not going to anyway,' he said. 'I'll wait until Mum comes down.'

'Oh,' she said. She went into the kitchen and brought back the cake tin and a knife. Bridget had made a Victoria sponge the day before. Amanda put it on the coffee table as though it would protect her from the conversation she was about to have.

'Want some?' she said to me.

I shook my head. She and David Steel might have disagreed with me, but it didn't seem your average cake day.

THURSDAY 8 JULY

After school, I was putting away some clothes that Bridget had ironed and wondering whether ironing pants was something anyone else did.

Amanda knocked at my door and said, 'Can I come in?'

She shut the door behind her, taking the seat that was fast becoming hers. She was wearing a tee shirt with a picture of the Aristocats on it. Despite her bid for independence from her parents, she was still fiercely loyal to Disney.

'Why do you keep coming in if you hate me?' I said.

She didn't answer.

'Say hello to Weston now you're here,' I said, shutting the wardrobe doors.

'Get lost.'

'Say it or you can't stay.'

She rolled her eyes but said, 'Hello, Weston.'

'Okay, what do you want?'

'They won't back down,' she said. 'A whole week.'

Amanda had been grounded again after parents' evening. Her protest about it seemed futile to me. She hardly saw friends now anyway.

I sat on the bed. 'You could see this positively. Anyone who does go outside gets sunstroke.'

'No, they don't.'

She really did not get jokes, the same way Bridget didn't. I hadn't realised there was a jokes gene, as there is for hair colour and hand shape.

'I'm not selling the make-up any more,' she said. 'I haven't stolen any for ages.'

I wasn't sure what she wanted me to say.

She said, 'I'm not smoking. Much. I can't afford it.'

'Right.'

'The teachers won't give me a chance. All because of passing a few notes in class and not working very hard. It's not my fault if I don't understand.'

'Your mum wants you to do well,' I said. 'She's being cruel to be kind.'

'It's not Mum!' she said, animated. 'That's the thing! Apparently, this is Dad's decision. He's suddenly come over all Hitler as Mum is backing off.'

It was true. Bridget was backing off, like a car after an accident, reversing away from the scene and hoping no one had noticed it being there.

'And he said he wished I could have your attitude,' she said. 'Same old story. Be more like Jackie. You're the golden girl. The angel.'

'I've got black hair,' I said.

SATURDAY 10 JULY

Uncle Nick said to me while we all ate breakfast, 'I've got the tune for your ballad repeating inside my head.'

The day before he'd brought me home from a rehearsal after school but had arrived early to fetch me from the hall and heard Kim and her brothers rehearsing it.

'It's not a happy tune exactly,' he said.

'It's not meant to be,' I said. 'Ballads aren't laugh-a-minute.'

'Doom-laden,' he said. 'But the lyrics are clever.'

I spooned up the last of my milk from the cereal bowl. I wanted to thank him for the praise, which did something to my spine, but didn't want to provoke Amanda.

He clearly didn't have the same scruples as he then asked her whether she'd completed all her homework for the week, and not in a gentle way.

'Stop interrogating me about homework,' she said. She glanced at me as if to say, 'See? I told you!'

'Not another argument, please,' Bridget said.

'What do you expect?' Uncle Nick said to Amanda. 'Someone's got to remind you, otherwise it doesn't happen.'

'I've only got my English left,' she said, presumably relying on me not to say that I'd helped her with her summary. 'I've nearly finished. It's on Sherlock Holmes. I need to write it out in neat.'

His face brightened at the thought that Amanda was voluntarily doing homework. 'Hey, I think I have a collection of his stories. I can search them out for you.'

She buttered a piece of toast. 'Already have it,' she said.

'I went to your shed. I couldn't find it on the bookshelves in the house.'

'Show it to me when you're finished. I'd be interested,' he said. I could hear him trying to make an effort, perhaps regretting his earlier harshness, but even trying to make an effort seemed an effort.

'I don't think so,' she said. 'I'm not five.'

'Of course not, darling,' Bridget said. 'We only want to help.'

Amanda chewed on a mouthful of toast then said, with her mouth full, 'That reminds me. Who's Trudie?'

I stopped eating my own toast. Bridget put her cup of tea down. Uncle Nick held a jar of jam mid-air.

Things set in aspic must feel similarly.

'What are you talking about?' Uncle Nick said.

Amanda didn't seem to sense the atmosphere. 'Trudie,' she said. 'When I was looking for the Sherlock Holmes, a piece of pink paper fell out of one of the other books in the box.'

'You went in the box?' he said. 'How did you know about the box?'

'Jackie said.'

I looked down at the table. I didn't know what I'd done wrong.

Amanda continued. 'It said, 'To *darling* Nick. Love and memories. Trudie.' She laughed. 'Was she your girlfriend before Mum?' she said.

He put the jam down as though he'd gone off the idea.

Surely she'd heard us mention Trudie, I thought. But when I remembered back, she'd either not been in the room or we'd spoken of her as Cynthia's sister. She wouldn't have known the connection.

'I put it back where I found it,' Amanda said. Maybe she thought this was her father's main worry. And maybe he was wishing it had been.

Bridget stood and said, 'I'll go and refill the teapot.'

Uncle Nick's face had turned the colour of putty.

Amanda said, 'Pink paper!' and took a giant bite out of her toast.

* * *

I spent the morning cleaning my room, accompanied by Amanda's music through the wall, and wondering what the outcome of the morning's conversation would be. My stomach felt the way it used to when I'd been alone in Dad's house in the evening, waiting for him to roll home from the pub, or when on my way home from school, knowing that I'd done something which had irritated him that morning.

I wished I hadn't mentioned the box of books. I wished I'd never seen it.

Before lunch, I went to find Uncle Nick in the shed. I wanted any potential telling-off over with.

He was sitting on the stool, a book on his lap. At first, I didn't think he knew I was there. He had to snap out of some other place where his mind was.

'Can I come in?' I said. 'I brought you a Coca Cola. Careful. It's wet and cold from the fridge, so it's slippy.'

I handed him the bottle.

He gulped half the cola and then stood up. 'I ought to be mending Mr Potts' bike. I'm trying to persuade myself into it.'

I sat on the stool as he picked up tools. The shed was airless, but at least it provided shade.

He didn't say anything about the box. Perhaps I wasn't in trouble after all. But it was clear that Uncle Nick was, and knew it. Amanda was oblivious of the impact of her announcement, but it seemed the rest of us were not. Like an active landmine that cars drive over, it was a case of when, not if.

There was strange comfort in it. It was familiar ground – parents who had flaws – and I was beginning to feel more myself in their company, in the same way people get used to litter or a messy bedroom and feel incongruous in tidiness. I was sorry for them and wondered about the outcome.

But I felt more sorry for Amanda than for Uncle Nick or

Bridget. They were old enough to take responsibility. None of the sadness should have belonged to Amanda, but she would be given a dose of it. In my recent experience, parents were more than happy to divvy out the pain.

'What have you been up to?' Uncle Nick said, pulling a rusty old bike into the centre of the shed but wearily.

'Cleaning my room,' I said. 'Sweating. Reading a book. And finishing some chemistry homework.'

'What was the chemistry about?'

'Something about different types of bonding. It doesn't grab me. I can't say I'll write a poem on it.'

He smiled, but his smile was lukewarm.

I looked up at the shelf but decided not to investigate any of the books myself in case of pink paper. 'Is there anything else you think I should read?' I said.

He pointed. 'Have you tried *The Catcher in the Rye*? It's on the end.'

I slid the book off the shelf.

'You'd like the narrator's sarcasm,' he said.

'What happens?'

'He gets expelled from school,' he said, 'and doesn't want to go home and admit it. He stays a few days in New York trying to be grown-up.'

I laid it on the shed floor, ready to take back into the house.

He took another gulp of the cola.

We heard Bridget call his name and both looked back at the house. She was standing at their bedroom window. 'Nick!' she called again, louder.

'Nick, Nick, wherefore art thou, Nick?' I said.

But his face was sickly-green.

Jackie, your big mouth.

'I'd better go and see what she wants,' he said, but, as he moved, the bottle slipped from his grasp and smashed on the floor of the shed.

'Don't go near that,' he said. 'I'll clear it up later.'

When he'd gone, I picked up the glass, binned it and

fetched a cloth and the dustpan and brush to clear up the rest. Already, a posse of curious wasps was beginning to gather.

When I'd finished, I stayed in the shed and began to read the Salinger book, falling in deep and fiery love with Holden Caulfield from the first page, even while aware of events at the other end of the garden. The window to the main bedroom had been slammed shut, then quickly opened again. I'd heard Bridget shout, 'No, I'm sure you don't want people to hear. But it's a bit late for that.' Then it was shut again.

Even with the window closed, I could hear the raised voices, although I couldn't hear the words. Bridget and Uncle Nick's voices were muffled like those of the divers in the Jacques Cousteau documentaries.

I heard footsteps on the path. It was Amanda. She stepped into the shed. She was crying. A handkerchief was balled up in her palm.

Reluctantly, I put Holden on the floor.

'They never have fights like this,' she said. 'I'm scared.'

It was true. There were cross words between them, and the odd gripe, increasingly so these days, but full-on marital rows weren't their style unless they were doing them in whispers at night and neither Amanda nor I had realised. Still, maybe that was because, until now, the secrets had stayed secrets.

'Don't be scared,' I said.

'But it's my fault, isn't it?' she said. 'And I've been listening at their door, not that I needed to.'

I waited.

She sat cross-legged on the floor of the shed and blew her nose. 'Who's Trudie?' she said. 'What did I say?'

It wasn't my place to tell her. 'I'm sure they'll explain.'

She was looking at the floor of the shed. 'They don't need to. I've heard them. Dad had an affair.'

'Right.'

'I hate adults.'

'I can see why you'd think that.'

'Don't you, though?'

I thought about this. 'They can be disappointing,' I said. 'But there are some good ones. Your mum and dad aren't bad people. They're faulty, but not bad.'

She sniffed, horribly. 'I heard Mum say, "So that's why you left the school so suddenly!" He's always told us a pupil complained about him, without reason, and that's why he left.'

'Maybe that happened too.'

'I was three. Or four,' she said. 'And he was seeing this Trudie woman.'

She started crying again.

'I suppose it's out in the open now,' I said.

'But how could he do that to Mum?'

'Adults do stupid things sometimes.'

Amanda went back into the house once the shouting had stopped. I watched her go inside. Thirty seconds later, Errol Brown began to tell me, the neighbourhood and perhaps people in the next town that 'Everyone's a winner, baby,' which, despite what he was insisting, right then, felt very far from the truth.

I heard the garage door slam. It was nearly one o'clock, which was Saturday lunchtime, but it sounded as though Uncle Nick was going out for a bike ride. It seemed reckless in the heat of the day, but perhaps, I thought, he would cycle to the woods and sit in the shade.

Half an hour after he'd gone, Bridget came to find me in the shed. Her face was marked and swollen with grief. I could barely look. It reminded me of my mother's face, which had ballooned with the drugs they gave her until it seemed as though she had someone else's face laid over her own.

'Jackie,' Bridget said. Her voice was hoarse. 'There's plenty of food in the fridge. Could I ask you to put lunch together for you and Amanda?'

'Sure,' I said.

'I'm meeting a friend,' she said. 'I need to talk to them. I won't be long.'

This was the first time she'd asked me to prepare lunch.

I went back into the house and put Holden Caulfield on my pillow. 'Don't be jealous,' I said to Weston. 'You're still high on my list too.'

When I came back downstairs, Bridget had already gone. I'd expected a guided tour of the fridge at least – 'On the left, you'll see cold sausages. On the right, slices of ham.'

Later, I knocked on Amanda's door. 'Lunch is served,' I said.

The music stopped. She opened the door. 'What?'

'I've made lunch. Your mum asked me to.'

'Where are they?'

'Both gone out.'

'Together?'

'No.'

She stared at me. 'What is happening?'

I sighed. 'Hard-boiled egg salad, that's what's happening. And I found some cold new potatoes. We could have lunch and pretend everything's hunky-dory.'

'Salad?' she said.

'I've unearthed a packet of cherry pies as well.'

'Okay.'

When Bridget returned, she behaved as though it was a normal Saturday afternoon, although it must have been a strain. The more she tried to preserve normality, though, the less normal the household seemed. Soon, I thought, the walls of the house themselves would shout out, 'Stop pretending! We all saw. We all heard.'

She sat reading a magazine and knitting and later made a meat loaf. Uncle Nick hadn't returned by teatime. She put a plate over his meal and put it in the fridge. She'd set his place for tea and I marvelled at this. Even though she had discovered his unfaithfulness and that he'd hidden the fact all these years, meat loaf and potatoes it was.

On the other hand, she could have poisoned his.

While Bridget was cooking, the telephone rang. I was giving Spotless his tea, spooning dog food into his bowl on the floor while he pestered my shins. Bridget picked up the phone then silently shooed me out of the kitchen, shutting the door, but not quite in time to stop me hearing her say, 'No. I told you earlier. Why can't you accept it? Don't ring me at home.'

She must have replaced the receiver almost immediately because the door opened again as I was about to sit on the sofa. I was still holding the dog food spoon.

'Sorry about that,' she said.

Spotless had already eaten the spoonful I'd served him and was looking at me as if to say, 'Since when did my meals include a starter?'

Uncle Nick returned at 8. He looked exhausted. Not only hot but disordered.

He went upstairs for a bath then came down in shorts and a vest. I hadn't seen him in a vest before. He reminded me of Dad and that hadn't happened often.

He sat at the dining table, silently eating his tea which Bridget had reheated. They didn't speak to each other.

Notably absent was Spotless, who had stayed in his bed in the kitchen as though he wasn't sure where his loyalties should lie.

That night, I lay awake listening to an insomniac house as doors opened, people went to the bathroom or downstairs. Amanda had carried on sleeping downstairs most nights. At one point, I crept down to the kitchen to fetch a glass for water and noticed that a lamp had been turned on. I found both Bridget and Amanda sitting side by side on the sofa, spooning ice cream from bowls.

SUNDAY 11 JULY

Everyone slept in on Sunday but without the sleep. I think the household was hesitant to begin another day in case it offered the same unpleasantness as Saturday. But lying in bed was uncomfortable with the sun so high in the sky already, heating the roof of the house so that it permeated throughout its rooms without compassion.

I couldn't see evidence that Uncle Nick had eaten breakfast. He was already in the shed. Amanda and I sat with Bridget to eat ours. None of us mentioned the events of the day before, and Bridget didn't seem to want eye contact with either of us, staring down the garden instead or into her bowl of Bran Flakes as mystics gaze at tea leaves.

I was due to spend the day with Kim. It had been arranged by telephone the week before. It seemed rude to mention something so trivial, like talking about a shopping trip during prayers in church. But Uncle Nick had promised he would drive me.

I said to Bridget now, 'Is it okay if I still go to Kim's?'

She put down her spoon and looked blank.

I said, 'We're rehearsing for the arts evening. Do you remember?'

I saw a look of panic cross Amanda's face. This would leave her alone with her parents. There was nothing I could do about this and, as far as I was aware, I'd been brought into the house to be looked after, not to act as Amanda's surrogate carer.

Bridget said, 'Go and remind Uncle Nick.'

'I could get the bus into Warwick. I know the way.'

'If he can't take you, I will,' she said.

I'd have been surprised if she'd let me go on the bus. In some ways, it was reassuring that not everything had changed.

I ventured down to the shed. Uncle Nick was bent over, working on Mr Potts' bike.

'Aren't you having any breakfast?' I said.

'It's too hot to eat,' he said. 'I don't have an appetite, to be truthful.'

I wondered if that was an invitation to talk. I declined it. Leave them to their adult worlds.

'Bridget said to remind you that you were taking me to Kim's this morning. I could go on the bus, though.'

He straightened up. 'Could you, this once?' His face looked fast-forwarded ten years. 'I'm sorry.'

The apology felt as though it stretched much wider than my cancelled lift.

'Uncle Nick says to go on the bus,' I said to Bridget in the kitchen.

But she said, 'I'll drive you,' and pursed up her lips as though resolving never to let words escape them again in case they were little bombs.

The car was like the inside of a blacksmith's forge. We wound down both passenger and driver windows. I leaned towards the window as we drove, trying to get even a suggestion of wind on my face.

As we navigated down the main road that linked Leamington and Warwick, I saw a tall man in jeans and a tee shirt walking along the pavement, towards us. As we drew nearer, I realised that it was Doctor Kite, but without the suit.

'Wind up your window,' Bridget said. She was driving with her left hand only, winding up hers as though she couldn't do it fast enough.

I did the same.

As the distance between our car and the doctor narrowed, a family with three small children was attempting to cross the road. They'd misjudged the traffic. Bridget had no choice but to slow the car and wait for them.

The man came closer to the kerb.

'No,' Bridget said. I didn't know if she'd meant to say it aloud.

He rapped on my window. 'Bridget,' he called. His face was strained, desperate. 'Bridget.'

She shook her head as people do when insects flit about their hair.

'Bridget!' he shouted. 'Pull in for a second.'

Her hands were gripping the wheel as though she was afraid of losing control of the car.

The family reached the other side of the road safely and Bridget let out the clutch, accelerating away, the engine complaining, 'What's the rush?'

The man had to step back quickly.

Neither of us spoke until we arrived at Kim's, apart from Bridget checking the directions with me. She stopped the car outside the house.

'Five o'clock pick-up?' she said.

'Thanks.'

'Jackie.'

'Yes.'

'Don't mention that incident with the man to anyone,' she said. She'd turned her head to look out of her own window while she said it.

'I won't,' I said. 'I think it was some crazy weird person anyway.'

She breathed out. 'I'm sure you're right. That's exactly what he was.'

A crazy weird person who happened to know her car and her name, but I glossed over that.

At 5, Uncle Nick arrived for the return journey. Amanda had come for the ride and was in the front seat, crunching boiled sweets.

Neither of them said much on the drive home. I wondered if they'd been having a father and daughter conversation which I'd interrupted. I could sense myself babbling about my time at Kim's, trying to fill a space that seemed larger than the inside of the car.

'We practised Kim's song that she's singing and my ballad. The one you heard.'

'Lovely,' Uncle Nick said.

'David and Kevin played us the song their band is performing. They're called The Stagers.'

'Good name,' he said.

'And then we had sausage rolls and Scotch eggs. Afterwards we played board games.'

'Sounds fun.'

'Board games?' Amanda said as though mocking the idea, but she didn't convince me. Ludo with friends versus time at home with disappointing parents. There was no contest.

I left out some details about my day, however.

While I'd been in the kitchen helping Kim slice up tomatoes, she had said, 'Kevin wants to ask you out.' I'd dismissed it as her imagination and told her so. But later, I'd found myself in the garden with Kevin and he'd asked if I would go to the cinema with him to see a new film called *Bugsy Malone*.

My mouth went to dust. I'd never had a boyfriend and, as I hadn't so far been surrounded by convincing examples of the pleasures of romance, I wasn't sure I wanted one.

'I don't think so,' I'd said.

He said, 'What if Kim comes?'

'I heard my name,' she said, stepping outside.

He told her his proposal.

'You're kidding,' she said. 'That wasn't the plan. I don't want to be the gooseberry. But if it means she'll say yes, I'll come. Just the once.'

'I'll have to ask my foster mum,' I said.

'I'm not paying for her ticket as well,' Kevin said.

'I mean for permission.'

'Don't worry. I got it,' he said, play-punching me on the arm. 'I'm teasing.' I couldn't look him in the eyes because otherwise my tummy felt weird.

I wasn't used to being the one outside of the joke.

'I'll get Mum to call her,' Kim said.

'Kim's got a lovely singing voice,' I said to Uncle Nick now. 'She wants to be on *Top of the Pops* one day. As the lead singer in a band.'

'That's nice,' he said, his tone as flat as if it had been sat on, perhaps by regret.

I went upstairs when we got home and ran a bath. Kim's house had been airless, plus I needed time to think.

After my bath, I sat on my bed, not feeling much cooler.

Amanda knocked and I let her in. I'd been reading about Holden Caulfield sending for a prostitute in New York then asking if they could just talk, and it was making me even more in love with him. I'd also been trying not to pick at my scabs. But there was blood under my fingernails. I sat on my hands.

'I've hardly seen Mum and Dad all day,' she said, shutting the door.

'How come?'

'They've been talking in their room.'

'Having a row?'

'No. Quietly. I couldn't hear what they were saying even when I leaned hard against the door.'

I couldn't help smiling.

She said, 'I think they were trying not to argue the way they did yesterday.'

'Did your mum make you lunch?'

'A cheese sandwich.'

'Just cheese? No tomato or lettuce?'

'Plain cheese.'

I had never expected to live in a family where an unadorned sandwich would signify the collapse of the status quo. But there was the evidence.

'Didn't your dad tell you anything in the car?' I said.

'He said I wasn't to worry. They were working things out. That was all.'

'That's something,' I said.

'Is it? I'm glad you think so.'

There was no doubt. Amanda's new scepticism suited her.

Bridget cooked chicken drumsticks for tea and made a salad, but the meal was later than usual, so she allowed Amanda and me to eat from trays in front of the TV so that we didn't miss *How Green Was My Valley*. Standards at the Walls' were slipping in the same way bits of earth fall off a cliff and then, whoosh, so does a house. She and Uncle Nick sat at the table to eat, but they didn't talk much. From what Amanda had said, I wondered if their tongue muscles had needed a break.

But when Bridget had washed up, and the closing credits went up on our drama series, she stood at the French windows and called Uncle Nick back from the shed.

He wandered towards the house, wiping his hands on a piece of old flannel. 'Now?' he said.

'Let's get this done,' she said, as though she was going to extract one of his teeth or perhaps make him undergo a punishing schedule of sit-ups.

Amanda and I looked at each other. She was cross-legged on the floor as usual. 'What's going on?' she said.

'We want a little talk. As a family,' Bridget said, although strangely Amanda had addressed the question to me.

'Do you want me to go to my room?' I said.

'No, stay,' she said.

'We said, "as a family",' Uncle Nick said.

I really wished they wouldn't do that. Not only was I

clearly not part of their family, but even those who *were* weren't doing family very well.

Amanda came to sit next to me on the sofa. Bridget and Uncle Nick sat in the armchairs. I felt as though Amanda and I were being interviewed for a job share.

Spotless loped in as if he'd noticed a family meeting in his diary. He sat next to Uncle Nick, his bulk leaning against his leg.

'Girls,' Uncle Nick said. He looked tortured. 'Mum and… Bridget and I have decided it's best to come clean with you about my… about my past.'

I wondered what else there was to say and Amanda seemed to agree. 'Don't say it, Dad,' Amanda said. 'We know.'

'I realise that,' he said to her. 'We know you must have heard us arguing yesterday. We lost control of ourselves a little.'

Bridget's neck and upper chest were bright red. I'd not seen that happen to her before.

Uncle Nick said, 'We owe it to you both to be honest.' He cleared his throat as though he'd rehearsed. 'As you may have gathered—'

'From the name on the pink paper,' Amanda said, not only acknowledging the elephant in the room but giving it a big hug.

'As you may have gathered, I had a relationship with Trudie, the lady I worked with at my first school. Cynthia's sister.' He was trying to meet our eyes, perhaps in the interests of transparency, but he couldn't maintain it for more than a few seconds. 'The relationship lasted a year and then I ended it.'

Was that supposed to give him Brownie points? I hoped he was telling the truth. I needed him to be telling the truth.

'Well, it got complicated. The pupils at the school had found out about it and one challenged me. I did not behave very well to that pupil. The headteacher of the school asked me to leave,' he said. 'I left teaching altogether. Until recently, of course.'

Amanda was looking at the carpet. She said, 'Why didn't you tell Mum *then*?'

'I didn't want to hurt her,' he said. 'And I suppose I was…
am… a coward.'

He looked shrunken, defeated. I remembered the affable,
smiley-eyed man I'd met when I first arrived, and I realised
that his decline had been happening over the past month since
Cynthia had first mentioned her sister. The facts about his
past had been gradually revealed in the way a sculptor chips
away at excess clay to release the shape of the truth beneath:
an ugly truth, like a monster or a troll.

'What happens now?' Amanda said.

Uncle Nick didn't look capable of saying much more, as
though he'd emptied himself.

'Is this all my fault?' Amanda said.

Uncle Nick shook his head. 'The fault is mine,' he said. 'If
you hadn't said anything, it would merely have delayed the
inevitable.' He had his hand on Spotless's head, feeling the
velvet of one of the dog's ears.

'It's all out in the open now anyway,' Bridget said. 'We
need a new start, and we can't do that until there are no more
secrets and the slate is wiped clean.'

I thought this, bearing in mind what I'd heard and seen,
an odd thing for her to claim, and I realised it went some way
to explaining the meat loaf and potatoes and the way she'd
heated up his tea even though he had committed adultery
with Trudie.

MONDAY 12 JULY

I was lifting up my satchel ready to head for the school bus when, through the front window, I saw the postman approach the house. Seconds later, the letter box clattered.

I picked up the envelopes. Two were brown and the other was a thin white one addressed to me in Dad's spiky handwriting.

Bridget arrived to look over my shoulder.

'I've got a letter from Dad,' I said. I slid it into my satchel and gave her the others.

She watched me tuck the letter away, her face anxious as though she would rather I read it in front of her, supervised.

'It's okay,' I said. 'Letters get checked.'

'I'm not worried,' she said, looking worried. 'As long as he hasn't said anything that might upset you.'

I waited for the irony to transfer from my brain to hers, but it didn't.

On the bus, the girl from my form wanted to chat about her tennis match at the weekend, so I didn't have a chance to open the letter until I reached school. 'It's too hot for lessons,' everyone on the bus was complaining. It had become a mantra we fatalistically chanted every morning.

We had two more weeks to endure until the summer holidays.

I climbed off the bus and sat on the wall by the car park, away from the stream of pupils arriving.

I unfolded the thin piece of lined paper cautiously, worried about tearing it. Her Majesty's Prisons' budgets clearly didn't stretch to Basildon Bond.

Someone, not Dad, had written at the top, in a different pen, a tick and Dad's prisoner number: Chadwick 74396.

Dear Jackie

Thank you for writing. I hadn't expected it, and didn't deserve to, but it really cheered me up that you did.

Don't worry about me. Things aren't so bad in here if you keep your head down and behave. I'm doing my best.

It hasn't been easy to stop drinking, but I wasn't given the option. They helped me through the worst. I won't bore you with gory detail.

When you came to visit, I was still having withdrawal symptoms and probably looked a state, but I'm glad I told you the truth about your mum. At least you know now and when I get out of here, you can decide whether you still want to see me. I would understand, whatever you decided. I feel better in myself physically – in fact, I feel like a different person – but there's a lot of time to think in here and I can't say that's easy, with all the things I have to regret.

I don't know whether you have heard from your grandma in Devon. I wrote to her to try and make amends, but she replied to say that she didn't want anything more to do with me and that I was a disgrace to the family. I suppose that's true. But I can't help feeling sad. I don't think you'll be getting Christmas socks from her any time soon.

I have shown your poems to my cellmate. He writes stories. He says you are an excellent poet and that I should be proud of you. I am. I liked the one about the picnic best. I am sorry (I am sorry about a lot) that I didn't pay much attention to them before. Whisky dulled my poetry appreciation skills. Don't ever start drinking it. Send me some more poems, if you'd like to.

My cellmate has forced me to start reading, mainly to shut me up, I think. There's plenty of time, as you can imagine, and there's a library here. I'm reading Huckleberry Finn *by Mark Twain. Have you read it? I think you'd like him.*

I'd better go. No peace for the wicked (your mum would appreciate that joke, bless her). Write to me again.

Good luck at your school arts evening. Are the Walls coming to see you? I'm sorry I can't. Evenings out are rare here.

I hope you're happy in your foster home. I'm sure it's more peaceful than the home I made for you and I'm sorry about that. I wish I had my time again.

I said I was going, didn't I? Bye.

Love, Dad

I read it again, three times, trying to work out why it didn't sound like my dad. Then I realised. He'd made some jokes. He was funny.

It had been a long time.

In the café after school, I told Cynthia about the letter as the waitress brought us ice-cold lemonade in tall glasses. 'Do you want to know what he says?' I said.

'Only if you're happy to tell me.'

I began to pass the paper over. She waved it back. 'Read it to me,' she said.

It would have been a flawless and articulate performance except that I started crying halfway through and something the size of a golf ball lodged in my throat. I think it had been sitting there all day since I'd first read the letter, waiting for its chance.

I blew my nose, took some deep breaths and managed to read the rest.

'Well done,' she said.

'Can I go and see him?'

'I can try to arrange it.'

'Will you come?'

'Of course.'

I put the letter back in the envelope.

'Are you all right?' she said. 'It must be upsetting to think about him in prison.'

I examined my feelings and realised I'd cried because the letter had made me feel closer to him, not further apart. I wasn't sure how to say it.

She stirred the ice in her lemonade with a straw. 'How is life at home?' she said. A shadow came over her face. Guarded, I think it's called. The name 'Trudie' hovered in the air between us.

I thought back to the weekend. Notes on pink paper. Arguments in bedrooms. Confessions. Suspicious phone calls. Tears. Doctor Kite banging on the car window.

I wondered how much Cynthia knew or suspected.

'I went to my friend, Kim's,' I said, 'and we rehearsed for the school arts evening that Dad mentioned in the letter. It's on the 22nd. Do social workers come to events?'

'The 22nd?'

I nodded.

'I'm sorry. I have something else happening. You should have mentioned it before. What a shame.' She sipped at her lemonade.

'I think I did mention it before,' I said.

She said it must have slipped her mind.

Amanda had kept saying to me, 'I hate adults.' I didn't, but I did resent the way that even people whose job was to forge a relationship with you turned tail when their own interests intruded.

Cynthia was paying our bill at the counter and buying herself a scone to take home when the door went 'ting' and in came Doctor Kite, this time in his work trousers and shirt, his tie loose.

Would he recognise me from Sunday? I shifted position so my back was to him.

I heard the scrape of a chair as he sat down in the corner and the waitress called, 'The usual?'

'That's us done.' Cynthia had come back to the table and was putting her purse back in her handbag. 'Ready?'

I let Cynthia go first so that she couldn't see me sidling out of the café crab-like.

'Let me find my car keys,' Cynthia said outside, and I waited. It gave me a chance to glance through the window.

He was reading another of Bridget's colourful notelets. I saw his shoulders rise and fall in what looked like a sigh and then he began to shake his head backwards and forwards as in a slow no. He put the notelet back on the table.

'What have I done with them?' Cynthia was saying, scrabbling in the bottom of her bag as a slim, red-haired woman in a flowered dress passed us and went into the café.

'Thomas! I *knew* I'd find you in here, darling,' I heard the woman say as she went inside and I watched Doctor Kite pick the notelet up and tuck it swiftly in his shirt pocket. But she'd have seen him do it, I was sure.

WEDNESDAY 14 JULY

I let myself into the house after school, called hello and went straight upstairs to change.

Later, I found Bridget in the kitchen, packing sandwiches into Tupperware and snapping on lids. Her face was flushed with the heat and her forehead sweaty.

'What's happening?' I said.

She said, 'I thought it might be nice to go for a picnic when Uncle Nick gets home. A surprise.'

Surprise was an understatement. The word 'picnic' didn't seem to fit well into the current Wall crisis. Imagine a pink flamingo in the lion enclosure.

Amanda came in. 'What's happening?' she said.

Bridget said, 'I thought it might be a nice surprise to go for a picnic when Dad gets home.'

It was as though she'd been practising lines for a play.

'It's too hot for picnics,' Amanda said. 'You're mad.'

'We'll find some shade in Victoria Park,' Bridget said, 'by the river.' She opened the cupboard under the sink to fetch a water bowl for Spotless.

Amanda breathed in deeply and let an enormous sigh escape, her whole body slumping like a puppet let go. 'The car will be *roasting*.'

Bridget ignored her, checked a list she'd written and opened the fridge. She brought out four tomatoes which she put in a box – snappety snap! – and added to the picnic bag. Amanda and I watched as she then made up a plastic jug of orange squash, dropping in cubes of ice. Into the bag went melamine picnic cups.

Bridget seemed to have decided on a plan of action and was not to be deterred.

'What if Dad doesn't want to go for a picnic?' Amanda said.

'He will,' Bridget said, as though she'd also packed a gun in between a couple of lettuce leaves.

There was an air of 'new start' around Bridget. It hung about in her bright smile, despite the suffocating heat, and her efficient organising of the picnic bag. She seemed to be ignoring the fact that the whole household was as tense as bootlaces.

I'd heard stories of people whose wives or husbands had died and, within days, they had cleared every sign of the deceased from their houses – clothes in carrier bags ready for the jumble sale, shaving cream and toothbrushes swept from the bathroom sink into bins – as though this would help with the grieving, moving on rapidly into new territory. Perhaps this was how Bridget was dealing with Uncle Nick's infidelity. Put it in the coffin, bury it and get rid of any reminders. Snap an airtight lid on it.

But how could Bridget move on? She had a secret of her own. If I'd had a secret like hers, even though I wasn't sure of its exact nature, it would weigh me down like a sack of coal and 'surprise!' picnics would be the last thing on my mind.

She suggested we sit in the garden, in the shed's shade as usual, waiting for Uncle Nick to come home. The three of us ate ice lollies whose juices dripped down our wrists within seconds and drove wasps mad with lust.

After a sustained wasp attack, Amanda said, 'I've had enough of this,' and headed inside. 'The wasps will probably follow us to the park.'

Bridget had sunglasses on, so when she looked at me, I couldn't quite see her eyes. 'Isn't this nice?' she said.

'The lolly?' I said. She'd finished hers and was waving the stick around as though conducting an orchestra. She looked happy. There was something film star about her with the sunglasses and her sandals kicked off. Not a natural Brigitte Bardot, but with potential.

'Not just the lolly,' she said.

'What, then?'

'Oh, I don't know,' she said, and suddenly I realised she was going to make some kind of confession. I don't know how I knew. The heavy air, something about the still lawn, perhaps the wasps buzzing around as though expecting gossip. She said, 'It's… it's lovely to be free of things that have been troubling you, isn't it?'

I deftly caught the last piece of my lolly in my hand and ate it before it slid into my lap. 'If you say so.'

She sighed. 'I should have done it months ago.'

I stood up, in case she said more. Why did she feel she could unburden, even in vague statements? I wondered whether the heat had got to her brain and fried it at the edges, like the lacy circumference of a pancake. I wasn't qualified to be anyone's counsellor and even if I had been, I would have told people like Bridget that my books were full.

When I said, 'I'm going in,' her eyebrows rose in a V as though she'd been woken from a trance. Perhaps she had. 'Do you want me to take your lolly stick inside?' I said. I thought I'd offer something in lieu of a listening ear.

She handed it across. 'It's sticky,' she said.

'The whole world is sticky,' I said and went indoors.

Half an hour later, I heard the garage door slam. Uncle Nick appeared in the living room where I was watching TV. I think Bridget had fallen asleep in the garden. Spotless was lying at my feet. He whined as Uncle Nick came in but was clearly too hot to respond further.

'Phew,' Uncle Nick said, dropping his briefcase on the coffee table. 'Am I glad that day is over. All I want to do now is have a bath and slump in a chair.'

Spotless whined again and I think it was dog for 'Who's going to tell him?'

We drove into the car park. 'Did you invite the whole town to this bloody picnic?' Uncle Nick said.

It took him ten minutes to find a space. Round and round, with Bridget saying, 'There! There! He's backing out.'

On the journey, Amanda had moaned about the heat so often that even Spotless looked annoyed with her and, with beautiful doggy eyes like his, that wasn't easy.

Eventually, Bridget turned out to be right, because someone did back out, although her hit rate had been about one in ninety.

Uncle Nick nestled the car into the space, and we all piled out, but he'd nudged the car too far back, so they couldn't get the boot open for the picnic. 'Bugger,' he said.

'Darling,' Bridget said. 'You're swearing a lot.'

'Bugger, bugger,' he said.

She didn't darling him again, which I thought a wise move. When you've press-ganged a sweaty, tired man into a picnic in tropical conditions, what can you expect? He'd only agreed, I was sure, because he felt he owed her some favours in return for his betrayal. I hoped he had more ideas up his sleeve because otherwise that would be a lot of cheese and tomato sandwiches eaten before debts were paid.

He took the handbrake off and shifted the car forwards again. The back of his shirt was spotted with damp. In the car, we'd been able to smell his body odour. Bridget had said at home after announcing her plan, 'You can have a quick bath first, if you like,' but he'd said, 'No, let's go and do it,' like people do when psyching themselves up for a tough exam.

We gave Spotless a bowl of water by the car as he was panting like someone in labour.

'I can carry the picnic bag, if you like,' I said to Bridget.

'Creep,' Amanda said.

'Thank you,' Bridget said, handing it to me. 'Can you carry the games bag, Nick?'

'Games?' Amanda said. 'What do you mean, games?'

'Simply a couple of tennis rackets and a ball,' Bridget said optimistically. 'And I popped the frisbee in too.'

For a moment, Uncle Nick, Amanda and I couldn't speak. Was she really imagining that we would hurl ourselves around after a frisbee or a ball under a sun this fierce? I was fully intending to lie on the grass under a tree and go to sleep.

'Who wants me to bring the games bag?' Uncle Nick said. 'Let's have a vote.' He didn't even wait half a second. 'I thought not. It can stay here.' He slammed the boot down. 'Let's go and catch sunstroke like all the other bloody bonkers families parked here.'

Uncle Nick's swearing interested me. It was as if, having admitted to one major flaw, he felt more free to curse, as though he'd been tamping down his real self for years and now it was leaking out.

He put Spotless on the lead and started walking towards the river. Amanda, Bridget and I trailed behind. Bridget said to us, 'I thought it would have been lovely to play a game.'

'Well, you should have brought Happy Families,' Amanda said, and when Bridget wasn't looking, I punched Amanda's arm to congratulate her on the joke. Despite herself, she grinned.

THURSDAY 15 JULY

The following day I was in the kitchen. Bridget had asked Amanda to dry the dishes, but Amanda had invented some science homework and earned her reprieve that way, bolting for her room.

'I'll do the drying up,' I'd said. Repetitive, mindless tasks such as drying up reminded me that somewhere in the world there were patterns and routines.

'You are a sweetie,' Bridget said, handing me a clean tea towel. 'I'll go and get the washing in.' She seemed light of heart, perhaps because after the rocky start to yesterday's picnic, we had found a spot by the river near some willows and grudgingly accepted our fate as she'd passed round the sandwiches and tomatoes and said, 'Isn't this lovely?' many more times than necessary.

I also wondered whether she was feeling a teeny bit smug. Her friend Gloria, her fostering role model, had telephoned the day before while Amanda and I were at school. I'd heard Bridget telling Uncle Nick about it while we were at the river and Amanda had wandered off to buy an ice cream from a van. I'd been on my back with my eyes shut, so I imagined they thought I was asleep.

'What do you mean, he's had to be fostered elsewhere?' I heard Uncle Nick say to Bridget. They were keeping their voices low.

'Apparently, they've had trouble with him from the start,' Bridget said. 'He's been bullying their own children, for one thing.'

'I thought it was all going perfectly. Idyllic.'

'That's what she's been telling me. She was the one who urged me to carry on with… you know.'

'Bloody hell,' Uncle Nick said. 'And it was all a sham.'

But today's happy mood could also have been explained by the fact that Bridget loved to collect washing in, fold and iron it. 'I feel as though I'm putting the world to rights,' she'd say, which I thought put a lot of obligation onto some nighties and a few shirts.

I set about drying plates and dishes. Uncle Nick came in to make a pot of tea. 'You don't have any homework?' he said, opening a cupboard.

'I do,' I said. 'Some questions about Isambard Someone Someone and a few bridges.'

'Kingdom Brunel. I have a book about him upstairs,' he said. 'I'll fetch it.'

He turned to go upstairs while the tea brewed, but then the telephone rang. He picked up the receiver, said the number, and listened.

'Yes,' he said. 'She does. This is her husband. Who's speaking?'

I could faintly hear a woman's voice at the other end.

'I don't think we know a Thomas Kite,' he said. He shook his head at me as if to say, 'Some madwoman!'

The woman's voice continued.

'Your fiancé?' he said. He listened for a few seconds. 'Look, are you sure you don't have the wrong number?'

I stood, holding the tea towel and a bowl. The tizz-tizz-tizz of the voice on the other end of the line seemed to get higher.

'I don't know what you're talking about,' he said. 'What notelet?'

He turned to face the wall of the kitchen as though he didn't want me to see his reactions.

'She doesn't work there any more,' he said. His voice had

an edge. 'I'm ending this call.' He replaced the receiver but kept his hand on it, as though to make sure it didn't spring back into his face.

Bridget appeared at the door of the kitchen, her arms around a basket of dry, innocent washing. 'Who was that?' she said.

He turned to face her. 'Do we know someone called Kite?' he said. 'A doctor?'

The contentment in Bridget's face fled with its colour. She looked as though she wasn't sure she could hold on to the basket. She bent to put it on the floor, so it stood between her and Uncle Nick, who said, 'He did some locum spells at your old surgery.'

'Yes,' she said.

'That was his fiancée on the phone.'

I thought Bridget's face couldn't have gone whiter but, as had happened on a few occasions now, I'd underestimated her. 'Fiancée?' she said, as though needing a definition.

They seemed to have forgotten I was there, but there was no way for me to escape, as I'd have had to negotiate a washing basket and a woman whose shame was filling the doorway.

'Tell me,' he said.

Her lips lost their shape. 'You think you have the monopoly on exciting secrets.'

'What a ridiculous answer,' he said.

'I told him it was all over,' she said. 'I didn't know about a fiancée.' Her face crumpled. She covered it with her hands. 'I even left the surgery,' she said from behind them.

Amanda came down the stairs and appeared behind her mother. 'What's happening?' she said. 'Can I get through, please? I want some biscuits.'

At this, Bridget let out a wail that didn't sound quite human, or even if she didn't mean to let it out, it escaped. She turned, leaving the basket, and ran up the stairs. Uncle Nick hurdled over it and followed her, saying, 'All this time? And *I'm* the criminal?'

Amanda brought up the rear and I watched them go upstairs in convoy. 'Dad?' she shouted, trying to tug at his shirt. 'What's going on?'

But her mother and father went into their room and slammed her out, which I knew because I could hear her on the landing, crying.

I'd been hoping to mention *Bugsy Malone* to Bridget, but he'd have to wait alongside Isambard and that was probably the first time anyone had thought of the two in the same sentence.

Uncle Nick and Bridget stayed in their room. After the initial shouting, their voices calmed, although I could hear their hum from downstairs. I couldn't help thinking how hot their room must have been with them shut in there, like a sauna but with the atmosphere heated up even further by revelations.

I'd switched the TV on to mask the noise. *Top of the Pops* had started.

I wasn't sure now whether Amanda was in her room or with her parents. But she came downstairs, her face bleak, and said, 'Do you know what this is about?' so I guessed she hadn't been enlightened.

I didn't trust myself to speak. I shook my head. She sat next to me on the sofa, and we watched TV, but the exaggerated cheerfulness of the presenters seemed not to belong in the Walls' living room. 'You to me are everything,' sang The Real Thing, swaying from side to side in their flares and oversized soft hats.

At around nine o'clock, Uncle Nick called Amanda upstairs. She glanced at me before going up. She looked anxious and I thought again how unfair it was. She'd played no part in her parents' infidelities and yet doubt and fear would now stick to her like burrs.

I heard low voices and then Amanda yelling, 'I hate you both! You're like *children*!' then first one door – slam! – then another, I presumed Amanda's bedroom.

I was thinking about taking myself to bed when Bridget

came downstairs. She looked like a ruined version of herself, her eyes puffy and ugly, her hair disarranged, and with no lipstick, like someone wiped clean of pretending.

She sat on the edge of a dining chair, as if she didn't deserve soft chairs now. She looked out at the garden and said, 'Do you remember the man who knocked at the car window?'

'You don't need to tell me,' I said. 'I know about him.'

She turned. 'How do you know? When?'

'It doesn't really matter.'

'I want to know.'

I went over to the TV to switch the *Nine O'Clock News* off. At the Walls', we had a surplus of our own news, so, plenty to keep us going. It felt strange, turning off Bridget's television, as though I were the one in charge.

I told her that I'd seen her and Doctor Kite arguing near the shopping arcade and about the times he'd come into the café.

'You won't have seen him in the Happy Plate,' she said. She looked puzzled.

'No, Simpsons we go to now.'

'I didn't know that,' she said. 'You didn't say.'

'I didn't think it was relevant,' I said.

We paused, both of us realising, I thought, how very relevant it had been.

'Simpsons,' she said eventually. 'It's his favourite haunt when he finishes work.'

I told her about the notelets. There were other details, but I didn't need to fill those in, like one of those dot-to-dots which has fifty points but once you've reached thirty, the rest is clear.

Bridget's face was already red with the ache and distress of it all, but it darkened further when I said I'd recognised the notelets.

'It didn't matter what I did,' she said. 'Write to him. Meet him. He was hard to persuade that it was over. I suppose I can't blame him for that.' She gazed at me for so long I dipped my head down, embarrassed by the surveillance. 'And you haven't said any of this to Amanda? Or Uncle Nick?' she said.

'It wasn't my place.'

'You are a very unusual girl.'

'Not really.'

'Self-sufficient,' she said. 'Composed.'

'Maybe on the outside,' I said, and she smiled, a tragic smile that seemed more authentic than many of Bridget's happy smiles.

'On the outside,' she said. 'Yes, we're all different on the outside. Or so we're discovering.'

Suddenly, she remembered she was meant to be my parent, but it had been refreshing for once to be treated like someone who had successfully navigated puberty. 'Are you saying that you feel worried on the inside?' she said.

'Well,' I said, 'the house hasn't exactly been an oasis of calm.'

'No. I'm so sorry,' she said. She took a handkerchief from up her sleeve and blew her nose spectacularly. It was so unlike her and immensely reassuring.

'I guess this means you and Uncle Nick are quits,' I said.

She said, tucking her handkerchief up her sleeve, 'I had no idea about a fiancée. I hope you believe that.'

'I'm not sure that's the main issue,' I said.

She bit her lip. 'You're right. It isn't.'

We both watched as Spotless wandered out of the kitchen and into the garden, lying down in the grass near the shed.

I said, 'Can I ask a question?'

She sighed. 'Of course.'

'Okay. Why did you start up with him in the first place?'

'Oh, now, you're probably too young—'

'To understand? Try me. I wouldn't be living with you if I'd been sheltered.'

'I suppose. Well, I'm not telling you anything I haven't said to Nick today.' She was turning her wedding ring round and round as she spoke. 'It was vanity,' she said. 'I lost all that weight. I showed you the photo.'

I nodded.

'Nick wasn't noticing,' she said, 'even though it took huge effort. Neither did Amanda care. Both too tied up with their own lives, more *fascinating* than mine, no doubt.'

'You've remedied that.'

She gave a rueful smile and continued. 'In fact, Amanda seemed to resent it. Then, someone started showing interest – a locum at the practice,' she said. 'It could have been anyone. I didn't even like him at first. But I was giddy with the weight loss and being... wanted.' She shook her head as though she couldn't believe what she was saying. 'It was the thrill.'

'You're the opposite of me,' I said. 'I want an ordinary life, the way things used to be before my mum died. Each day the same. You can keep thrills.'

She looked at me. 'I'm sorry,' she said again.

'I think excitement is overrated.'

At that point, Amanda walked downstairs. 'Don't talk to me, Mum,' she said. She went into the kitchen. We heard a cupboard door being opened.

Bridget stood and said, 'Anyway, Cynthia is coming round tomorrow afternoon.'

'Why?' I said, and Amanda had clearly heard what Bridget said as she emerged from the kitchen to listen. She was holding a jam tart in each hand.

Bridget didn't comment on the jam tarts but said, 'Uncle Nick rang Cynthia to say that he'd confessed to us about the relationship with her sister. It's clear she'd been told all about it. And he wanted to apologise for his previous rudeness to her.'

'Oh,' I said.

'She doesn't know, yet, about... about more recent developments. But she will.'

'Is she going to take me away?' I said.

'Actually,' she said, 'can I be honest and say I don't know what's going to happen?'

Amanda said, 'Will Jackie switch to another family?' but her voice was flat, so I couldn't tell what was behind the words.

FRIDAY 16 JULY

When I came home from school, there was a letter from Nanna. I put it upstairs to read later. There was too much on my mind.

Bridget was in the garden, staring at a flower bed that didn't deserve its name any more. We weren't supposed to use hosepipes now and if a neighbour saw you using up water for anything unnecessary, it was a matter for shame. The grass was browning and crackly, each day less of a lawn.

I wandered outside.

'Remember Cynthia's coming today,' she said, without her usual greeting.

'I remembered,' I said.

'Good.'

When Cynthia's mustard car drew up at 4.30, we were all waiting in the living room. Bridget had told me and Amanda that they intended to give Cynthia the whole picture and hold nothing back.

'Clearly, this is awkward for me on a personal level,' Cynthia said, even before sitting down. She was dressed in more muted tones than usual and wore a summer jacket. 'But I suggest we forget that connection and deal with what we have in front of us.'

I think she'd rehearsed in front of the mirror.

'Thank you,' Uncle Nick said and Bridget echoed him.

Cynthia sat down and took the offered cup of tea, stirring sugar into it. The spoon went round and round and round.

Bridget and Uncle Nick were both holding their bodies stiff and alert as though afraid that if they loosened them, they might not be able to put them back together again.

'This... revelation of Nick's has come as a shock, no doubt,' Cynthia said, sipping her tea. 'It must have disrupted family harmony.'

This was understatement at its finest.

She continued, 'And the main reason we need to discuss it at all is Jackie and the effect on her.'

'Before you go on, Cynthia,' Bridget said, 'there's something else.'

Cynthia's eyebrows and forehead took this in.

I looked at Bridget. She'd clasped her hands together as if in prayer.

Upstairs in my room was Nanna's letter. I knew it would be about which flowers she had in her garden and a trip to Marks and Spencer to buy Grandad some new braces for his trousers or something similar. I had a sudden appetite for that slice of ordinariness and fought an impulse to get up and fetch it.

Instead, I watched Cynthia's face as Bridget briefly explained that she had been having a recent extramarital relationship which had ended before I'd arrived but which had just been revealed to Nick. And to Amanda and me.

After her initial reaction, Cynthia had composed her face into the one I assumed she was taught at social worker training college for these occasions.

'I see,' she said.

Amanda had started crying.

Spotless appeared as if to see what was happening and lay on his back showing off his belly, joining in with the general trend of exposure happening in the Wall house.

Uncle Nick said, 'We're aware that we have let the girls down.'

Cynthia was writing in a notebook. She looked up. 'May I have a word alone with Jackie?'

'Of course,' said Uncle Nick, looking out at the garden and then up the stairs as if accepting the embarrassment of being displaced in his own house. He seemed to feel he deserved it. 'Where do you want us to go?'

But Cynthia said, 'It's okay. We'll sit in the car for a few minutes. You stay where you are.'

In the car, Cynthia flapped at her face with a cardboard folder. She said, 'You need to tell me now whether you want me to find you somewhere temporary until we decide what to do next.'

'What do you mean?'

She asked me whether I felt safe.

'Of course I feel safe,' I said. 'They're not bad people. They've got secrets, like everyone else. And when one came out, it looked as though the others were waiting in the queue.'

'Let's hope there are no more,' she said.

'I don't think so,' I said. 'I think it's all out now. Like bursting a carbuncle.'

'Lovely,' she said.

'It is, though.'

'So you're not unhappy?'

I examined myself for unhappiness. 'No, that's not the word for what I'm feeling.'

'Worried?'

'I am for them. More for Amanda. Not for me.'

'What is the word for how you're feeling, then?'

'I don't know.'

'That's unlike you,' she said.

'Words come easily in poetry,' I said. 'Real life is trickier.'

She said, 'I'm afraid what happens next isn't my decision. There'll need to be a meeting with my superiors.'

'I thought you'd say that. Don't let them be too harsh on Uncle Nick and Bridget.'

'You're a kind girl,' she said.

'It's not that,' I said. 'I've got used to them. Like getting used to being sweaty.'

'You're full of wonderful analogies today,' she said. 'So much for not being able to express yourself.'

Spotless trotted across to welcome me back as we stepped inside the living room. All three of the Walls looked our way, like a family in a hospital corridor waiting to hear whether someone has turned the corner overnight.

Cynthia picked up her handbag. 'I'll be in touch very soon,' she said. 'Probably Monday or Tuesday. For now, I'll leave you in peace.'

It seemed a high aim, but I went upstairs to read Nanna's prosaic news in an attempt to give it a chance.

SATURDAY 17 JULY

On Saturday, Uncle Nick restored bikes in the shed and Bridget went shopping then spent her time in the kitchen, making ice cream and producing meals at the allotted times. I offered to help make the ice cream and she nearly died from gratefulness, so I grabbed my moment.

'Can I go to the cinema with Kim and her brother Kevin?' I said, stirring cream into mashed strawberries. 'In a fortnight's time, when school's broken up. That's assuming – you know – I'm still here.'

'I hope you will be,' she said.

I waited.

Eventually, she said, 'What's the film?'

'*Bugsy Malone*. It's not X-rated or anything.'

'I've heard of it,' she said. 'How would you get there?'

'Kim's mum says she'll take us and collect us.'

'I'll phone her,' she said, but I could tell it was a yes because she then said cinema ice cream wouldn't taste as good as our home-made, to which I hastily agreed in order to strengthen my case.

Amanda stayed upstairs most of the day, treating us to some T-Rex for a change. Her record player's output meant that I'd rarely had to use my transistor radio since Uncle Nick had bought it, except for Radio 1 in the mornings while I dressed for the day and occasionally on Saturday mornings while I cleaned.

At one point in the afternoon, Amanda knocked on my

door to ask the difference between a simile and a metaphor, but otherwise she kept to herself. I suspected she'd been crying again.

A letter came from Auntie Pat in New Zealand. *I'm so sorry you've learned the truth about your mum's cancer so late*, she said, after a few paragraphs about other things. *Even if your dad had let me speak to you, I'm not sure I could have brought myself to tell you. I would have been worried about the consequences. Maybe it was the wrong thing. I was trying to keep you safe. I live too far away. Please write back.*

'What did she say?' Bridget asked me.

'They've got snow on the mountains near their house,' I said.

MONDAY 19 JULY

Cynthia picked me up from school on Monday afternoon.

'What's happening?' I said.

'Nothing yet. There's a meeting late tomorrow afternoon. Bridget and Nick have been asked to come along.'

'Are we going to the café?'

'We're going somewhere,' she said. 'It's a surprise. Don't worry. I've told the Walls about the change of plan, so they know where you are.'

'It's not a new foster home?'

'I wouldn't do that to you at such short notice.'

'I didn't exactly get much warning before I was trundled to the Walls.'

She couldn't answer that.

'You're abducting me?' I said. 'Are you going to hide me in your cellar?'

She said yes and that she had drafted the ransom note.

The surprise was a visit to see Bobbie at her house in one of the villages near Warwick. She was wearing a bright-yellow cotton maternity dress and a straw hat. She sat in her tiny garden with her feet up on a stool. Her hands stroked her bump as though it were a cat curled up. Cynthia and I sat on the brown postage-stamp lawn and drank lime cordial with ice.

'Where's your beret?' I asked Bobbie.

'It'll be back on when it cools down.'

'I nearly didn't recognise you,' I said.

'Sorry there's nothing home-made,' Bobbie said as we

munched on Fig Rolls. 'I've been told not to stand for long, so baking is out.'

'How long until your baby is born?' I said.

'Three months or so,' she said.

'Can I come and see it?' I said. 'I could get Uncle Nick to bring me.'

I saw Cynthia glance at Bobbie and that's when I knew Bobbie had been told everything. I suspected that she couldn't admit this as she wasn't technically involved in my case.

'Of course,' Bobbie said. 'Perhaps you could write me a poem for the baby.'

'I wrote a ballad for the school arts evening,' I said.

'Could you do something happier for the baby?' she said.

We stayed half an hour. ('You're lucky to find me awake,' Bobbie had said.) As we left, I said to her, 'My dad wrote to me from prison. He has a sense of humour when he's not drenched in whisky.'

She smiled. 'That is good news.'

Back in Hollybush Close, as I climbed out of the car, Cynthia said, 'Anyway, I don't have a cellar. I live in a third-floor flat.'

When I came downstairs, having changed out of my uniform, I saw a leaflet on the table entitled 'Marriage Guidance'. On its front was a photograph of a couple who looked as though they'd been very satisfied with their guidance indeed.

I picked it up.

Bridget came out of the kitchen wielding a whisk. I put the leaflet down, afraid I'd been prying.

'It's okay,' she said. 'It's not a secret.'

'What is it?' I said.

'We've made an appointment next week to see a counsellor.'

I had a vision in my head of a horse running off and someone bolting a stable door.

'You're probably thinking isn't it too late for that,' she said.

'Not in those terms.'

'We want to get things right,' she said. 'Put things right.'

'Cynthia says you've been called to a meeting with Social Services tomorrow.'

'Are you feeling worried? Can I give you a hug?' she said.

'Thanks, but no thanks,' I said.

'How would you feel,' she said, 'if they said you could stay with us?'

I looked down the garden at Uncle Nick's shed, at Spotless, who was lying on his back on the carpet with four feet in the air, and at Bridget's whisk. They'd all become part of my routine.

I was about to reply when Amanda came downstairs and said, 'There you are.' I waited to see why she'd come out of her room but, no, apparently she'd come to acknowledge my arrival. It was the first time. Perhaps she planned to squeeze in a few greetings before I disappeared from their lives in case she became 'the girl who never said hello'.

'Can I get you something, Amanda?' Bridget said, maybe to stop Amanda from getting it herself in truckloads.

'Is there any news about whether Jackie is staying?' Amanda said.

'No, darling,' Bridget said.

'Don't darling me,' Amanda said. 'If she does go, it'll be yours and Dad's fault.' She walked back up the stairs but stopped halfway. 'Then you'll be sorry, Mum, seeing as she's your favourite.'

TUESDAY 20 JULY

On Tuesday morning, Bridget told me and Amanda while we were clearing up after breakfast in our school uniforms that she and Uncle Nick were eating at a restaurant that evening with friends. I'd noticed it on the calendar. 'It's their tenth wedding anniversary,' Bridget said. 'We can't not go. We promised.'

'Why *wouldn't* you go?' I said.

'We're not exactly in the mood,' Uncle Nick said, picking up his briefcase.

'And whose fault is that?' Amanda said.

'Obviously, ours,' he said.

'Obviously,' she said.

'There's no need to rub salt in,' Bridget said.

'We've said we're sorry,' Uncle Nick said. 'We're doing our best.'

'So you claim,' Amanda said, picking up a jar of jam.

'But we've also got this meeting with Social Services this afternoon,' he said.

'Your interrogation,' Amanda said.

I wished she'd stop. There was no need. I felt she was using them as a punchbag and, although I understood her disillusionment in her parents, they looked broken, wincing at her comments. No wonder they didn't feel like celebrating someone's wedding anniversary.

At least, I thought, it wasn't theirs.

'I wish *I'd* been invited to a restaurant,' Amanda said.

'I bet you do,' Bridget said recklessly, wiping the dining table free of crumbs with extravagant sweeps of the cloth.

Amanda turned on her. 'What's that supposed to mean?'

'Nothing,' Bridget said. She went into the kitchen. Amanda followed.

Uncle Nick trailed them, carrying his briefcase. 'Stop this, you two.'

'I want to know what Mum was getting at,' Amanda said.

'She wasn't getting at anything,' he said.

Bridget said, 'It's not fair, Nick. She thinks she can say anything she likes and no one can object.'

'You meant because I'm greedy, didn't you?' Amanda said.

There was a pause. 'Actually,' Bridget said, 'I was thinking that you seem to have lost all your friends. But now you mention it.'

Spotless had been under the dining table. He wandered out and came over to where I was standing by the stairs, about to go up and fetch my satchel. I patted his head. We listened together to a long silence, waiting.

'I can't believe you said that. I hate you both!' Amanda said, her voice building to a crescendo for 'You are the worst parents in the world!' She ran out of the kitchen, past me and up the stairs. She was still holding the jam.

Bridget emerged too and yelled upstairs, 'You forgot to take a spoon!' and although I was shocked to hear her say it, it was the best one-liner she'd come up with yet. But she returned to the kitchen, her shoulders slumped, as though being that witty had proved a strain.

Amanda came down almost immediately, her satchel slung over her shoulder, and I wondered if there'd be more confrontation. But she took the stairs fast and headed for the front door, saying as she passed me, 'And what do you think you're staring at?' even though I'd been looking the other way so as not to catch her eye and show my pity.

'I'm really late,' Uncle Nick said, his voice sounding tired as though it hadn't slept well. 'I've got a staff briefing before school and I need to leave at lunchtime for the meeting at Social Services. I have a lot to get done.' He checked his watch. 'Jackie, I might as well take you.'

'Okay. I'll get my satchel.'

As Uncle Nick and I left the house, Bridget was sitting on the sofa, looking out of the French windows at the brown lawn, as though she might be there all morning, wishing it could be green and fresh again.

When I came home from school, Bridget was cleaning a kitchen that didn't need it, bending to wipe inside the cupboard under the sink. I was sure she'd be the only housewife in the Midlands cleaning. Surely all the others were sitting in gardens, fanning their faces with a magazine. 'How did the meeting go?' I said. 'Is there any news?'

She straightened up and brushed hair from a moist forehead. 'They asked us so many personal questions,' she said with a shudder. 'Even more than when we first applied to foster. But I suppose that was to be expected.'

'What was the outcome?' I said, hoping for news about me and not more about Bridget's embarrassment.

She looked at the cloth she held as though she couldn't meet my eyes. 'We don't know yet. We're hoping they will be merciful. They liked the fact that we've booked marriage counselling. They said it was a good sign.'

Amanda came into the kitchen. 'Shouldn't people go to marriage counselling *before* they get married, so they don't mess up and ruin things for their families?'

'That's harsh,' I said.

'You're not their child,' she said. 'What would you know about it?'

'You seem to have forgotten what brought me here,' I said.

She didn't answer as she passed me to go upstairs.

I left to change out of my uniform. Bridget resumed her

cleaning as though disinfecting cupboards could also scour away regrets.

Before they went out that evening, Bridget grilled Amanda and me some fish fingers for tea. While we ate, Uncle Nick went for a short bike ride even though it was still aggressively hot. I wondered to what extent he was punishing himself, like those monks who whip themselves, only he was doing it with low gears and the sun's rays.

They left just before 7, having alerted the next-door neighbours, Ken and Irene, and telling us we could call on them if we needed to. I went up to my room when they'd gone and wrote a letter to Dad. When I'd sealed and stamped it, I went downstairs to sit in the garden, passing Amanda, who lay on the sofa in her Donald Duck nightie.

I was trying to read *Huckleberry Finn*, having finished *The Catcher in the Rye*, but found it hard to concentrate. Hankering after Holden Caulfield wasn't helping matters, no offence to Huck.

Spotless lay on the patio by my side, his tongue hanging out of his mouth. I'd brought him a bowl of water, but he was too lazy or too hot to get up and drink from it.

I must have drifted into a doze. I woke to hear the sound of chopping coming from the kitchen. This confused me. Only Bridget chopped.

I went inside. The clock in the living room said it was eight o'clock. Amanda was in the kitchen, using Bridget's bread board to slice clumsily peeled potatoes into chips. Bubbling on the hob was the chip pan, its oil furious. On the kitchen counter were the salt cellar, a bottle of vinegar and a loaf of white bread. Also there was a bottle of vodka and, beside it, a tumbler half-full of clear liquid.

She turned to face me. 'Don't even start.'

I raised my hands in surrender. 'I wasn't going to. I wondered what was happening.'

'Well, this is happening,' she said.

'Isn't it a bit hot for chips?' I said. The kitchen was smoky and her face was sweaty. I decided not to mention that she'd already had four fish fingers and demolished a piece of Black Forest gateau the size of her head.

'I said don't start,' she said.

'Okay.'

I watched for a minute, wincing as she wielded the chopping knife like someone who'd never held one before.

She said, 'I know they hate me for getting fat, but I hate them, too. At least I've been honest about it.'

I wasn't sure what to say.

'Do you want some chips when they're done?' she said.

I said, 'Maybe a few.'

I thought I'd better help her out. She'd chopped enough for six weightlifters. And then there was empathy.

'I'll bring them outside,' she said.

I went back into the garden to carry on reading, but I was uneasy. Amanda was hardly Fanny Cradock. And I wasn't sure how much vodka she had drunk.

I could hear the spit and angry sizzle of the fat as she dropped the chips in. I wondered whether she'd patted them dry in a tea towel the way Bridget did.

Spotless looked up at me, his eyes anxious.

'I know,' I said to him. 'But what can you do?'

Then Amanda screamed.

I flung my book down and rushed inside. She was still yelling, like in a horror film, standing by the hob, her arms helpless in the air. The pan had a lid of flame. And in another few seconds, the flames would begin to nibble at the front of her nightie.

I took hold of her arm and hauled her away from the cooker, then stretched to turn the hob off. Grabbing the hand towel that hung on a hook on the wall, I ran it under the tap until it was sodden then flung it over the pan. I did the same with the tea towel and threw that on top, too. The fire hissed and spat like a witch for a few moments while I waited, then it gradually calmed until only smoke was left.

Amanda stood by the kitchen door, staring.

I breathed out a long breath and realised I must have been holding it in.

'Are my chips ruined?' she said.

'Are you kidding? I think you mean, thank you for saving me from being burned alive.'

She folded her arms. 'You want a gold medal, I suppose.' But she couldn't fool me. Her eyes were wide.

'If you're offering.' I looked at Bridget's towel and tea towel, blackened and sooty. 'That could have been your nightie,' I said.

'I suppose.'

'I know.'

'How did you know what to do?' she said.

'My dad was a fireman.'

'Oh.'

'Thank you, Jackie's dad,' I said.

'I guess so.'

I looked around the kitchen at the mess. 'We'd better clear this up.'

'Let's not tell them what happened,' she said.

'Don't be an idiot.' Didn't she know her own parents? Bridget would have been suspicious if a tea towel had been moved an inch to the left, let alone scorched and binned. Plus, there was the small matter of a heap of half-dead chips.

'Mum and Dad are going to kill me,' Amanda said.

I poured the vodka from her glass into a jug then back into the bottle. 'Put that away in the cupboard for a start.'

'You're such a goody-goody,' she said. But she took the bottle and went back into the living room, I assumed to obey my instruction.

'We'll tell them we were trying to make chips together,' I said when she came back. 'It's nearly the truth.'

I waited for her to say, 'Would you really do that for me?' but she didn't.

The doorbell rang.

'I'm not getting that,' Amanda said, looking down at Donald Duck.

'I think it's the neighbour,' I said.

I was right. Ken from next door said, 'We heard someone shouting. Is everything okay?'

'We were playing a silly game,' I said. 'I'm sorry. We'll try to be quieter.'

He looked doubtful, but I was wearing my honest youngster face. It had served me well while shoplifting, or pretending to be sixteen at off-licences.

'If you're sure,' he said reluctantly and walked away down the path.

I press-ganged Amanda into helping me rescue the kitchen as far as we could. She owed me that. I noticed her hands trembling as she put away the vinegar.

'I think you might be in shock,' I said and put an arm on her shoulder.

She shook me off. 'Don't touch me,' she said. 'I don't need your help.'

We sat in the living room and switched on the TV. The *Nine O'Clock News* had started.

'You're supposed to have sugary tea if you're in shock,' I said. 'I can make you one.'

'In this heat?' she said.

'You were about to eat steaming hot chips.'

'That's not the same.'

'Fine.' Leaving her to her unreasonableness, I made two tall glasses of lemon squash which I put on the coffee table, with no thanks from her, and went through to the downstairs toilet.

Although it was evening, there was no sign of the air cooling or of any freshness and being cloistered with Amanda's ungratefulness didn't help. I needed a break from her. I went back into the living room, drank my lemon squash in one go and said to Amanda, 'I'll be upstairs for a while.'

'You gulped that down,' she said.

'I was thirsty,' I said. 'What's it to you?'

I sat on my bed for about fifteen minutes and tried to read, but the walls of my room began to seem as though they were nearer to me than usual. The skin under my hair itched.

I went into the bathroom, splashed my face with cold water and took Dad's letter downstairs. 'I need air. I'll walk round the corner with Spotless now the pavements are cooler and post this.'

'You can't.'

'What's the problem?' I said. 'I'll only be ten minutes.'

'I'll be on my own.'

I nodded towards the newsreader on the TV. 'You've got Angela. I'm not your babysitter.'

'Mum and Dad won't like you going out.'

'They won't know. Would you really split on me when I'm covering for you about the fire?'

'No,' she said. 'I won't. Go and post your stupid letter, then.'

'It's not stupid. It's to my dad.'

She had the decency to look ashamed.

I called Spotless inside, told him that proper dogs went for walks willingly, slipped a lead around his neck and let myself out of the house.

Approaching the post box a few minutes later with Spotless beside me, I thought I'd be feeling better for being outside, but instead I was light-headed, as though I was trying to stay awake but couldn't. The heat seemed to push against me so that every step needed a decision.

I posted my letter in the box and peered at the next day's collection times but found it hard to focus. Was that an 8 or a 3?

I bent to pat Spotless and said, 'Come on, boy, let's get home,' but, as I stood upright, had to put my hand out to the post box to orientate myself.

Suddenly, there was an urgency about getting home. I

was about to be sick. An elderly woman approached and I realised I couldn't see her face properly. A moment later and there were two of her, then one, then two. 'Are you okay, love?' I heard her say and she put a hand (or two) towards me, which was when I lost balance altogether and fell, letting go of Spotless's lead. He gave a woof and ran off, ungainly and directionless and, somehow, even though I knew I needed to call him back, I couldn't think how.

I decided not to stand up as it seemed beyond the energy I had, so I sat cross-legged on the pavement, vaguely aware of the woman watching me and sometimes unaware of much at all. Then I realised Amanda, now in shorts and tee shirt, was bending over me, weeping like a drain, and a policeman was saying to her, 'Is she your sister, love?' At that point, I leaned over and vomited on the policeman's boots.

'Thanks, pet,' I heard him say.

I tried to say sorry but was sick again. I was tasting Black Forest gateau for a second time. The first time had been more enjoyable.

'Does she have some kind of health condition?' I heard him ask Amanda. 'Do we need to get her to hospital?'

'No, she's had some vodka,' Amanda said.

'How much?'

'Not too much.'

'I have not,' I tried to say. How dare she? But my words didn't want to come out separately, and they got lost anyway in a conversation she was having with the policeman about where we lived and where our parents were.

'Hollybush Close? That's only round the corner,' the policeman said. 'I'll get this party girl home. Up you come now.' He tugged me to a standing position and handed me a giant square handkerchief to wipe my mouth with.

'She was going to the post box,' Amanda said. 'I followed her because I was worried.'

'Worried?' Since when?' I said, but no one heard. Perhaps I hadn't said it at all and the words were still in my head.

He led Amanda and me towards a police car.

I couldn't shake off the feeling that I wasn't awake and although I wanted to ask where Spotless was and what the hell Amanda was playing at saying I was drunk, the words wouldn't form coherently, so in the police car I just put my head back and stayed silent, as did Amanda.

At home, Amanda used her key to let us in.

The policeman guided me to the sofa and lifted my legs so that I could lie back. 'Sleep it off,' he said.

Somehow, from an officer of the law, it seemed more a command than a suggestion, so I closed my eyes. It was welcome. I had lost Spotless, Uncle Nick's dog, and put him in danger. That much I knew for sure. But I felt too helpless to do anything about it.

As I began to drift, the doorbell rang and I heard the voice of the same neighbour who'd visited earlier, talking to the policeman. Ken was saying, 'I'll go and look for the dog. I'll send Irene to mind the girls.'

I wasn't sure how much time had passed when I resurfaced. Inside my head was like mulch. Bridget and Uncle Nick were side by side, looking down at me as though I were an alien, newly arrived on Earth. I slowly turned my head. I could see Irene knitting in one armchair and a white-faced Amanda in the other.

Bridget was saying, 'Brought home by the *police*?'

The telephone rang. Uncle Nick went to answer it. As he entered the kitchen, he said, 'I *thought* I smelled smoke. What the bloody hell's been going on?' He picked up the receiver, recited the telephone number, and then we heard more alarm in his voice with every word.

Coming back into the living room, he said, his voice unsure of itself, 'That was an emergency vet. He says Spotless has been hit by a car.' I struggled up to a sitting position. Uncle

Nick's eyes were round with the news. 'Ken arrived on the scene just after it happened,' he said.

'No!' said Bridget.

'Oh dear,' Irene said.

Amanda ran upstairs, her face in her hands. Above us, we could hear her wailing as her door shut.

'How bad is he?' Bridget said.

Uncle Nick said, 'His leg is broken, but they don't know how seriously. He might need an operation tomorrow. They think they can save him.'

'They *think*?' Bridget said.

She and Uncle Nick sat down on two dining chairs as though their bodies had given them no option.

I tried to force myself up to a standing position. I felt fragile as though I might break if I did anything sudden. But some clarity had returned to me, not that I wanted it. 'It's all my fault, Uncle Nick,' I said, pushing back tears. If I started crying, I wouldn't stop, and I didn't deserve anyone's pity. 'I took Spotless out for a walk to the post box,' I said, 'but I fell over. I let his lead go.'

I couldn't maintain the standing position. My body reacted as though it had put on weight or was carrying something heavy, which could have been Uncle Nick's disappointment. I slumped back down onto the sofa. The room was swirling around me and I felt as though I were on a boat.

I was dropping into sleep again when I heard Uncle Nick say, somewhere in the distance, 'Is that our bottle of vodka by the sofa?' and, straight afterwards, Bridget calling from the kitchen, 'My chip pan!'

WEDNESDAY 21 JULY

I woke on Wednesday in my bed, in Tuesday's clothes, but with no memory of the journey from the sofa. My pillow was blotted with bloodstains. How disconcerting it is to find that you've gouged pieces of yourself away in the night without knowing.

I flipped the pillow over.

In my mind, the events of the previous evening were sketchy, as if I'd seen a film three years ago and could only remember random highlights.

My clock said nine. I hadn't set the alarm.

Nine?

I was sure Weston's face was disapproving as he looked down at me from the chest of drawers.

'What are you looking at?' I said. I felt bad enough without his censure, and, scene by scene, I was beginning to recall why. My gut tightened as though someone had put a large fist against it and pushed.

A knock at the door was followed by Bridget saying, 'Who are you talking to, Jackie? Can I come in?'

I sat up. My head pulsed like a drum.

She came in carrying two mugs and handed me one. 'I've brought you some tea. It will help.'

I sipped at the tea while she sat on my bedroom chair with her own mug. I waited for the telling-off, or the grounding, or the banishment.

'It's a school day,' I said. It was all I could think of.

'You can always go in later. Amanda hasn't gone in either, and Uncle Nick has rung in too because of Spotless.'

I took a huge gulp of tea. It burned my mouth, but I was glad. I took another gulp. I said, 'Could Spotless die?'

'We'll know soon. You mustn't worry,' she said, her face marked with worry.

'Am I still allowed to go and see *Bugsy Malone*?'

'Oh, Jackie,' she said.

I held my mug against my chest to feel its warmth. 'I can't remember exactly what happened last night. I felt so poorly.'

'Don't you know why?' she said.

'No. I thought maybe it was the gateau.'

'It wasn't the gateau. I'm not in the habit of poisoning people.'

'You must hate me,' I said.

'No,' she said. 'You're not to blame for anything that happened yesterday.'

I remembered Spotless running off, the lead slipping from my fingers. 'Of course I am.'

'No, Jackie.'

'Who, then?'

'Amanda woke us first thing and told us everything. She's been downstairs, awake all night, frantic.'

'She told the policeman I'd had vodka.'

'I know.'

'We were making chips together,' I said.

'No, you weren't,' she said. 'You don't have to pretend.'

'Oh.'

'She says you saved her from being burned.'

I put my empty mug next to Weston on my chest of drawers. 'She was angry about that for some reason.'

'She was jealous.'

'I don't know why.'

'Neither does she. Not that she can explain. Or wants to admit.'

I decided to help Amanda out. 'She thinks you like me better,' I said.

Bridget sighed. 'That could well be our fault.'

I let that hang in the air.

She said, 'But, anyway, that's why she put vodka in your lemon squash.'

'What? So I *was* drunk?'

I thought back. The possibility that Amanda had put vodka in my drink had not occurred to me, would never have occurred to me, and even now it seemed like someone else's story that I might read in a magazine.

'Why would she risk that?' I said.

'She's not sure herself,' Bridget said. 'She knows it was stupid. That's why she followed you when you went out. She was genuinely frightened about what she'd done. Then things got out of control.'

The tea was unravelling my brain. 'I was sick on a policeman's boots.'

She smiled. 'I'm sure he's seen worse.'

'Where is Amanda?'

'In her room,' she said grimly, 'probably wondering how she's going to face you.'

'She didn't mean for Spotless to be injured.'

'I'm sure she didn't,' Bridget said. 'But she did mean you to get drunk.'

'She didn't know I'd go out.'

She stood up. 'Would you like me to bring you some toast and jam?'

'To eat in bed?'

'Just this once,' she said, 'so long as you're careful about crumbs.'

The word 'toast' made me salivate and I realised that it was what I wanted more than anything else at that moment, if you don't count stability, for Spotless to recover, and an international reputation as a poet.

When Bridget returned with the toast, she told me there'd been a phone call and that the vet would be X-raying Spotless that morning. 'We'll know by lunchtime how it went,' she said. 'They're hoping they can save his leg.'

As she went out of my room, she left the door ajar. I heard Amanda come out of her own room and say on the landing, 'What do you mean, save the leg, Mum?' Her voice sounded thick and weary.

'They're not sure how much damage there is,' Bridget told her.

There was a silence, but then I heard it, and I think they did too: Uncle Nick in his bedroom, crying, the sound low and somehow primitive. I stopped nibbling at my toast out of respect. This was like the end of the world.

'Mum,' Amanda said hoarsely. 'What can I do? What do I do?'

I thought she would start crying, but she didn't. For once, she wasn't trying to suck up all the pity in the house and I put that down as progress.

I finished my toast and went into the bathroom to wash and to clean my teeth. When I returned to my room, Amanda was sitting on my bedroom chair in the same Donald Duck nightie she'd worn the evening before.

'Right,' I said.

'I know you despise me,' she said.

'You fed me vodka.'

'I didn't mean it to go wrong.'

'What could have gone right about it?'

'You're always such a good person.'

'And you tried to get me into trouble? That's twisted.'

I sat on my bed.

'I know,' she said. 'I see that.' She was looking down at Donald Duck.

'You'll get no sympathy from him,' I said. 'You nearly set him on fire.'

'And if you hadn't known how to…'

'Let's not go over it,' I said. I started brushing my hair. 'I did what needed doing. I wasn't trying to be a hero, or a good person. There was no need to corrupt me.'

I could see that she was biting the inside of her mouth. 'I don't want you to go and live somewhere else,' she said.

I put my brush down. 'Are you trying to be funny?'

'No.'

'You have a very strange way of communicating your true feelings.'

She walked to the window and looked out. 'I hate myself.'

'There's no need to go that far. Everyone makes mistakes. Everyone does wrong.'

'You don't.'

'You already know I used to steal food. And I've done plenty else wrong. You've got yourself a very strange view of me.'

'You had no choice about the stealing. Dad told me.'

I scanned my sunflower room for inspiration. 'Look at this, then,' I said, and she turned round. I picked up my toast plate and upended it onto the bed so that crumbs scattered onto the eiderdown, and even though she was proving a terrible sister, and Spotless might lose his leg, and Uncle Nick was already grieving in his bedroom, we giggled, because it seemed the thing to do. And something else that seemed right to do, although I would never have written Amanda down as my confidante, was to tell her about my dad and what he'd confessed to me about contributing towards my mother's death.

Amanda sat listening, her mouth an O and her hands folded in her lap. 'When did you find this out?' she said.

'When I visited him in prison.'

'And you haven't told anyone? You should have told someone.'

'There you go,' I said. 'You just said I never made any mistakes.'

She was looking at me now, properly. 'He didn't mean for that to happen, though.'

'No,' I said. 'I suppose not.'

'You should tell Mum and Dad.'

'What's the point? I might not even be staying.'

'You told me, though.'

'You look as pleased as punch,' I said, 'at my terrible news.'

'Not your terrible news,' she said, 'but the fact that you told me, after everything.' Her cheeks were rosy-pink.

'I know,' I said. 'No doubt another mistake. Slap it on your growing list.'

When Amanda had disappeared to her room, I lay on my bed, looking at the ceiling, and fell asleep again, the heat of the day and perhaps my debut hangover making me listless. I woke to see that it was eleven o'clock. The telephone was ringing. I went to the top of the stairs and met Amanda there. We listened.

Uncle Nick had answered it. We heard his low tones and then a louder 'Thank you. Thank you.'

He came to the bottom of the stairs and Bridget followed him.

'Was that the vet?' I said.

'It's good news. He's going to be fine. It's a clean break. Nothing more complicated.'

'Isn't that a relief?' Bridget said.

'I'm weak with it,' Uncle Nick said. 'My legs don't belong to me.' He put a hand to the banister.

Amanda ran down the stairs. 'Dad,' she said. As she reached the bottom stair, she hesitated, as though she wasn't sure of his reception, but he put his arms out and she dived into them. I watched as she pushed her head into his chest, saying, 'I'm sorry, I'm sorry,' and he laid his hand on her head. I felt envy the way people feel punches. *She* jealous of *me*?

Uncle Nick looked up. 'Come here, you,' he said, and I walked down the stairs towards him, warily as Amanda had done but for a different reason. But Amanda stepped away from him and went to stand by her mother.

I gave myself up to his hold and realised when my cheek touched his that, for the first time since I'd moved in, he hadn't bothered to shave.

I wanted to go into school. 'It's Poetry Club at lunchtime,' I said to Bridget, who was in the kitchen trying to resurrect her chip pan with determination and a Brillo pad, 'and there's a full rehearsal for the arts evening later.'

'Do you feel well enough?' she said.

'I feel fine,' I said. It wasn't strictly true. I still had a headache. 'Actually,' I said, 'can I have an aspirin and then go?'

'I thought as much,' she said. 'Let me talk to Uncle Nick. He's in the shed.'

When she came back, she said, 'Nick will drive you in. He's visiting Spotless on the way back. Amanda's going with him.'

'Isn't Amanda going to school?'

'We need her here,' she said. 'We still have some talking to do.'

'She's really sorry about everything. She's told me.'

Uncle Nick walked in. 'She's made some terrible errors of judgement. But she's not the only one. We are as much to blame.'

After Poetry Club at lunchtime, Mrs Collingworth asked me to stay behind. 'You didn't seem yourself,' she said. 'You look what the poets would call wan.'

She was wearing the green skirt and blouse again, the outfit that gave me peace when I looked at her.

'I wondered if that poem had upset you,' she said. Another member of the group had written a poem about a funeral and read it out.

'No,' I said.

She perched on the edge of the teacher's desk, unhurried. 'I know your mother died because of cancer.'

'I think so,' I said.

She looked at me quizzically but didn't push for information, which is when I decided she could have it anyway. I explained to her what I'd told Amanda earlier.

When I'd finished, she said, 'Your father must wake with regrets every single day. What a punishing load to bear, and that's without being in prison.'

I hadn't considered this.

'I'm glad you felt you could tell me,' she said. 'It must have been hard to say.'

'I had a chance to practise this morning with someone else,' I said, 'so I'd warmed up. You can tell Miss Jones what I told you. I don't know if I want to say it all a third time.'

She smiled. 'Is there anything else you want to tell me so that I can tell Miss Jones what you don't want to tell her?'

I shook my head. 'I think that's enough for today.'

I grabbed some roast pork and mashed potato in the school dining room in the last ten minutes of lunchtime, sitting with Molly, who was scraping up the dregs of her rice pudding.

'Do you think anyone's told the dinner ladies there's a heatwave?' I said.

'Ham salad and ice cream would be more suitable,' Molly said.

'But not as tasty,' we said at the same time and laughed.

'Don't forget the rehearsal,' she said.

'I won't,' I said.

'I was worried,' she said, 'when I didn't see you at break.'

'Thanks,' I said. 'I could get used to this, having people to worry.'

On my way back for afternoon lessons, I saw Cynthia walking towards me in the corridor near the school reception. At first, I couldn't place her. She'd turned up out of context, as people do in dreams. It didn't help that she was wearing a loud pink mini dress, kitten heels and sunglasses and had never looked less like a social worker.

She waved. 'I've been to see Miss Jones,' she said as I drew nearer.

'Oh.'

'I understand last night was eventful.'

'How did Miss Jones know about that?'

'I assume Bridget rang to let her know, as she did me.'

I said, 'I think we're all adopting a new "honesty is the best policy" policy.'

'Including you?'

'It seems so.' I felt myself redden, though, as I remembered her personal involvement in the Walls' honesty campaign.

'I have some news for you,' she said. 'I wanted to tell you face-to-face.'

The school bell rang.

'Is it about me and the Walls?' I said.

'It is.' She took a handkerchief from her dress pocket and dabbed at her face. The corridor had a glass roof and we were being braised.

'Is it time to pack my bags?'

She examined my face as though testing my reaction.

'In case you missed it, I said that forlornly,' I said.

She smiled. 'No. The feeling is that we'd prefer you to stay with them. If you're happy. It hasn't been an easy start. But it would be more disruptive to move you.'

'Does that always happen,' I said, 'when people move in with foster families? Suddenly everything goes tits-up?'

We were being edged to the margins of the corridor as pupils with hot faces from careering around in the sun began to herd through, checking their timetables and calling to friends.

'There usually are teething problems,' she said.

'Teething problems?'

'The Walls have excelled themselves, it's true,' she said.

'What about Amanda?'

'I spoke to her on the phone. I think you may be winning her over.'

'I admire your optimism.'

She tucked her handkerchief away. 'You don't have to make a final decision right now.'

I dipped into my satchel for my maths book so that I was ready for the lesson. 'That's okay. I don't have to make a decision at all.'

Bridget served gammon steaks with chips at teatime, having scrubbed and scraped the chip pan clean of its unfortunate recent history. She brought the plates to the table. 'Amanda helped me make the chips,' she announced, although we already knew this. 'We've had an impromptu cookery lesson.'

Amanda looked embarrassed but said nothing. I'd overheard the conversation from upstairs when I was changing out of my uniform after Uncle Nick had brought me home from the arts evening rehearsal. Bridget had suggested she teach Amanda how to make chips safely, Amanda had said not in a million years, but Bridget had insisted, her voice firmer than usual. 'We've left this too long,' she said, and Uncle Nick had backed her up, saying, 'Everyone should know how to cook chips without razing a house to the ground.' They'd left Amanda little choice.

Soon, though, I'd heard her say, triumphantly, 'Look how crispy they are!'

'They look absolutely perfect,' Uncle Nick said now, picking up his knife and fork.

'They are,' Bridget said. 'She did really well.'

'That's my girl,' Uncle Nick said.

'Can we just *eat* them?' Amanda said.

She was right. Her parents were overdoing it. Any moment now, I thought, they'd start listing my faults and tutting.

'I made lemon meringue pie, too,' Bridget said. 'We have some things to celebrate.'

'One being Spotless,' Uncle Nick said. He'd told me in the car that Spotless had been wild on seeing him and Amanda that afternoon, jumping up clumsily on his splinted back leg and licking them both over and over. 'Like an absolution,' he'd said reflectively, turning into Hollybush Close.

'What's an absolution?'

'What priests give you. Forgiveness when you've done wrong.'

I thought he'd over-estimated Spotless's talents, but I understood why he might.

'And,' Bridget said now, 'something else to celebrate is that Jackie is staying with us.' Her tone was very muted and un-Bridget.

'You don't *have* to say it like a robot as though you're not pleased,' Amanda said. 'I can take it.' She turned to me and rolled her eyes as if to say, 'Parents!'

THURSDAY 22 JULY

I came down for breakfast before Amanda on the day of the arts evening, the penultimate day of term.

In the kitchen, I was buttering toast. Bridget said, 'There's something I need to say.'

I turned to her. 'Am I using too much butter?'

She shook her head. 'Why do you always think you're getting told off?'

I let that sit.

'I'm sorry,' she said eventually.

'It's fine.'

Her eyes were wet. 'We are so pleased that you can stay with us and that you told Cynthia that's what you would like.'

She moved in for a hug, but I stepped back. We'd made progress, but there were limits and I still wasn't ready for Bridget's ad-hoc embraces. I let her pat me on the arm as a compromise.

'After the messes we've made,' she said, 'it's lovely that you are prepared to give us a chance. It made me cry.'

'Really?'

'Yes, buckets!' she said.

I put the lid on the butter dish. 'Well, so long as you know, it's on condition that you don't make me eat the yolks of eggs.'

Uncle Nick walked into the kitchen, doing up his tie. 'I think we can make that concession.'

I said, 'Can I ask something while you're both here? Please promise not to over-react.'

'Of course,' Uncle Nick said, although it hadn't been him I was worried about.

'There's no easy way to say this. I'll just say it. I need to see a doctor.'

Bridget glanced at my abdomen.

I said, 'No, I'm *not*!'

'Oh.' She said nothing more and waited, to her credit. She had a tea towel clenched in her hands.

Somehow, the truth didn't seem so hard to say now, having been suspected of a secret pregnancy.

'I need help,' I said, 'because I've been picking at the skin on my head when I'm worried about things, and it keeps bleeding and getting infected.'

'Oh dear,' Uncle Nick said. 'How long has that been happening, pet?'

'Since before I came,' I said. 'Don't worry. It's not your fault.'

He looked sad. 'I expect it is,' he said, 'to some extent.'

'Well,' I said, 'I've got no appetite for recriminations. I'd rather have a doctor's appointment.'

'I'll telephone the surgery first thing this morning,' Bridget said, squeezing the remaining breath out of the tea towel.

'Don't mention it again,' I said, 'until the appointment, if that's okay.'

'That's fine,' Uncle Nick said.

'Thank you for telling us,' Bridget said. 'Would you like—'

'Bridget,' Uncle Nick said.

She looked hurt. 'I was going to ask if she'd like some marmalade.'

When Uncle Nick had taken a bowl of cereal to the dining table and I was spreading marmalade, Bridget whispered, 'Even if it had been a baby, we would have looked after you.'

'I know,' I said. 'But it would have been a miracle baby.'

I could tell she tried hard not to look relieved.

At school, Kim wasn't in maths.

Outside the dining room at break time, I saw her brother

David, standing close with a group of friends. I approached gingerly, but he peeled himself away and came over.

'I saw you hovering,' he said. 'I assume you're wondering about Kim.'

'Is she poorly?'

'Her throat,' he said. 'She's hoarse but desperate to be okay for tonight. Mum thought if she spent the day in bed, she'd have a chance.'

'What if she can't make it?' I said.

'Cross that bridge later,' he said and patted me on the head. It cheered me, because even though his friends were watching, he wasn't ashamed to acknowledge me.

The arts evening began at 7. Performers had been asked to arrive by 6.30.

Bridget had prepared an early tea of tinned tuna, bread rolls and salad. We ate it while trying to reconfigure ourselves into an everyday family sharing a pleasant meal before heading out for an evening's entertainment.

'Could you pass the basket of rolls?' Uncle Nick said.

'Of course,' Bridget said. 'Would anyone like more tomatoes?'

'Please,' said Uncle Nick. 'They are lovely and sweet.'

'May I have the salt?' I said.

'Here you are,' said Bridget.

Amanda looked particularly uneasy. I knew she was nervous about coming to my school and I thought she might find an excuse not to. I would have felt the same.

'Do I need to dress up?' she said. 'It's too hot.'

'Of course not,' I said. 'It's not formal.'

'What are you going to wear?'

'My blue dress,' I said, 'but remember, I'm performing.'

'I don't know how you have the courage,' she said. She was buttering a bread roll but very thinly: a scrape. I think Bridget was trying not to notice and, wisely, hadn't commented.

'I might bottle it and collapse,' I said.

'I'm sure you won't,' Bridget said.

'Of course she won't,' Uncle Nick said.

'Stop reassuring me,' I said. 'It's scary.'

When we were ready to leave, Bridget called upstairs, 'Come on, Amanda. It's time to go.'

There was a long silence and I thought, this is when she'll say, 'Go without me,' and there'll be a scene.

But she appeared and walked downstairs in a new lilac cotton dress, flower-patterned, and with a square neckline. It was pleasantly loose on her. Bridget had been shopping and Amanda's wardrobe now contained pretty clothes a size bigger. She was wearing soft-grey eyeshadow and a dab of lip gloss. With her long legs and swinging blonde ponytail, she looked beautiful to me.

'Darling!' Bridget said.

'Say nothing,' Amanda said. 'I mean, nothing.'

We all made our way to the car, our lips obediently sealed. But she'd made a huge effort and I was proud of her. I took it as a sign that she deeply regretted having poisoned me for fun.

At the entrance to the hall, pink-faced pupils dished out typewritten programmes in return for ten pence. I found seats for Bridget, Uncle Nick and Amanda. 'You'll have a good view from here. And you're near one of the doors for some air.'

A line of chairs at the front was filling up with teachers and governors of the school. Miss Jones and Mrs Caine were there, sitting together.

I said to the Walls, 'I need to find Kim. We were told to gather in the geography classroom down the corridor.'

'We'll be fine,' Uncle Nick said. 'Break a leg.'

I said, 'That's for actors.'

But I was reluctant to leave them just yet. They seemed a little lost, unfamiliar with the territory. On the way, Uncle

Nick had said, 'It's the first time I've been to the school as a parent,' and Bridget had said, 'Well, at least you'll know your way around, unlike me and Amanda.'

Some sixth formers were serving tea from an urn and selling orange squash at the back of the hall. 'Shall I fetch some drinks?' Uncle Nick said and went off to join the queue as if pleased to have a mission.

Amanda looked around her. 'This hall is definitely smarter than my school's.'

'Is it?' I said, looking round at its smeared windows and faded wall displays.

'Ours is a dump, though,' she said. 'It wouldn't take much.'

Mrs Collingworth appeared at the door and waved. 'Come on, Jackie,' she called. 'We need you now.'

'I'll see you at half-time,' I said to Bridget and Amanda.

'Surely it's called an interval,' Amanda said.

'Who's posh now?' I said.

In the geography classroom, I steered my way round the milling pupils and the instruments to find Kevin and David, both holding their guitars and standing with Molly. She wore green eyeshadow and a cheesecloth blouse and full skirt. Her hair was slightly wet as though she'd washed it but had no time to dry it before leaving.

She looked quite different out of uniform. For the first time, like a fourth-year girl, older than me.

'Here you are,' Kevin said. He laid a hand momentarily on the back of my neck in greeting and I thought I might tip over with the rush of feeling. It wasn't unlike being drunk.

Silver linings. I wouldn't have known that without Amanda's help.

'Is Kim here?' I said.

David shook his head. 'She did try to ring your house.'

'We must have left already.'

'Here, she wrote you a note.' He passed me a piece of paper torn from a notebook.

On it, Kim had written, *Bad news. I've got larinjitis. I hate the whole world. Good news. Molly will do us proud.*

Molly said, 'Is that all right, Jackie? I promise I'll do it justice. I know the tune from rehearsals. I've been singing it to my mum.'

'We've played it to Mrs C,' Kevin said to me, 'while we waited for you. We're on after the break. You're on third.' He pointed to a schedule that Mrs C had pinned up.

David said, 'Wait until you hear Molly!'

I put my arms around Molly and said, 'This is going to be good, I know it.'

She smelled of soap.

A calamitous punk band of sixth formers kicked off the evening followed by a solo girl singer who calmed everyone's blood pressure with a love song.

I was the third act, so, the first poem. I walked from the front row reserved for performers to the spot in front of the microphone. In rehearsals, Mrs C had told us, 'Remember you'll face an audience on the night, not a hall full of wooden chairs. Prepare yourself.' Still, when I turned to announce my title to the expectant faces, my knees threatened to forget that they were knees.

'This poem is based on Edward Thomas's "Adlestrop",' I said. 'It's about a place I remember. It's called "The Picnic".'

I barely needed to check my sheet of paper. The poem was written into the middle of me like words in Blackpool rock.

When I'd finished, I said, 'That's the end,' and there was eager applause. Miss Jones shouted, 'Bravo!' I saw Bridget stand up to clap, but she was grabbed by Amanda by the back of her blouse and tugged down again.

The last act before the interval was The Stagers, who sang their own composition, a love song called 'When Your Heart is Broken'. Kevin and David both played guitars alongside a drummer and a keyboard player. When Kevin sang, 'When your heart is broken/and your love unspoken,' I looked at my lap and my heart jumped around in my chest as though set free from its tethers.

In the ten-minute break, people wandered out onto the school field next to the hall to gulp air. I took the carton of Kia-Ora that Mrs C had provided and went to locate the Walls. I saw them before they saw me. They looked separate from each other even though they were standing together. They reminded me of winter trees in a copse.

'Here she is,' Uncle Nick said as I approached. He seemed glad of an intervention. 'Our very own bard.'

'You made me feel quite emotional,' said Bridget, as though it were a rare event that had taken her by surprise.

'When is the ballad happening?' Uncle Nick said.

'Straight after the interval,' Amanda said. 'You'd know that if you'd read the programme, Dad.'

I was touched.

After the interval, Molly made a shy walk to the front and took her place at the microphone. Her face was pale, but she looked less shaky than I had felt in the same position.

Mrs Collingworth explained that Molly was standing in for Kim Price. 'She's rescued us at the last minute to sing a ballad written by our poet Jackie Chadwick, with its tune composed by Kevin from The Stagers. I think you'll find Molly a worthy understudy.'

It was the first time I'd heard Molly sing. Her voice differed from Kim's, being sweeter and higher, and, combined with Kevin's soft guitar, it made my throat constrict. My lyrics seemed to grow into something more as she told the story. Maybe singing did to her what writing poetry did to me.

When the audience was silent after Kevin played the final chords, I wondered what was happening. Why was no one applauding?

But then the entire hall stood and cheered. The clapping

was like a rainstorm. I looked behind me and wondered whether Molly's parents were there.

Later, after a performance by a string quartet concluded the evening, Mrs Collingworth and Mr Court stood together to receive flowers from Miss Jones, who made a brief speech of appreciation.

The string quartet continued to play quietly as the audience stood and stretched or flapped at their faces. Even though the doors had been open, the stifling air had weighed on us all.

I went to search out the Walls again. Bridget was in the drinks queue, Uncle Nick was pretending to read displays about good behaviour at mealtimes, and Amanda stood alone.

As I joined her, Molly arrived at my side. 'I have to go soon, Jackie,' she was saying. 'My mum's waiting.'

'Say hello to Amanda first,' I said. 'She's my—' I stretched for a definition. 'I'm staying with her family.'

Molly didn't miss a beat. 'Hi, Amanda,' she said, giving a mini-wave. 'I love that dress. Is that Dorothy Perkins?'

Amanda reddened. 'I think so.'

I turned to locate Kevin and David, who were putting their guitars into cases. I waved them over. 'Say hello to Amanda.' I liked my new explanation. 'I'm staying with her family.'

'You poor suffering thing,' Kevin said to her.

'More like, poor Jackie,' Amanda said.

'Not really,' I said.

She said to the boys, her voice shy, 'I like your band.'

'Come and watch us in October,' David said, as though he'd known her for years. 'We're doing a gig for charity.'

I could see she was speechless at the invitation.

Kevin said, 'We'd better go and finish packing up before Mr Court has a seizure.'

They wandered back.

Molly said. 'I really have to go.'

I followed her gaze to a woman who looked Bridget's age but carried a walking stick. She stood, supporting herself by holding onto the back of a chair.

'Is your mum okay?' I said.

'She has multiple sclerosis,' she said. 'But she has better days. Today's a bad one, but she wanted to be here.'

'That's sad.' I'd seen a TV documentary about multiple sclerosis. 'Is your dad here?'

'There isn't one,' she said bluntly. 'I'd better get Mum home and into bed. Our taxi's waiting. I'll see you tomorrow.'

I watched her as she drew alongside her mother, putting an arm under hers to lead her towards the exit.

Bridget came back, just about managing to wield four cups of squash. Uncle Nick re-joined us.

Mr Court approached. He shook hands with Uncle Nick and said, 'I'm teaching Jackie's ballad in my singing lessons. I'm sure she'll agree that it's about time "Speed Bonnie Boat" hit the dust.'

Uncle Nick said, 'I sang that when *I* was at school.'

'Quite,' said Mr Court. 'You know, I'm surprised Jackie didn't sing the ballad herself, knowing how singing is her over-riding passion.'

'Is it?' Bridget said, sounding affronted. 'We had no idea. Jackie, you didn't tell us!'

Amanda said, 'Oh, Mum!'

Kevin reappeared. 'We're off in a minute,' he said. He nudged me playfully. Again, I felt weakened and thought, If this happens to lovers every time they touch, how has the human race stayed on its feet?

I said, 'Kevin is Kim's brother.'

'Kevin as in the *Bugsy Malone* Kevin?' Bridget said, looking from me to him. I could tell she was trying her hardest not to see him as a potential serial killer.

I said to Kevin, 'This is my uncle Nick and auntie Bridget. They are my foster parents.'

ACKNOWLEDGEMENTS

I'm reminded of the old joke: A selfish young man (let's call him Colin) continually badgers his dying father. 'Dad, acknowledge me in your will, won't you?' Every time he sees his fast-failing parent, he repeats it. 'Dad, acknowledge me, won't you?' The father says, 'Yes, yes, son. Of course.' The father then dies and the solicitor reads the will aloud. Colin excitedly awaits the good news but is not mentioned until money and property have gone to his siblings and a cats' home. Finally, the solicitor reads, 'And now to Colin, who was desperate to be acknowledged. Hello, son.'

I hope you won't be disappointed, unlike Colin, with what I offer here, because nothing can reflect my true appreciation of the part you've all played in seeing 'Cuckoo in the Nest' devised, planned, written, improved, improved again, improved again, produced, published, and now in the hands of readers.

So, *much* more than acknowledgement goes to, in no particular order –

The foster parents whose names I haven't retained but who took me in for a short time in the 1970s to live with them, their daughter and a Dalmatian. I remember few details about my stay, the reason for it or why I had to leave, which is why I can confidently state that 'Cuckoo in the Nest' is a work of fiction. If you're out there, and you remember me, I can only hope I did you no lasting damage.

Those who saw the manuscript before it reached Legend

Press, either for editing help or beta-reading: Caroline Bacon, Lisa Carey, Poppy James, Deborah Jenkins and Liz Munslow. Each of you said things that re-shaped the book in big ways and little ways and, frankly, all the ways.

Cari Rosen, fabulous commissioning editor for Legend Press, who read the first 10,000 words and wanted to see more. Your first emails were so enthusiastic, Cari, I had to keep re-reading to make sure I wasn't being spammed by someone exploiting the vulnerabilities of wannabe novelists.

Everyone at Legend Press who agreed that my novel was worth a punt and then worked hard to make it happen. Special thanks go to Lucy Chamberlain and Olivia Le Maistre in Publicity and Marketing; Sarah Nicholson, Rights Manager; Sam Rennie for digital wizardry; Liza Paderes in Sales; Ditte Loekkegaard for typesetting and putting it all together, and, of course, the inimitable MD Tom Chalmers, without whom there would be no Legend Press at all.

Catriona Robb, copy editor, for eagle-eyed editing.

Clare Stacey at Head Design for all sterling work on the cover design. I love my cuckoo.

Each author, book blogger and reviewer who received a pre-publication copy then posted or messaged reactions, comments or endorsements. Most of you do this for very little reward (be more like these people, Colin) and you are astonishingly generous.

All the networks of writers providing bursts of encouragement and valid reasons for me to procrastinate via social media chats, online and face-to-face meetings and conferences. Special mention goes to the Association of Christian Writers; the @womenwritersnet Twitter network; everyone at Writing West Midlands including its irrepressible Chief Executive Jonathan Davidson; the Room 204 emerging writers' scheme alumni; and the Warwickshire chapter of the Society of Authors.

The fearsome threesome that is Ruth Leigh, Georgie Tennant and Deborah Jenkins (so good I've named her twice).

All the members of my family, or, more accurately, families: those I'm related to and those I'm not but who welcomed me in anyway. I'll include my church family here, too. Many of you have keenly followed my writing journey – or practised your keen faces very effectively - and offered all kinds of support, although my offspring will right now be making disgusted vomiting gestures because I've called it a writing journey.

My husband Paul. You get a paragraph of your own because, well, frankly, you suffer the most.

There's bound to be someone I've forgotten and who is feeling, like Colin, spectacularly unacknowledged. If that's you, *waves*.